Praise for [

"Gritty and loud, raucous and real, but still somehow hushed and holy—like a love story told in the blacklight room at the back of a Spencer's."
—Ben Loory, author of *Stories for Nighttime and Some for the Day*

"*New Jersey Me* is, like Ferguson's poetry, funny and heartsick, breathless and bent. An inspired debut novel and a wonderfully twisted love song to wounded souls in dead suburbs in forgotten corners of America."
—Brad Listi, author of *Attention. Deficit. Disorder.*

"In *New Jersey Me*, the lyrical new novel from Rich Ferguson, there is a roll call of icons and time-and-place markers: Mary Kay cosmetics, Count Chocula, TV dinner trays and cars long since rusted to nothing. Springsteen and Bruce Lee posters preside over the room, mind, and heart of Mark, the wounded and wandering young man at the novel's center. Ghosts abound in this novel, in the form of the men Mark wishes he was—the Bruces—and the men he fears ever becoming—his ferocious cop father, the piggish bully Terry, the disease-riddled father of his secretive best friend Jimmy. Mark roll calls the iconic into existence whenever he faces down the bleakness of his present life, anchoring himself lest he fades to nothing. In prose as furious and rhythmic as freely flowing poetry, Ferguson pinballs his characters between the intractable poles of their lives—death-dealing power plants, drugs, abandoning mothers, futile jobs, and futureless friends—and dares them to find their way out. And you root for them to make it, which is no small feat. It's a tough, raw, and ultimately compelling piece of writing, and it matters that it's found its way into your hands. A must-read."
—David Rocklin, author of *The Luminist*

"The perfect mating of poetic noir and a carny barker's banter. Ferguson's unique vision sounds the death toll of the American suburban dream as it slowly overdoses in the back seat of a smoldering Chevy Vega. Fiction doesn't get any better than this, and if did, it'd be illegal."
—Patrick O'Neil, author of *Gun, Needle, Spoon*

"Those of us fortunate enough to have seen the legendary spoken word artist Rich Ferguson perform are familiar with his mastery of the language. I'm happy to report that in *New Jersey Me*, Ferguson's soaring debut, that mastery is on full display, and in the service of a killer story that has all the cool, soulful flavor of an epic Springsteen deep cut, a "Rosalita" in novel form. (And if you're from Jersey, like I am, you know that praise doesn't get any higher than that)."

—Greg Olear, author of *Fathermucker* and *Totally Killer*

"Rich Ferguson's *New Jersey Me* is an incredibly powerful debut. Ferguson creates a world unlike any you have ever read. This is raw, powerfully moving, darkly funny, and original. The full throttle prose is lapidary in its precision, and unique in its execution. A stunning novel."

—Rob Roberge, author of *Liar*

"If you've seen him perform it's no surprise, but for those not lucky enough to have witnessed LA spoken word legend Ferguson in action, his debut novel *New Jersey Me* delivers the literary version of a manic burst of joyful optimism in what can sometimes be an unfriendly and complicated world. His endearingly eccentric characters lovingly display the humanity all around us, while the story, almost secondary to these beautiful people he's created and allowed us to know, mimics the internal chaos with which we all struggle—and catches the reader off-guard by offering peace in such chaos."

—Lenore Zion, psychologist and author of *Stupid Children* and *My Dead Pets are Interesting*

"*New Jersey Me* is a gripping novel full of heartbreak, awkward sex, and violence. The underlying heart and humor will keep the reader utterly engrossed. Ferguson's prose is lyrical and gripping. One of the best coming-of-age novels I have ever read. A fantastic debut novel from an amazing veteran poet."

—Tony DuShane, author of *Confessions of a Teenage Jesus Jerk*

"A novel rife with Ferguson's sharp, verbal gymnastics that'll keep you locked in and hungry for more as you're driven brilliantly through a beautiful tale of lost souls."

—Adrian Todd Zuniga, founder of Literary Death Match

"Richard Ferguson is wonderful—his book is playful, grand, and disturbing. His words flow like a new Cadillac driving down Killer Highway 9—"Decked out in a pearl-white blouse, fuchsia skirt, silver high-heeled pumps, and still sporting the remnants of a tan from her last Mary Kay–sponsored vacation to the Bahamas, all she said was: 'Well? What do you think?'" I think it's brilliant."

—Jack Grisham, author of *An American Demon* and *Untamed*

"An unforgettable, wild romp through one boy's coming-of-age. But it isn't only fun and games, for behind the chimp, the Mary Kay Cosmetics, the two Bruces (Lee and Springsteen), the coffins, the bongs, the booze, and the girl with one leg is a whole lot of tenderness, heart, and soul."

—Jessica Anya Blau, author of *The Trouble with Lexie*

"Like one long double live Springsteen LP—if Springsteen had suddenly gone gonzo grammatical magician singing about one-legged lovers and kidnapped chimps, Joan Jett strippers and Mary Kay Cadillacs, the taste of Count Chocula and cigarettes…Ferguson's debut novel burns with big-hearted life."

—Jamie Blaine, author of *Midnight Jesus*

"A weary mother leaves her goodbye note by the vodka bottle and bails in pink suede pumps with a Vicodin in one hand and suitcase in the other. Her young son Mark buzzes with adolescent grief that only teens who downed SpaghettiOs, Ozzy Osbourne, and David Lee Roth records in equal parts can understand. While Mark's mother dreamt of dumpier pastures three towns away, our sharp protagonist hurls defiantly towards loserville. In *New Jersey Me*, you don't want to be anyplace else. Ferguson's easy prose is a sly ride from the flirty Charlie perfumed Cotton Candy girls at the local circus to a motherless place of anxious rage fueled by sadness. Ferguson captures what Joan Didion refers to as "The loneliness of the abandoned of whatever age." For, in *New Jersey Me*, we are left looking for clues of how you lose someone: in the old man's recliner, in the lazy umbrella's of a mother's *Beach at Cannes* print, in a one-legged girl's heart, in the remnants of puke in the white shag carpet, or in the way she silently stepped out the door."

—Antonia Crane, author of *Spent*

"In the tradition of Michael Chabon's *The Mysteries of Pittsburgh*, David Mitchell's *Black Swan Green*, and the best parts of JK Rowling's *The Casual Vacancy*, this remarkable first novel from poet Rich Ferguson is in one sense a classic coming-of-age, finding yourself story in which a young man plagued by soul-crushing small town ennui and a pervasive sense that his family are not really his people struggles to both embrace and transcend his own roots. Being a poet, Ferguson makes full use of his unflinching lyricist's voice to create a stylized, symbol-rich imagining of this literary archetype as an evocative and darkly witty portrait, perfect in its imperfections, not only of a dysfunctional adolescence but also of a specific time and place in American culture—the hopeful, hardscrabble, self-medicating New Jersey that gave the world *Born to Run*."

—Shana Nys Dambrot, art critic and curator

"Anyone who's ever grown up, had parents, been in love, loved rock and roll, done drugs, not done drugs, heard voices, spoken in tongues, driven too fast, puked too long, heard two hearts beat as one, seen shooting stars over an open road on the way to find themselves will love this first novel by poet and musician Rich Ferguson. I read the entire book with a smile on my face. It reminded me of some of the best novels I read when I was his protagonist's age, masterpieces by Tom Robbins, Ken Kesey, Ishmael Reed, William Kotzwinkle, and Kurt Vonnegut.

It's an earworm of a novel, nesting in your head when you put it down and then singing to you like a siren until you pick it up again. A masterfully painted portrait of coming-of-age in eighties America, of dysfunctional domestic derangement, teenage rage, rabid restlessness, sweet adolescent strangeness. And love. Hopelessly hopeful, soulful, and life-altering love. When I read Rich's prose I feel like a new language has been invented just for me. Like the best I've ever read, I was sorry to see it end but grateful it'll live with me 'til I die. He paints with his prose in varying styles and from an infinite color palate as your mind's eye draws across his pages: abstract expressionism, Impressionism, cubism, surrealism, photo-realism, lyrical abstraction. They all meld and become vividly accessible, crystal clear in their detail, drawn with a drummer's unerring sense of rhythm and time, as Modern Fergusonism. *New Jersey Me* belongs in the libraries, museums, and concert halls of every seeker's ever-expanding mind and heart."

—James Morrison, actor and singer/songwriter

"Ferguson's poetic prose takes us on a magical ride through adolescence, specifically the time when all you could dream about was leaving home, even if you didn't have the wherewithal to do so."

—Jodyne L. Speyer, author of *Dump 'Em*

"If you want to read a searing account of a hero's reckoning with a devastating childhood and subsequent redemptive wrenching from a hellish American hamlet, this is not your book. This is no *Bastard Out of Carolina*, it's more like *Accident Awash in Blackwater*—the narrator's hometown near the New Jersey shore. The hero is not one and his tale of growing up in a drab, industrially polluted town with a somewhat neglectful mom and abusive dad is neither brutal nor harrowing enough to be redemptive, but rather ordinary and even laughable. *New Jersey Me* is a paean to the everymen and women who live lives, not of quiet desperation but of grumbled quasi-shittiness. How do you strike out from a place that isn't quite there anymore, surrounded by people whose chronic mantra is to get out? How do you leave parents who never fully embraced *or* abandoned you? If Huck Finn had to exchange the Mississippi for a nuclear facility's runoff creek and his BFF Tom Sawyer was a sexually ambiguous basement-dwelling Italian kid with a passion for bongs, Tolkien, and Stevie Nicks, what adventures would they have? Rich Ferguson delivers the answers and then some with down-home wit, plainspoken insight, and a goofy, revelatory lyricism rendered true poetry by its earthbound origins in the armpit of America. This is a vision quest where epiphanies can only be glimpsed from one eye of dilapidated seaside Lucy the Elephant, over an ocean facing the wrong, backward-looking direction, or hinted at, on a littered rainy shoreline with the sun sinking behind America's western promise, walled off by a wasteland of postindustrial detritus. It's about insisting on staying in a place that has already deserted you, where you wish you were stuck but are merely adrift. It is the protagonist's gentle but persistent demand that beauty be accounted for and love confessed to that ultimately sees us through; his story eclipses the hero's journey and gives us instead a real boy's passage into actual, fumbling adulthood, all of it to a red hot soundtrack that includes The Clash, Black Sabbath, Nazareth, R.E.M., and of course, The Boss himself."

—Heather Woodbury, playwright and performer

"It isn't often someone can take on New Jersey with the kind of aplomb worthy of the Boss himself; the impressionistic, secondhand accounts of the place are every bit as legion as jokes about neighborhoods correlating to exits on its famed Turnpike. Which makes what Rich Ferguson has done, in his boldly-titled *New Jersey Me*, nothing short of a near-miracle: put bluntly, this is as authentic, as lived-in an account, as pitch-perfect a rendering of the Garden State's special brand of denizens as exists. So dust off your vinyl copy of *The Wild, The Innocent, and the E Street Shuffle*, crack open a cold one, and enjoy Ferguson's lovely, street-lyrical prose. I sure as hell did!"

—David Kukoff, author of *Children of the Canyon* and *Los Angeles in the 1970s*

"After meeting the stoners, misfits, and pill poppers who inhabit the radioactive, ghost-haunted pages of Ferguson's debut, you'll never listen to Bruce Springsteen the same way again."

—Jim Ruland, author of *Forest of Fortune*

New Jersey Me

New Jersey Me

Rich Ferguson

A Barnacle Book | Rare Bird Books
Los Angeles, Calif.

A Barnacle Book | Rare Bird Books
453 South Spring Street, Suite 302
Los Angeles, CA 90013
rarebirdbooks.com

More from Rich Ferguson at rich-ferguson.com

Set in Minion Pro
Printed in the United States

10 9 8 7 6 5 4 3 2 1

Publisher's Cataloging-in-Publication data

Names: Ferguson, Rich, author.
Title: New Jersey me : a novel / Rich Ferguson.
Description: First Trade Paperback Original Edition | A Barnacle Book | New
York, NY ; Los Angeles, CA: Rare Bird Books, 2016.
Identifiers: ISBN 978-1-942600-53-4
Subjects: LCSH Bildungsromans. | Rock music—Fiction. | Suburban life—
Fiction. | Nuclear power plants—Fiction. | New Jersey—Fiction. | BISAC
FICTION/General.
Classification: LCC PS3606.E7265 N49 2016 | DDC 813.6—dc23

This book is for those who've escaped, or those fighting to free themselves from their own Blackwater.

"In those days, there was neither here nor now, only there and the time it would take to reach it."
—*Marvin Bell*

"Talk about a dream, try to make it real."
—*Bruce Springsteen*

Chapter 1

JIMMY AND I DRIFTED through the circus crowd on a magic carpet combo of weed, brews, Jimmy's mom's codeine cough medicine, and the downers I'd swiped from my mom's medicine cabinet. All around us laughter and merry-go-round sounds filled the air with a lively music. Lion roars and trumpeting elephants made us feel like we'd been dropped into an episode of *Wild Kingdom*. Stuffed animals were being won, hot dogs and cotton candy consumed. High school girls—with their deliriously sweet scent of Charlie perfume and Double-Bubble bubble gum—hung out by arcade games, flashing teasing looks, taunting us to bet our last quarter to win them the latest Ozzy Osbourne or David Lee Roth record.

"Not bad," Jimmy mumbled through a mouthful of caramel corn. I agreed.

For a week out of every year, the Wilbur Brothers Family Circus transformed our little town from its drab and dreary self into a dizzy freefall down an *Alice In Wonderland*–style rabbit hole. Contortionists, human cannonballs, and fire breathers had us grinning like we were spun on laughing gas. The Zipper spun us until we didn't know which way was up. Bumper cars allowed us to ram head-on into friends, enemies, and strangers. So what if most of the animals looked like petting zoo rejects, and the workers like ex-cons ready to kick our asses? Even a ride on the Ferris wheel could lift us high into the sky, temporarily taking us out of Blackwater.

That's all I'd ever wanted—to escape my shithole South Jersey town any way I could. I'd tried sex, drugs, and music. All had helped me break out in some way or another. That evening at the circus, I had no idea that my greatest escape was only weeks away.

Jimmy and I continued floating through the circus crowd, occasionally brushing elbows or bumping into the usual assortment of townies: muscle-teed thugs and Springsteen wannabes, off-duty cops and dull-eyed strippers, the radiated and medicated. It felt like we were all engaged in a strange dance orchestrated by the merry-go-round's eerie, sickly-sweet calliope music that my weed, codeine, and pill-jangled brain had morphed into beat-heavy, psychedelic space rock. Around and round we went, where we stopped—who knew, who cared? For those few moments, gone were all my past problems: the car crash, the kidnapping, and the rest. Saved Me. Sky High on My Blackwater Ferris Wheel Me.

Jimmy and I continued drifting through the crowd. We ended up in a dirt lot behind the big top. Carnies rushed by, tending to rides, food stands, preparing animals for performances. A stringy-haired, pimple-faced girl approached us, gave us the once over. My Etch-a-Sketch scribbled mess of dirty-blond hair, ripped jeans, Who *The Kids Are Alright* T-shirt, along with Jimmy's dark, sleepy eyes, equally ripped jeans, and ratty Fleetwood Mac *Rumors* tee had us looking less like male-model material, and more like rock roadies in training.

The circus girl asked what we were up to.

Luckily, I was present enough to point toward the wooded area beyond the circus. "We're outta here," I said. "It's Miller time."

The girl nodded an approving *cool* then hurried off.

Jimmy and I passed exhausted, mud-covered elephants. Bears, lions, and tigers huddled into cages so small they could hardly move. A few bore visible whip marks. The sight of so many animals peering at us through their prison bars, flashing tragic eyes as we passed, undazed some of our drug haze.

"Hey," I said. "Check it out."

There was a lone cage behind an empty trailer. Inside that cage, atop a skimpy bed of piss-fouled hay, sat a chimp—dusty, unkempt. Was missing some hair on his arms and head, and across his chest. Was about the size of *Lancelot Link*, that secret agent chimp I'd seen on TV as a kid. He stared at us with big droopy brown eyes—eyes a lot like Jimmy's—and stuck a hairy hand through his cage bars.

I brightened slightly. "Looks like he likes us," I told Jimmy.

At that moment, we knew squat about primates; we were just taking a wild guess about its sex. But over the next couple days, after plowing through some Jane Goodall books we'd borrowed from the Ocean County Library, and talking to a friend of Jimmy's dad—the local vet, Doc Morton—we'd learn the chimp was indeed a male, about three years old, and surprisingly well-adjusted given what he'd gone through.

When Jimmy and I reached for the chimp's hand, he exhibited very little fear. Barely whimpered, only briefly made a pouty face.

Jimmy handed the chimp some of his salty, sugary caramel corn. The chimp bobbed his head, grunted, begged for more.

The more Jimmy and I fed him, the more he warmed up to us. He groomed Jimmy's arm, my arm.

"We should give him a name," I said.

In considering that one, Jimmy's face scrunched up like a crumpled beer can. It was only when he uncrushed himself that he said: "Mr. Jeepers."

I repeated the name a few times aloud. Those four syllables danced between tongue and teeth. Felt and sounded like a circus in my mouth. "Sounds good," I said.

Once we'd handed over all the caramel corn to Mr. Jeepers, Jimmy said: "What now?"

I eyed a tire iron leaning against another trailer's back tire. Then I glanced around—not a carnie, human cannonball, or contortionist in sight. "Let's take him," I said.

Those words flew in the face of the pet jinx Jimmy and I had repeatedly experienced when we were younger. No matter what types of pets we'd owned, no matter how well we'd cared for them, they'd always wound up belly up.

Looking more at Mr. Jeepers than me, Jimmy said: "You sure about that?"

I told him absolutely. Said it had been years since either of us had owned a pet. Surely we must've grown out of that phase. Besides, I added, jinx or no jinx we could give the chimp a way better home than these skeevy circus people. Then I grabbed the tire iron. The crowd noises and circus music were so loud I couldn't even hear the cage lock pop.

Once I opened the door, Mr. Jeepers just stood there, wobbling slightly on his feet, and looking at us all loose-lipped. There was, however, a moment where his brow furrowed, his lips pulled back, baring teeth. At the time, I thought it meant he was pissed. But later, after going through a chimp behavior book, I'd realize it meant he was scared shitless. "Maybe we should sing to him," I whispered. I woozily crooned Steve Miller's "Jungle Love."

Jimmy joined in.

By the time we hit the chorus we had Mr. Jeepers smacking his hands against the floor of his cage, and spitting the occasional Bronx cheer through his lips.

"*Now*," I said.

We each grabbed a hairy arm, hoisted the chimp from his cage. Upright, he was a little over two feet. Around twenty-seven pounds I'd later learn—slightly less than a flat tire. At the time Jimmy and I were foolish enough to believe all chimps were like the trained, docile ones we'd seen on TV. We'd soon read how chimps were naturally territorial, stronger than humans comparable to their size. Given our wasted state at the circus, Mr. Jeepers could've easily inflicted some serious wounds. But that night, and for all our time together, the chimp remained chill.

I grabbed Mr. Jeepers' hand. While wrinkled and leathery in appearance, it was soft to the touch. Jimmy grasped Mr. Jeepers' other hand. With unsteady voices we warbled through "Jungleland," "Welcome to the Jungle," "Bungle in the Jungle," "Telegram Sam," "The Lion Sleeps Tonight"—any song we could think of that had the word *jungle* in the lyrics as we stumbled along, not sure of where we were going, just knowing we had to stay clear of the main roads.

We bolted along side streets dotted with vacant lots and shotgun-blasted stop signs, cars propped up on cinder blocks on dirt lawns and shabby trailer homes where no lights shined through the windows at any hour of the day. We roared past oak trees riddled by gypsy moths and dilapidated shacks where beer-guzzling Pineys lounged in easy chairs, completely mesmerized by alcohol and the TV's dull blue flicker.

We continued running. Breath panting. Shoes and bare feet slapping against road.

Whenever Mr. Jeepers needed a rest, Jimmy or I would carry him in our arms. Whenever we heard a barking dog or squealing tires, the chimp would briefly hoot, holler, and latch his arms tighter around our necks. Between all our singing and gasps for air, Jimmy and I assured Mr. Jeepers everything would be okay.

Through the streets we continued running.

The warm and clear, pine-scented air, riddled with cricket chirps and bullfrog grunts, felt good against my face. Mosquitoes buzzed the dark like tiny winged torpedoes. From inside one of those trailer homes we passed, a radio cranked Tom Petty's "Refugee." Just like all those evening sounds and smells, I felt completely electric and alive.

The three of us paused to rest in the alley behind my work—the Rainbow Casket Company, which was owned by one of my old man's drinking buddies, Mr. Delaney. In that dreary alley, Jimmy, Mr. Jeepers, and I were blanketed mainly in shadows. Only a thin sliver of moon grinned down on us.

Jimmy let go of the chimp's hand so he could inspect a wadded-up Kleenex someone had tossed out in the alley. Mr. Jeepers brought that tissue to his nose, then extended it toward the night sky. He repeated the gesture, as if he were not only trying to blow his own nose, but a ghost's nose. As he did so, I flashed on all those caskets filling the Rainbow showroom. Especially my nemesis: the child-sized Heaven-Sent. How I'd managed to spend so much time around that casket, and all the others, without slitting my wrists, was a complete mystery to me. I gave the chimp's hand a squeeze. He glanced up at me, mimicked that squeeze.

"Here's the deal," I told Jimmy. "We'll have to keep Mr. Jeepers at your place."

"What about all the stuffed animals?" Jimmy asked. "Think that might freak him out?"

I shrugged. "Not as much as a pissed-off cop."

We continued our singing and running through the streets, only now in the direction of Jimmy's. As we did so, I told Jimmy that for Mr. Jeepers' food and upkeep we'd need to kick in cash from our jobs, in addition to selling all our crappy footwear to Mad Man Milligan—a crazy local that, for years, had been buying our old socks.

"Speaking of which," I said. "Let's make a pit stop."

◆ ◆ ◆

WE ENDED UP IN a dirt lot across from Mad Man's squat shoebox of a shack, located in a wooded area dotted with other ramshackle homes, alongside the town's Third Lake.

About Blackwater's three lakes.

The First Lake was a summer Siberia. It's where all the overweight, zit-faced, and socially awkward orchestra and glee club geeks got stuck. Also the moms and their little runts. Every year they'd all end up with pink eye and hellacious earaches from so much rancid bacteria in the water.

The Second Lake was a step up. There you'd get better looking people. *JC Penney* catalog model types. Wholesome boys and girls with clear skin and all their teeth. Every so often you'd get a wild card—a bikini-clad tourist girl from out of town who didn't know the scene.

But the Third Lake: not only was that where Mad Man lived, but it was also the place where the slutty ex-cheerleaders, washed-up jocks, and guys like Jimmy and me hung out. Our common bond: booze and drugs. Every summer—in our weed, pill, and JD haze—we'd strut around like the beautiful Venice Beach–bronzed gods and goddesses we'd seen on TV and in the movies.

Dotting the Third Lake's perimeter that evening were souped-up muscle cars—Camaros, Mustangs, Pontiac GTOs—where equally muscled and tattooed dudes, along with their halter-topped and bikini-bottomed sweethearts, were either leaning against vehicles, downing brews and listening to stereos blasting classic rock, or huddled inside, making out—windows fogged.

Since Jimmy and I had already sweated and sung out most of our drug haze from running through the streets with Mr. Jeepers, I was relatively clear-headed when I called out the title of an old Clash song: "Julie's Been Working for the Drug Squad." That was our signal to inform Mad Man we were ready to do business.

Burly as *Gentle Ben*, he ambled out of his shack. Highlighted in the streetlight glow was his face: pockmarked as the bullet-blasted road signs lining the highway. There was also his Flock of Seagulls sweep of dyed blond hair, *Magnum, P.I.*–style Hawaiian shirt, Sex Pistols–style ripped and safety-pinned jeans, and Doc Marten boots.

"Well if it ain't *The Really Wild Show* meets Blackwater," Mad Man said, eyeing Jimmy and me, then focusing on Mr. Jeepers. "What have you gents done now?"

"We stole him from the circus," I said.

"Yeah," Jimmy tailgated. "He's our monkey, Mr. Jeepers."

Mad Man shook his head. "If you're gonna keep him as a pet, Bucko, you better get it straight. He's a *chimp*, not a *monkey*." With a meaty hand, he clapped Jimmy on the shoulder. "Don't worry. Lots of people make that mistake." Then Mad Man flashed a smile that accentuated the lines around his eyes—eyes as blue as the ribbon on Pabst Blue Ribbon beer. He looked at me. "How's it hanging, Spicoli?"

Jeff Spicoli: Sean Penn's character from *Fast Times at Ridgemont High*. For years, Mad Man had said that my shaggy dirty-blond hair and spaced-out grin reminded him of that Southern California stoner.

I motioned toward Mr. Jeepers, then said: "Looks like we might need to reestablish sock detail."

"Anything to help out a fellow primate," said Mad Man. Whether due to instinct, or because he'd watched tons of nature shows, he seemed to have a natural rapport with the chimp. He knelt down, gently extended a hand. Even though that hand, along with the rest of Mad Man, reeked of spray paint, he must've had some strong, subliminal pheromones giving off positive vibes. Mr. Jeepers jerked free of Jimmy's grasp, lazily extended his hand in a begging gesture toward Mad Man.

Mad Man let Mr. Jeepers latch onto his hand, then said: "He seems pretty cool right now. Probably a little drugged. But you better be careful." He warned us that while chimps were in the same family as us—the great apes—and that they were social creatures, and shared 96 percent of our DNA, they could still be easily angered.

I was foolish enough to say that we had everything under control. Everything would be okay. Said Mr. Jeepers especially liked it when we sang to him. Then I added: "You know how music soothes the savage beast and all."

This time, Mad Man clapped me on the shoulder. "Actually, Spicoli, the phrase is 'music has charms to soothe a savage *breast*.'"

"Whatever," I said. "Shakespeare, right?" I'd paid enough attention in high-school English to learn that he'd penned most every cool and noteworthy phrase.

"*Ehhh,*" said Mad Man, sounding like a game show buzzer. "It's actually from *The Mourning Bride* written by William Congreve."

◆ ◆ ◆

Once through the door of Jimmy's place, we were slammed by the usual olfactory stew of Ben Gay, Lysol, and stale cigarette smoke. Jimmy had grown immune to it all. As for me, while I'd hung out with him for over ten years, the stench still made my eyes water, my nose scrunch up like a piece of tossed litter. It had a similar effect on Mr. Jeepers. He alternately rubbed his nose, and swatted at the air as if trying to make those smells go away.

Jimmy gathered the chimp into his arms and led him through the vestibule where an assortment of his dad's bowling trophies and Korean War memorabilia lined the walls. Mr. Jeepers hooted softly and smacked his lips as he touched the gold-plated bowling trophy tops, along with the framed war certificates: US Army Korean Service and the Silver Star.

Upon entering the living room, however, the chimp got quiet. Surrounding him was an odd assortment of stuffed animals—a sleek gray fox, a huge striped bass, a ten-point buck head, a lumbering black bear, and more—all orders that customers had never picked up from Jimmy's dad's taxidermy business.

We let Mr. Jeepers roam through that quiet jungle. He did this slightly wobbly three-legged walk toward the stuffed fox. He got in its face, carefully observing its marble eyes and snarled expression. Ran a finger along the fine muscle detail Jimmy's dad had built into the animal's legs and back. Mr. Jeepers picked at its fur, sniffed it, licked it, murmured in its stiff raised ear.

I motioned toward the empty reclining chair.

Jimmy and I thought it odd. His dad was hardly ever gone. Normally, he would've been sitting in that recliner, watching the tube or admiring his animals. Since we'd been worrying about his health, we scoured the house. Jimmy's mom was snoring like an asthmatic muffler in her bedroom, but no Mr. Gigliotti. At least his portable oxygen tank was also gone, so that was a relief. After we'd fed Mr. Jeepers some apple juice and celery sticks from the fridge, we carefully led him down to his new room.

Jimmy's basement room was a toxic waste dump, but in a good way.

Three pot plants—Larry, Moe, and Curly—sat atop an old pool table, a constant sixer of Rolling Rock by a crappy Sears turntable, some of Jimmy's mom's sickly-sweet codeine cough medicine beneath his pillow, and the latest killer batch of homegrown was stashed inside the sleeve of his Tubes album, featuring the song "White Punks on Dope." It was all right there: everything we needed to make the walls throb, the music shimmer, and the rest of the world—no matter how tragic or mundane—seem like one long, laugh-your-ass-off episode of *The Three Stooges*.

Unlike those upstairs smells, the basement smells were altogether different: old bong water and Nag Champa laced with a tinge of musty basement puddles. Those smells never really bothered me. The same could be said for Mr. Jeepers. He jerked free of Jimmy's grip, extended that hand, grabbed at the air—like he wanted to bottle those smells, take them with him everywhere.

Jimmy sparked up a fresh stick of incense. Then he sparked up Rhiannon. That was the old dented dryer by his bed. Jimmy never used the puke-green appliance for drying clothes. He'd just turn her on for her warm, soothing white-noise song. While he did that, I cued up Pink Floyd's *Animals* on the crappy Sears. "Pigs on the Wing (Part One)" scratched through the speakers.

With our downstairs soundtrack established, Jimmy rushed back upstairs to search for his dad. I gave Mr. Jeepers a quick tour of his new home. The chimp sniffed and picked at everything: Rhiannon; the pot plants; the grow lights—two, sixty-watt bulbs clamped to busted microphone stands; the old pool table with the felt all fucked up from places where pool cue tips had repeatedly dug into it; the oddball poster collection slapped up onto cinderblock walls; the BB-cracked window looking out onto a grim, gravel lawn; the ceramic gnome whose pointy hat doubled as a coat rack; and the tower of plastic milk crates filled with a various assortment of family photos, bongs, and board games. Mr. Jeepers even explored a portion of the basement just out of reach of bare-bulb light. The spot was cold, shadowy, cobwebby. Jimmy and I rarely hung out there. We called it The Dark Side of the Moon. That's where his parents stored stacks of water-stained boxes stuffed with family junk, moth-bitten clothes, rusted tools, and banged-up kitchenware.

When the tour was complete, Mr. Jeepers and I plopped down on the concrete floor right by Rhiannon. At first, the chimp was freaked by her warm white-noise hum. He'd touch the pulsating appliance with a craggy finger, then pull away. Touch, pull away. Eventually, the chimp chilled out. He groomed himself—licked his fur, picked out bits of circus dirt and debris; the whole time his jaws worked, making chewing, clicking sounds. Once done, he leaned against Rhiannon, got still and quiet. Had an elbow propped atop his knee, chin resting in hand. He was a spitting image of Rodin's bronze sculpture—only much smaller and hairier. The chimp sat there, all dozy eyed, staring straight ahead.

I couldn't tell whether he was missing someone or something, wondering what to do next, or perhaps still under the effects of some mild circus tranq. I mirrored Mr. Jeepers' pose, doing my best to remain as still and quiet as possible.

The chimp sniffed the air between us, puckered his lips. Gradually, his dozy eyes opened into a more natural and enlivened expression. His mouth eased into a slack wide grin, bottom teeth barely showing. Later I'd learn that was his expression for Play. At the time, however, I had no idea what he was trying to tell me. I did my best to mirror his look.

He panted, hooted. Slapped a hand against Rhiannon.

I panted, hooted, slapped a hand against Rhiannon, too.

Mr. Jeepers' eyes grew as wide as the eyes on one of those wind-up, cymbal-crashing monkeys. He sprang to standing and wobbled through the room, a combination of knuckle-walking and hulking along upright.

Around that time, Jimmy returned to the basement. He didn't have to say a word. His wadded-up facial expression translated into: *No pops.*

I did my best to take his mind off the situation. I had him join me in imitating Mr. Jeepers as he roamed through the basement. The three of us bounced up and down on Jimmy's smooshy-springed lumpy bed, played Twister. We even rolled around on that basement floor littered with musty puddles, dust bunnies, and black smudges from where Jimmy and I had squashed out joints too tiny to smoke anymore.

After what must've been hours of play, Jimmy, Mr. Jeepers, and I collapsed onto the ratty sofa. The chimp crawled into my lap. A faint whiff of mud, circus hay, and clear night air still clung to him. He was all huge ears, bulging mouth, fleshy belly, and soft, dark hair. Had a nose so alert, seemed it could sniff in the entire world at once. His bright brown eyes were perched beneath a massive brow. Beneath those eyes, an intricate webbing of wrinkles. Those age-old eyes looked right into mine. Then he reached for my hand. Later, I'd learn how chimps were far less aggressive than humans in resolving disputes. Rarely would they go to bed mad. Just a touch could chill them out. Once Mr. Jeepers cleaned bits of trash from my hair, then stroked my arm with a weathered hand, I felt a sense of peace I hadn't in some time.

Forget all the death, odd shadows, cryptic Ouija board messages, and pet jinxes I'd experienced in the past. I drew Mr. Jeepers close. He puckered his thin pink lips into a kiss, gave me a hug. That's when I noticed morning light spilling through the BB-cracked window. I glanced over at Jimmy, who'd just awoken from a brief sleep. "So," I said. "What now?"

Chapter 2

BACK IN 1975—LONG BEFORE that night at the circus, long before my twentieth year alive—I didn't have Mr. Jeepers or anyone else to help chill me out. There was just Six-Year-Old Me surrounded by what felt like a very haunted Jersey. There was the Jersey Devil—the legendary flying biped with hooves, a forked tail, and blood-curdling scream—that roamed the Pine Barrens. There was also Blackwater's huge, scarred white oak, Satan's Tree. Over a hundred years ago people had been hanged from it. But when I lived there, all I saw, every day, were the newly posted photos, along with the weathered notes, wreaths, and crosses left by the heartbroken parents, friends, and siblings of victims that had crashed their cars into that tree.

There were also the ghosts. Jersey was full of ghosts—the Atco Ghost, the Parkway Phantom of Exit 82, the Ghost Boy on Clinton Road, and the Ghost of Annie on Annie's Road. But those ghosts weren't like the one closer to home. My mom would eventually become my ghost. Not literally. She didn't die. But she always seemed to be there and not there whenever we were together.

My ghost story first began that one Saturday morning in '75. It was spring. A bright blast of sunlight shone through the front living room windows, turning my mom golden as I watched her take part in one of her favorite rituals: housecleaning. Dusting, Pledging the furniture surfaces, arranging and rearranging her Hummel figurines. When she wasn't looking, I bit into a celery stick from her Bloody Mary sitting atop the driftwood coffee table, a cork coaster beneath it. That celery stick: a tangy burst of bad medicine. I dipped it back into the drink. Took another bite. And another. It sent a shock through me. Made my eyes go high beam, body rubberbandy. Then all at once, everything eased into a peaceful, giddy glow. That glow: the equivalent of what Mom would experience after downing a couple drinks. There'd be more music in her voice. She'd hold me close, kiss me repeatedly on the cheek, tell me how much she loved me.

I'd never accuse Mom of turning me into the partier I'd later become. Even if she'd grounded me right then, I still would've found my way back to the bottle. But she never saw a thing. She was too busy singing along with Olivia Newton-John's "Have You Never Been Mellow" blaring over the living room stereo, and gliding through that room, the roaring vacuum cleaner her dance partner.

I swiped another bite of celery. Even took a sip of her drink. The smear of her red lipstick on the glass tasted waxy like birthday candles, but sweet—the perfect chaser for that bitter shock of vodka. Next thing I knew, I was dancing through the living room, and everything spun. The ceiling. The Windsor Cherry grandfather clock with the astrological blue moon phase hovering above the twelve. The display shelf holding Mom's Hummels.

Everything shimmered, blurred. Gone my parents fighting. Gone my only-child loneliness. Merry-Go-Round Me continued spinning. The white shag carpet spun. The hickory liquor cabinet spun. I called out to Mom. Told her I loved her. Twisting, glittering Mom asked if I was okay. I told her yeah. Everything was fine.

That's when all my spinning dropped me to the floor, and the sparkly room went black.

From that moment on, well into my teens, it felt like all I did was stumble from one dark moment in life to the next: Getting My Lights Punched Out Dark. Partying Till I Couldn't See Straight Dark. Maybe that's why I never really got those clues Mom had been leaving along the way.

The first clues: starting when I was thirteen, Mom began spending more time away from home. Beds unmade. Dishes unwashed. At the time, I figured she was just working her usual Mary Kay overtime, or having a blast joyriding in the big pink Caddy she'd recently been awarded for being top-selling regional sales director.

Next: her suppers were often late. And when they were on time, meals were off—lukewarm TV dinners, Tater Tots, or cold pizza as the main course.

I didn't pick up on that either. I could go for days living on little more than the good times and the occasional brew I'd share with Jimmy.

As for my old man, he was another story. Like always, when dinner wasn't sitting in front of him, piping hot, promptly at seven, he'd holler.

When I was little, Mom would just retreat into her dark bedroom to cry and pray. But that had changed, too. For years, she'd busted her ass, working her way through the Mary Kay ranks of Independent Beauty Consultant to Senior Consultant, then on to Team Leader, Future Sales Director, Sales Director In Qualification, and finally Sales Director. The grueling process had made her an armed and armored Wonder Woman. Whenever she was home, she'd stand her ground and fight my old man.

Still another clue I didn't completely get: I rarely heard my parents argue anymore. Back in those days, I'd lock myself in my room and blast my bedroom stereo. I used to refer to my music as my sonic walls, the way that sound would rise all around me—thunderous drums, thumping bass, wailing guitars. Whether it was the Clash singing "Should I Stay or Should I Go," or Springsteen sending me hopeful greetings from Asbury Park—"I strolled all alone through a fallout zone / came out with my soul untouched"—my music shielded me from the outside world.

The last clue, and perhaps the trickiest: Mom's hugs came less frequently. That clue was the hardest to detect, as she'd never been big on physical displays of affection. But on those rare occasions when she'd expressed those emotions, she could never hold me long enough or close enough. So unlike my grandmother, where I'd be gathered into thick arms and pulled so close that I was no longer outside, but in.

Some months after I turned fifteen came that dreaded day I stepped out of one dark and into another far greater. That's when I finally put all those clues together to form the picture of Mom leaving me.

It was a Sunday morning. Like most Sundays, my old man should've already been at work filing the week's police reports and accident records, which meant the only sounds filling the house would be those usual Mom sounds: her NASCAR-sounding hair dryer; the asthmatic coffee maker; and her merciless critique of her Jackie O-like, widely set, stunning brown eyes, high cheekbones, and crisp bouffant hairstyle in the bathroom mirror. On that particular Sunday, there were no Mom sounds, so I slept right up until the last minute, when I thought she'd shake me awake to accompany her to church. Upon rising, the place was quiet: loud quiet. Eerie quiet. All I could hear was the soft burble of birds outside, and the low, steady hum of the neighbor's lawn mower. I lay there, bristling to the densely charged electricity of my old man moving through the house, he and Mom not so much arguing as simply not talking. Then, with the slam of a door, he was gone.

I hopped from bed. Didn't bother flipping on my stereo or lava lamp. Didn't even engage in my morning ritual where I'd face down my two Bruce posters—Bruce Springsteen *Darkness on the Edge of Town*, Bruce Lee *Enter the Dragon*. Instead, I dug deep into my dresser, threw on the first couple things I found—jeans and a Superman T-shirt—then stumbled down the hall. When I reached the living room I spotted Mom. As Catholic as she could be at times, she never bothered with a rosary. Cigarettes were her worry beads. Decked out in a V-neck, shoulder-padded, floral knit dress and pink suede pumps—not her usual sober, business-like church attire—she was sitting on the faux leather love seat, huffing a Virginia Slims. The cigarette's fiery red tip pulsed like a full-on cop siren.

Afraid to move any closer, I asked: "What's up?" My voice felt like something limping out of my mouth and staggering over to my mother.

Mom wasn't as cold as Jimmy's basement's Dark Side of the Moon, but she did possess her own icy calm. Without responding to my question, she just kept huffing her cigarette.

At her feet, I spotted the baby-blue Samsonite suitcase my old man had given her on their first wedding anniversary. Over the years Mom had taken many things to church—her sins, my sins, even my old man's on those rare Sundays when he wasn't working. All those things and more she'd taken to church, but never luggage.

Mom snubbed out her cigarette in the coffee table ashtray, then said: "Your mother needs to go."

"When will you be back?" I asked.

She shook her head.

I wondered if that meant no, she didn't know—or no, no.

A bit of her iciness melted away. Her chin quivered; her eyes grew red, strained.

I took that as no, no. I froze. Couldn't speak or move. All I could do was go camouflage with the living room's off-white walls.

Mom's lips were moving, but I couldn't hear her. It was a bit like how I'd get in math class: simple addition, subtraction, division, and multiplication problems I could handle. But word problems and math formulas—volume, surface area, laws of exponents—always numbed me out. Spun my mind off into a black hole. I was better versed in the mathematics of life: partying times ten equaled Me. Lipstick plus leaving: Mom.

"Did you hear me?" she said. "It's not your fault, honey. I just need to go." She stood, brushed her hands along her dress, then picked up her suitcase. Switched it to the opposite hand, then back again, then sat it down by her feet.

Both of us stood there staring at that suitcase.

"So what is it?" I asked. "Is it Dad? Is he cheating on you?"

That one made Mom almost laugh. "Heavens no. Your father's far too busy for that." She grabbed the suitcase, clutched it tightly in front of her heart.

Later, when talking with my old man, he'd tell me how criminals could rat themselves out without ever saying a word. I'd realize that Mom had done that, too. And while I didn't have the cop jargon to explain her behavior in that moment, it was obvious that her suitcase translated into *I'm already gone*. I stormed across the living room, got in her face. "You *suck*."

"How dare you talk to your mother like that," she blasted.

"I'll talk how I want," I counter-blasted.

She sat the suitcase down, then reached out a hand to touch me, but withdrew it. In a voice there and not there, she said: "You and your father will do okay without me."

I figured she must've downed a couple Bloody Marys because she was talking nuts—Code 10-37: *mental case*. No way would my old man and I survive on our own. With him working so much, I'd have to manage things alone. But I'd never be able to accomplish what Mom had done before going AWOL on housekeeping duties. I was clueless when it came to making the place smell like that wonderful blend of garlic, bacon, and onions whenever she'd whip up her special home-fried potato recipe. Wouldn't be able to make the kitchen sink dishwater that perfect blend of sudsy and hot. I'd forget to put lemon pieces through the garbage disposal for a clean fresh smell. Wouldn't bother using that gross paste of cream of tartar and water to clean the porcelain. All those things and more Mom had done perfectly, and for very little reward, to keep my neutron-bomb old man from blowing up in our faces. Once she left, though, he'd explode in full force. Only this time I'd be his only target. "Please," I said. "Take me with you."

"It's best this way," Mom said, still maintaining most of her icy calm. "A boy needs his father."

I gave the coffee table a solid sidekick. Books, votive candles, and a bowl of sickly sweet potpourri went flying. "What're you crazy? He's an *asshole*."

"How dare you talk about your father like that," Mom said.

"You're one to talk. You're the one leaving him."

Next thing I knew: *slap!* Felt like a sudden rush of bee stings and flames had ravaged my face.

I raised a hand to hit her back, but punched my thigh instead. "Don't *ever* hit me again. I get enough of that shit from Dad."

Mom pressed a French manicured nail into the center of my chest, right over my Superman S. Lines bunched up around her mouth, as she seethed: "Now you listen, young man. No matter how upset your father gets with you what he's really trying to tell you is how much he loves you."

I snorted a sound halfway between a laugh and a sob.

"It's true," she said. "He needs you."

Based on past experience, that sounded like total crap. But I didn't say so. Still stunned by her slap and threat of leaving, I stood there quietly, awaiting her next move.

Looking more at her suitcase than me, Mom managed to say: "I was only twenty-two when I had you. I wasn't even sure I wanted kids. But your father did."

That one snapped me out of my stupor. "You're saying I was an accident?"

"I'm just saying I was too young, honey. I wasn't ready. I don't think I've ever been ready."

She had it all wrong. She'd been a fine mom. And once gone, a big part of my life would be gone, too. No more beauty. No more prayers. No more smiles and tears to fill the house. Gone color. Gone cleanliness. Ditto with that voice calling me *honey* when I hurt. No more advice about girls. Gone heart. Gone kisses. And while she'd never done any one of those things that great, she'd done just enough to keep me happy.

"So what?" I said. "You were just gonna leave and not say nothing?"

"I left a note for you and your father in the kitchen."

"Where? By the vodka bottle?"

Right then, I wanted my words to pack more of a wallop than the smack she'd delivered. But if she was feeling any pain, she didn't show it. My words barely watered up her eyes. Not even enough to shed a single tear. She swiped a Vicodin from her purse, downed it, then grabbed her suitcase, and headed for the door.

Without looking back, she said: "I'm not leaving *you*, Mark. I'm leaving your father." She paused, then added: "You may as well get used to it. This is what people do best. Leave." She continued to the door. As she opened it, golden October light spilled into the room.

"Wait," I said. "Where'll you go?"

"Harborville."

Harborville was only three towns away. It was a dump, though not as big a dump as Blackwater. Screw Mom for going to that lesser dump without me. "If you leave," I said. "Dad'll find you, you know. He's a cop."

"Doesn't matter," she said. "He already knows." Then she gave me a look: looking right at me, looking right through me. On. Off. Total Mom.

"Fine," I said. "Then go already."

She placed a hand on the screen door handle, but couldn't bring herself to open it.

Later, when recalling that moment, I'd be reminded of a Bruce Lee quote: "Optimism is a faith that leads to success." While I'd often tried to live by that creed with mixed results, right then I was a goner. Once Mom walked through that door, all I wanted to be was a loser in spades.

I started my new life by grabbing one of Mom's cheery Hummel figurines—a pigtailed girl playing a violin—and whipping it across the room. It rocketed past the floor lamp, the grandfather clock, my old man's recliner, and slammed into Mom's LeRoy Neiman print, *Beach at Cannes*. Like the Bruce Lee quote, that print—filled with colorful umbrellas, blue skies, and sunbathers strolling by an even bluer ocean—was a constant reminder that happier days were just ahead. Screw that. Along with the shattered figurine, the picture frame glass and print were totally smashed and torn apart.

If, on any other day, I'd smashed one of her Hummels like that, Mom would've grounded me for a month. But on that day, she just silently stepped through the door.

She was gone. Gone for real. I was so frozen with fear that I couldn't even pick up the phone to call Grandmother for support. All I could do was puke all over Mom's white shag carpet. That puke was chockfull of her lousy Spaghetti O's dinner from the night before, along with the beer I'd later downed at Jimmy's place. In the past, whenever I'd thrown up due to stress, Mom had been there to help clean up. Now there was only me.

My gut knotted up even more. Felt like I was giving birth to a brand new me: Nowhere Me. Blown To Bits Me. Like Mom, that new me just wasn't there anymore.

Chapter 3

ONCE MOM LEFT, THE last shreds of home sweet home vanished, too. Family photos in the living room appeared sadder, grayer. The toad lilies out front wilted. Dust conventions gathered on every furniture and décor surface—from the charcoal-gray, wide-wale cord sofa to the creepy porcelain harlequin wall mask. The rich brown and red rag rug in the hallway now seemed a total sham. I'd once read in history class that female settlers had woven those rag rugs as a way of dealing with the sadness of their husbands being away hunting.

Certain aspects of Mom still remained, or at least seemed that way—the Sweet Bay Magnolia scent of her hair, and the music of her voice drifting through every room—but the house told a different story.

Most days the place was quiet: faded tombstone quiet. Wilted flower quiet. All that quiet recalled an old Irish saying my old man had once told me while we were admiring a winter night sky: "The stars make no noise." My house was even quieter than those stars. And when it wasn't, it creaked and groaned. Maybe those noises were due to the water pipes or the house settling. But back then

I thought differently. There were ghosts roaming the halls. No matter how high I cranked my sonic walls I could still hear them. They let it be known they were there to stay.

I did my best to battle the ghosts.

Within a few days of Mom's leaving, I began dusting, vacuuming. Even put lemon pieces through the garbage disposal, and made that nasty paste of cream of tartar and water to clean the porcelain. It was all so time-consuming. What I'd normally seen Mom do in a few hours took me almost an entire day, not including feeding my old man and myself.

So I put out a call for reinforcement.

The very next afternoon—a Thursday—my grandmother showed up. Sturdy, broad-chested, refreshing: a beer keg with appendages. She was armed with a load of dust cloths, towels, colorful plastic buckets, sweet-smelling cleansers, and other supplies. Once plopping them down in the front hallway, she gathered me into a huge hug that reeked of menthol and bacon grease. Her black wool coat scratched at my face. Her shoulders clicked when she hugged me tighter. Those sky-blue, lined, and wizened eyes of hers sparkled a hello behind librarian-style glasses. She asked in that sandpapery Irish brogue of hers: "How are you, sweetie?"

Not only had it been another day of battling ghosts, it had also been a day of battling school. Mainly math. I could only muster a shrug.

Grandmother swiped a kitchen timer from one of her plastic buckets. "We're gonna play a game to help cheer you up."

I told her unless it was called Get the Hell Outta Blackwater it probably wouldn't do much good.

"It's called Beat the Clock," she said. She tossed her coat over the living room sofa, then spied the surroundings—the white shag carpet, the Hummels, the grandfather clock, and other items—

some belonging to Mom, some to my old man. As she focused on Mom's furniture pieces her forehead creases deepened. Maybe she was imagining how to properly clean them, or recalling past run-ins with Mom. Whenever they'd gotten together, they were all pleasant smiles at first. But those decayed far faster than the half-life of uranium. Grandmother would attack Mom's mothering skills, railing on how she was far more absorbed in housecleaning and Mary Kay than me. Mom would say she was nuts. That she should mind her own business. Whether or not Grandmother was recalling those fights, all she said was: "How long do you think it'll take to clean the room?"

I recalled my past cleaning ventures, how time-consuming they'd been. With Grandmother helping, I figured we'd achieve much better results. "Four hours?"

Grandmother cracked her knuckles. Made a sound like her bones were tap dancing. "Let's cut that in *half*," she insisted. The excess fat under her arms shook as she flashed me double thumbs up.

All I flashed back was a smirk. "You're nuts," I half-laughed. It was the first time I'd uttered anything close to the sound of happiness in days.

Grandmother winked. "That's why you love me."

I retrieved the vacuum from the closet. We laid out the Pledge, Windex, Woolite carpet cleaner, and other items. Before we set off, Grandmother said: "We need some cleaning music. Something upbeat."

I immediately flashed on Springsteen's *Born to Run*. I retrieved it from the pile of records in my room, slapped it on the living room stereo. Cranked it.

Grandmother set the timer and off we went.

I began vacuuming. She began scrubbing at the rust-red blotch on the carpet; the puke stain I hadn't been able to totally eliminate after Mom's leaving.

As for Bruce, he began with "Thunder Road." It started out slowly at first—just piano and his voice. While he was singing about Roy Orbison singing for the lonely, I cleaned beneath the coffee table and around the sofa, careful not to clank the nozzle too harshly against the pristine furniture legs. The whole time my eyes remained on the cleaning, but my ears were tuned to the song. The drums kicked in all mellow at first while Bruce continued singing about staying hidden beneath the covers and studying pain, making crosses from lovers, and throwing roses in the rain. Though I'd heard those words countless times before, right then they sounded different. Sure it was cheesy as hell, but it seemed like Bruce was singing directly to me. Something like a wake-up call or warning. So when the drums kicked in full throttle, and Springsteen said the night was busting open and the two lanes could take us anywhere, I took that as a direct cue. Latched onto the Electrolux, zoomed across the living room. Suddenly, that vacuum didn't sound like a vacuum anymore. More like a high-performance engine. The power nozzle banged into Mom's grandfather clock, my old man's La-Z-Boy recliner, and the liquor cabinet. It wasn't like I was trying to hit them. But it wasn't like I was trying to miss them either.

Over Springsteen and the vacuum, Grandmother called out: "That's the spirit. We'll be done in no time."

She was right. We finished all our cleaning, were even able to take a snack break a good half-hour before we heard the timer ding.

Then, like she'd often done before, she assisted me with math homework. She'd studied the subject in college. Had even continued challenging herself long afterward. While on walks around the neighborhood, she'd pull a pad and pen from her purse, jot down random house addresses—add, subtract, multiply, and divide them. Would take note of all the geometric shapes. Stop sign: octagon. School zone: pentagon. She knew all about functions and derivatives. Factoring and algebraic expressions. No matter how often Grandmother tried passing her math gene on to me, the end product was usually zero.

That most recent tutoring session involved a word problem— something about a six-foot tall guy named Joe that cast a five-foot-long shadow. He noticed that the shadow cast by his school building was thirty-feet long. Given that, I needed to figure out the height of the building.

Before even knowing how to solve the problem, my mind was already spiraling off on a Tilt-a-Whirl daydream powered by those words. That name Joe recalled all kinds of Joes: the singer Joe Jackson. Shoeless Joe Jackson. Joe DiMaggio, which led me to Marilyn Monroe. Pills and death. "Candle in the Wind." All kinds of winds: breezes, gales, hurricanes. "Rock You Like a Hurricane." What about that building of unknown height? Buildings got me to cities. "Detroit Rock City." "It's Hard to be a Saint in the City." There'd also been that mention of shadows. "Moon Shadow." Also *Dark Shadows*, that vampire soap opera I'd seen in reruns. It had featured zombies, werewolves, and ghosts. Ghosts and shadows brought me back to Mom. With or without sunlight, her shadow spread far and wide throughout my home. Once my brain had spun through that entire thought process, I didn't give a shit what the height of the damn building was, and I told Grandmother so, only in slightly kinder words.

She sat me down at the kitchen table, pulled her pen and math pad from her purse. Flipped through a few of the small lined yellow pages that had random numbers and equations scrawled all over them. Once she landed on a blank page she drew a stick figure of Joe and labeled his height—six feet. Then she scribbled back and forth, creating his shadow—five feet. Next she sketched a building with a question mark next to it. Afterward, she scratched its shadow: thirty feet. She stopped there. "Know what to do next?"

I made a couple lame attempts to figure out the answer. But no matter how hard my tongue drilled the roof of my mouth, I couldn't figure it out. I flashed Grandmother a look. Code for: *I have no fucken idea what to do next.*

So she continued. She drew a line from the top of Joe's head that extended to the end of his shadow. Then she drew a line from the top of the building that connected with the tip of its shadow. That's when she asked: "What do those look like?"

Didn't need to tongue-drill the roof of my mouth to answer that one. All those extending and connecting lines began taking shape in my brain. "Triangles?" I said.

Grandmother peered at me over the top of her glasses perched low on her nose. "Ex*act*ly!" she said. "Know what to do next?"

Again, I made a couple futile attempts to solve it. And again I shot her the look that made her continue on her own.

With her pen, she traced down the length of Joe, then along his shadow. Did the same with the building and its shadow. She explained how they both had right angles, and since the shadows were cast at analogous angles, the angle-angle postulate proved they were similar. Then, as if I weren't lost enough already, she said something about six is to X as five is to thirty. Then six times thirty: one-eighty. After she'd spun that ball of confusion into a tangled web of bewilderment, we were left with the following equation:

$5x = 180$

"What next?" asked Grandmother.

For a change, I thought I knew. My old man—taking a rare break from his mountain of paperwork—had once assisted me with that very type of problem. "Divide both sides by five so X is by itself?" I said, with a slight rise in my voice at the end of that question.

Grandmother flashed another double thumbs up. "Now *do* it."

Once I'd completed my calculations, I said without any sign of question or hesitation: "The building is thirty-six feet tall."

Grandmother didn't have to say a word. Her huge smile said it all. That smile split her face wide open and gave the wrinkles around her nose, mouth, and cheeks their own wrinkles. Screw Mom's Mary Kay products to make those wrinkles go away. Grandmother's smile was a blast of pure light. Chased away all the ghosts and shadows in my home, if only for a little while.

Chapter 4

OVER THE NEXT COUPLE weeks I did my best to build upon that happy home Grandmother had helped to create. Cooking. cleaning. Was doing it even when I wasn't doing it. With Springsteen as my soundtrack, I had nightly dreams of scrubbing the toilet and cleaning tracked-in dirt stains from the carpet. Dreams of boneless chicken breasts, lemon juice, and olive oil. Those were just a few ingredients in Mom's prized Mother's Day Lemon Chicken recipe.

Through it all, my old man doled out an occasional thank you, but was generally oblivious to how hard I was working. He was so buried in paperwork, and studying old photos of him and Mom in their younger, happier days that he'd become almost as much a ghost as her.

Then there was that one Saturday morning, nearly three weeks after Mom's leaving.

I'd just awoken from dreaming my same old dreams. I slapped on a U2 *War* T-shirt and a pair of jeans. Then I flipped on my lava lamp. Staring at those glowing blobs of red wax for hours on end had always allowed me to feel stoned even when I wasn't.

Once I'd caught a buzz, I sparked up the stereo. While Hüsker Dü's *Everything Falls Apart* soared through the room, I engaged in that morning ritual—facing down my *Darkness on the Edge of Town* poster. Tried mastering Springsteen's hands-in-pocket relaxed but solid stance, that don't-fuck-with-me look—one eyebrow slightly raised, mouth somewhat open, gaze unwavering. Imitating Bruce Lee was even trickier: knees slightly bent; evenly balanced between ball of left foot and right; left shoulder back; right arm—loose, relaxed, extended; hand out and up, but not so far up that it blocked my vision. Some days, when I'd almost mastered the Springsteen stance, Bruce Lee would be a total car wreck. Other days when I'd almost perfected Bruce Lee, the Springsteen stance would look like I'd gone Code 10-24: *intoxicated*. It was all so involved and demanding, that morning ritual. But that was the kind of shit I needed to do back then to get along.

Another thing that helped: my Ouija board. I'd often referred to it whenever faced with problems. Sometimes it was way off. Like once it told me I'd marry Farrah Fawcett. Other times it was spot on. The day before Mom left, when I'd asked the board what that Sunday would bring, it spelled out: T-R-O-U-B-L-E. I laid the board out on my bed, placed the inverted heart-shaped pointer between my hands, then asked: "When will everything be okay?"

The pointer didn't move right away. Just hovered on the word GOOD BYE. Then it gradually wobbled upward, past 5, over R, finally landing on E. It then wiggled upward toward the smiling moon, but sailed back down to rest on A. Then it glided down across the O, alighting upon 2, but then immediately floated back up, sharply to the right, finally coming to land on T.

E-A-T. What the hell did that mean, I wondered. All I'd been doing for the last couple weeks was cooking or dreaming about it. The last thing I wanted right then was food. I stuffed the board back in my dresser, stumbled down the hall. Everything was cold and shadowy—my home bitter home's version of Jimmy's Dark Side of the Moon.

I peered through my old man's slightly ajar office door, spotted him at his desk.

He was studying a photo of Mom. It was a picture of her at nineteen: doe-eyed, ruby-cheeked. At the time, she was working as a waitress at a seaside North Carolina diner. That's where my old man had first met her. Once that Jersey-raised, twenty-three-year-old, rough-and-tumble Marine, newly released from Camp Lejeune, first heard Mom ask whether he wanted his eggs scrambled or sunny-side up, he was hooked. After just two dates, he was already promising her a home, money, and stability. Then it was back to Jersey, where he enrolled in the police academy. Not long afterward, he gave Mom a ring, a City Hall marriage, then me kicking around in her gut. And while the pressures of marriage and family had them continually growing further apart, they'd always shared something in common—in their own ways, they'd both wanted to clean up Blackwater. I knocked on my old man's study door. "Can I come in?"

He turned from the photo, snatched up a pile of papers. "Make it fast. I'm busy."

I stepped inside. Plastered all over the walls were his photos: one of him in the Marines, brandishing an M16 marksman rifle; another of him receiving Officer of the Year award; still another of him receiving a gold medal of valor. There were others: him after passing his sergeant's test, lieutenant's test, captain's test, and finally being sworn in as Police Chief. Those photos were a constant reminder that no matter how Bruce I became, I'd never add up to my real-life-hero old man.

Another thing about my old man.

Normally, he resembled that badass Sergeant Carter on *Gomer Pyle, U.S.M.C.*: gravelly voice, buzz-cut brown hair, intense blue eyes. But with Mom gone, he'd changed. The hair around his temples: grayer. The starched beige button-up, which he'd worn for the last couple days: sweat-stained, wrecked. Equally as wrecked: his face. The lines across his forehead and around his mouth—lines that Mom had once said the underlying collagen holds a memory of in each crease—were even more pronounced.

My usual hatred gave way. "You all right?"

My old man could see that my whole body was a billboard for worry: muscle tension, tired eyes. Also a few extra zits; nowhere near as many as those poor socially awkward First Lakers possessed. "Yeah," said my old man. "What about you?"

I shrugged. Spotted a few boxes on the floor containing Mom's Hummels; Mary Kay awards, outfits; and other prized, personal possessions. Written across each of those boxes in my old man's meticulous print were the black magic marker words: *Sylvia's Items.* "Taking those to Mom?" I asked.

"At some point."

"Need any help?"

"Sure you want to do that, Mark?"

That's when I recalled the note Mom had left my old man and me. It reminded me of certain caves in North Jersey. Legend had it those caves were filled with all kinds of primitive paintings. A dragon here. A centipede-looking creature there. Some stick man hauling ass from a blood-red bull. That's how Mom's note had been—as cryptic and unable to prove true as those paintings. All she'd said was she was sorry for leaving, but needed to be on her own to find herself. She ended it all with the word: Love. "You're not gonna stop her," I said to my old man, "are you?"

In a voice sounding more dead than beat-down, he said: "Nope."

That didn't surprise me. Like Jack Lord on *Hawaii Five-O,* my old man was a tough Irish cop that had served warrants, tracked down criminals, and directed investigations. When it came to

Mom, though, he had little authority. Suddenly, I wanted to curse and scream. Demand what he'd always demanded of me—to be a man. That's what we most needed at home right then: a man. But I was afraid if I started yelling, I'd never stop. Next stop: Trenton Psychiatric Hospital.

"I just don't get it," said my old man. He tried to say more, but couldn't. Instead, his hands did all the talking: those fingers clenched into fists then relaxed. Fists, relaxed.

I studied my old man's hands. Those were the hands that had beat on tables, beat on me, and had held Mom. Those were the hands that had fired guns, collected trophies, and dragged criminals to jail. Those were also the hands featured in that dreaded photo on his study wall. It summed up our relationship. Snapped only hours after my birth, the picture featured my old man's beefy hands frozen in the moment of handing First Born Me back over to Mom.

"Now what?" I asked.

After more hand clenching, and brow furrowing, my old man said: "We'll have to pull together to make things work around here."

It had been tough for him to say that. It was equally as tough for me to say: "I know."

That's when I got an idea, right after I'd spotted a photo on my old man's study wall. A photo just above the one of him handing me back over to Mom. This other photo featured a younger version of him during his marksmanship training at the police academy. "Let's go shooting tomorrow out in the Dump," I said.

"Not another one of your bright ideas, Mark."

He had it all wrong. Over the years, we'd often discussed firearms, but I'd never shot one. Mom would never allow it. This was our big chance for some serious .38 caliber male bonding. "I'll bet you're a better shot than Dirty Harry and Jesse James all rolled into one."

That one softened my old man up a bit. But he still didn't go for it.

I gave it one last try. Told him we needed to be real men. Blow some shit to pieces.

That one made him almost laugh.

"So?" I said. "Deal?"

After some serious brow furrowing, he said: "Deal."

◆ ◆ ◆

THE DUMP WASN'T REALLY a dump. It was just a huge undeveloped wasteland area. Seen from one angle it was nothing more than a huge sandbox filled with tons of tick-infested pine trees. From another angle it was the last bastion of freedom on the edge of a dead-end town. For as far as the eye could see—spent condoms and bullet casings, empty beer bottles, blackened and abandoned bonfire pits, tire donuts dug deep into dirt. Cops rarely patrolled the area. They'd often park just outside the Dump's entrance, along the highway shoulder. Once partiers were gutsy or stupid enough to leave, the rules changed. The boys in blue would set off their cherry tops, light up the night like a disco, pull them over, and dance them down to the station house.

Yet while in the Dump, it was white-trash Disneyland all the way—teenagers hopped up on black beauties and raging hormones screwing like jackhammer jackrabbits in the back of parked cars; hard rockers blaring Black Sabbath and Rainbow from muscle cars, tripping balls, barking at the moon; Bud-guzzling, redneck Pineys zooming along in reverse in rebel flag-decaled, souped-up street racers, while blasting Bulldog revolvers, and Vietnam-era M 36 handguns out open windows.

The best time to have any privacy in the Dump was on Sunday mornings. That was when everyone else was either at church confessing their sins, or at home sleeping off massive hangovers.

My old man produced a pistol from his shoulder holster. "This is a Smith and Wesson K-38 Masterpiece Model 14 target revolver," he said. "It has a six-inch barrel and adjustable sight." As he extolled the gun's virtues, there was no longer any hint of that downtrodden, wifeless man from the night before. Weapon in hand, he was back to full-on cop mode. He aimed the revolver at a distant bottle target we'd set up, and squeezed off a shot.

The bottle exploded in a boom of glittery bits. A spooked blue jay cut across the ashen November sky. It passed pine tree after pine tree casting dull shadows, just like that math word problem and my home with all their shadows. My old man squeezed off another shot.

This time, a forest rabbit—a rabbit not much unlike the one I'd briefly owned as a child until my pet jinx got it—skittered across the landscape.

My old man continued firing shot after shot. Bottle after bottle exploded.

As he continued shooting, I recalled something he'd once told me about guns. How when a round fired that meant it was a good round. But if the hammer fell and there was no explosion, it was a dud. On the other hand, if the hammer fell and you only heard a pop, it was a squib. That meant there wasn't enough gunpowder in the cartridge casing. That was a dangerous situation because it meant the bullet was still lodged in the barrel, and if you fired off another round that bullet would impact upon the squib and the gun would explode from the built-up energy that hadn't been released.

All that built up energy. "C'mon," I said. "Hurry up already. Lemme shoot."

My old man reloaded the pistol, handed it over.

I held it like it was a newborn baby.

"Jesus Christ," he said. "You're a teenager. Grip it like you mean it." My old man—all 5'11" of muscle and stoic looks that I got gypped out of in the womb—pulled me close. Braced his right shoulder against mine, reached around with that hand, wrapped my fingers securely around the revolver's rosewood grip, and repositioned my shooting arm. He slung his other arm around my scrawny left shoulder, grabbed my free hand, and cupped it beneath my shooting hand for support.

As we aimed at another bottle target, my eyes watered, palms sweated, trigger hand trembled.

"Take it easy," said my old man. "I got you."

He held me tighter. For a change, his meaty grip on me felt warm and reassuring. So was his scent of sweat and Old Spice. He began giving commands: "Maintain a strong stance. High hand grasp and hard grip on the weapon. Keep your eye on the front sight. Gun steady on the target. Depress the trigger with the end of your finger."

I did my best to obey. Squeezed off a shot. The noise was far louder than the sonic walls I'd built with my bedroom stereo. This new noise filled my ears with high, sustained, feedback fuzz. Made my head heavy metal. The gun's recoil sent a sharp jolt up my arms, traveled deep into my shoulders, my brain, and ignited brilliant, blinding fireworks behind my eyes.

"*Wow*," I said. "That was intense."

My old man gave my shoulder a squeeze. "Not bad. But you were nowhere near the target."

He continued offering suggestions. But each time I'd get one thing right, another would go wrong. Right then, my head felt as cluttered and jumbled as all those boxes my old man hadn't yet delivered to Mom. My ears ached from all the gun noise. My hand

and arm ached from the kickback. I couldn't have hit the target if it were right in front of me.

For a while, my old man kept cool, probably more out of pity than anything else. Like me, he'd been an only child. Part of him sympathized, knowing how difficult it had been to grow up feeling lonely and frightened. Then there was another part of him, the part that seemed to hate my guts for having to watch me live through that hell all over again. Eventually, the sweat stains beneath the arms of his starched button-up grew much larger than normal. "Goddammit," he finally snapped. "Wake up. You're off in your own world. Just like your mother."

Just like your mother. Four words he often used when we fought. Because I slightly resembled Mom in looks and manners this was his way of battling her without battling her.

"I'm trying," I said. "Just relax already, will ya."

"Don't tell me to relax, Mark. I'm in no mood to cater to your bullshit."

I recalled something Mom had once read to me from the Book of Corinthians—how love was supposed to be patient and kind. Obviously, my old man had missed that lesson. I tried to bolt, but he clamped down on me.

I struggled to break free.

He clenched tighter, forced my shooting hand into the air. "Easy. You're holding a loaded weapon."

What a load of shit. I stomped on his foot, then quickly applied a handgun disarming technique he'd once taught me. Had I executed the reverse wristlock perfectly, I would've dislocated his shoulder or broken his wrist. That wasn't the case. Still, I'd performed the move well enough to serve its purpose.

Code 10-47: *subject armed.* Gun in hand, I took a few steps back.

"You sonofabitch," said my old man, shaking the pain from his hand. "Drop the weapon."

I didn't budge. I just stood there recalling a time when I was nine. My old man had whipped the shit out of me after discovering that still another one of my pets—a guinea pig—had died. My old man called me a lazy, irresponsible little shit. But I'd saved up weeks of allowance to buy that animal a top-notch aquarium home, complete with a drip water bottle, along with fresh litter, fruits, and vegetables. No way could I begin to explain my pet curse to my old man, when I couldn't understand it myself. Even if I'd known what to say, my old man wouldn't have listened. For days after that beating, I had black-and-blue belt marks on the backs of my legs.

Shaking me from that memory was my old man saying: "I'm serious, Mark. Drop the gun. *Now*." He took a step forward.

I gripped the .38 tighter.

He took a few steps back. "Just relax, Mark. There's no need to do anything foolish."

Back in those days, I figured my old man to be the root of all my problems, especially when it came to Mom's leaving. So I let him have it way louder than that gun. "Screw you," I railed. "I *hate* you."

If that wasn't nuts enough, things got even crazier. Felt more out of my body than in it. I trained the gun on my old man's heart, pulled the trigger. First there was the boom. What I heard next was the keening, dying cry of *me, not me*. With that cry, my old man was down on the ground, ribs heaving, body shuddering. His blood was redder than the sumac leaves that lay around his body. All that red—red the color of emergencies and rage—kept pouring from his chest, all over those red, red leaves.

I blinked once, twice, rattled myself from that murderous vision.

There I was again, still holding that gun on my very alive old man. And while I'd often secretly wished him dead, no way could I actually make it happen. I dropped the gun to the ground amidst those red, red leaves.

My old man holstered the weapon. Then he seized me by my white sweater, dragged me to his off-duty Chevy Caprice. Once there, he got in my face and flared: "Listen good, shit for brains. You have no idea how much I loved your mother." He dosed me with a couple smacks upside the head.

To a degree, I figured I deserved his abuse. But after he continued dosing me, enough was enough. I tried hitting back, but he blocked the shot, punched me in the gut.

I doubled over. All the air left me.

He slammed me up against the car, and said: "If you *ever* point a gun at me like that again you're dead. Got it?"

I didn't respond. I just stared at all the wrinkles across his forehead. Since Mom had left those wrinkles had multiplied by ten.

My old man smacked me again. "*Got* it?"

"Got it," I choked out.

He shook his head. Then he glanced down at the ground, then up at the clear blue sky, then back at me. "Get in the damn car."

Once inside, my old man jammed it into drive. We sped off in a kicked-up cloud of dust.

When we reached blacktop, he power-punched the gas. Kicked the V8 into overdrive. The speedometer climbed to sixty-five. Seventy. We zoomed past shotgun-blasted road signs, past a shotgun-blasted, ten-point buck strapped to the hood of a pick-up, ready to be stuffed by Jimmy's dad, or turned into venison stew. We barreled past the Rainbow Casket Company, the cemetery, and, looming ahead in the distance: the Crab Creek Nuclear Power Plant. As a child, I'd often tried running away from all of Blackwater's death and destruction. But each and every time, I never got very far. Even before reaching the end of my block, I was always stopped by the same old fears—the fear of being alone, or of losing Mom's dinners like Easy Chicken Cordon Bleu with Buttered Rice. As for Grandmother, once I left her, I figured I was a goner. The thought of that alone was scarier than my scary town. I was always back home before my parents ever knew I'd left.

My old man locked eyes with mine in the rearview mirror.

"Well?" I taunted. "You gonna hit me again, or what?"

He reached back to do so, but instead offered a different kind of jab, more like a knock-out punch: "Your mother got off easy when she left."

Chapter 5

THE WHOLE DRIVE HOME after our Dump incident, my old man had only gotten quieter and quieter, meaty hands gripping the steering wheel tighter and tighter. That was when he was to be most feared. Not when he'd flare and rage like a roaring .38. But when he was like a squib, when all his unreleased emotions were shoved down deep inside. Then, there was no telling what the next trigger would be that would blow everything to shit.

As for me, no amount of quietly humming Springsteen, Pink Floyd, or any one of my other sonic walls bands had been enough to shield me from my own anger. I banged my fist against my thigh. Cursed my old man under my breath. By the time he'd skidded into the driveway—leaving burnt rubber on an otherwise pristine, oil-stain-free driveway—my jaw ached, my thigh: bruised. But that didn't stop me from bolting from the car, running to my room, and locking the door behind me. I plopped down onto the warm carpeted floor, grabbed the phone, punched numbers.

Grandma picked up before the first ring had completed. "Hello?" Her voice seemed slightly more ghost than gregarious.

"You okay?" I asked.

She told me she was fine, but I could hear some odd rustling over the line. "Everything, alright over there?"

"Sorry, sweetie. My skin's been a little itchy lately." Normally, Grandmother might've cracked wise, saying maybe she should get some Mary Kay hand cream from Mom, but instead she said: "How are things with you and your father?"

I couldn't so much hear as feel my old man angrily pace the carpeted hall to shreds just outside my room. I lowered my voice. "Not so good."

"How do you mean?"

"Let's just say we're not seeing eye to eye."

"You can stay with me if you need."

I considered that one. Then I recalled Mom's words before she bolted: how I needed to get used to people leaving me. I knew Grandmother would eventually do the same, except for different reasons than Mom. No way did I want to be there when that happened. Then I thought of Jimmy. "Thanks anyway," I said. "I gotta go. I love you." I hadn't even given my grandmother a chance to say I love you back. I'd already disconnected the line.

But just as I was about to phone Jimmy, I recalled our most recent argument. A week prior, the prized Lee Majors *Six Million Dollar Man* action figure Mom had given me back when I was ten had gone missing. I'd accused Jimmy of the theft. Told him to keep his greasy Italian fingers off my things. The very next day I noticed the neighbor's dog dragging his butt all funny across the lawn while taking a dump. After he'd finished, I spotted a plastic arm sticking up out of the dark, steaming pile. It was Lee Majors' arm.

I was about to pull out my Ouija board, ask it whether or not I should phone Jimmy when I figured, screw it. Way too much work. Besides, it would probably give me that weird E-A-T response anyway. So I punched numbers. Jimmy picked up on the third ring. Before he had a chance to say hello, and before I had a chance to worry any further about his response, I was already saying: "I nearly shot my dad."

Jimmy didn't respond.

Great, I thought. *Lee Fucken Majors.* "Didja hear me?" I said.

Finally, Jimmy said, "So wait. Was it an accident, or were you *trying* to kill him?"

I didn't know how to respond. While my old man and I were filled with more conflict than cordiality, talking any further about shooting him was way too weird—the type of crime Blackwater's brain-nuked, inbred Piney locals committed against relatives on a fairly regular basis. "Look," I pleaded. "Can I stay at your place for a while?"

Jimmy could've easily said no. Ever since meeting back in fourth grade, we'd had our history of brawling and branding each other with ridiculous names. Like one time in fifth grade: Jimmy bought a turtle that soon died of unknown causes. I'd bought a hamster that soon died of a respiratory infection. For a good year, whenever we got pissed at one another, I'd call Jimmy *Jack the Ripper*. He'd call me *Son of Sam*.

Still, our bond was tight. Besides our shared pet jinx, we also loved martial arts and getting wasted. We were also both only children in our own way. Jimmy's older brother had moved up to Hoboken that year. And another thing: we shared a common nemesis, Terry. Every summer, he was one of the drunk, muscled thugs that would hang out at the Third Lake alongside the likes of Jimmy and me. Eventually, Terry would stop harassing Jimmy. I wasn't as lucky.

After some dead air in telephoneland, Jimmy said: "Lemme talk to my pops."

Within minutes, his dad was out front in his tobacco-brown, black-interior, '55 Chevy pickup called Bessie, after the blues singer Bessie Smith. Bessie was equipped with an original V8 engine, wrap-around windshield, egg-crate grille, 80-watt in-dash speakers, flame-cut steel spider web gauge panel, stainless steel skull gearshift knob, and running board behind the cab door.

Bessie was very cool, but not as cool as Jimmy's dad.

As a young man, Mr. Gigliotti had served in the army during the Korean War. Wielded a Thompson .45-caliber sub-machine gun with far more ease than I'd handled my old man's pistol. Now in his early fifties, Jimmy's dad was still lean, agile, strong-armed, partly from brandishing that submachine gun, partly from being a semi-pro bowler in the fifties and sixties, and partly his rigorous taxidermy work. He sported a thin inky mustache, an intense, self-assured gaze, and slicked-back, salt-and-pepper hair. He also wore basically one style of clothes—flannel shirt and overalls. Why waste any time worrying about what to wear, he'd always say, when he could instead utilize that brain space pondering his family and taxidermy. Mr. Gigliotti's badass attitude plus that standard outfit of his made him a rural version of the suave and menacing John Dillinger from his FBI wanted poster. This was before the poor health, before the oxygen tank. He seemed almost happy to be at my house, even though it couldn't have been easy. Jimmy's dad stepped out of his pickup.

Once my old man spotted him through the front living room window, he said: "What the hell's he doing here?"

"Helping." I opened the door for Mr. Gigliotti.

My old man shot him an interrogation-room glare.

Jimmy's dad flashed back his own searing, gray-eyed gaze. "How you doing, Chief McDaniel?"

My old man kept up his glare. "That isn't alcohol on your breath is it, Ray?"

"No, sir. I'm clean as a whistle."

"I highly doubt that," said my old man.

My old man always gave Jimmy's dad the third degree. Not only did he think Mr. Gigliotti was a lousy bum, unworthy of my adoration, but he'd also busted me a couple times for having beer on my breath when returning from Jimmy's—no matter how much Binaca I'd blasted or how many Tic Tac's I'd eaten.

"Well you better not be drinking and driving, Ray," my old man continued. "The Blackwater Police Department has very strict rules about that, you know."

Mr. Gigliotti swiped the filterless Camel from behind his ear and stuck it between his lips. The cigarette bobbed up and down, as he said: "Yes, sir. I'm well aware of the rules." Then he looked at me. "You ready?"

My old man folded his arms firmly across his chest. "Wait a minute," he interrupted. "Where are you going, Mark?"

More cigarette bobbing from Mr. Gigliotti. "With everything going on around here, Chief, I figured you and your son could use some time apart."

"I can take care of my own damn son," my old man blasted.

I wondered what my old man was thinking. Maybe he was too proud to let Mr. Gigliotti take me, or perhaps it was that I was the only one left to cook and clean for him.

Mr. Gigliotti gently raised his hands, soothed the air as if it were one of the taxidermied animals I'd often witnessed him masterfully paint and varnish. "Easy, Chief. I ain't saying you can't. I'm just saying a little space might help clear both your heads."

Again, my old man got that wrecked look on his face, the one I'd witnessed after Mom first left home. Just then, I almost changed my mind. Told him I'd stick around. But then his look flashed back to that badass sergeant on *Gomer Pyle*.

"I've had enough of this shit," he said. Then he tossed out a threat he'd uttered to me umpteen million times in private, but was now only saying to Mr. Gigliotti for the first time. He meant every damn word of it when he said: "You better watch yourself, Ray. I know where your pick-up is parked every day at five."

He was referring to Duffy's Bar. Jimmy's dad was a regular Happy Hour fixture.

"Just drinking Cokes," said Mr. Gigliotti.

"We'll see about that," said my old man. He flashed another round of glares, then said: "The two of you. *Go.*"

I quickly grabbed some clothes, my lava lamp, Ouija board, and my two Bruce posters. Once outside, I said to Jimmy's dad: "Sorry about that, Mr. Gigs."

"Don't be," he said. "I get worse shit from my wife for drinking outta the milk carton."

I placed my belongings in Bessie, then said: "I wish you were my dad."

Mr. Gigliotti rested a hand on my shoulder. "Your father might have his faults, but he's a good man."

"Not as good as you," I said.

He considered that. Then, in a comforting and scratchy voice, like one of my old Bob Dylan records, said: "Let's just say I'd never give you shit for drinking outta the carton."

He glanced up and down my block, observing my neighborhood filled with posh ranch- and colonial-style homes and well-tended lawns, along with Buicks, Chryslers, and other big American cars parked in oil stain–free driveways. Then he observed my freshly skidded-up driveway. He shook his head, then sparked up his filterless Camel. Through a cloud of smoke, he said: "Whudya say, son. Let's get the hell outta here."

Chapter 6

WHEN I WASN'T ALTERNATELY missing and hating Mom, or on the phone, checking in on my grandmother, or arguing with my old man as to when I'd be returning, I was adjusting to my new life in Jimmy's basement room.

Bongs, beer bottles, and pot plants; leaky overhead pipes; Rhiannon; The Dark Side of the Moon; the ceramic gnome, whose pointy hat now held an extra coat; the oddball assortment of *Lord of the Rings*, Stevie Nicks, and Chuck Norris posters—everything from Gandalf and Saruman to *Bella Donna* and *Lone Wolf McQuade*. It was all fine while visiting, but now it was my home. And while I'd hoped my lava lamp, Ouija board, and Bruce posters would improve the situation, it still felt like Tolkien repackaged—not so much a world of Men roaming the lands of Gondor, just two drug-hungry, music-loving teenagers exploring our own cold, damp, and creepy Jersey Middle-earth.

When Jimmy and I weren't arguing over matters like who'd sleep in the bed versus the lumpy sleeper sofa Mr. Gigliotti had lugged into the basement, or who was a more kickass singer—

Chrissie Hyndes versus Stevie Nicks—I also had to deal with the smells.

Besides the musty puddles, Nag Champa, and old bong water downstairs, combined with the combative odors of BENGAY, Lysol, and stale cigarette smoke lurking upstairs, there were also Mrs. Gigliotti's cooking smells. The pervasive, heady, and soulful aroma of simmering garlic, sausage, onions, and tomatoes would recall what my house used to smell like before Mom left.

Just a week into my stay, I walked through the door after school. Mrs. Gigliotti was in the kitchen whipping up some sausage, peppers, and onion hoagies. All those smells sucker punched me. I steadied myself against a vestibule wall, took a few deep breaths, wiped at my burning eyes.

Mrs. Gigliotti approached me, studying me long and hard. "What's the matter, son? You been drinking?"

I blinked once, twice, studied Mr. Gigliotti's Korean War medals lining the walls. Thought *machine guns* instead of *Mom*. "I'm just a little dizzy."

Jimmy's mom wiped her hands on her apron, then dug inside the pocket of her shabby flannel housecoat, pulled out a pack of Lucky Strikes, and sparked one up.

Though veiled in a noxious cloud of smoke, I was still able to get a good look at her. With Mrs. Gigliotti, it was like watching TV with lousy reception. Her big teeth, lined and nervous face, and graying hair recalled a more haggard, staticky version of Alice from *The Brady Bunch*.

I coughed out a "how are you today?"

Between puffs off her Lucky Strike, Mrs. Gigliotti croaked: "I've been better." Her voice was far more rough-edged than my grandmother's voice—a cross between nasal North Jersey and a smoker's rasp. "This fall's been playing hell with my arthritis."

While Jimmy's mom was fifty-two, her liver-spotted hands, physical ailments out the wazoo, and a parade of wrinkles marching over her brow and around her eyes, had her looking at least fifteen years older. That made sense. She'd given birth to Jimmy's brother back in her mid twenties. All the diaper changing, extra cooking and cleaning had been tons more work than she'd expected. Once Jimmy's brother turned nine, Mrs. Gigliotti insisted that Mr. Gigliotti get his tubes tied. Just as he was about to do so, she discovered she had another pie in the pizza oven. Enter Jimmy.

I glanced down the hall, through the kitchen window. Spied the distant image of the Crab Creek Power Plant. That evil radioactive specter with its massive hourglass-shaped steam towers recalled a recent report I'd heard on the news: how radon had recently been detected in numerous Jersey basements. I turned back to Mrs. Gigliotti. "Quite the view you have there."

She sighed out another cloud of smoke. "Beats Newark any day of the week."

Still, Missing Mom smells, radon, and the occasional bickering aside, life at Jimmy's wasn't bad. There, at least, I didn't have to worry about hiding my beer breath or stoned-out eyes. And while Jimmy's parents weren't keen on his partying, they didn't put the kibosh on it. They figured if they did he'd just rebel and continue anyway. So rather than having him get wasted out in the real world, where lurked dangers such as my cop old man, Jimmy's parents condoned his activities within the confines of his basement room.

One Friday night, a couple weeks before Christmas, we were plopped down on Jimmy's cold cement floor. We were seated right by Rhiannon. As usual, she was humming warmly and steadily. For additional warmth we had Jimmy's bong, his Tubes record jacket, some of his mom's codeine cough medicine, a sixer of Rolling Rock, and a holiday tree we'd fashioned from an old hat rack with cutout cereal box fronts folded into cone shapes and attached as ornaments. There was also my Ouija board sitting between us.

"Let's do some looking into the future," I said. "You first."

Jimmy placed his hands on the inverted-heart pointer then asked: "Will I ever get married?"

At first the pointer did nothing. Neither did we. Jimmy and I just sat there stone quiet. All we could hear was Rhiannon's warm song, along with faint gunshots and tire squeals from the upstairs TV.

Gradually, the pointer drifted upward from GOOD BYE, past the 4, the Q, the C, finally ending its road trip on YES.

Jimmy blushed, though it was a little hard to see the red due to his olive-brown complexion.

I raised my beer in a toast. "Way to go, Casanova. Who's the unlucky girl?"

Once Jimmy asked that question, he again rested his hands on the pointer.

This time, it took off almost instantly. It floated downward, coming to rest on S. Then it wobbled next door to land on T. After that: a short trip upward to the left to land on E. Once done, it spelled out: S-T-E-V-I-E.

What a surprise. Jimmy's favorite singer: Stevie Nicks. "The board's been known to lie," I said.

"You wish," he shot back. He tossed me the pointer, flipped the board around. "Your turn, buttmunch."

Aloud, I asked that first question Jimmy had. But the truer, more secret question I said to myself was the one I'd asked in my room just after Mom left: *When will everything be okay?*

It didn't take the pointer long to spell out the word it had before: E-A-T.

Jimmy howled over that one. "Dude, you're gonna marry EAT. Like *eat* my dick!"

I flipped the pointer at him like a Chinese throwing star, then huffed: "Like I said, its been known to lie."

We grabbed our beers, downed them in a few huge gulps. Then we chased it all with a couple swigs of his mom's cough medicine.

"Hey," said Jimmy. "Check it out, Pac Man." Pac Man. That was one of his most recent nicknames for me. He called me that because of the *wah-uh, wah-uh* sound my ratty black Converse high tops made when I walked.

I countered with my own nickname: Pong. That seventies video game. Like that game, Jimmy could be boring as hell. Especially with how he'd spend so much time in his basement room, getting buzzed, and reading *The Hobbit*. Said he loved it for the treasure hunt and adventure. I figured he was secretly in love with the Wargs, Wizards, and Elvenkings. Me, I was never into that fantasy crap. I craved grittier, more streetwise things: Springsteen's *Greetings From Asbury Park*. "Dude," I said. "You're so blinded by the light."

"Whatever," said Jimmy. "Listen to this." He plopped his Stevie Nicks *Bella Donna* record onto the turntable and cued up "Edge of Seventeen."

The tune started slowly with a chugging guitar and drummer playing four on the hi-hat. Not long after Stevie had sung, "Just like the white winged dove..." Jimmy stopped the record with his finger.

"Not this again," I said. One of his favorite pastimes: looking for hidden messages in rock songs.

"Serious," said Jimmy. "It's a good one this time." He spun the LP counter clockwise.

To me, it sounded as cryptic as Mom's goodbye note and every math word problem I'd ever encountered. "I don't hear nothing," I said. "Just backward shit."

"You got it all wrong," said Jimmy. "Check it out." He spun the record again, then added: "She's saying dump the crocks in a boiling bowl. Pound them up with a thumping pole."

Another *Hobbit* reference.

I responded with a choice Bruce Lee quote I'd often used in similar situations: "As you think, so you shall become."

"Bullshit," said Jimmy, plopping back down on the cold floor. He grabbed his brown glass bong—brown like the color of Stevie Nicks' eyes, he'd once told me. He sparked up, drew in a long bubbly hit. He tightened his mouth closed, made that coughing sound, which also sounded a lot like suppressing a sneeze. He took in a few sips of air. Then, still holding in the smoke, he managed to say in a choked-off voice: "Chuck Norris could kick that guy's ass any day of the week." With that, he exhaled a great gust of smoke that drifted up toward the mildewy cedar wood rafters.

Minus that bong, Jimmy was a carbon copy of his dad—green flannel shirt and overalls. As for me: ratty jeans and a Def Leppard *Pyromania* long-sleeve shirt, nothing like my old man's crisp white button-ups and slacks. I observed our funky Christmas tree—a Captain Crunch here, a Tony the Tiger and Count Chocula there. But no amount of silly cereal box fronts could make me forget that this was going to be my first Yuletide without my family. I recalled past Christmases: the family gathered around a tree—a real tree, a Douglas Fir—that filled the house with heady whiffs of green. There'd been glittering lights, loads of carefully wrapped presents, Bing Crosby on the stereo, eggnog dosed with rum. But all that cheer never lasted. Mom and Grandmother would argue. My old man would rail about the turkey being over or undercooked. My grandfather—before he died—was civil enough when sober, but belligerent after a few belts of Jameson. None of those Christmases had ever been perfect. But at least we'd all been together.

It was right then—right when that family memory got all tangled up in my mellow beer and codeine high that a few tears leaked from my eyes.

Jimmy asked: "What's up?"

"Whudya mean, 'What's up?'"

Jimmy's eyes got all broken. I couldn't tell whether he was about to bawl himself, or if he was just mirroring my expression.

"Fuck you," I said. "It's just the smoke."

Jimmy scooted closer. He reached out a hand like he was going to place it on my thigh, but stopped. Through a mess of black curls, his stoner brown eyes peered right at me—blinking once, twice—flashing an overly attentive Mother Hen Morse code. And if that wasn't uncomfortable enough, there were also those overhead bare bulb lights—more like interrogation lights—blazing down on me. To top it all off: Stevie Nicks on the crappy Sears with "How Still My Love." The scratchy track was all sexy croons, slick bass, and guitar.

"*Jeez*, you fag," I said, scooting away from Jimmy. "Stop looking at me like that. I told you I'm *fine*."

Jimmy's shoulders slumped. His already sleepy eyes, dozier. But that didn't last. He sat bolt upright, shoulders back, fists up, eyes alert—his version of Chuck Norris fighting mode. "Speak for yourself," he spit back. "You're the one that fights like a *girl*." He punched me in the shoulder.

I punched back.

Then, without a word, we just sat there, hands to ourselves. All we could hear was Stevie Nicks along with faint screams and dramatic music from the upstairs TV.

When I couldn't stand our uncomfortable silence any longer, I said: "Stop Bogarting the bong." I swiped it from Jimmy; pulled out a healthy green bud from the record jacket. Just as I was about to pack up, I heard the toilet flush upstairs. That was followed by water whooshing through the overhead basement pipes. No way could I get wasted while Jimmy's parents' waste products whizzed along just above my head. "Dude," I said. "Road trip."

Jimmy brightened. "You mean what I think you mean?"

I nodded. "Grab your old socks. Let's Speed Racer."

◆ ◆ ◆

Bundled up in puffy down coats, and armed with the six pairs of ratty socks we'd managed to scrape together, Jimmy and I trudged through the dick-shrinking, see-your-breath-turn-to-smoke, unseasonably frigid night. All around us, snow fell plentifully, peacefully—*It's a Wonderful Life* snow. We blinked nonstop to remove the falling flakes from our eyelashes and clomped along the highway shoulder, passing busted beer bottles, wrecked hubcaps, sheered-off lug nuts, and spent bullet casings laced in icy white. Those random glittery objects served as stars—the makeshift constellation leading us faithfully toward Mad Man.

Once we reached the dirt lot across from his shack, I spied the surroundings. Had it been summer, the air would've been filled with the stench of street racer burnt tire rubber and the sounds of cranked stereos blaring from the muscle cars of those Third Lake denizens. That night, however, the accumulating blanket of snow had tucked Blackwater into bed, made everything smell clean, and sound so quiet.

I shattered the serenity by calling out our signal: "Julie's Been Working for the Drug Squad!"

Mad Man emerged from the shadows. His Flock of Seagulls dyed-blond hair was tucked beneath a Santa hat. In addition to his usual Sex Pistols–style jeans, he was sporting a *McCloud*-era sheepskin coat, and *Flashdance* leg warmers partially concealing his Doc Martens.

Jimmy brushed a mess of curls from his snow-stung eyes to get a better look. "What a freak," he muttered.

I agreed. While there were tons of weird mutations being passed down from generation to generation in Blackwater—everything from radiation-linked cancers to a ravenous love of firearms—we had no clue what original mutation had created Mad Man. It was bad enough that he was in his late forties, and dressed like a pop-culture car crash, but he was also buying the town's old socks. What twisted shit he did with them, Jimmy and I could never figure out. No matter how often we pressed Mad Man for an answer, he'd never confess.

"Sleazons greetings," he said, his breath reduced to smoke as it met with the cold night air. "How're you juvenile delinquents doing?"

Jimmy flashed a thumbs-up.

Mad Man flashed one back. Then he excavated a wad of grimy bills from his pocket. "All right, Spicoli," he said, waving the dirty money in my face. "You know the drill."

Jimmy and I handed over the socks we had stuffed in our pockets.

Mad Man examined each pair carefully—determining the wear, smell, and fabric.

Another thing about Mad Man.

He didn't buy socks from everyone. Some of the more bigoted and hateful, redneck, Piney locals he steered clear of. Said their footwear was filled with bad vibes. As for our own socks—the ones we could spare from time to time—Jimmy and I had first figured Mad Man bought the dirty cotton because he was queer for us. He said no way. He just thought we had some righteous foot-funk going on.

Once Mad Man finished inspecting our socks, he said: "Ten."

"Forget it," I said. "Fifteen."

Mad Man spit out a laugh. "I was trying to be generous with the holidays and all, Spicoli. But forget you." He turned to walk away.

Jimmy flashed me a look: wide-eyed, open-mouthed. It was definitely an addled expression, but nowhere near as freaked as that guy in the Edvard Munch *Scream* painting. Jimmy's look was code for: *What now?*

I flashed him my own worried look: *We need booze.*

"All right," I called out to Mad Man. "Deal."

Once we made the exchange, Jimmy and I schlepped down to the liquor store. We convinced some guy hanging out front to buy us a quart of Rolling Rock and a pint of off-brand schnapps. Per the agreement with his parents, Jimmy stayed drink-free until returning home. Not me. The rest of my evening was spent like all those falling snowflakes. The more I drank the more I drifted along in a dreamy white haze. Even when I stumbled to the ground my fall was soft. I never felt a thing.

Chapter 7

THE NEXT DAY—SATURDAY—WAS A different story. I didn't get up until almost noon that day. When I was at home, and Mom was around, she'd wake me much earlier on the weekends to help with chores, or go to church. With me at Jimmy's though, I could sleep as late as I wanted. But the extra Zs hadn't allowed me to skip out on a hangover. I had the spins. Dry heaves. Couldn't walk a straight line to the bathroom. Around four that afternoon, when most of the shadows had cleared from my head, Jimmy's dad rousted me from the couch.

"Alright, son," he said. "It's time to take part in a Gigliotti family tradition."

Jimmy and I snagged our jackets from the gnome. Threw on scarves and boots. Mr. Gigliotti grabbed a long-handled fishing net, cigarettes, and a couple sixers. Jimmy swiped a Styrofoam cooler. Forget riding in super-cool Bessie that day. Mr. Gigliotti had her stored away in the garage, warm and under wraps. So the three of us trudged alongside Route 9, through the frigid, back-hunching air toward Crab Creek Power Plant.

About the power plant.

It was gray and weathered, loomed over my little town like a giant tombstone. Built in just four years, it had been birthed a few months before me—back during the height of the Vietnam War, when astronauts were only steps away from walking on the moon. Within the walls of the power plant's thousand-megawatt facility was enough long-lived radiation to equal a thousand Hiroshima bombs. Maybe all that radioactive waste was good for certain superheroes, but not for me. Over the years I began to feel contaminated. Was sure I glowed like a night-light in my sleep. Stick a plug up my ass, watch me power New York City for days.

Once we reached the icy creek alongside the power plant, I noticed a few other fishermen—some with poles, some not—dotting the frozen landscape. There wasn't a crow, grebe, or gull in sight.

Jimmy's dad sparked up a Camel. Between drags, he said: "Time to catch some fish, boys."

"What about a fishing pole?" I offered.

"Not necessary, son." Mr. Gigliotti pointed to a cluster of dead fish floating belly-up in the creek. Told me how they'd migrated to Blackwater in cold weather due to the power plant flushing water that had been used to cool the reactor back into Crab Creek. The newly warmed creek must've felt like a hot tub to those stupid fish. But on wintry days, when the power plant would occasionally shut down for routine maintenance, party time was over. The creek was back to icy cold, and the vacationing fish would go into shock and die.

All those duped fish: those were the ones Jimmy's dad wanted. They were the easiest to scoop up in his net. He hauled in a load, dumped them into the cooler. Then he handed the net to Jimmy.

Jimmy held it high above his head and called out another *Hobbit* reference: "Here is my dagger, Sting. It glows blue in the presence of goblins like you." He dipped the net into the creek, scooped up a mess of fish. "See," he said. "A, B, C. Easy as 1, 2, 3." Once he'd dumped the stiff catch into the cooler, he got in my face.

I could still smell lunch on his breath: tomato soup, creamed corn, ground-beef tacos.

He pushed the net into my chest. "Your turn."

I could've easily refused. Ever since I was twelve, I'd read all kinds of articles about nuclear power and radiation I'd dug up at the library. Like how radioactivity is often measured in rems. The nuclear waste from a reactor gives off about 10,000 rems per hour. When exposed to 500 rems at one time, a human will die. By those standards, we were all doomed. There was no use fighting it. Even if I had, I was clueless as to whom I'd go after. Forget the corporation that built the power plant, or the ghost of Enrico Fermi, father of the atomic bomb. In Blackwater, it was much easier for residents to visit the strip club, blast off guns in the Dump, or get completely trashed to help forget about the huge nuclear device in their backyard. I dipped the net into the icy waters and hauled up my poisonous load.

After a while, Jimmy, Mr. Gigliotti, and I took a break, cracked open some Rolling Rocks. The beer melted the last remnants of my hangover headache.

I noticed one of the milky-eyed catfish in the cooler. It recalled a time I'd visited Mr. Gigliotti in his shop. Over the course of a few days, I'd studied him stuffing a largemouth bass. He first laid the fish out on a sheet of cardboard, traced around it, made a stencil. Then, with a caliper, he measured the width of the fish in various positions—tail area, belly area, gill area—to determine its various thicknesses. Then, with a couple pairs of scissors—one to cut bones, one to cut scales and skin—he cut straight up the side of the fish. Used a butter knife to separate the outer scaly hide from the inner meat. He scraped out all the meat, muscle, tough tendons, and bone. Took another tool, popped out an eye, and measured it so he'd know how big the glass eye should be. Then, using the stencil he'd made, along with his measurements, he created a Styrofoam form. After soaking the fish skin in a 50/50 mixture of denatured alcohol and water, he fit it around the form. Got a handful of clay, packed it inside the head and cheek pad area to fill it out. The side of the fish that wasn't the "show side" he sewed shut with spider wire. He trimmed the fins, painted them with a material to ensure that they'd dry out properly. Then he painted those fins with a clear caulk compound to make them durable and flexible. Spray sealed it all to lock in the fish smell, and ensure that the paint wouldn't peel off. Then he airbrushed it, carefully fading the brown, yellow, ochre, and other colors into one another. Lastly, he sealed it all up with a clear lacquer to make the colors burst. It was all such an involved process for such a small creature. Then I recalled the moose head he'd stuffed which was on prominent display at the liquor store. A bobcat at the gun and ammo store. Also that quiet jungle in Jimmy's living room. None of those creatures seemed beautiful to me—just dead, stiff, glassy eyed. I could never figure why Mr. Gigliotti loved the work so much. "So what's so great about it, Mr. Gigs?"

"Great about what, son?"

"Stuffing dead animals."

Mr. Gigliotti downed more brew, swiped a drag off his Camel, then said: "It's a beautiful thing."

"Fucken A," Jimmy chimed in. "Tell him about it, Pops." Jimmy was well aware of his dad's take on taxidermy, and wanted me to know, too.

Like Mr. Gigliotti had often done with Jimmy, he explained to me how taxidermy was an art form. How preserving and displaying animals was an ultimate form of respect. But when it first began back in the early nineteenth century, it was a crude process. Animals were gutted, hides tanned, stuffed with straw, paper and rags, without any regard for the animal's actual anatomy. Unnatural preservatives like arsenic made their teeth, eyes, nose, and tongue rot. Skins would dry, tighten, crack. Natural muscle tone: obliterated. Mr. Gigliotti paused, scuffed a boot toe against the hard frozen ground, then added: "But all that changed in the seventies."

"Why's that?" I asked.

"That's when we began stretching animal skins over sculpted molds." Then he ruffled my mess of hair. "That's why you should never refer to an animal as stuffed, but mounted."

"Yeah," Jimmy echoed. "They're *mounted*, not *stuffed*, you *fag*."

"Look who's talking," I shot back. "You Hobbit-loving Bella Donna."

That one made Mr. Gigliotti crack a smile. But it quickly crumbled into a more serious look: Dillinger lean and mean crossed with cemetery somber. "You might be surprised," he said. "Taxidermy isn't just all blood, guts, and death. It's one of the finests ways I know to honor a life well lived."

◆ ◆ ◆

THAT EVENING, A NEW odor skulked through Jimmy's house— Crab Creek fish. Smelled like fried corn meal crossed with armpit sweat. Mrs. Gigliotti—constantly veiled in her own stench of cigarette smoke and BENGAY—didn't like the fish stink either. She went to her sister's house for dinner.

Jimmy's dad slid a plate in front of me. "Dig in, son."

As I stared at the seafood waste dump, I wondered how those fish could've been so foolish, how their innate sense of survival could've tricked them into believing that any kind of warmth and comfort could last forever. I thought of Mom, my old man, and

Grandmother. Wondered how they were doing at that moment. Wondered if they'd been thinking of me. Or had they been like me, filling their time with numerous activities, trying to forget the fact that our home sweet home had rarely been that at all? The equivalent of screwed: Me. Me plus radioactive fish: family. I dug my fork into the seafood waste dump.

"Way to go, son," said Jimmy's dad. "Now you're a true Gigliotti." He cracked open a Rolling Rock, handed it over.

As I downed brew, Jimmy said: "Guess what we did last night, Pops?"

"Besides getting wasted?"

"We sold socks to Mad Man."

Mr. Gigliotti choked out a piece of fish. It landed on the red-and-white checkered tablecloth, right between the three of us. Without missing a beat, Jimmy's dad picked it up, popped it in his mouth, and said: "I've told you to stay away from that guy. He's a *whack* job."

Jimmy waved his fork back and forth, indicating no. "Forget about it. He's harmless."

"So, Mr. Gigs," I barged in, "whudya think he does with all those socks?"

Before he could respond, Jimmy had already dropped his fork and was pumping his fist in the air. "Beating meat mittens," he declared.

"Or fucked-up sock puppets," I shot back.

Mr. Gigliotti waved his skinny arms about. "*Dio Caro.* Shaddup, you meatballs. I hear something else."

Jimmy zipped it. So did I. The only sounds: the hum of the fridge and the wall clock going *tick, tock, tick, tock.*

"My friend, Bill, over at the power plant, tells a different story. Says he's heard Mad Man's been sewing socks into blankets to protect himself from the power plant."

Jimmy cackled. "That's nuts."

"Yeah," I said. "That's nuts."

"Yeah," said Jimmy's dad. "Bill says Mad Man's supposedly found a way to use sock stink to ward off radiation."

Jimmy and his dad howled over that one.

As for me, I kept quiet. Sure a vest of dirty socks sounded insane. But the more I thought about it, the more I realized maybe Mad Man was onto something. Maybe even a genius. And maybe *I* was the idiot. Instead of selling all my socks, I should've been stitching them into my own stinky quilt.

"If you ask me," said Jimmy's dad, "the power plant's safe. It'll be here long after I'm gone."

"Don't talk like that," said Jimmy. "You're gonna be around a long time, Pops."

"Yeah," I said. "You'll outlive us all, Mr. Gigs."

Jimmy's dad shrugged. "The power plant ain't gonna kill us. We're more likely to die in a car crash."

He had a point. Plenty of Blackwater Pineys—in their hopped-up Fords and Chevys blaring Lynyrd Skynyrd and Molly Hatchet—drove like reckless maniacs. Either out in the Dump or through town, where they'd often crash into Satan's Tree.

Deep down, though, I knew the power plant would kill us first. There'd be the power surge, followed by the steam explosion, the rupture of the containment vessel, then the melting of the control rods. All that released radioactivity would light up the night like hell's raging rock club. The inferno-like atomic winds would turn everyone to ash. Ashes mixing, friends and enemies coming together as one. *Maybe that was it*, I thought. Forget everything Mr. Gigliotti had said about taxidermy. Forget stitching our skins around foam-sculpted molds, or treating us with preservatives as a way to honor our lives. Maybe obliterating us to ash was the only way to go. Maybe then my old man and I, or Mom and I, or even

Mom, dad, Grandmother, and I could finally rest happily together forever.

"I dunno," I said. "One day the power plant is gonna get us good."

"You got it all wrong," said Mr. Gigs.

"Maybe," I replied. "But if it did?"

Chapter 8

AFTER NUMEROUS PHONE ARGUMENTS, and a Christmas spent without one another, my old man and I gave the living-together thing another go. But we made some changes. We began by delegating household responsibilities. My old man: yard work, laundry, taking out the garbage. Me: cooking, cleaning, making beds. Nightly, we shared dinner to discuss the day's events. Had even set up a punching bag in the garage to hammer out our aggressions. But whenever our tempers or fists hadn't gotten a good enough workout, we got better about storming off to our separate rooms— my old man to chip away at his mountain of paperwork, me to crank my sonic walls. Sometimes we'd forget our agreement. My old man would raise a fist to clock me if I'd gotten a D on a math quiz. Or I'd call him a son of a bitch if he'd cracked wise about Mom. With time, however, things got better. Never perfect, but at least bearable.

On one of our calmer evenings—an unusually warm Tuesday in mid-April—my old man and I were seated at the dinner table. We were chowing down on one of Mom's simpler recipes I'd prepared—Hamburger Helper Stroganoff. Through a mouthful of food, my old man mumbled: "What's that?"

"What's what?" I said, thinking I'd set the table wrong, or something.

My old man pointed out a bruise on my arm.

Usually, I'd been good about covering my bully bruises in the past, either with long-sleeve shirts, or using Mary Kay concealer that I'd swiped from Mom before she left. But I'd been in such a rush to prepare dinner that I'd forgotten to unroll the sleeves on my Deep Purple *Perfect Strangers* shirt after browning the ground meat. "It's nothing," I said, looking more at my heap of steaming beef and noodles than my old man.

Just as those words had flown from my mouth, I knew it had been useless trying to lie to him. He was a master at noticing when I was avoiding eye contact, or when my gestures were stiff, or when facial expressions were limited to mouth movements, instead of using my entire face.

"It's Terry," my old man said. "Isn't it?" Not only had he witnessed prior Terry-inflicted bruises I hadn't concealed well enough, but he'd also hauled Terry to juvi court on numerous occasions for theft, disorderly conduct, truancy.

"It's fine," I said. "I got it under control."

My old man studied the bruise, studied my arms, which hadn't beefed up much despite all my punching bag whacks. He got a look on his face like he was about to slug someone or something, but instead repeated the words he'd often uttered: "Want me to handle it?"

I gave him my usual response: "Then I'll be in even more trouble."

My old man downed another couple forkfuls of food, and a few swigs of Guinness. The whole time I could see he was considering my situation. The rate of his eyeblinking decreased. Mouth:

hard set in a grimace. Forehead creases: tense. Eventually, those creases diminished, and his mouth relaxed into a slight smile as he jokingly nodded in the direction of his study, where his .38 sat atop his desk. "If you need any reinforcement," he said, "let me know."

Again, I told him everything was fine. I had it under control.

But that wasn't the case the next day at school.

It was between third and fourth periods. Flooding the school hallway were students of all shapes and sizes decked out in spandex, polyester, feathered hair, scruffy hair, and black jackets over T-shirts—all fashion offshoots of *Charlie's Angels*, the disco craze, and that pensive, gritty Springsteen-look circa *The Wild, the Innocent & the E Street Shuffle*.

Over the D-flat drone of the morning bell, I continued down the hall to my locker. Just as I'd spun out the last number on my combination lock, I heard: "Yo, faggot."

Generally, the halls reeked of sour milk, cleaning products, and hairspray applied one too many times to achieve the perfect Farrah Fawcett feathered hairdoo, the Dorothy Hamill wedge, or the spiky, asymmetrical New Wave look. Added to that noxious stew of smells were two new ones: weed and Brut cologne. I knew that stink all too well, along with the stench of those two all-too-familiar words. I wheeled around, spotted Terry.

He slammed me against my locker, got in my face.

Since I'd recently had a growth spurt, I was almost his height. I got a close-up of circles beneath his intense brown eyes. Mouth carved into a pout. Pretty-boy looks flown south. A young James Dean after a weeklong drinking jag.

Terry seized me by my Pink Floyd *Wish You Were Here* sweatshirt.

Not only was that sweatshirt one of my most cherished ones, but *Wish You Were Here* was also one of my favorite sonic wall records. "Fuck off," I said, struggling to break free.

Terry doubled his grip on me. "Just 'cause you're in tenth doesn't make you a big man. Remember, I'm in eleventh."

"Technically," I said, "you're a senior. Don't forget. You flunked second."

He fired off another locker slam.

As we continued tangling, some students stopped and stared. Most kept walking. They'd already witnessed our ritual.

About our ritual.

Back when Terry was seven he woke one morning to find his old man sitting in the kitchen, .22-caliber pistol in hand. When Terry asked what was up, his old man couldn't even look at him. Couldn't say a word. All he did was stick the gun in his mouth and pull the trigger. After that, Terry began terrorizing kids throughout elementary, middle school, and into high school. Most would fight back. They didn't give a shit about what Terry had experienced. As for me, I hated his guts, too. Hated all the times he'd punched me in the arm, the gut, slapped me upside the head, locked me in chokeholds, or fired off locker slams. In those days, whenever he'd knock the shit out of me, all I wanted to do was fight back. But then I'd flash on his dad's horrible story, and I'd just let him continue abusing me.

But our most recent tangle had taken things too far. "You know what?" Terry blasted. "I ain't playing no more, faggot." He seized me by the throat. He squeezed hard, harder than he ever had before.

He was, in fact, not playing. I could barely breathe. The hallway spun. I struggled to break free, but that only made Terry angrier.

"I don't got all day," he said, maintaining his grip on me. "And neither do you. So you gonna be a good little faggot and shut the fuck up?"

More spinning. Things grew dim, cold. Dimmer and colder than Jimmy's Dark Side of the Moon. I nodded.

"I can't *heeeeeear* you," Terry said almost sing-songy.

I barely managed to choke out an okay.

He shoved me to the floor.

I struggled to catch my breath, massaged my aching throat.

Once I'd worked my way upright, I spotted this incredible girl walking toward us. I'd soon learn her name: Babs. Babs Kozlowski. But everyone would come to know her as Baby. She'd just transferred from Harborville High. Had moved to town with her mom after her father walked out on them. And while most girls at Blackwater High were 34Bs or less, slender-shouldered and small-backed Baby was a solid 36C. Her looks were straight from the Susan Dey *Partridge Family*–era songbook: long, straight brown hair; angel face; blue eyes you could drown in. What intrigued me the most, though, were her legs. Lean legs that poured into corduroy pants in a way that made you rethink the material. When it was wrapped around Baby's twelfth-grade legs it wasn't all sandpaper sounding, like it was on most students that cruised the halls. On Baby, that corduroy song was sleek and wistful. I heard that song loud and clear as she glided down the hall toward Terry and me.

"Check her out," I said, my voice all raspy from that choking. "She's hot."

Terry glanced back over his shoulder. "Not bad."

As Baby approached, she locked eyes with Terry.

Terry's mating call: another locker slam.

Baby smiled, kept walking.

Noting the chemistry between the two, I told Terry: "You should go for her." The way my crazy logic worked back then, if a guy like me didn't have a chance with Baby, then at least someone I knew should, even if that someone was my dreaded enemy.

Terry flashed me a greasy grin. "I'll keep that in mind, faggot."

I kept it in mind, too, as a miracle happened: once Terry had fought off all the others—practically every junior and senior at

Blackwater High, with the exception of the Chess Club and Drama Club males—to win Baby's heart, he left me alone. For a while, at least. Finally, I could breathe more easily. In just a couple weeks, the bruises on my neck went through the color wheel of pain: faded from purple and black to a jaundiced yellow, then to nothing at all. Like a different type of Ouija board, I wondered if those bruises were sending me a message. Something I could rely on—a sign, perhaps, of better days to come.

Chapter 9

BECAUSE OF MOM'S QUESTIONABLE mothering skills, any sign of protection a woman offered me—no matter how purposeful or accidental—genuinely felt like love. So it's no surprise that once Baby's legs and the rest of her had come between Terry and me, I worshipped her. Proclaimed her my savior. I spun mental movies of her in bed at night: everything from G to Triple X. At school, I sketched pictures of her in my textbooks and notebook while teachers blathered on about photosynthesis and the fall of the Roman Empire.

One Thursday during math, while I was creating my latest Baby masterpiece, my teacher, Mr. Gibbons, said: "I don't suppose that's something you'd like to share with the class, is it, Mr. McDaniel?"

I covered the drawing with my hand, glanced up from it. Noticed the day's word problem on the dusty chalkboard—the one I hadn't been able to solve since first walking into class. It had concerned a cell that divides into two cells every thirty minutes. At that rate, the problem asked, how many cells would there be after ten hours. That word *hours* got me to days. *Days* got me to songs with Monday in the title: "Blue Monday," "I Don't Like Mondays," and one of Jimmy's favorites, "Monday Morning." There was also Saturday: "Saturday Night's Alright For Fighting" and "Almost Saturday Night." Immediately following Saturday: "Sunday Morning" and "Sunday Morning Nightmare." *A Nightmare on Elm Street.* Streets got me recalling postmen, and how I never receive letters in the mail. Blackmail. Mail fraud. Sigmund Freud. Fred Astaire. Lighter than air. Then there was that word *cells*, which got me spinning on red blood cells. White blood cells. Words like *canceled, cellar,* and *cell blocks. Cell blocks* got me to Terry. Terry got me, once again, to Baby.

Then there was my math teacher—a photocopy of that goofy TV cartoon character Mr. Magoo—repeating his question, and walking straight toward my desk. He passed student after student whose bodies and faces puberty had transformed into war zones of acne, scraggly mustaches, blossoming breasts, periods, and uncontrollable erections pressing against jeans.

Looming over me, Mr. Gibbons slid my hand away from my notebook, spotted a naked Baby sporting a halo and devil tail. With his rental car–smelling breath, he said: "Let's stick to the work at hand, shall we? Otherwise, I'll have to call your father. And you don't want to end up in *jail*, do you?"

A stinging ripple of *oohs* ran through the class.

Those *oohs* were cut short by our regular afternoon announcement.

Over the intercom came that familiar and soothing voice: "Good day, fellow students. Welcome to Eye on Blackwater High."

Eye on Blackwater High was fellow tenth-grader, Callie McCarthy. She'd provide the student body with daily motivational speeches and updates regarding sporting events, after-school programs, and extracurricular activities.

"After school in the library today," she said, "there'll be a meeting of both the junior and senior student councils…"

Many students figured Callie got the job because the administration pitied her after she'd lost part of her right leg in a car crash the previous year.

"Girls' cheerleading tryouts will take place in the gym…"

But I disagreed. She got the job because of her voice. It was a bit like that siren song from the *Odyssey*. Once I heard that voice I couldn't escape her.

"Drama club tryouts for *West Side Story* will take place in the auditorium…"

Something else about her voice: it was a bit like Mom's, soft and sweet around the edges, while deeper down lurked something sad.

"Don't forget, French Honor Society, it's picture day tomorrow…"

Sure, Callie and I had a history. Back in elementary school, she'd always rat me out to teachers whenever I'd curse or draw dirty pictures in textbooks. But every time I heard her speak, I forgave her for everything.

"And that's been your latest edition of Eye on Blackwater High," she concluded. "Have a *great* day."

At the end of that day, just after I'd dumped my math book in my locker, I again heard that special voice, but this time right behind me.

"Hi, Mark."

Callie McCarthy. Beneath the fluorescent lights—lights that made most students look like pale, washed-out suspects in a criminal lineup—her sad, watery hazel eyes sparkled. Her long, straight blonde hair shimmered. Never mind the scar that ran from the right corner of her mouth to down beneath her chin. It was merely a small crack in her finely polished alabaster beauty. Had she ever allowed herself to sunbathe during the summer she would've reigned queen supreme at the Second Lake. For she was Ophelia repackaged: made saner, stronger, less suicidal.

"I liked your announcements today," I said.

Callie's lips turned up into a smile; the left side a little more than the right. As she continued speaking, her hands moved in front of her, as if she were playing a game of Cat's Cradle with invisible string. "Yeah," she said, "what with student council, Drama Club tryouts and all, it's gonna be a busy day."

Up until that year, Callie had rarely spoken to me. But now she'd often say hello and ask about school. Maybe she was genuinely interested. Or maybe she was trying to make amends. Or maybe that fake leg of hers had brought her down to my level.

"What are you up to today?" she asked, stepping closer.

Her hair always smelled like she'd washed it a couple days prior—a hint of sweet strawberries laced with a natural oily scent that drove me wild. That scent eclipsed the hallway's usual stench.

"Not much," I replied. "How 'bout you?"

She reached down, knocked on that fake leg beneath her jeans. "Gotta go get refitted. Growing pains."

As she turned to hobble away, I said: "Wait."

She glanced back over her shoulder.

I took a deep breath and let fly: "I was wondering if…you know…if maybe sometime you'd like to—"

Callie brightened. "Yeah?"

Suddenly, I couldn't muster up the courage to finish asking her out. I grew dry-mouthed, tongue-tied. In a cracked voice—a voice like I'd had when going through puberty—all I could manage to eek out was: "Can I carry your books?"

Callie's brightness dimmed slightly. "That's okay," she said, holding them close to her chest. "I can manage."

On the bus ride home from school I eventually decided to tell Jimmy about my Callie encounter. I left out all the stuff about me not having the balls to ask her out—an *intentional omission* my old man would've called it. I tapped Jimmy on the shoulder.

He continued staring out the window.

I tapped again. "Yo, Sleeping Beauty. Wake the fuck up."

Jimmy spun around, wiped a sweep of curls from his eyes. Normally those eyes appeared sad and dozy. Now they were that times ten.

When I asked if he was alright, he first said yeah. Then he flashed his nervous smile, where only his bottom lip joined in, sunk down below his gum to reveal slightly crooked teeth. I'd first noticed that smile back in fourth grade. Through the years, the smile would come and go, depending on the weather or how much Jimmy had been partying. That smile broke my heart if I stared at it too long.

"What gives?" I asked.

Jimmy shrugged. "Just thinking about my pops."

Back then, that's all Jimmy did. Especially since his dad's doctor had recently told him his lungs sounded awful and that he wanted to take more tests and X-rays. But Mr. Gigliotti had refused. He'd refused to quit smoking, too, no matter how many times Jimmy asked.

After that Jimmy and I fell silent: Six Feet Under Silent. Not Knowing Why Your Parents Do The Things They Do Silent. All we could hear was the wet, sputtery hum of the bus's diesel engine, and white-noise chatter of the surrounding students.

Jimmy broke our silence by saying: "Whadja wanna tell me?"

"Forget it," I said. "It's not important."

"Go ahead. Tell me."

"Guess who I saw today?"

Jimmy's nervous smile eased into a genuine one. "Better not be Stevie Nicks, you fag. She's my future wife." He proceeded to take other wild guesses that got us both smiling: "Cookie Puss? Boy George? Richard Simmons?"

I finally told him: "Callie."

His eyes grew as wide as a Smurf doll. "That *freak*? I thought you *hated* her."

I shrugged. "She's not bad."

Jimmy got quiet. That's what he usually did whenever I'd mention girls. Then he'd change the subject. "Wanna come over? I got some killer weed." It was a mindbomb batch he'd just harvested. Created from seeds he'd scored from a Trekkie classmate, and some sleazy disco creep he'd encountered at the Seaside Heights boardwalk, he called it *The Wrath of Chaka Khan*.

"Lemme think about it," I said. I eased back into my seat, surveyed the other students on the bus. Many were members of various cliques: jocks, cheerleaders, nerds, burnouts, metalheads, video arcade gamers, guys into Rush and D&D, girls that wore Spandex, and others that collected Cabbage Patch dolls.

Jimmy and I borrowed certain elements from certain cliques—a love of loud music, martial arts, and getting wasted—but we never belonged to any one particular group. We were our own.

"Hey," I said to my one and only clique member. "When're you gonna get a girlfriend?"

"Fuck off," Jimmy said. "You always ask me that."

He was right. Even during times when I didn't have my own girlfriend, I'd often tried to help him score to stop him from spending so much time alone in his room. But each and every time he seemed more interested in sucking on his bong than a tit.

"I just ain't found the right girl yet," he said. He went back to staring out the window.

So did I. Over the next few miles, I watched Duffy's Bar, the Blackwater Diner, and the cemetery drift by.

About the cemetery.

Some of its tombstones dated back to the late eighteen-hundreds. Over time, many of the markings on those decrepit headstones had worn away. *Dying in Blackwater was bad enough,*

I thought. But to do so without a name seemed far worse. It was no wonder why flowers rarely grew there. Still, fading flowers and faded tombstones aside, Jimmy and I had snuck in there many late nights over the years to bury various hedgehogs, parrots, and frogs—all animals that had been victims of our unfortunate pet curse. I tapped Jimmy on the shoulder. "You ever wanna get out?" I asked. "Out of Blackwater."

"Dude," said Jimmy. "You're such a broken record."

It was true. Pretty much ever since I was twelve, all I could talk about was heading out to LA at some point and leading a life full of action and adventure like I'd seen in those movies: *Grand Theft Auto* and *To Live and Die in L.A.* There were also bands like X and T.S.O.L. wailing livin'-on-the-edge songs like "Code Blue" and "Johnny Hit and Run Paulene." And those Pepsi commercials I'd seen as a kid, where everyone's on Venice Beach playing volleyball, skateboarding, lifting weights, and looking beautiful. "I'll get out someday," I said. "What about you, Hobbit Lover?"

"Just because Frodo Baggins left home," said Jimmy, "doesn't mean I have to." He shifted in his seat, then added: "Guess I never really thought about it anyway."

He went back to staring out the window. Ditto with me. A busted-up and abandoned pick-up floated by. The words *Everything Lost, Everything Broken* had been scrawled into the dirt on the hood. Jimmy and I saw that pick-up every day that week, until it was towed away. There was also the huge, scarred, and scary white oak—Satan's Tree. Every time we passed that tree, either while on the school bus or with our parents, Jimmy and I wondered if that would be the day we'd end up the next photo on it. Most days the two of us, along with everyone else on the bus, including the driver, would shrug it all off, claiming it was just another one of Jersey's weird, old legends like Dempsey House or the Gates of Hell. We'd all be lying, though, if we said there'd never been a day when we'd held our breath, said a quick prayer, or gripped the edges of our bus bench seats a little tighter until we'd passed safely beyond its reach.

Whether or not it was truly haunted, it occurred to me that before Satan's Tree or the rest of Blackwater erased me off the map, I needed to work up the guts to ask out Callie. But I'd need date cash.

"Gotta go take care of some business," I told Jimmy. I hopped off at my stop, bolted to my place. Once there, I rifled through my sock drawer. Grabbed what few ratty ones I had available, then rushed to my old man's room. His drawer was an Ellis Island of socks: casual, dressy, sporty. Mid-calf, crew, over-the-calf. Acrylic, wool, cotton. Browns to whites, blues to golds. Every style, every material and color imaginable were all right there. I grabbed a couple pairs of each, shoved them into a Shop-Rite grocery bag, and Speed Racer'ed.

◆ ◆ ◆

"Julie's Been Working for the Drug Squad!"

Mad Man was his usual sweep of blond hair, ripped and safety-pinned jeans, and Doc Martens. Some new additions: a Dead Kennedys T-shirt beneath a white suit coat that made him resemble an older, burlier, more punk, less pastel version of *Miami Vice*.

"How's it hanging, Spicoli?" he asked.

"Not bad." I handed over the sock bag.

He rifled through the contents, produced a pair of my old man's freshly washed ribbed black dress socks. "Going uptown on me?"

"They're my old man's," I said.

"Ah, cop socks. That's a first." He tossed them back into the bag. Then he held up a few that had been clumsily stitched together. "What's with these?"

I shrugged. Even if the rumors had been true, that he'd actually created a radiation vest from socks, I was too embarrassed to reveal that one night while stoned I'd attempted to do the same. But all I'd ended up with were needle-stuck fingers covered in Band-Aids, and a vest that didn't resemble a vest, but a huge mess when I'd tried it on.

After careful inspection of the footwear, Mad Man said: "Twelve."

This time I didn't argue.

"What's the special occasion, Spicoli? Got a date?"

"Maybe. Howdja know?"

"You've got that dopey grin of yours. Plus, you're without your partner in crime."

"It's Callie," I said. "Callie McCarthy."

Mad Man nodded in approval. "The pretty girl from the car accident. Good taste, Spicoli. Just be nice to her. Seems like she could use a good guy in her life." After that, he got quiet.

Me too.

All we could hear was the breeze whistling through the pines, and rippling across the lake. That breeze blew at Mad Man's super Aqua-Netted hair. The 'do wavered back and forth, but mostly remained in place. Glancing at that crazy hair, and Mad Man's hard-worn looks, I was reminded of something he'd once mentioned. How he'd been all around the country. Even to California. I didn't know it then, but the main reason he'd returned was because his mom had contracted leukemia. "Must've been pretty wild," I said. "All the traveling you've done."

He flashed a wicked grin. "T'was a blast." Then that grin faded; his pockmarked face, more like those grim shotgun-blasted road signs. He looked down for a moment, scuffed one of his Docs through the dirt. Then he shrugged, looked back at me, a bit more at ease. "It's not too bad being back. Blackwater's got some righteous foot-funk going on." He picked up a rock, whipped it toward the lake. Kept staring at the water as ripple after ripple bloomed from the place where the stone had met water.

It was plain to see he was growing tired of all my questions, but in a genuine tone, he asked: "Do much traveling?"

I shrugged. "Just a few trips to New York and Philly with my parents. You know, tourist crap."

Suddenly, Mad Man's demeanor changed. He fixed me with a solid stare—his Pabst Blue Ribbon eyes grew brighter, as he said: "You got that bug, doncha, Spicoli? You want out."

"Was it hard?" I asked. "Getting out."

"Not at all. I just packed my bags and split. You can do it, too, when you're ready."

I must've had one hell of a look on my face, because he laughed. "Trust me," he said. "When the time comes, there'll be nothing left to do but leave."

◆ ◆ ◆

THE NEXT DAY, FRIDAY, I hadn't yet worked up the guts to break out of Blackwater. But I did manage to thank Baby for saving me from Terry.

Just before second period, I was heading to French when I spotted her in her usual hangout in the woods behind school. It was one of those rare moments when she was alone.

I bolted across the yard. At my feet, the grass glistened. Up above, big white clouds drifted through the April sky, a blooming blast of blue. I ran faster, across the soccer field and baseball diamond. No way was I all headspun like I'd get when encountering math word problems. I knew exactly where I was going and why.

When I reached Baby, she was smoking and leaning against a maple tree that had her name carved into the bark along with

Terry's. She had crushed-up leaves and dirt stuck to the back of her sweater and jeans.

Baby.

She had a glow about her, like she was the earthbound version of moonlight. Just looking at her made my heart and eyes ache. She was everything I'd ever wanted in a girl—the intersection of Chrissie Hynde and Joan Jett. The exponentiation of every rebel girl I'd seen on TV after-school specials about drug or alcohol abuse. Had she given a shit about hanging out at the lake during the summer, she would've ruled the Third. For she was mind-numbing, heart-pounding, quadraphonic rock-n-roll cranked to ten. And she hadn't even spoken yet. When she did, her breath reeked of Marlboro Reds, not Boone's Farm Apple Wine. She didn't start drinking until after lunch.

"What's up, kid?" She brought the Marlboro to her cherry lip-glossed lips, swiped a drag.

Had that been Mom smoking, I would've snatched the cigarette away. But not with Baby. She looked too damn cool.

As for me, I was light-years from cool. I could smell my sweat, could taste the Count Chocula I'd had for breakfast that morning. I jammed my hands into my pockets, stood tall, tried striking that Springsteen *Darkness on the Edge of Town* stance. What a mistake that was.

Baby asked, "You okay, kid?"

Doing my best to hold what I'd imagined to be that classic Bruce stance—slightly raised eyebrow, sort of open mouth, neutral gaze, I asked Baby what she'd meant.

She swiped another Marlboro drag, turned her head to blow out smoke, then said: "Looks like you just ate cafeteria food or something."

I desperately gave it one more go. "*Merci de m'avoir sauvé la vie.*"

When Baby didn't respond right away, I figured I'd totally blown her away with all my French cool. Instead, she tapped ashes from her Marlboro, while saying: "Look, kid. I didn't save your life. I just told Terry to go easy on you."

In a rush and jumble of words, I told her all about my years of Terry abuse, and how she'd been the only one to make it stop. Right then, I must've looked completely ridiculous—some gangly guy in green cords and a Springsteen sweatshirt, babbling on and on about how I hadn't been able to deal with my own shit. Still, Baby just stood there, patiently smoking, always turning her head to the side to exhale.

When I was finished, she said: "I'm glad I could help you, kid. But really, it was nothing."

I didn't know what she was talking about. In my mind—the mind of a lovestruck, hormone-driven, starry-eyed tenth-grader—what she'd done had been everything. It was no wonder that, despite her protestations, I still held tight to the idea that a miracle had taken place, and she was, indeed, my savior. Yet the longer I marveled at my savior, the more I noticed a more vulnerable and human side. Slightly more moon-faced than Susan Dey, Baby sported a smattering of pimples beneath her jaw line covered in barely matching flesh-tone concealer. Her left eyebrow was plucked a little farther away from her nose than the other. Tiny clumps of mascara were lodged in her eyelashes. She tugged at the frayed hem of her black sweater with fingers that had purple polish chipped off bitten nails. Had Mary Kay Mom been there she would've had a heart attack over how poorly Baby managed her appearance.

Yet, imperfections and all, I wasn't shocked or disappointed. Those imperfections made Baby even more holy.

Right then, I recalled a Bible passage I'd once heard in church: "Remain in me, and I in you. As the branch can't bear fruit by itself, unless it remains in the vine, so neither can you, unless you remain in me." The way I interpreted it, that's how I wanted to be with Baby—the two of us blooming wildly together. I reached out a hand to touch her.

She smacked it away, crossed her arms in front of her chest, and rocked slightly on her feet. "You got a lot to learn, kid."

Maybe I did. Maybe I didn't. Still, I had to figure out whether or not a guy like me would ever have a chance with her. "You think someday we might be able to…you know."

Baby laughed.

"What's so funny?" I asked.

"Looks like you're doing all you can to survive. Besides, you're not my type."

"What type's that?"

"A real man." She swiped a final drag off her cigarette, then tossed it to the ground, crushed it with the toe of her fiery red Converse. "Get back to class, kid. Go learn a thing or two."

I did as she said. And later that day, just as I'd swiped my math book from my locker, I caught that familiar scent of strawberries and naturally oily hair. I wheeled around, was face to face with Callie McCarthy.

Her hazel eyes sparkled more golden brown than green as she said: "Hi, Mark. What's up?"

I was about to respond when I spotted Baby down the hall. As she drew closer, she flashed me a look: *C'mon, kid! Grow a pair already!*

Had I taken her look the wrong way, it could've easily had me feeling as small as the midgets up in Midgetville—an area in North Jersey where P. T. Barnum had once housed the little people that worked in his circus. Instead, quite the opposite occurred. In response to Baby's daring glance, I did what I hadn't been able to do before. I didn't even need to strike a Bruce pose, was just totally myself when I asked Callie: "Would you like to go out tonight?"

"Really?" she beamed.

"Absolutely," I said. I glanced back over my shoulder, noticed Baby continuing down the hall, but glancing back at me. She blew a teasing kiss. I looked back to Callie. "Well?" I said, feeling ten feet tall. "Do we have a date?"

"Sure," she said. "I was hoping you'd ask." Then again, she said my name: "Mark."

About my name.

Originally, Mom had wanted to call me Ty, after the old movie star, Ty Power. My old man had wanted to call me Kilian. Neither parent liked the other's name. Mom said Kilian sounded too Irish and violent. My old man thought Ty was way too light in the loafers. An odd thing, though: hardly anyone ever called me by my first name—mainly just my old man and Callie. Whenever my old man called me Mark it sounded like its Roman origin: Mars, the God of War. That made sense. Back then, I was constantly battling him to prove my strength, and that I could ultimately amount to something more than a loser. In Callie's case, whenever she called me Mark, it sounded much different. Like X marks the spot, I've found treasure. Or that one day, I'd make my Mark on the world.

Chapter 10

ONCE THE SCHOOL BELL rang, I made a beeline home, dusted, vacuumed, then whipped up one of my old man's favorites—mushroom pork chops. After he'd eaten and was sitting at the table polishing off a cup of coffee, I told him I was heading over to Jimmy's to do homework, wouldn't be out too late. I made sure I'd said all that while I was in the kitchen scrubbing dishes; wanted the running water and Brillo scritch-scratch to obscure any flutter my old man might've detected in my voice, and to also make sure he didn't have a direct line of sight with my eyes, or any other body parts that could rat me out.

Then I grabbed my schoolbooks, bolted through my neighborhood, out to Route 9. I promptly hopped a bus to Mom's place. From what my old man had told me earlier in the week, she wasn't even home. She and her latest boyfriend were off on another Mary Kay expense-paid trip to the Bahamas. I didn't need Mom anyway.

For my Callie date, all I needed was her car: Mary Kay Pink Cadillac. Sure that white-trimmed Hostess Snowball on

Wheels was a lame choice for a first-date vehicle, but it was all I had available.

As for my old man, he had his own opinions about that car. He'd say it was the hit-and-run that had driven right over his marriage. Represented all the cash he'd sunk into helping Mom launch her cosmetics career, in addition to all the years Mom had shirked on wife duties—spending day after day selling lipsticks, moisturizers, and recruiting new sales reps—just to score that Caddy. If you asked Mom, she'd say it was payback—the dues she had to pay for all the years of my old man being a bastard.

For sure I could understand Mom wanting to ditch my old man and Blackwater. But when she left without me that was another story.

Once at her place—a modest, gravel-yarded, boxy two-bedroom, one bathroom house at the end of a cul-de-sac—I scanned the block. In most homes, lights glowed warmly through living room windows. Happy families were seated around dinner tables; others were huddled together on couches, glued to the tube, ready for an evening of *The Dukes of Hazzard*, *Knight Rider*, and *Miami Vice*. I crouched down by the Caddy's front driver-side tire, recalled that before leaving home, Mom used to keep a spare key stashed in a magnetic box inside the wheel well. It was still there.

While I'd never taken the Hostess Snowball out for a spin, driving wasn't a problem. Starting when I was six, my old man would occasionally strap me into his off-duty ride, and drive me through the Dump, showing off various cop driving techniques: skid pan, controlled braking, evasive simulator, and serpentine. Between that and the R-rated car chase movies I'd snuck into—*Vanishing Point* and *Bullitt*—in addition to the racing car video games I'd played—*Pole Position* and *PitStop*—I figured myself a regular Steve McQueen. Once again, I scanned the block. Then I scraped the dirt from my ratty black high tops, clicked my heels together three times, said a quick Hail Mary Kay, and unlocked the door. I tossed my schoolbooks on the back floor, hopped behind the wheel. I turned the key in the ignition, adjusted the seats, and flipped on the radio, but not too loud. I eased out of the covered driveway, and down the street. And though that Hostess Snowball was nowhere near as cool as Bessie with her black interior, 80-watt in-dash speakers, and stainless steel skull gearshift knob, she got the job done. At the end of the block, I cranked the stereo. Punched the gas. Made those Caddy whitewalls squeal. Made those 350 horses under the hood rear up, go wild.

◆ ◆ ◆

CALLIE'S NEIGHBORHOOD WAS FILLED with unadorned one- and two-story cedar and aluminum-sided homes. Their yards—some grass, some gravel, some dirt—were littered with children's bikes, toys, plastic flamingos, and goofy ceramic gnomes, like the one Jimmy owned. Sedans, station wagons, and other nondescript cars—nowhere near as classy as Mr. Gigliotti's tricked-out Bessie—were parked on dirt lawns, and in oil-stained driveways. The heady aroma of pitch pine filled the air. The bright chirp of crickets mixed with the throaty hum of the Caddy's finely tuned engine, and Bob Seger on the radio singing "Shame on the Moon." And standing on a shadowy corner, a few blocks away from her home, was Callie.

I pulled over.

As she stepped carefully toward the car, I noticed her blue and black striped skirt, over-the-knee socks, buckle-up shoes, and Go-Go's T-shirt beneath an unzipped sweat jacket. Nowhere near as sexy and rebellious as Baby's cranked-to-ten looks. And while I couldn't express it so clearly then, I'd later realize Callie's song was softer, sweeter, something I could easily listen to while sleeping, incorporate into my dreams, then wake up in the morning with the song of her still floating through my head.

I hit the electronic switch, cranked down the passenger-side window. Got a refreshing blast of salt-air from the nearby Barnegat Bay. "Climb in," I said.

Callie stuck her head through the open window. Half laughing, half not, she asked: "Where did you *get* this?"

"It's my mom's. She sells Mary Kay."

Stepping away from the car, Callie's once sweet looks turned sullen. She glanced down at her fake leg.

"Don't worry," I said. "It'll be okay."

"I don't know," she said. "Maybe this isn't such a good idea."

I tried putting myself in Callie's shoes. Since her accident, it must've been difficult to get in a car—especially a stranger's car. Each ride must've constantly brought up so much anger, so much shock and pain. That and the constant reminder of how, in an instant, a charmed life could suddenly vanish. "Look," I said, "if you don't wanna that's fine. I'll just park and we can talk."

Across her face flashed a series of emotions—shame to fear, then full-blown giddiness. It was when she was at her calmest that she asked: "Will you be careful?"

I chimed in with a lame response that still makes me wonder why she ever put up with me: "You're in good hands with Allstate."

Callie flashed her wobbly smile. "If anything goes wrong I'll never talk to you again."

"Won't happen," I said. "I plan on hearing your voice for a long time."

◆ ◆ ◆

For the next half hour or so, we drove around our dumpy little town. Nowhere to be found were the stunning vistas I'd seen in those LA movies; where people would drive high into the late-night Hollywood hills and in less than a blink of an eye could witness a stunning view of downtown then, far across that jeweled and glittering city, behold starry-skied Santa Monica. In Blackwater everything was grim, flat, boxed in. Maybe it had been a different story in the eighteen hundreds when the town was founded. Dense groves of pines, crystal-clear creeks, lush farm lands. Back when I lived there, though, my little town was just strip malls, gun shops, radiation, and funeral homes.

Callie and I held our breath as we passed Satan's Tree, rolled our eyes as we cruised by the high school, and shook our heads as we passed Piney shacks with concrete-reinforced bomb shelters dug deep into backyards, in preparation for the power plant's eruption, or World War III. Had I been alone, or with Jimmy, I might've pounded a couple brews, smoked a fatty, or downed some cough medicine to make the ride more interesting. Not that night, though. I wanted to stay clean for Callie.

At one point, I noticed her good foot pressing into the floorboard. I motioned toward that foot. "Brake or gas?"

"Gas," she said.

"You wanna go faster?"

She nodded.

"You sure?"

"Yeah. Just a little."

"No problemo," I said. "But only a little." I inched the car up to fifty. We sailed past Duffy's Bar and the place I'd eventually come to love and hate—the Rainbow Casket Company.

We ended up out in the Dump. I killed the lights and engine, but left the radio playing low. Normally, I would've popped a tape into Mom's cassette player, but I was so nervous about my date that I'd spaced on bringing any tunes.

About my tunes.

Ever since I was a kid, bombarded by K-Tel Records ads I'd seen on TV, I'd learned early on the power of rocking tunes. The right tune at the right time could totally make a date. Take a song like The Kinks' "Give the People What They Want." It got girls' libidos moving faster than a Corvette engine flywheel. And another: Pink Floyd's "Wish You Were Here." It was great for wooing slinky stoner chicks. Aerosmith's "Toys In the Attic" could tame the most rebellious, feather-haired rocker babes.

That night, however, all I had was WMMR, the Caddy, and the Dump to provide my Callie first-date soundtrack—Culture Club's "Do You Really Want To Hurt Me" playing low, the ticking of the car's cooling engine, cricket chirps, the burble of frogs, along with the whoops and hollers of distant partiers drifting in through the open windows.

For a moment, Callie just sat there, staring out the window and quietly humming a tuneless song. No way did it match the sweetness of her face. She motioned toward the sky, pointing out a snaky line of stars stretching across the night. "Know what constellation that is?"

In school I'd learned a few things about the heavens—like how there were eighty-eight constellations, and the sun was the only known star in our galaxy that wasn't part of a constellation. But Callie's constellation eluded me.

"Hydra," she said. "It's a weird one."

I must've given her a completely clueless look because she proceeded to tell me the whole story. How Hydra was the largest constellation in the sky. A beast with the body of a hound and one hundred serpentine heads. Had poisonous breath and was so ugly that it caused people to die from seeing it. One of Hercules's great tasks was to kill it. But when he began fighting it, he discovered that every time he cut off one of its heads, three grew back. Eventually, he had his charioteer, Iolus, burn the headless stumps, which prevented regeneration. The last head, however, was immortal, so after cutting it off, they trapped it under a rock.

Callie stopped there, shook her head. "Sorry. Sometimes I can talk a lot." Then she turned in her seat to face me. "How's school?"

School was like always, math was Public Enemy Number One. But I excelled in classes like geography, world history, and French; classes that swept me far, far away from Blackwater. "It's fine I guess."

"What about Terry?" she asked. "I don't see him bothering you anymore."

"It's taken care of," I said.

"Good," said Callie. "I hated how he'd hit you. Especially your face."

After that, we stared at each other so intently it almost scared me how I felt like I was falling into her deep watery eyes. Drowning in Pale Jade Rivers Me. Never Want to Resurface Me. But then she looked away and my falling stopped.

Callie glanced down at her fake leg.

So did I. "If you don't mind me asking, what happened?"

At first she didn't respond.

"Look," I said, "if you don't wanna talk about it—" My words fell away. I didn't know how to pick them up from there.

Callie helped me by saying: "It's fine. I've spoken to so many people about it so many times." She readjusted herself in her seat, then began. "I was with my mom. She was driving to the cleaners. She wanted to get there before it closed so she was in a hurry. Since then, she keeps telling me she never saw the stop sign. Said it was hidden behind a tree. But that's crazy. We'd driven that road so many times. She should've known. Anyway, the last thing I remembered seeing was this car outta the corner of my eye. After that, the doctor telling my parents they'd have to amputate my leg because my femur had been shattered so badly."

I didn't know how to respond. My mom was reckless. But Callie's situation was far worse. If I'd been telling that story, I would've been yelling my head off. She, however, spoke in little more than a whisper.

Callie let fly a nervous flutter of a laugh. It spilled from her mouth like a tiny bird. "It's definitely been a big adjustment," she said.

"Do you hate her for what happened?" I asked.

Callie got a look on her face like she'd been asked that question a million times, or had at least considered it that many times herself. "For a while," she said, "no matter how many times my mom apologized I hated her. Now I don't know what to think. Sometimes I try to forgive her and everything's okay. Well, sort of. Then there are other times…" Her whispery voice trailed off like smoke, then began again. "All I know for sure is that my parents argue a lot and aren't happy here anymore. Neither am I." She stopped.

Sure, there was the radio and usual evening Dump sounds. Otherwise, the car had become so quiet I could hear my ears ring.

Callie leaned into me as if she'd been blown there by an invisible wind. "You can touch it if you like," she said. "My leg."

I must've had a look on my face—part fear, part curiosity—that caused Callie to add: "Go ahead. I do it all the time." She pulled down her sock to reveal a portion of her fake leg.

I rested a hand on it. It felt like the top of my school desk.

She guided my hand just above her knee, to that place where fake flesh met real. "You can go higher if you like," she said.

Her real flesh was soft, smooth, and warm. As my fingers inched beneath her skirt, her flesh grew warmer and warmer.

Callie brushed strands of blonde hair from her mouth. "That feels nice," she sighed.

I rested my forehead against hers, breathed in her usual scent. But there was also something new, something electric and fresh—thunderstorms and new babies.

"Tell me something," she said. "Why did you ask me out?"

That didn't take long to answer. Sure, part of me had done it to prove myself to Baby. But mainly, I adored Callie for a very different reason. I gave her another one of my lame lines, only this time in French, which still makes me groan a bit. At the time, however, it was absolutely heartfelt, for real. "*Parce que tu es un diamant*," I said.

Also a student of French, Callie understood that I'd told her she was a diamond. But she didn't get the full meaning.

So I explained. "No matter how much life knocks you around, your strength keeps you shining."

Callie flashed that wobbly smile of hers that'd always make me weak-kneed. "That's the nicest thing anyone's ever said to me." She touched my hand resting on her thigh. "You can go higher if you like."

I recalled how she'd treated me back in elementary—the snide comments and ratting me out to teachers. When I reminded her of all those moments, she scrunched up her nose, and said: "It was only because I liked you, Mark. Sorry it came out all wrong."

I inched my fingers a little further up her thigh. But when I reached the place where her warmth grew too intense, she shook her head.

"Maybe we shouldn't be doing this," she said. "I thought I was ready. You're the first guy I've been with since—"

I was torn. I'd had my share of making it to second base, sometimes even third, with random girls out at Dump parties. Right then was my chance to do as much, or more, with someone better than all those Dump girls combined.

"You better stop," Callie said, her voice cracking.

Back when I was almost sixteen I thought I knew a lot. Mistook the accumulation of odd facts for true knowledge. I'd acquired a whole laundry list of random information—like if you installed an Indy Car engine into a riding mower, it could cut a half-acre lawn in about 5.6 seconds. Also, the only guy in ZZ Top that didn't have a beard was the drummer, Frank Beard. And because Grandmother had been suffering from so many heart problems as of late, I'd also learned that cardiovascular disease killed more women every year than the next sixteen causes of death combined. But when it came to knowing what to say or do to make a girl feel better, I was completely clueless. I removed my hand from Callie's thigh, put my arm around her.

"Please don't hate me," she said.

I told her I'd never hate her, pulled her close.

In a small voice, she said: "Maybe we should go."

I didn't argue. I started the car, got us out of the Dump. Luckily it was still somewhat early in the evening, so there wasn't a police cruiser parked by the entrance—takedown lights blazing—waiting to pop wasted partiers. Sure I'd developed a certain amount of cachet with Blackwater's finest. But that cred wouldn't have saved my ass for driving around without a license in Mom's hijacked Caddy.

Just as I pulled up to the main road, Callie said: "Go left."

"But right's the way home," I said.

Her brow furrowed. Her soft, watery eyes were like blazing bonfires. "What're you waiting for? The way you talk about leaving. You want this, too."

I sat there, struggling with what to do next. Just then, I recalled another one of my old man's Irish sayings: "When God made time he made plenty of it." *That was bullshit*, I thought. Bruce Lee summed it up better when he said: "If you love life, don't waste time, for time is what life is made of." More than wanting to do this for me, I wanted to do it for Callie. I wanted to give her the gift of a long and happy life. "Strap in," I said.

She buckled her seatbelt.

I did the same. Then I punched the gas, spun the wheel to the left. In a kicked-up cloud of dust, we rocketed down the highway.

Shadowy trees whipped by. So did gun-blasted road signs and deer grazing by the side of the road.

"Faster," said Callie.

The wind rushing in through the open windows had turned her straight and shiny blonde hair into a brilliant and spinning array of firework sparklers. She was laughing. She was the happiest I'd ever seen. I leaned on the gas. The speedometer climbed to seventy. I cranked the radio.

Whether it was dumb luck, or the Music Gods smiling down on us, Springsteen's "Born to Run" blasted through the speakers.

Over the music, over the rushing wind, Callie called out, "I hate my mom!"

"I hate mine, too!" I hollered.

Once we crossed the train tracks skirting the edge of town, Callie pointed up ahead.

Within the headlight's glow was the distant image of the *You Are Now Leaving Blackwater* sign.

Right then, I figured it to be the moment Mad Man had referred to—that I'd leave when the time was right. I didn't let off the gas. We were Code 10-56 to paradise.

The Blackwater sign drew closer. Throughout my life, that sign had represented a huge obstacle in my mind, marking a border that had imprisoned me. That night, however, I coolly glided out of town with Callie at my side. The ease of it all surprised me. I let fly a whoop, as a crushing weight lifted from me.

Callie let fly her own whoop. She reached out a hand for mine.

"You don't want me to have two on the wheel?" I asked.

"One's fine," she said. She took my free hand in hers.

I continued driving. Though we were only doing seventy, it felt much faster. Or I should say, *I* seemed to be moving faster. Like I was a piston, sparking inside life's great big engine. That engine was well-oiled. It hummed and revved. Was ready to take Callie and me anywhere. And all the roads in front of us were wide open.

For two sheltered teenagers from the Pine Barrens, we had such big aspirations that evening. We couldn't stop all our optimistic dreaming out loud.

"Where to now?" Callie asked.

"How 'bout LA?" I said.

Callie stuck a hand out the window, swished it through the mild night air. "What'll you do there?"

"Maybe I can become a stunt driver. Or a bongloader to the stars."

Callie made an *euw* face. "Or maybe we can keep driving until we find a place where we can start our own city. We'll call it No Parentland."

"And the skies will be clear," I said, "no radiation."

"And there'll be tons of stars in the night," she offered, "so many that we can create our own constellations."

Mile marker after mile marker, we continued our dreaming. It was all as fast and frenetic as the wheels against road. Gradually, that energy diminished. The inertia made the world around me feel strange and overwhelming.

"You okay?" Callie asked.

I said yeah, but the truth was I wasn't so sure anymore. I didn't know how I'd take care of us. Back home, I'd only made cash working crappy summer jobs: cutting lawns, delivering newspapers, selling old socks to Mad Man. As for responsibility, I'd mostly spent the last few years in a wasted haze with Jimmy. In regards to relationships, the only physical intimacy I knew was: Grandmother's hugs and my old man's abuse.

Of course I'd do my best to better my life, I thought. Yet what if it didn't look much different in another town? Being a fuckup in Anywhere USA might be a small improvement over being one in Blackwater. But I didn't want to live that way anymore. Still, I had no idea how to change. I couldn't find that place on a map, even if you drew a straight line to it. That realization scared me so much I slammed on the brakes.

Callie screamed, braced her hands against the dash.

I safely skidded over to the side of the road.

For a moment, we didn't speak. Just sat there as a kicked-up cloud of dust surrounded the car.

Tears flooded Callie's wild eyes.

"I'm sorry," I said. "I didn't mean to scare you." I clicked off the radio, looked right at her and spoke the truth. "I don't know where to go. I don't know what to do. I don't know how I'd take care of you and your leg."

"Forget my leg," she cried. "It's gone."

I tried taking her into my arms, but she pulled away. Choked out how she'd never be able to run again. Didn't trust stop signs. Or her mother. Hated her smile, and how everyone looked at her funny. Couldn't stop having nightmares about the crash—how her leg was there one moment, then in a flash, gone. Through it all, I didn't interrupt her. Just let her say all that needed to be said. Once she'd exhausted herself, she collapsed into her seat.

I collapsed into my own seat, sat staring straight ahead. That first-date Friday night with Callie, I was clueless as how to explain what had just taken place. Some time later, though, I'd recall Callie and me sitting in that Caddy alongside the highway shoulder, totally lost in the dust cloud surrounding us. As it diminished, we could see the wide-open road ahead of us. All that leaving—and everything it meant to Callie and me—was right there. We just didn't know how to reach it.

Chapter 11

THAT SUMMER BETWEEN ELEVENTH and twelfth grade was filled with all kinds of bizarre shit: Richard W. Miller became the first FBI agent convicted of espionage. Cyanide-laced, Extra-Strength Tylenol was in supermarkets. President Reagan's "Just Say No" to drugs was everywhere. That summer was also when I got a call from Mom.

"Get over here," she said. "*Now.*"

That one puzzled me. Since she'd left home, I'd only seen her a couple times. Each visit had amounted to nothing more than the two of us sitting on her couch, drowning in silences, unable to discuss the past. But with this call, Mom had that old music in her voice—honey-slow and sweet. It was the music that had made my old man fall in love with her. And though it was the music that made me miss her all over again, I had my doubts. Through a lumped-up throat, I said: "Gimme one good reason."

"I've got a plan," said Mom. "A way for you to make some money."

"Money?" I said.

"Money," she said.

I recalled how Mom used to sit at the kitchen table around tax time, armed with a calculator, punching in numbers, going through the figures aloud. How she'd rake in over $40,000 a year in commission. Add to that her $9,000 monthly check, and her average monthly "love check" which was around $2,600. That was pretty good, but there were expenses: leadership conferences, career conferences, incentives, customer gifts, postage. The list went on and on. When she was done with all her calculations, she was lucky to end up with little over $30,000.

When I reminded Mom of this, she got all defensive, and said: "Now you listen, young man."

Then she threw back in my face the bits and pieces of my life she'd heard through the strained and infrequent phone calls with my old man. Her laundry list summed up my summer: working odd jobs weeding and cutting lawns, evenings spent hanging with Jimmy or Callie, the occasional bus ride to the Toms River Branch of the Ocean County Library to search out nuclear power articles. And when I wasn't doing those things, I was at home alone, watching the tube, cleaning the house, raiding the fridge. And when I wasn't alone, my old man and I—back to our old ways— were often arguing. "Some money," Mom added, "might change all that."

Part of me figured she was lying through her teeth. But another part of me wanted to believe her. If for no other reason, the extra cash could finally allow me to take Callie out on a real date, and to also afford me a set of wheels. "Fine," I said, overcoming my lumped-up throat. "I'll be right over."

◆ ◆ ◆

ONCE THROUGH THE FRONT door, Mom barely uttered a hello. Like our previous visits, she didn't even offer a hug. Decked out in a pearl-white blouse, fuchsia skirt, silver high-heeled pumps, and still sporting the remnants of a tan from her last Mary Kay–sponsored vacation to the Bahamas, all she said was: "Well? What do you think?" She spread her arms out wide, as if she were Vanna White displaying a solved puzzle on *Wheel of Fortune*. Except with Mom, all she was displaying was her lousy living room.

Gone were the off-white walls, driftwood coffee table, and bile-green ruffled curtains my old man had said filled the room when he'd brought over the divorce papers for her to sign. Currently, Mom's living room reflected her desire to express her true inner self. The walls screamed pink. There was crap all over them. Mom pointed out each and every adornment.

On one wall was a poster for the Broadway play, *Cats*. Mounted on another wall were hand-stained shelves sporting barf-inducing Hummel figurines; photos of women's rights activists Gloria Steinem and Bella Abzug; cosmetics executives Mary Kay Ash, Elizabeth Arden, Estée Lauder; along with photos of Mom receiving this Mary Kay award and that Mary Kay award. On still another wall was a cheesy Nagel print, featuring a mysterious hooded woman with a horse. By her living room window, covered in pale yellow curtains, was an oversized sofa, featuring a garish Laura Ashley floral print. Displayed on a sparkling glass-topped coffee table were copies of *Jonathan Livingston Seagull* and *Broken Patterns: Professional Women and the Quest for a New Feminine Identity*. But the real kick in the ass was a framed poster for *Terms of Endearment*, which I'd later discover had been a movie about a mother/daughter relationship.

Mom led me into the kitchen. Gone were all the wonderful cooking smells from my youth. It reeked of stale cigarette smoke and potpourri air freshener. That kitchen was also fiftiesed-out with a vintage Coca-Cola vending-machine-style illuminated wall clock, a black and white checkered floor, a pink Formica table, and matching vinyl-cushioned chairs. "Here," Mom said. "Sit."

As I did so, she grabbed some vodka, tomato juice, and horseradish from the fridge, along with some Tabasco sauce, and other ingredients from the counter. She whipped herself up a Bloody Mary. With drink in hand, she sat across from me at the table. Watched me eye the celery stick in her drink. "Don't even think about it," she said.

Like so many other times, I recalled the first time I'd downed booze. That electric shock of vodka from Mom's Bloody Mary had gone straight to my six-year-old brain, sent me spinning through the living room—everything a shimmery blur. No more parents fighting. No more only-child loneliness. Only Mom's voice asking if I was okay. Then everything went dark, and seemed to stay that way. "What about this business proposition?" I asked.

Mom swished the celery through her drink, took a couple sips, then said: "I want you to help me with Mary Kay."

I stomped a black Converse against the floor. "I *knew* I shouldn't have come over. No way I'm selling Mary Kay. That shit's for *fags*."

Mom took another hit off her drink, then cracked open a fresh pack of Virginia Slims. She sparked one up, huffed smoke.

I snatched the cigarette from her lips. Snubbed it out in the half-filled black ceramic ashtray sitting between us.

She sparked up another. "About Mary Kay," she continued. "I don't want you selling. I want you doing something *different*."

The way she said that last word worried me.

Mom must've detected my concern because she added: "I want you to be my male model."

That one confused me. No way did I resemble the fashion model types I'd seen on the cover of *GQ* and other mags at 7-Eleven. All I had was my mess of shoulder-length hair and wild brown eyes—the kind you'd find on criminals in wanted posters. "Forget it," I said. "I'm not model material."

Mom thought differently. She leaned across the table, launched into a sales pitch so perfect, it seemed as if she'd rehearsed it numerous times before my arrival. "Think of it," she began. "There's hundreds of men out there still using products like Aqua Velva and Lava soap to stay clean. Maybe they want to try something new, but don't know where to turn next. You'll be the one to show them and their wives the Tribute line of men's products, along with moisturizers and deep cleansers to help their skin stay fresh and wrinkle free."

That was total Mom. While she'd often doubted her skills in the Mothering Department, she never doubted herself with Mary Kay. Spouting company catch phrases like, "You can have anything in this world you want, if you want it badly enough and you're willing to pay the price," she always knew what to say and do to make the sale. And while her speeches went over well with new Mary Kay recruits, and the old blue hairs and desperate housewives in town, they didn't fly with me—especially in that moment. "You got the wrong guy," I insisted.

Mom coolly swiped a couple sips off her drink, a cigarette drag, then said: "It all depends on how you look at it." Then for a kicker, she added: "Honey."

But I wasn't buying her saccharine. It had left a truly bitter taste in my mouth in the past, and would continue to do so long after that day sitting at her kitchen table. "How do you figure?" I asked.

No way did my question throw Mom off. It was like another one of her well-rehearsed responses. "The way I see it," she said, "you'll be a trendsetter. You'll boldly go where no man around here has ever gone before with skin-care products."

Now she sounded like an episode of *Star Trek* on the Planet Mary Kay. I snorted a nervous laugh. A snot rocket shot from my nose and nailed her white blouse, right below the ruffle-trim collar.

"Oh shit," I said. "Sorry."

Mom got up, grabbed a napkin. She dabbed it with her tongue, and rubbed out the stain. In a matter-of-fact tone, she said: "I've had much worse stuff of yours on me than this." She balled up the napkin, tossed it into the trash. Then she grabbed a compact sitting atop the counter. Flipped it open, quickly surveyed herself in the mirror. She puckered her lips, did this little left to right movement with her face, picked away some tiny bit of something just to the right of her nose. Once satisfied, she smacked closed the compact, then sat back down at the table.

She took another drag off her cigarette. Didn't even have the civility to turn her head to the side to exhale like Baby had done that day I'd first met up with her in the woods behind school. Mom just casually blew smoke between us.

Like I'd done before, I snatched the Virginia Slims, snubbed it out in the ashtray.

Both of us sat there quietly observing that dead cigarette.

As Mom was about to reach for a fresh one, I swiped the pack away, got in her face, and said: "How much you gonna pay me?"

With a voice sounding more business-like than musical, she replied: "Forty bucks per modeling session. And every time a customer buys over a hundred dollars worth of supplies you'll get an additional twenty-five percent commission. Plus," she continued, her voice growing slightly vulnerable, "this could give us a chance to spend more time together." She took my hand in hers. Even though her hand was cold it still felt good.

Mom gave my hand a gentle squeeze. "Do we have a deal?"

For a change, her pitch seemed heartfelt. But I wasn't totally convinced. She'd left me once. She could do it again. I reached for her Bloody Mary.

She slapped my hand away, then reached for the celery stick. Not to stir her drink, but to hand it over. Perhaps she was hoping it would make me equally as dopey as when I was six. I took a bite. No go. I eyed her Bloody Mary.

Mom eyed me eyeing her drink. She shook her head no.

I just shrugged. Code for: *No drink. No deal.*

It went on like that for a while—me eyeballing Mom's Bloody Mary, Mom eyeballing me eyeballing her drink. Neither of us said a word the whole time. The only sound: the tick-tock-ticking of that Coca-Cola clock.

Mom finally rolled her eyes, slid the drink in front of me.

I downed what was left. While it was nowhere near as mindbomb as Jimmy's killer homegrown, or the codeine cough medicine he kept stashed beneath his pillow, the Bloody Mary offered enough of a mellow shock for me to say: "You got a deal."

◆ ◆ ◆

THERE WERE THREE PEOPLE I couldn't tell about my new business venture.

First: my old man. Seeing as he bled police blue through and through, he would've killed me had he found out I'd gone pink.

Next: Callie. She already thought I looked ridiculous in Mom's car. If she caught me modeling mud masks and moisturizers, I just knew we'd be history.

Last: Jimmy. If he spotted me lugging around Mom's cosmetics cases, he'd start asking questions. And though I could be a good liar when needed, I often confused fact and fiction after one too many beers and bong hits. If I let slip my male modeling, Jimmy would call me an even bigger fag. Queerbait. Butt Munch Deluxe. And while they were only words, we had ways of branding each other with nicknames that stuck. Like one time in seventh grade: he thought Duran Duran kicked ass. I told him the definition of kickass was Led Zep. For a good number of months, whenever we got annoyed with each other, I'd call him *Rio*. He'd call me *Moby Dick*.

That's how I came up with Operation Pretty In Pink.

Every morning, I'd wait until my old man left for work. Once his tank-tough Caprice had glided out of the driveway I'd count to a hundred forward and backward. That would give him plenty of time to be far from the scene.

I'd hit the streets. Jog through my neighborhood of large, well-tended ranch and colonial-style homes complete with Kentucky blue-turf lawns; past Jimmy's neighborhood of shoebox-sized, aluminum-sided houses with gravel lawns; ending up in Terry's neighborhood full of run-down shacks with rusted-out cars propped up on cinderblocks in dirt yards. That was the perfect place for Mom to pick me up. Around there, no one woke until after noon.

But to insure my anonymity, just in case I recognized someone from a Dump party, I'd also wear a John Deere cap, brim pulled down over my eyes. Even after I'd climbed into Mom's Caddy, all sweaty and stinky, I didn't remove the cap.

"Do you know how foolish you look?" she said on that first day of modeling.

She was one to talk. There she was dressed in her knock-off Chanel suit and fancy black pumps—an outfit she had five copies of back at her place. When Mom did Mary Kay she went all the way: Stepford Mary Kay.

"Take it off," she said, referring to the cap. "It's messing up your hair."

"Can't," I said. "I gotta stay in disguise." I cracked open a window to take in the clear pine air instead of the Caddy's stale cigarette stench, and my BO faintly reeking of my fried Spam breakfast. Then I flipped my *Greetings From Asbury Park* tape into the cassette player.

Bruce's "Blinded by the Light" had barely begun jangling through the speakers when Mom popped it out, and tossed the tape into my lap.

"Whydja do that?" I said. "It's getting me psyched."

"Figure out another way," Mom said. She swiped off my cap, threw it to the floor, then clicked on the radio. It was the usual 1986 pop-bubblegum stuff: Wham!, Whitney Houston, and Bryan Adams.

When Don Henley began singing "All She Wants To Do Is Dance" I tried flipping off the radio, but Mom smacked my hand away. "Don't," she said. "It's getting me psyched."

Our sparring went on for days. Often I threatened to quit. More often, Mom threatened to fire me. Neither one happened. That's how badly we wanted to be in one another's lives again.

So we reached an agreement. On Tuesdays and Thursdays, Mom begrudgingly allowed me to wear my cap and listen to my own tunes. On Mondays, Wednesdays, and Fridays I had to go John Deereless while being pummeled by Top-40.

As for Mom's customers: none bore Baby's pedal-to-the-metal sex appeal, or Callie's quiet charm. Most were splotchy-skinned, dumpy-looking housewives with faint mustaches and coffee breath. Total doppelgängers for the moms that toted their sniveling, earaching runts to the First Lake every summer. They had homes that reeked of Mr. Clean, fish sticks, and Glade Air Freshener. Sported stretch pants, ill-fitting polyester dresses, and variations of the Farrah Fawcett *Charlie's Angels* feathered hairdo, a coif that had long died out with disco. I prayed to God that if my old man was dating on the sly, none of those women resembled these.

Once I'd dragged a comb through my mess of hair, Mom and I would step inside each customer's home. With her well-practiced smile, she'd promptly introduce me as her male model.

With those two magic words—male model—the customers' faces would brighten. "Really?" they'd say. "An *actual* model?"

"Sure," I'd respond. "*Formé et tout.*" French for *trained and everything.*

This one woman, looked to be around thirty-five, sported a midriff branded with the words *Foxy Lady* in glitter. Her huge hips spilled over the edges of her stretch pants like a fleshy high tide. When she heard those two magic words she flashed me a wink while Mom was admiring a baby Jesus Hummel figurine on the woman's coffee table.

I winked back. That's how much I wanted her to buy Mary Kay.

Mom continued her pitch. "You're easy to make look radiant," she said to the customer. "With only a few products you're well on your way to being the beautiful you that you are."

The woman giggled, flashed me another look.

I looked away. Stared at the black dog hairs littering her beige carpet.

"But as you know," Mom continued, "men are different. That's why you called me. We both know they don't take care of their skin like we girls do." She pointed to a picture perched atop the mantle. In it, a man was standing on a fishing dock, sporting a Kelly green windbreaker, plaid shorts, and boating shoes. His sun-damaged face was more lined and worn than beef jerky. "Your husband, right?" said Mom.

Eyes downcast, the woman said: "That's my Paulie."

More genuine than rehearsed, Mom said, "He's a good-looking man. How old is he?"

"Thirty-nine," the customer sighed. "But he already looks fifty."

This was when Mom was at her best—whenever she spotted a chance to clean up Blackwater's ill-scrubbed residents. She rested a hand on the customer's shoulder. "Don't worry. I have the perfect product for your Paulie. It's a gel that helps reduce the visible signs of aging. It'll take years off his appearance."

While Mom rummaged through her bag for the product, the woman batted her eyelashes at me. They were super-long, hairy awnings perched over small, bright eyes.

The sight of her looking so aroused, even before I'd modeled any products, made me feel like a super stud, better than Richard Gere in *American Gigolo*. I licked my lips. If the woman ratted me out and accused me of getting fresh, I'd lie. Say I was removing a piece of my Count Chocula breakfast.

Again, the customer batted her hairy awnings. This time Mom caught her. But instead of going ballistic like I thought she would, she encouraged the woman. "My son's handsome. Isn't he?"

"Ah, c'mon, Ma," I said, feeling my cheeks fire up.

But she'd have nothing to do with my pleading. "Really," said Mom. "It's okay." She repeated her question to the customer.

The woman blushed. "Yes," she replied meekly. "He is."

Mom pinched my cheek. "You see, honey? I told you my customers would adore you."

She sat me down in the customer's love seat. Grabbed a cotton ball from her bag and applied gel to it. When she reached out to dab my face, I backed away. It didn't matter that we'd already gone through our routine countless times in her living room, and in other living rooms. I still couldn't relate to this kind of physical attention from her.

"It's okay," Mom said. "Just relax. This won't hurt a bit."

Maybe it was the sound of her voice right then, or the way she applied the gel to my face—whatever the case, I completely zoned out. Could see Mom's lips moving, speaking to the customer, but I couldn't hear her. Instead, I sat there recalling a time when I was seven. I'd just thrown up after hearing my parents fight. In one of her more tender moments, Mom was wiping my face clean with a warm rag, and telling me how much she loved me.

Mom smoothed more Mary Kay gel into the area around my eyes. Now I was ten. My old man had just smacked me for getting still another D on a math test. I couldn't stop bawling. "I know you're hurting," Mom had said. "But the hurt won't last forever." She wiped my eyes dry, eased my lips into a grin. "There," she said. "Think happy thoughts."

With each new application of Mary Kay gel product, I relived more Mom memories. Each one made me more and more wistful for the old days. I bit my quivering lip and gripped the sides of the love seat tighter. My Converse high-tops fidgeted back and forth.

Mom in the present, which sounded tons like Mom in the past, said: "Easy, honey. Stay still."

I did as she said, but it wasn't easy. I was sweating, heart racing. *Get a hold of yourself,* I thought. *You're a tough, straight, seventeen-year-old male with a solid track record of getting wasted and making-out.* But no matter how much I tried to convince myself of my manliness, it was no good. Being Mom's Mary Kay modeling bitch seemed a far better trade-off than sitting at home alone, or in the bowels of the Ocean County Library, my head filled with radiation and death.

Once we'd left the customer's house, and were back in the Caddy, Mom said: "I'm proud of you. I told you you'd be great at this."

She was right. The customer had purchased over two hundred bucks worth of products—everything from purifying fresheners to age-fighting moisturizers, to most of the entire *Tribute* line for men.

"It wasn't easy," I said. "That woman was way too K-Mart. I like my ladies Macy's."

That one made Mom smile. "Then you did an especially good job."

It was like that everywhere we went. Word quickly spread through the Mary Kay community that Mom and I were revolutionizing men's skin care. If it kept up, I figured, I'd be LA-bound in no time.

◆ ◆ ◆

"WELL?" MOM SAID, PICKING me up one late-July morning. "Ready for a big day?"

That I was. Since it was Tuesday, I popped The Who's *My Generation* into the cassette player, leaned back into the fine, white leather seat, and pulled my John Deere cap down over my eyes. Fresh pine air rushed in through the open window. Keith Moon wailed on the drums, Townsend jangled the guitar, and the soaring harmonies of "The Kids Are Alright" sailed through the Caddy. Everything was pitch perfect until Mom clicked off the stereo, and said: "We're here."

I lifted the cap. Noticed we hadn't traveled out of town like we had with a number of other customers. We were still in Blackwater, cruising one of its few well-kept streets bordering the Second Lake. "What's the deal?" I said.

"We have a big meeting with the local ladies auxiliary club," said Mom.

As we neared the customer's place—a sprawling ranch-style brick home with a gleaming lawn—we passed a baby blue Chevy Impala parked out front. It seemed vaguely familiar. Then it hit me. "We can't go in," I yelped. "It's Jimmy's mom's car."

Mom dismissed my comment with the wave of a hand. "She isn't even *in* the ladies club. She's not *rich* enough."

When I insisted it *was* Jimmy's mom's car, and that he'd give me endless shit about modeling for Mary Kay, Mom pulled over alongside the road's narrow shoulder, shifted the Caddy into park. She turned in her seat to face me. "Even if it *is* her car," she said, "and Jimmy *does* find out, *so what*? He's got *nothing* on you."

Ever since I'd been in fourth grade, up until Mom left home, she'd met Jimmy on numerous occasions—when he'd visited for weekend sleepovers, or had needed my assistance with homework. From those meetings, Mom had formed a very specific impression of him. She let me have an earful there in the car. "His dark curls," she said, "and his big brown eyes like a young Sal Mineo. Plus, practically all he talks about is Stevie Nicks *this* and Stevie Nicks *that*. Don't you think that's a little *odd*?" Then as if it wasn't obvious enough as to where she was headed with all her insinuations, she held up an arm, let her wrist go limp.

Sure Jimmy had messed-up tastes, I realized. But he'd always thought the same about me. There was also that night when I'd stayed at his place, when he'd flashed me that Mother Hen Morse code while we were sitting around our makeshift Christmas tree. But no way had I chalked that up to him being gay, so much as way too overly concerned about my well-being. "Look," I said. "Let's just go to the next customer."

Mom didn't see it that way. She checked both mirrors, dropped the Caddy into D, then eased back out onto the road. Though barely moving faster than a drugged bug, she clutched the wheel as if she were doing ninety. The customer's driveway—with scattered patches of grass growing up in-between the concrete cracks—drew closer and closer.

That day I'm sure there was a breeze blowing off the Second Lake and through the trees. I'm sure there was a raucous opera of warblers and chickadees playing full blast in those trees. But all I heard in my head was Jimmy laughing his ass off, calling me every name in the book. His taunting grew louder and louder as the driveway grew closer and closer. That's when I reached over, grabbed the wheel; veered us away from the customer's home, and across the road toward the lake's edge. It was a truly ass-headed move on my part. At the time, however, a car crash seemed far more appealing than taking Jimmy's shit.

Mom slammed on the brakes. We sat there in the middle of the road, struggling for control of the wheel.

"Stop it!" Mom screamed. "You'll get us killed!"

Maybe she truly feared for our lives, but I think she was more worried about the Caddy. Truth be told, that "free" Mary Kay car wasn't so free. If Mom didn't meet her minimum monthly or quarterly production, she'd have to make copays that exceeded its true value.

Mom's black pump slipped off the brake. The Caddy lurched forward, straight toward an oncoming car. The siren-red Mustang swerved sharply to the right, momentarily going off the road, into the dirt and low-lying shrub area bordering the lake. Then it deftly shot back out onto pavement, sailing off behind us, barely missing a beat.

That was so Blackwater. While many of the town's hot-rodders had failed out of high school, their driving skills were A+.

Mom managed to get her foot back on the brake, then hissed: "I should've had my head examined for wanting to help you."

I let go of the wheel. "What's *that* mean?"

Mom delivered the perfect KO: "You're just like your father." She got us back over to the side of the road, jammed the Caddy into P. Then she sat there, head bowed, like she genuinely felt bad about what she'd said. Just when I thought she was going to apologize, she reached over, threw open my door. "Get *out*," she snapped.

"What the hell?" I said.

"Get *out*!" Mom repeated, with bite times a thousand.

"You see," I shot back. "I *knew* you never wanted to be with me. All you needed me for was your faggot Mary Kay crap." I jerked my tape from the cassette player, seized my cap, and leapt from the Caddy.

Mom peeled out, leaving me alone and without pay until further notice.

The rest of the week I spent in a blur. Beer and weed at Jimmy's, going to third base with Callie in the woods near her house. At home: episodes of *Cheers*, *Twilight Zone*, and *Friday Night Videos*. Those were the things I filled my head with instead of all that Mary Kay nonsense, like how plum lipstick, not red, was best suited for pink-complexioned women, or how exfoliation was the step most people skipped in their skincare routine.

Come Sunday, Mom phoned me. "Well?"

"Well what?" I said.

"I think we owe each other an apology." Mom's voice lacked its usual Mary Kay confidence. She sounded frail and far away, like she'd downed one too many Bloody Marys before phoning.

"You first," I said.

"I'm sorry I said you were like your father. I didn't mean it."

"Seriously?"

"Seriously."

The two of us fell silent. All we could hear was a distant hum over the line. Then came Mom's voice, a little less distant than that hum. "We don't have to work together, you know. We can just try being mother and son."

That would be a tough one, I thought. The closest I'd ever felt to her hadn't been in the real world, but in the wonderful world of Mary Kay. "Here's the deal," I said. "I think we can make this working together thing work."

"Think so?" said Mom.

It didn't take long to answer that one. Just like Mom had always been a natural when it came to selling Mary Kay, I figured that to be the time to close my own deal. "Absolutely," I said. "See you tomorrow."

That next day, and for the next number of days, I was back in my groove. In fact, I was better than ever. Instead of doing the usual—partying or *Twilight Zone*ing in my off-hours—I was doing massive amounts of homework. Armed with various Mary Kay brochures and samples I'd swiped from Mom's place before she'd canned me, I was locking myself in the bathroom for hours on end, either reading brochures on the crapper, or standing in front of the mirror, modeling products. Through it all, I learned how the men's facial bar cleaned and buffed the skin while reducing the visible signs of aging, the woman's Moisture Rich Mask Formula Two could remove environmental elements that clogged pores, the all-in-one mascara formula could deliver long, thick lashes without clumping. And while there were times when my old man would bang on the door, wondering what the hell was going on, while my face was slathered in Balancing Moisturizer Two for oily skin, I never let up.

All my hard work was paying off. Mom and I began spending quality time together outside of Mary Kay—sharing an occasional dinner, attending church. Her once grim-smelling kitchen became filled with all her old, wonderful cooking smells. Her living room was even bearable.

But one day at her place, while she was making us lunch— Philly steak sandwiches—I sensed a sudden chill in the air. Maybe it was a breeze drifting in off the Barnegat Bay, and sailing through the back screen door. Or much worse, I feared, Mom was brewing up another leaving storm. So I swiped her key ring from her purse, and called out, "Gonna take a quick walk around the block to check out the neighborhood."

I Speed Racer'ed to a hardware store I'd seen by my bus stop. Got her house key copied. When I returned, I snuck the keys back into her purse, and strolled into the kitchen, sporting a huge grin.

"What are you so delighted about?" Mom asked.

What I told her was that I was just happy to be in her life again. What I didn't say was that she'd left me twice, it could happen again. If it did, next time I'd have the key to her magic kingdom. More specifically: her medicine cabinet. And if she did, indeed, leave me again, I'd at least have a little bit of her, and all her downers, rushing through my blood.

Chapter 12

NOT LONG AFTER REJOINING forces with Mom and Mary Kay, I'd not only earned enough to put away some cash in the bank, but to also buy a beater—a Chevy Vega—from the *Asbury Park Press*.

About that car.

It had sweet pinstriping, chrome-plated wheels, and blow-your-eardrums-out Kenwood speakers. Back then, I thought those were the things that made a car go. Really go. But what the owner didn't tell me was that the radio would cut out when it hit potholes. Also had a slightly warped aluminum block engine. Was a real oil-burner. Had to carry around a case in the back because I'd go through a quart just pulling out of the driveway. But by the time I'd learned that one from the guy at NAPA Auto Parts who sold me my first case of Valvoline, it was much too late to get my money back.

Since tunes were key, I bought one of those AM-FM cassette jobbers. Quad stereo speakers. Even paid to get it installed. As for the case of oil in the back, I grabbed some sheets from the linen closet—a couple colorful, shiny ones my old man had bought at

Gimbels after Mom left home—and tossed them over the box. I tried passing it off as a damned expensive piece of equipment: the subwoofer for my kick-ass car stereo. But that shit-for-brains charade didn't last long. Just a few days later, while cruising Blackwater with Jimmy—Hoodoo Gurus' *Mars Needs Guitars!* cranked loud—he totally busted me; said speakers didn't leave oil stains on sheets.

I officially christened that Vega by taking Callie out on a proper date.

It was a Friday night, early August. The humid air was sugar drunk with Summersweet. Crickets, bullfrogs, and mosquitoes sounded their rackety symphony. Night hung over the sky like a black sheet riddled with holes, allowing tons of starlight to shine through. Amidst it all, Callie was waiting for me at our usual meeting spot. She emerged from the shadows just beyond the streetlight's glow, and hobbled toward the car.

For a while, I'd had my doubts as to whether another car date would ever happen. There'd been that knuckle-headed stunt I'd pulled when cruising with Callie in Mom's Caddy. Plus, her parents had become extremely overprotective due to a recent spike of tourists crashing into Satan's Tree that summer. Nonetheless, I'd begged, pleaded. Told Callie I'd been working all kinds of jobs to earn the money to take her out in style. So she lied to her parents, told them she was spending the night with a friend that was willing to cover for her.

She stuck her head in through the open window. Instead of giving me shit like she'd done after seeing Mom's Caddy, that trademark wobbly smile of hers crept across her face. "Nice," she bubbled.

Her voice was as effervescent as her outfit: a black Madonna "Live To Tell" T-shirt, a long flared polka dot skirt, equally polka-dotted Keds, white knee-high socks, and an unzipped pretty purple sweat jacket.

I hopped out. *"Bonne soirée, mademoiselle,"* I said.

Callie let fly a small curtsy. "And a good evening to you, too, sir."

I opened her door. Helped to ease her sidesaddle into her seat. She swung her good leg around; then carefully eased her right leg inside.

Once back behind the wheel, I reached behind my seat, produced a red-rose bouquet.

Callie gushed, snuggled them to her chest, and breathed in their potent scent. Then she scoped me out. "Looking good."

That night I'd gone out of my way to win her approval. Not only was I wearing my freshly washed Cult *Love* T-shirt, brand-new Converse high-tops, and my one-and-only pair of unripped jeans, but over the last couple months, all the Mary Kay products I'd been modeling had made my skin clearer, eyes brighter. I told Callie she always looked good.

We leaned in, shared a shy kiss. Never mind that we'd already gone to third base out in the woods, it was strange being in a car again. Callie glanced out the front window. Not so much noticing the patch of streetlight hitting the pavement just in front of the car, but quietly contemplating something only she could see. Then she turned back to face me. That sweet smile of hers had gone into hibernation. "You'll be careful, right?" she asked.

This time I didn't offer any lame lines. I simply told her absolutely. Then I motioned toward her seatbelt. Once we were fastened in, I asked: "Where to?"

Her smile came back out of hiding. "How 'bout the beach?"

I made a beeline for the Garden State Parkway. Once there, I inched the Vega up to sixty-five. Seeing as I'd dumped in a few quarts of oil before leaving home, the normally rackety engine purred. All the mile markers—from the seventies up into the eighties—blurred by.

I grabbed one of my favorite tapes—*The Wild, The Innocent & the E Street Shuffle*—and slapped it into the deck. "Rosalita"—with its bright sax riff, driving beat, and Springsteen's urgent vocals—filled the car.

Spread out now, Rosie, doctor come cut loose her mama's reins / You know playin' blind man's bluff is a little baby's game.

I inched the car up to seventy. Windows down, the boisterous, pine-scented wind whooshed through the car, transforming Callie's long silky hair into that brilliant array of sparklers that had dazzled me on our very first date.

Dynamite's in the belfry, baby, playin' with the bats / Little Gun's downtown in front of Woolworth's, tryin' out his attitude on all the cats.

While I hadn't been able to bust Callie and me out of Blackwater on our first date, that night was different. Well, sort of. Forget trying to imitate that Springsteen pose, which I could never cop anyway. For those glorious seven minutes and four seconds—the length of "Rosalita"—I imagined Callie and I were living that song. We were on the run, escaping the swamps of Jersey, heading out California way, trying to find a peaceful place where guitars played night and day.

Then the chorus kicked in.

Rosalita, jump a little lighter / Senorita, come sit by my fire / I just want to be your lover, ain't no liar / Rosalita, you're my stone desire.

Recalling that moment, maybe Callie was also living my escape dream. She was bobbing up and down in her seat, beaming. Gave me a smile so sweet and tart it was like she had the juice of Pine Barrens blueberries running through her blood. Gone her sad, watery eyes. Gone the forehead creases she'd sometimes get when thinking too much about her fake leg or her mom. There were no vacancies in her shine hotel. Everything about her was electric and alive. I pressed my foot a little deeper into the gas. The engine revved, hummed. Sounded better than it ever had before. I cranked the stereo louder.

Parkway trees blurred by. Ditto with the occasional deer grazing by the side of the road. Callie was weightless. So was I. We sailed through all the trails of taillights and headlights from passing cars as if they were dazzling liquid streams.

But once the song ended, it was as if we'd suddenly lost that buzz of our lovers-on-the-run electricity, and had been dropped from a great height back down into our regular lives. I clicked off the stereo. Callie and I sunk a little heavier into our seats.

We sat there quietly. The only sounds: that whoosh of wind rushing in through open windows, and my Vega. No longer did it hum like a finely tuned high-performance engine, one you'd hear about in a Springsteen song. Instead, the aluminum-block's valves were back to their tapping. I eased my foot slightly off the gas; crossed over into the slow lane. I glanced over at Callie. A crease or two had bloomed back across her forehead. I gave her hand a squeeze. "You okay?"

She nodded, squeezed back. "It'll be nice to see the ocean."

At Exit 82, we headed east toward Seaside. As we crossed the bridge connecting Toms River to the barrier island, Barnegat Bay's musky, marshy stink gradually eased into the clear scent of sea salt as we drew closer to the beach.

We ended up in Seaside Park—dilapidated beach houses, fleabag hotels, meth-head surf punks. It was the twisted stepsister to the neighboring, way-too-glitzy and touristy Seaside Heights boardwalk. Still, it possessed a certain charm. From Memorial Day to Labor Day, Seaside Park's blinker traffic light was changed to a regular traffic light. The population would jump from 1,800 to 18,000. Certain shops and stands would only open for the summer.

Sweet corn and Jersey tomatoes, miniature golf and arcades everywhere. Come winter, though, the place was a ghost town.

Callie and I cruised the chaotic streets until we discovered a fairly remote portion of town. Armed with a huge blanket I'd brought from home, we walked out onto the beach. A slight breeze sailed in off the ocean. That ocean: a shimmering, semi-slumbering beast whose steady hum reminded me of that final sustaining chord in the Beatles' "A Day in the Life." I took off my Cons, helped Callie remove the shoe from her good foot; the other sneaker, she kept on. I tied all the laces together, slung the shoes over my left shoulder. And while Callie had been taught over and over in physical therapy how to walk, fall down, and safely get up, I slipped my right arm around her waist, drew her close. She shivered briefly, then rested her head against mine. We walked through the sand, careful to avoid the occasional broken bottle and crushed, jagged beer can.

Waves continued their working song against shore. The apparitional strains of arcade music and roller coaster screams floated over from the Funtown Pier.

Like she'd done so many other times, Callie motioned toward the night sky. She singled out three bright stars. "There's the Summer Triangle," she said. "Lyra the Harp, Aquila the Eagle, and Cygnus the Swan."

Since I'd brushed up on my stargazing skills since my last Callie date, I was able to tell her a thing or two. I pointed to the right of that triangle. "There's the Big Dipper." Then I pointed to a red giant star amidst a cluster of other stars just bellow the Summer Triangle. "And there's Scorpius the Scorpion."

Callie kissed my cheek and told me she'd been reading up on music, said we should quiz one another.

I started easy. Some music I'd heard earlier drifting over from the pier—music that reminded me of Jimmy—gave me my first question. "Who sings 'Nightbird'?"

Callie squeezed my waist. "Way too easy. Stevie Nicks."

Then she shot back: "Name a band whose name is a palindrome."

That was a no-brainer. "ABBA," I said. Then I added the cherry, told her that the band's self-titled album released in '75 also featured another palindrome. Track four: "SOS."

We paused so Callie could take a breather, and readjust the waist belt that attached her fake leg to her body. Then she said: "Jerry Lee Lewis married his cousin in 1957. What was her name?"

Another no-brainer. "Myra Gale Brown. She was only thirteen, and was the daughter of the bass player in his band." Then I soared us into the heavens. "In what constellation can you find the brightest star in the night sky?"

Far faster than my Vega could ever rev up to twenty miles an hour, Callie said: "Canis Major. Sirius, the brightest star in the night sky is only eight light-years away." Then she shot back: "What's so interesting about the songwriter David Rose?"

That one stumped me.

Callie explained that he'd not only scored a Billboard #1 hit with a 1962 instrumental called "The Stripper," but he'd also written the theme for *Little House On The Prairie*.

With all our quizzing, we'd hardly noticed that we'd ended up on a remote little sand dune, the Funtown Pier far in the distance. That evening breeze made a patch of dead dune grass around us come alive with a dry rustle of music.

I spread out the blanket, then eased Callie down onto it. She kept her fake leg straight, while her good one, she twisted under her for support. She observed the dark stretch of beach and ocean that bloomed out from us in all directions. Callie picked up a stick, etched a heart in the sand. For a few moments, she admired that heart, eyes beaming. Then she tossed the stick aside, glanced out at the dark waters. Her eyes were slightly more maudlin than moonglow.

I asked what was up.

At first she didn't say anything, just played with the zipper of her sweat jacket. Finally, not so much out of pity as simple observation, she offered, "I used to come here with my family. Running along the beach." She glanced down at her fake leg, then back up at the vast stretch of ocean. "Wow. That seems so long ago."

She kept staring at the ocean. Had her head turned in a way so I couldn't see the scar on her face. That flawless side of Callie was the side I'd imagined she'd always wanted in life. The Callie of Purity and Promise. The Callie of Unblemished Porcelain Skin. Then she turned back to me, and I, once again, witnessed the Callie I so admired: The Callie of Damage and Dignity. The Callie of the Huge Heart, Wobbly Walk, and Off-Kilter Smile.

As for the way I'd always viewed myself: just some flesh-and-bones version of Muzak—some drippy person that trickled into the environment without anyone really noticing at first. And when they did, all they saw and heard was some paltry, watered-down version of something they may or may not have enjoyed in the first place. Which would pretty much leave everyone, including myself, pissed off and disappointed—plugging their ears, and running for the exits. But that wasn't how Callie viewed me. In fact, it was right at that moment she turned to me, and said: "I think I love you, Mark."

"I think I love you, too," I said. I gathered her close.

She took my hand, slipped it beneath her skirt. Took me to that place where fake flesh met real. And while I'd traveled to that place many times before, that evening her real flesh was almost hot to the touch.

I worked my fingers beneath her panties.

That's when Callie said all warm and breathy against my neck: "Let's go all the way."

"You sure?"

She nodded. "Just be careful."

All the R-rated movies I'd snuck into back in those days— *Catch-22*, *M*A*S*H*, *Performance*, and more—had me stupidly believing going all the way was easy. That practically all I had to do was snap my fingers, and there I'd be—awash in a sea of bare flesh, with moves smoother than Adonis. The reality of the situation, though, was much different.

I was in such a hurry to strip that I ripped my *Love* tee while pulling it off. My Levis got bunched up around my ankles; I flopped around like a fish washed ashore. Between Callie's peals of laughter, and all my huffing and puffing, I finally tore myself out of my pants. Those once unripped jeans: shredded in the knees.

As for Callie, while removing her sweat jacket, her right arm got caught in the sleeve. She struggled so much to free herself she elbowed me in the nose. "Oh my God," she gasped. "I'm so sorry." When she tried to examine my nose more closely, I told her to forget about it. There'd been no blood. Only a few moments of me seeing my own stars. Her "Live to Tell" T-shirt, however, was much easier. "Here," she offered. She raised her arms. I clutched the tee at the bottom hem, just below Madonna's image—all golden hair, blue-eyes gazing toward the heavens—and slipped it up and over Callie's head and outstretched arms. I tossed it to the side of the blanket. Then I helped remove the sneaker from her right foot; her skirt, she left on. She gathered all those pretty polka dots up around her waist.

From there, we quickly stripped out of our remaining clothes as if trying to outrun any shyness and fears that might've made us think twice about it all.

Callie pulled her good leg out from under her, then the two of us eased down until we were lying on the blanket, all goose bumps and shivers. I slipped her a kiss so heavy with tongue it made her cough. She hugged me so tight I also coughed. Getting hard wasn't a problem though. Once she'd said she wanted to do it, I was ready. But finding my way inside her was another story. The first time, I poked her just above the ass. She got a look on her face like she'd seen a beach rat. "Higher." Then another time: "A little lower."

When I finally found the sweet spot, I slid inside her. We avoided eye contact. My hips didn't pump jackrabbit fast, like I'd seen in so many movie sex scenes. I took it slow.

"That feels nice," Callie sighed.

Still more goose bumps and shivers, but now for reasons other than the cool night air.

My left leg kept brushing against her fake leg. At first, I'd readjust my body, trying to avoid it. Callie got wise to my moves. A crease or two spread across her forehead. Her eyes appeared sadder, lonelier than Seaside Park in the winter. "Should we stop?" she asked.

I told her no. Said everything was just so new and all, and to give it another chance.

So we did.

I'm not sure how it happened, but right then, all our ineptitude slipped away. Callie's body: a warm, slow-flowing river. Her hair: radiant as Vesta's sacred flame. Her scent: sweet and earthy, bonfire smoke laced with freshly spun cotton candy. And every soft something she uttered: holy. A parish of whispers between her lips. Our breathing, which had at first been choppy and out of tune, merged into one shared breathing in and out. When I noticed my shadow slowly cross over her belly, small breasts, and face, I forgot about all the ghosts. And when our glances finally locked, and Callie's eyes swallowed me whole, I was freefalling through a continuous field of diamonds. The whole world was spinning, far greater than any ride on Funtown Pier. No conception of loss or fear. Only possibility. At that moment we didn't need French. Didn't need Ouija boards or Mad Man's wise words to determine the future. Didn't even need to fool myself into believing my life was a Springsteen song. Callie and I were that song. That night I could've lived and died in her arms. I could've stormed the Pearly Gates with a wide grin slapped across my face.

Chapter 13

IN BLACKWATER, PEOPLE WANTED out. Out of debt. Out of trouble. Out of marriages and relationships. Sickness and sadness. For a few, it was as easy as packing their cars and heading out. Others died of natural causes.

That winter during twelfth grade, for example. It was about five months after that summer when Mom and I had first kicked ass with Mary Kay.

She'd just pulled up to our usual meeting spot. Never mind it was an icy January Saturday morning. We were all about making the sale. I hopped into her warm car. Right away I knew something was up. There were half moons of darkness beneath Mom's eyes, like she'd been wiping at the concealer that generally covered them. And instead of greeting me with that music in her voice, she said flatly: "We can't do this anymore."

When I asked what I'd done wrong, all she said was, "You've done everything right, honey. I just don't think I'm cut out for this." Then she swiped a pill from her purse, popped it.

Up until that moment I'd managed to stay fairly cool. But forget that. I was pissed. Super pissed. I didn't know who to be more pissed at—Mom for leaving me again, or me for believing she'd stay. I punched the glove compartment. It sprang open. Mary Kay samples, bunched-up tissues, along with insurance and registration paperwork tumbled to the floor.

Mom didn't flinch. Didn't even bat a mascara'd eyelash when she said, "Please try to understand."

I understood all too well. This had been our lifelong game: love tug-of-war. Right then, I recalled a Bible quote. How Jesus had said something like: *Yes, I am with you always, until the very end.* "Why do you even go to church?" I asked.

The half moons beneath Mom's eyes grew a little darker. "Excuse me?"

I spit that Bible quote in her face, then added: "If you're so damned God-like, you should've at least followed that one." I stormed from the car.

Mom stuck her head out the window. Even stuck out an arm, frantically swished it through the frigid, teeth-biting air. Normally, she never raised her voice in public. But that day she just kept waving and hollering: "Get back here right now, young man!"

I ignored her, kept hunching my way through the chill.

She called after me a few more times. But when I flipped her off, she peeled out in the opposite direction.

I continued skulking through the maze of wintry residential streets. Above, the sky was withered, ashen gray. Below, the lawns were sprinkled with a light powdering of snow that sparkled like shattered glass. I continued replaying the blowout with Mom. It was the same endless loop. The same breakdown song with the same old words and melody I'd heard for years.

After that, things only got worse. A few days later, I visited Grandmother in the Blackwater Medical Center.

She was hooked up to all these sci-fi looking machines that beeped, whirred, and groaned. A snaky maze of tubes and wires ran from them, went up her nose, connected to her arms and chest. Her flesh, like a bad thrift store dress, hung loose and rumpled from her frame. Milky eyes. Tissue-thin speech. She was light years from the Grandmother I'd known as a child: the hefty, fearless woman with the husky voice, beautiful sky-blues, and perfect hug.

I pulled up a chair alongside her bed, smoothed the matted white hair from her face. Gave her a kiss on the forehead. In the old days she smelled of menthol and bacon grease. Now: antiseptic and death.

Her eyelids fluttered open. The creases across her forehead and between her eyebrows deepened. Her lips pursed so much she sprouted a wrinkle mustache. "What are you doing here? You should be in school."

Truth was I'd skipped that day. I'd twenty-five mphed my Vega along the frosty Garden State Parkway to reach her. I recalled one of the many medicine bottles I'd spied sitting atop the nurse station desk when I'd first checked in. "It's a holiday," I lied. "St. Procardia's Day."

"Oh," said Grandmother. "I've never heard of that one." She paused, took a few labored breaths, then said: "So you're doing well in school?"

"Absolutely. All As." Another flatline lie. In truth, the As were mostly Bs and in math I'd barely managed to score a C.

Some sky-blue drifted back into Grandmother's eyes. "You're doing better in math. I'm proud of you." Then, in that fragile voice of hers, she told me her bed was number twenty-seven, and the empty one next to hers, twenty-eight. "Quick," she said. "Multiply them."

Luckily, straight computation had never been too difficult. From her purse sitting atop the bedside table I snatched a pen and her math pad. Flipped to a blank page, got to work. Once done, I said without any hesitation: "Seven hundred fifty-six."

A tiny caterpillar of a smile inched across Grandmother's face. From beneath the sheets, she wriggled a hand free. It was badly wrinkled and covered with splotches of browns, reds, and yellows. It looked like one of the Christmas fruitcakes she used to make. She rested that hand on my own. While I'd expected it to feel cold and clammy, it was warm, reassuring.

That day, and long afterward, I'd wonder how a woman of such warmth could be dying on account of complications due to her heart. Another thing that would continually confound me: how had such a loving woman given birth to my bastard of an old man?

I dreaded bringing up that bastard's name for fear of conversation buzzkill. But I had to. I wasn't sure how much longer Grandmother would be around. "What was he like when he was my age? You know, Dad?"

Grandmother shook her head. "A real devil," she sighed. "Nothing I did could ever please him." Her eyes clouded slightly, welled up a bit. But not enough to blink down a storm. She gave my hand a pat. "Your father loves you very much."

I snorted a laugh.

"It's true," she said. She proceeded to tell me how, as a boy, my old man's cop father had constantly bullied him to be the best he could be. Sometimes my old man succeeded. More often than not, he'd failed miserably.

Great, I thought. It was just like that Springsteen lyric from "Adam Raised a Cain." Something about how you're born into this life paying for the sins of somebody else's past. If my relationship with my old man was forever dictated by the word of Bruce I was screwed. That decree was far bigger than anything I could change through sheer will or the right drugs.

"Don't worry," said Grandmother. "Things'll get better."

After that, she fell silent. All we could hear were the hurried voices of nurses out in the hallway, the sounds of a Code Blue and other commands crackling over the intercom, and the song of Grandmother's life-saving machines.

"Anything I can do to help you feel better?" I asked.

Grandmother flashed a weak smile. "Tell me more about your life. Do you have a girlfriend?"

I shrugged.

"Come on. You can tell Grandma."

"There's this one girl," I said. "Callie. She's a senior like me. She's got blonde hair and pretty eyes. And a nice voice. She was also in a car crash and has a fake leg. But you wouldn't know it. She's not all bitter. Just kind."

As Grandmother considered that one, her machines continued singing—beeps here, groans there. When she finally responded, I had to lean in extra close on account of all those machines. "Kindness," she said, her voice pale and delicate as her flimsy and faded blue hospital gown. "That's important. But do you trust her?"

At first I figured it was the near death and drugs making her ask such a strange question. To me, trust and kindness were the same. Yet the more I thought about it, the more I realized she had a point. For example, Mom could be kind. Though once she'd left me that first time, I never truly trusted her again. As for Jimmy, I trusted him with my life, but knew he could be a real pain in the ass. With Callie, I never questioned her kindness. In regards to trust, I recalled our first date, and how she'd tried to bust me out of Blackwater. Never mind that I was stopped by my own fears. "Yeah," I said. "I trust her."

Grandmother studied my eyes, and my hand resting on hers. Maybe she was thinking of what to say next. Or maybe, like my old man would often do, she was searching for any physical or emotional reaction that would contradict or corroborate with my statement. All she did was motion toward her purse.

I placed it between us.

She worked her hands through the maze of machine hoses, and fumbled with the purse clasp, but couldn't quite manage.

"Here," I said. I popped it open for her.

She fished around inside, dug past lipstick, ballpoint pens, Kleenex, and a mini sewing/repair kit to produce a small velvet drawstring pouch. From inside the pouch she produced a ring. It was a thin white gold band with a sparkling diamond center.

"It's beautiful," I said. "But you shouldn't keep it in your purse. Someone might steal it."

Grandmother said that was nonsense, that she always carried it with her. Then she told me a story she'd repeatedly told me through the years. Never once did I stop her; I just let her, still again, recount that sad and stunning tale about the young man named Reece that had given her the ring when she was eighteen. They'd met on the Asbury Park boardwalk. He'd been my grandmother's first true love. They had plans to get married. But then he went off to war. After that, she never saw him again. Throughout her story, her lifesaving machines beeped and groaned faster, then slower. Once done speaking, the rhythms of those machines gradually leveled out. Grandmother, however, appeared exhausted. Her rumpled flesh was even paler. Her arms: hanging limply at her sides. It took all her strength to motion with her head toward the plastic Pepto-Bismol-pink water pitcher sitting atop her bedside table.

I poured her a glass.

After a few sips and some quiet time, she again displayed the ring. "I want you to have it."

In those days, I was practically the definition of Teenage Wasteland. Was always partying. Couldn't hold down a job. Would lose track of time. Forget about knowing what to do with a fine diamond ring. "It's too nice," I said. "Besides, shouldn't Dad get it?"

Grandmother's milky eyes brightened slightly. "You have your whole life ahead of you, sweetie." She placed the ring in my hand.

As I marveled at the glittering band, I wondered why she'd never given it to my old man to pass along to Mom. I wanted to ask, but then I recalled all those past Christmases, and other occasions, when Mom and my grandmother had been together. When I was much younger, it had been so confusing to see them arguing. More times than not, I'd bolt to my room, bawl my eyes out. But as I grew older, the situation grew clearer. Grandmother—one of my greatest allies—was just looking out for me. As for Mom, she was simply clueless when it came to expressing her emotions. So she stuffed them into Mary Kay and housecleaning. Once I began understanding things in those terms, I'd no longer run off crying whenever they'd argue. I'd just lock myself in my room and crank my sonic walls. Between all those fights with Mom and having my old man as a son, I figured Grandmother must've learned very early on that true affection wasn't either of my parents' strong suit.

I wasn't sure if I'd mastered affection either. Maybe the ring would help. The way it sparkled and felt in my hand, it seemed all about warmth and true love. "So it's mine, huh?"

"Absolutely," said Grandmother. "But you can't tell your father."

"I won't." I swished an X across my Police *Ghost in the Machine* sweatshirt–covered heart to seal the promise.

"One more thing," she said, beginning to drift off. "Don't give the ring away until you find the right girl." Her eyes closed, then slowly opened. She pointed a withered finger at the ring. Sounding a lot like Jimmy's lousy Sears turntable, she said in a scratchy, nearly inaudible voice: "Let's see you with it."

I held the ring up for display.

Grandmother managed a parched smile. "It was meant for you. See how it shines?"

I was so worried about her health that I totally missed what she was getting at. Later, though, I'd realize she'd been right. While that ring was slightly smaller than a pellet of uranium, which contained more energy than six carloads of coal, it was far more powerful. Even beneath the hospital's stale fluorescent lights, the white gold band and diamond inlay had sparkled like stars, stars in the brilliant constellation of Grandmother Major.

Her eyelids fluttered shut.

When they didn't open right away, I said: "You okay?"

No response.

She was gone for real, I thought. I couldn't move. Couldn't cry or scream. All I could do was go camouflage with the room's stark white walls. There I was: just another lost ghost roaming Blackwater.

Gradually, Grandmother's eyes opened. "I'll miss you when I'm gone."

"Don't talk like that," I said, relieved she was still among the living. "You'll be okay real soon."

She extended her frail arms.

I fumbled through all the wires and hoses to ease into her hug. It sent shivers up my spine.

"Don't worry," she said, giving my back a gentle, reassuring pat. "Everything'll be fine."

"No it won't."

In a voice nearly drowned out by all her singing machines, she uttered something about poets saying wise things they don't comprehend.

I slipped out of her hug, flashed a curious look. I'd heard those words before. It was that Greek philosopher I'd learned about in school. "Plato?" I said.

Another patch of sky-blue drifted back into her milky eyes. "So you *are* doing well in school," she said. "Tell me what it means."

I asked her to tell me instead. Said it would sound much nicer, her saying it.

She motioned me closer. In a brittle voice, she said: "Sometimes we McDaniels can be thickheaded. It can take a little while for us to understand what's best." Once again her eyelids fluttered shut, then opened. "You should go, sweetie. I need to rest."

"I'll be back Saturday," I said.

"You don't have to."

"But I want to," I insisted.

"Good," she said, her voice growing extra weary. "That'd be nice."

Chapter 14

OME SATURDAY, I DIDN'T return to the Blackwater Medical Center. Sunday neither. Bong hits in Jimmy's basement. Going all the way with Callie out in the Dump. Even with the best of intentions of returning to see Grandmother, my whole weekend had sped by in a blur of partying. Partying to feel good. Partying to forget.

First thing Monday morning, well before I'd risen for school, there was a phone call. Despite my hangover I knew the sound of those bells. They'd rung the same way when Grandmother had called to tell my old man his father had died. I jerked the covers over my head, buried myself deep in my dank, dark grave. Yet all that darkness, all my head buzzing, ear ringing, and bed spinning couldn't drown out the sound of the phone hanging up, or my old man's footsteps coming toward my room, or his voice.

"I have some bad news."

Those five words, I'd later say, were like the studies of Fermi. In 1934, he conducted studies with nuclear fission—where he'd blast uranium with tiny neutrons to create a massive release of energy. All that energy was later used to create nuclear power and bombs. And that tiny neutron—how it could bore down deep into matter—was my grandmother's death. And the world around her, my world: uranium. Once her death bombarded my uranium world, things began blowing to pieces.

"It was bound to happen," said my old man. "I just didn't think so soon." He got quiet. Squib quiet. I poked my head out from beneath the covers to see if he was about to slug me. Instead he just stood there, head bowed. Like he was searching the floor, or searching somewhere deep inside himself for what to say next, or if what he'd just said was the right or wrong way to have expressed it.

I yanked the covers back over my head. That's when my radio alarm clock chimed in: The Clash's "Rock the Casbah." My shaky hand emerged from beneath the covers, hit the snooze button, then buried itself again.

My old man, suited up in his usual starched white button-up, and more highly starched attitude, said, "Get up. You'll be late for school."

"I'm not going," I muttered.

He repeated his command. It had sharper teeth, a bigger bite.

I still didn't budge.

Again, my radio alarm clock sounded. This time: The Talking Heads' "Burning Down the House." I slammed the snooze with a raging fist. The Talking Heads and the alarm clock flatlined.

My old man yanked me from bed, seized me by my flannel top.

There we were, face to face. Well, almost. While my old man clocked in at five-eleven, I was only a few inches shorter due to another growth spurt. But that wouldn't have saved my ass had we gone to blows. I was just a bag of bones and attitude up against a sixteen-cylinder engine of muscle and rage. I rubbed the sleep from my eyes, croaked out, "What now? You gonna hit me?" It wasn't so much a taunt, just what I'd been conditioned to expect in stressful situations.

My old man opened his mouth to speak, but instead remained quiet. I clenched my hands into fists, waiting for that squib to detonate.

Instead, he just stood there, looking at me. His expression was ninety-eight percent badass Sergeant Carter, two percent *Father Knows Best*. All he could say was, "Your grandmother was a good woman."

I agreed. "One of the best."

Still maintaining strict eye contact, my old man said, "I was with her on Saturday. She kept saying you'd promised to stop by. But you didn't."

Now I was the one bowing my head. "I tried. I just got busy."

"Well I hope the party was worth it," said my old man.

Up until that point, his physical restraint had been truly commendable. But his verbal digs were beginning to cut deep. So I tried defending myself. But seeing as I'd just woken, I wasn't doing such a hot job. "That's bullshit," I said. "I wanted to be with her. I just lost track of time." What I didn't say, though, not so much due to lack of sleep, but rather that I didn't understand it so well myself at the time, was that it scared the hell out of me to see Grandmother so close to death. Didn't want to be there when it happened. Didn't want to witness her becoming another ghost like Mom. The last thing I did utter, however, were those three very simple, but heartfelt words, "I loved Grandma."

That's when my old man delivered the worst blow of all, and I deserved every bit of it. "Then you should've been there," he said.

Now it was my turn to go ballistic. I sprang up onto my toes, eye-to-eye gaze. Spat out, "When I visited grandma she said you were the same when you were my age. Always pissed off. You treated her like shit." Then I scrambled for the nearest thing available: the three-foot-high red acrylic bong I'd recently won at the Seaside Heights boardwalk. I whipped the bong across the room. It whooshed past my two Bruce posters, my stack of records, one of my stereo speakers, and nailed my lava lamp sitting atop the dresser. Water, wax, broken glass, and carbon tetrachloride flew everywhere.

My old man pinned me against the wall. Not to fight, but to keep me from doing something even more asinine. His rancid coffee breath spilled all over me as he said with that taut, even tone of his, "I'm really trying here, Mark. But all you do is keep breaking my balls."

I struggled to break free, but he kept me pinned there. The more I struggled, the tighter he gripped me. The tighter he gripped, the less pain I felt, the more protected.

My old man surprised me still again. No savage punches like in *Fists of Fury*. Instead, his voice grew even quieter, words more measured. As if it were taking all his strength to speak. "I loved my mother," he said. "And I loved your mother, too."

Part of me wanted to say how much I loved and missed Mom and Grandmother, too. But another part of me still couldn't let down my guard. That part won. "Get out," I sputtered.

"Not before I get the ring," said my old man.

When I asked what the hell he was talking about, he said, "When I was with your grandmother I looked through her purse while she was sleeping. It wasn't there."

"Someone must've stole it," I said.

"Maybe you did, Mark. Or maybe she gave it to you." Again, my old man tightened his grip on me, more pain than protection. Maybe he wanted to turn up the heat or perhaps, I'd later consider, it had been a rare moment when he'd temporarily lost control of his own strength, or how to use it.

Either way, I barely felt the pain. He'd dosed me with far worse in the past. Instead, what struck me was his face. It was difficult to say what hurt him more—the idea of me swiping the ring, or

Grandmother giving it to me instead of him. If I handed it over, I realized, I'd probably never see it again. "Screw off. I don't have it."

"Sure you do," said my old man. "It's written all over you."

"Then you don't know how to read," I said. "Now *go*."

But he didn't. He just held me up against the wall, his face close to mine.

I caught a whiff of his musky sweat and Old Spice odor. While he'd changed a lot over the years—his hair had gone a little grayer, he'd gotten a little meaner, more melancholy—his smell had always remained the same.

He kept studying my face and physical reactions for any more signs that would rat me out. "I lost my mother today," he said. "I don't need your shit, too." He released his grip on me, then stormed off to work.

I crashed back down onto my bed. Or should I say, *into* it. I fell deep. Real deep. All that falling felt like flying, in a way. *Flying* got me recalling a math word problem I'd recently encountered at school. As I lay there, sinking deeper into my bed, I changed the wording of that problem:

Grandmother's spirit flies against the wind from Blackwater to Heaven in eight hours. Her spirit then returns from Heaven back to Blackwater in the same direction as the wind in seven hours. Find the ratio of the speed of Grandmother's spirit in still air to the speed of the wind.

Before I could even begin solving it, or my own problems, there were all those words in that problem: the phrase *against the wind* got me thinking of that Bob Seger song of the same title. Which led me to music, which reminded me of my sonic walls. *Walls* got me to Pink Floyd. *Pink* to Mom, which brought to mind how she and Grandmother never got along very well. *Spirit* immediately brought forth one of my favorite songs, "Spirit in the Sky." There was also my weird Jersey and all its ghosts—Spy House ghosts, Ghosts of Westside Tavern, and the Ghosts of Tennent Church. All those ghosts got me remembering the ghosts and shadows in my own home. Like all those ghosts, part of me wanted to just drift away, never to be seen again. But then another part of me recalled the deathbed promise I'd made to Grandmother. And so I lay there, sinking still deeper into my bed, wondering if I was becoming a ghost.

Chapter 15

I EVENTUALLY FOUND MYSELF PARKED a few houses down from Mom's place. I left the Vega's sputtery engine running. Sat slumped in my seat, John Deere cap pulled down low, maintaining a sharp guard on Mom's door. I spied the car's dash clock. Didn't doubt its time. Experience had revealed that spark plugs would blow, clutches would wear, valves would need replacing; the only two dependable devices in that Vega remained the clock and tape player. But I didn't pop in any tunes. I knew it wouldn't be long. My male modeling days had taught me that much. Sure enough, once the clock struck 8:30 a.m., Mom—all suited up in Stepford Mary Kay—was out the door, and gone.

Inside her house, I didn't bother scoping out the lame art and posters on the walls. Didn't even speak to the silence, like I'd done before and would continue to do, telling her all the things I could never say in person: how I hated her and loved her and missed her like crazy. Instead, I made a beeline for the bathroom. Bagged some downers. I popped two, placed the other four in a small baggie, and shoved that into my army surplus jacket pocket, the one not containing the velvet pouch with Grandmother's ring.

From there, I cruised the slushy winter streets toward school. Every so often, I'd reach into my coat pocket and touch that velvet pouch. It helped to set my head on straight, as straight as it could get at the time. I drifted past the cemetery, the closed-for-winter ice cream stand, and the Blackwater Medical Center. Glided effortlessly through traffic, dodging stalled-out cars and grizzled hunters with bow-killed deer strapped to the hoods of their slow-moving pick-ups. It was like I was inside a racing car video game: *To Live and Die in Blackwater.*

As I neared Blackwater High, I could feel my guilt and grief get all tangled up in the pills I'd taken. The downers kept trying to lift my head off my shoulders, soften the world's hard edges. But death kept dragging me back down to earth, or more like beneath it. Six feet under. No matter how many times I touched that velvet pouch, nothing changed. In fact, well after I'd parked my car behind the school, that tug-of-war continued.

Once I stepped from my car, I was immediately slammed in the face with fistfuls of winter chill. I spotted a crow sailing across the cadaverous sky, toward the place where pines and maples lined the vast school playground. I recalled my first meeting with Baby, how I'd made such an ass of myself trying to be a tough guy. Since she'd graduated two years prior, I rarely saw her anymore. Just here and there around town, or at an occasional Dump party. Last I'd heard she was working dayshift, stripping at the Little Red Dollhouse. The more I thought about her, the harder it got to tell whether it was the pills, or me just getting all lost in time, but that meeting with her seemed so long ago. At least it had all led to scoring a date with Callie.

I continued alternately floating and trudging through the school parking lot. Bitter winds cut me to the bone, hijacked my breath. Those ill winds whooshed in my ears, mixed with the lonely clang of the flag's metal halyard banging against the flagpole. I continued toward the main entrance, the air around me sounding like ghosts, my warm breath expelling ghosts.

I passed a couple wiry tattooed guys with severe, narrow faces. Gearheads. Always had dirt and grime under their nails. Survived on a regular diet of speed, weed, and *Hot Rod* magazine. No matter the time of year—be it the dead of winter, or hanging out at the Third Lake during the summer—the Gearheads sported worn flannel shirts, faded jeans, scuffed-up work boots, and denim jackets, sleeves hacked off. One was leaning against a metallic red Dodge Charger. The other, against a souped-up primer-blue Nova. MC5's "Kick Out the Jams" blasted through the Nova's open driver-side window. Shoulders hunched, the Gearheads bobbed their heads to the tune, smoking cigarettes, breathing their own ghosts. Those guys reminded me of Terry. But like Baby, Terry was also gone. He'd barely graduated the year before, and was working as a janitor at the power plant.

Once through the main doors of that bland two-story brick building known as Blackwater High, I was immediately slammed with the familiar stench of sour milk, cleaning products, and hairspray. That and the glare of fluorescent lights which made all students—even the cheerleaders and Honor Society—look like haggard suspects in a criminal lineup. I moved through the halls, passing room after room with words and numbers scrawled across chalkboards like all those mysterious letterings on my Ouija board. I kept my hands in pockets, head bowed slightly, eyes more on the dirty floor—a collage of grimy shoe prints of all shapes and sizes—than on any teachers or administrators walking by.

Once I reached Jimmy's American History class I paused, peered through the closed door's narrow glass window, chicken wire embedded in it. I spotted Jimmy. No matter how many times I'd assisted him with his current studies, the American Revolution, I could never get him to see how all those smaller battles—the

French and Indian War, No Taxation Without Representation, the Boston Tea Party, and the Intolerable Acts—had worked hand-in-hand to create one great big battle for freedom. I flashed him a thumbs-up immediately followed by a shrug. Code for: *Everything cool?* Jimmy rolled his eyes, shot me the finger.

When I reached Callie's first-period class, a class we shared—Honors Literature—I leaned against a locker just outside the door. Through that closed door, I could just make out a class discussion concerning Jack London's *The Call of the Wild*. I heard the teacher's boomy voice, the teacher's pet's whiny voice, and others. But nowhere in the mix did I hear Callie. That one threw me. Whether in person, or on the phone, we'd often discussed the book's story—how Buck the dog had been kidnapped from his California home and sold to Canadian postal workers in the Yukon; how that dog had to deal with his nemesis, Spitz; and how Buck eventually turned his back on civilization to join a pack of wolves. So many hours Callie and I had spent deliberating that book—all its metaphors and well-drawn characters—and also dreaming about our own hero's journey some day. I glanced up and down the hallway. With the exception of Mr. Dixon—one of the school's janitors—at the far end of that hall pulling mop detail, the place was empty.

But all that changed once the end-of-class bell rang.

A massive, swirling sea of students consumed me. There were the wild-eyed boys I'd seen at the Third Lake every summer—the Bud-toting, joint-smoking, music-blasting rabble-rousers clad in wifebeaters and Birdwell Beach Britches. But like me, they were now clad in heavy army surplus jackets, rock T-shirts, and jeans—their bodies growing taller, thicker with muscle, raging hormones sparking wild. And the girls' doughy baby flesh had slowly melted away like the winter snow to reveal radiant and wholesome catalog model types, future queens of the Second Lake come June. Other students—tweaked out on puppy love, acid, or family problems—

wandered lost. The rest—student council members, junior ROTC, Home Ec experts, and the occasional dreary-eyed wannabe devil worshipper with *Ozzy* scrawled all over notebooks and inverted five-pointed pentagrams scribbled onto the white tips of their sneakers—walked with purpose, as though once they graduated they already knew their path in life: college, the military, getting married, having babies, starting a band.

Hazy Me wondered about my own path. For years, my old man had harped on me, giving me the same old speech about the importance of education, saying how college was my ticket out. Maybe he was right. But I wasn't completely convinced education's road would lead me far enough from Blackwater. I'd seen too many people leave high school, go on to complete JC, even college, then end up back in town working long, grueling shifts at the power plant as secretaries, maybe even passing their NRC licensing tests to become dispatchers, or full-fledged operators. No way was that for me. When I busted out of Blackwater I wanted to be released into wide-open, radiation-free spaces.

The only trouble was getting there.

I continued staring at the ebb and flow of students. Gradually emerging from that sea was Callie. In a plain black sweater and plaid wool skirt, she clutched her books to her chest as she hobbled from class.

Though out of it, I could still sense something was wrong with her. Much like that night I'd taken her out on our first official date in my Vega, her red-rimmed eyes were staring off into space, seeing something only she could see. I didn't bother speaking French. Just got down to basics. I had to call her name twice before she spotted me.

When she did, she came back to life, but only a little. "Mark, where were you this morning?"

As the sea of students continued flooding past us, I fished the ring from my coat pocket.

I figured it would've dazzled her, just like it had dazzled me when Grandmother had first revealed it. But that wasn't the case. Callie's response barely registered a blip on the interest scale: "Where did you get it?" she asked vacantly.

I was just about to say *from my grandmother* when I was slammed with a sudden case of dry mouth, one of the common side effects of Mom's pills. At first, all that fell from my mouth were huge verbal cotton balls, nothing that made any sense. Callie cocked her head from side to side, not knowing what to make of my behavior. It only got worse when I began licking my lips and the inside of my mouth, trying to build up enough saliva to speak. To Callie, and anyone else walking by, I must've looked like a dog that had been fed peanut butter. *Lick, lick, lick.* Just when Callie asked if she should get an administrator's assistance, I'd built up enough spit juice to say, "The ring…my grandma…she died this morning."

That's when Callie—the Callie I knew and loved—reemerged, if only momentarily. She placed her books on the floor, took me in her arms, pulled me into her. "I'm so sorry."

I nuzzled deeper into her, placed the ring in her hand. "It's for you," I said.

At first she admired it like she'd received the finest gift on earth, something she'd believed no one would ever care to give her. But then that rare and precious look wilted into her shaking her head no.

When I asked what was up, she released her hold on me and took a wobbly step back. In a small voice—far smaller than the booming intercom voice announcing the two-minute warning before the beginning of next class—all Callie said was, "I can't."

While those pills and Grandmother's death had afforded me a certain numbness, Callie's words hit me hard. Had I been straighter, maybe I would've stumbled upon the right question to ask, or the perfect thing to do to get to the root of her troubles. But given my lousy track record with girls back then, even being drug- and guilt-free probably wouldn't have helped. Right then, I figured the only way to win Callie over was to confess everything—the deathbed promise I'd made; how she was the right girl; how I'd love, honor, and protect her. Everything. Yet when I opened my mouth to speak, cottonmouth free, all I did was say much louder than I'd wanted, "Just take the ring!"

A few students—some of the remaining members of that trickling sea—stopped and stared. While they'd become immune to me getting my ass kicked by Terry, it was a rare occurrence to witness me forcing a proposal upon my girlfriend.

The whole scene upset Callie even more. "Look," she said, staring more at that grimy floor than me. "Maybe I should—"

I hate to say it now, but back then, amidst those noisy students, the harsh lights, and the slosh of Mr. Dixon's mop, all I wanted to do was hurt Callie. "Fine," I said. I snatched the ring from her hand, stormed off down the hall. Didn't even look back when I heard her trembling voice call my name numerous times.

Chapter 16

STORMED OUT OF SCHOOL, hopped in my car, popped two more pills. From there, I continued floating through town past the gun and ammo store, the funeral home, and the Rainbow Casket Company. Some time around noon, when Mom's pills had fully kicked in, and temporarily freed me from that tug-of-war with death, my head lifted off my shoulders. Gone Me. Helium Balloon Me. All that dizzy free-floating reminded me of Baby. Since she was working dayshift, I figured her to be onstage at that moment. Her pale flesh, crazily thrown hair, and grinding hips—a dizzy, slow-mo flow. In the smoky spotlight she'd be shining like the countless saints I'd seen on Mom's prayer cards as a kid.

Truth was, I'd never stopped thinking about her, even with Callie. Baby's brightness, I was drawn to it. I floated over to the Little Red Dollhouse.

Once there, I cut the Vega's engine, but left the key turned in the ignition so I could listen to tunes.

I leaned into my seat, drifted away on my Vicodin flying carpet. But what I saw was not some euphoric floating dream. Just Grandmother in the hospital hooked up to all those hoses and wires. That disturbing image—a Code 10-40—kept breaking and entering my heart. Rearranging its furniture, knocking it over, knocking me out.

Knock, knock, knock.

I woke to hear someone knocking on my car window. Through all the fog, I spotted Hazy Baby. I clicked off the stereo and rolled down the window to get a better look. In jeans, boots, and a parka, she was brushing windblown strands of hair from her face. As she did so, I noticed a change in her appearance. All the drugs and alcohol she'd downed since high school had tarnished some of her illuminated beauty.

"What're you doing here?" she asked, her words turning to spirits as they met with the cold air. "Wanna thank me again for saving you from Terry?"

"I wanted to see how you were doing."

She crossed her arms in front of her chest. "Shouldn't you be in school, kid?"

"I'm where I wanna be," I said. I stuck a hand in my jacket pocket, touched the velvet pouch. It was smooth and warm, like how I'd imagined Baby's flesh might feel. I must've fallen too far into that dream because the next thing I heard was, "Yo, wake up."

I opened my eyes, was back in my car.

Baby fixed me with a solid stare. "What're you on?"

"Downers."

She pursed her lip-glossed lips, and cooed, "Got any for me, Sugar Smack?"

At least I was better at drug math. I ran the numbers in my head. Started with six pills. Downed two. Two for later. Last two for another day. "Nope."

Baby let fly an exasperated sound. "Hogging all your drugs. Reminds me of someone."

Not really giving a shit about his well-being, but at least grateful he was no longer around school, I felt obliged to ask, "How's Terry?"

Baby rolled her eyes. "Crazier than ever."

I shook my head. Just like my old man would shake his head when thoroughly disappointed in me. "You deserve better."

"Oh yeah, Sugar Smack? Like who? *You?*"

I shrugged a *why not.*

That one made Baby laugh. "Yeah, right, kid." She grew quiet. All we could hear was the occasional car slushing by on Route 9. Then she motioned back behind her. "Look, I gotta get to work."

Blame it on the pills, my teenage wasteland brain, or my on-again, off-again Terry rivalry, but all I wanted to do was prove myself to her. As she walked away, I produced the ring. "Bet Terry doesn't have one of these," I called out.

Baby glanced over her shoulder. Unlike Callie's lukewarm response, Baby's eyes lit up. She headed back to the car, scoped out the ring. "Nice rock. Looks about a carat."

"Howdja know that?" I asked.

"Practice, Sugar Smack. You wouldn't believe the stuff guys try to give me. Some's legit. But a lot's complete shit." She cupped her hands, blew air into them. Then she stuck those hands into her coat pockets. "You steal it?" she asked.

"It was my grandmother's. She just died."

"Sorry to hear that," said Baby.

Again, she grew quiet. Winter Silence. Feels Like a Million Years Before Spring Silence.

Baby broke that silence by asking, "Why'd she give it to you?"

"To give to the right girl when I found her."

Baby laughed.

"What?" I said. "It's true."

"I'm sure it is," she said.

The next thing I knew she'd snatched away the ring.

I reached a hand out the window to grab it.

She pulled away. "What? I'm not the right girl? You just said I was."

"Sure you are," I said. "I mean maybe. I dunno." I was way too pill-and-death jangled to fully get what I was saying. Later, though, I'd realize what was lying beneath my messed up words was that concept Grandmother had shared while on her deathbed: trust. Add to that: lust. While those two worked together, in some form or another, to create affection, I've always been pretty clueless as to how to untangle those emotions, and order them into a sensible equation that would equal true love.

Baby was about to try on the ring then stopped. "Why don't you put it on me, Sugar Smack."

Whether or not she was messing with me, that wasn't happening. When I slipped that ring on a girl's finger it would be for real.

Once Baby saw I wasn't budging, she slipped it on, flashed it in my face. "Looks like I'm the right girl whether you like it or not, Sugar Smack." Then she stuffed that hand, which had jade polish chipped off bitten nails, into her coat pocket.

Referring to the ring, I said, "Give it back."

Baby began walking away.

I leapt from the car. But Cloud-Legged Me wasn't prepared for touchdown on solid ground. My knees buckled. I fell against the hard, icy dirt. I struggled to my feet, stumbled after Baby. Caught her by the shoulder, spun her around.

She stared me down. Wisps of windblown hair streaked across her dim face. "Easy, Sugar Smack. I was just teasing."

Blame it on the pills, the guilt, or that deathbed promise, but I was determined to give the ring to someone that day. Since Callie wanted nothing to do with it, Baby seemed the next best choice.

Not only had she, in her own way, saved me from Terry, she also had a far hotter body. Not that that really mattered. But if Callie was going to blow me off, screw it. "Keep it," I said.

Baby was far wiser than me when it came to knowing the score. She scoped out my eyes, my manner, my ratty jeans, and dirty coat; she was just as good as my old man in the Sizing People Up Department. "Look," she said. "Get it straight, kid. You're not thinking right. A pretty ring like that shouldn't be for someone like me."

"What're you talking about? You're beautiful."

Baby shook her head. Slipped off the ring, placed it in the palm of my hand, closed my cold fingers around it. "You might be a mess, Sugar Smack. But not as big a mess as me."

Chapter 17

YET AGAIN:
I continued drifting through town, feeling more like the aimless spirit of some poor soul that had been wiped out by Satan's Tree than my flesh-and-blood self. The whole drive around Blackwater, I kept a hand on the velvet pouch containing Grandmother's ring. While the drugs kept trying to spin me off high into the sky like the Wilbur Brothers Family Circus Ferris wheel, that ring kept me grounded, steering me safely through the reckless wintry streets. *So funny*, I thought back then, *how only a few hours prior I couldn't even give that ring away.* Still, I couldn't stop thinking of Callie. Despite her odd behavior, she'd been the one and only girl I'd truly considered the right one. Maybe that's why when the Vega's dashboard clock read the end of the school day, I pulled myself together—the best I could at the time—and headed to her bus stop.

About Callie's bus stop.

A funky, blood-red house that also served as the Blackwater Diner. Had rusty pots, pans, skillets, saws, and knives hanging from the exterior siding. A string of tattered Budweiser and Coors flags—around the size of church bingo cards—ran along the sill. Worn carpets of all shapes, colors, and sizes were scattered across the barely exposed dirt lawn. The blue front door was covered in laminated photos of various locals and tourists that had eaten there. But the most notable feature was a wheelchair sitting by that front door. Sure, it served a purpose: an elderly person could rest there while waiting for a table, a patron could slump down into it, sleep off a drunk. But I always thought that wheelchair especially odd since Callie had to see it every day. Twice: on the way to school and home. When told by school officials that she could receive special consideration, get a stop closer to her house, she said she didn't mind the two-block walk. Said she didn't mind any of it at all.

Her bus—a huge monstrosity of a bruised banana beast, almost as sputtery as my Vega, and spitting out dark clouds of noxious diesel fumes—emerged from around the bend in the road. It puttered to a halt in front of the diner, grinding brakes shriller than a battalion of dog whistles. I helped Callie off the bus.

She wasn't as withdrawn as earlier, but she wasn't that sweet girl with the clear hazel eyes and wobbly smile either. At least she had the presence to notice that my frazzled pants, mop of wild hair, and wanted-poster gaze had marked me far more fucked up than earlier. "Mark," she said, "I've been worried about you."

I told her I'd been feeling the same way about her. "Here," I said. "Let's go to my car."

"Good," she said, warming up a bit more. "We need to talk."

The way she said *talk* seemed odd. Plus, her eyes appeared more red-rimmed than earlier. Had I been more with it, I would've immediately understood what she was getting at. Instead, I said, "Good. I like it when we talk."

We got in my car. I clicked on the heater, then popped The Replacements into the tape deck: "Here Comes a Regular." The clear chiming of an acoustic guitar, along with Paul Westerberg's heart-strained vocals, hovered low and mournful around Callie and me. Again, I fished the ring from my coat pocket. Just when it seemed I could actually say those words I hadn't been able to say earlier, Callie beat me to the punch.

"I'm leaving."

At first, my fuzzed-out brain heard that as she was *weaving*. *That was crazy*, I thought. *What did weaving have to do with not taking the ring?* I let a laugh fly.

"What's so funny?" asked Callie.

"Nothing. Wait. What did you just say?"

That's when I heard those words loud and clear. To those words, she added, "My family is heading to Arizona. My dad got a transfer." Those familiar worry creases bloomed across Callie's forehead. "You're mad, aren't you?"

I wasn't sure how I felt. All I knew for certain was that those I'd loved only seemed to leave. Part of me wanted to cry, but another part of me had forgotten how. So I just sat there.

Callie, however, cried for the two of us. Her body shook. No amount of me holding her could make her stop. The windows began fogging. It became harder and harder to see the diner, and the rest of the outside world.

Once she'd collected herself, she wiped at her face with her sweater sleeve, then choked out a laugh. I asked her what was so funny.

"Here I am a one-legged girl getting out of Blackwater before you." She paused. Maybe she was thinking of what to say next, or perhaps she'd detected a look on my face that made her add: "I'm sorry you're not leaving, too."

Just then, I caught sight of my eyes in the rearview mirror. Those numbed-out, broken eyes were like Mom's eyes the day she left home. What I could never bring myself to say to her then, I found myself saying to Callie, "I'm glad you're getting out."

"You mean it?" she said.

My feelings for her then, and long afterward, would never change: with all my heart, I wanted her to lead a good, long life. That meant getting far, far away from poisoned Blackwater. Yet again, I tried offering her the ring. "Please, take it. My grandmother wanted you to have it."

"I *knew* it," Callie choked out. "No one wants me. Only her."

Later, when my head was on straighter, I'd recognize how my feelings for her were a lot like that Bruce Lee quote: *Love is like a friendship caught on fire.* It was just too bad that that wildfire had burned me into a crazier mess than I normally might've been. I told Callie I wanted her too, then placed the ring in her hand.

She turned it in her fingers. The more she studied it, the more her downcast eyes brightened. "If I take it," she said, "you might meet someone else."

I considered that one. As the low, jangly strains of "Nowhere is My Home" ghosted through the car, I realized that in the long run, maybe she wasn't the right girl for me. More importantly, I probably wasn't the right guy. Between the downers and everything else, I was spun. The only hope I was still holding on to was of honoring Grandmother's wish.

"Here's the deal," I said. "Just take the ring. Even if you don't wanna be with me just hold on to it. You're the only person I can trust to keep it safe. Plus, if you have it that means I'll have to leave some day to get it from you. Or maybe you can still keep it if you want. I dunno. Whatever."

Between sniffles, Callie said: "Listen to what you're saying."

But I couldn't. The crude equation of Mom's pills plus Grandmother's death times Callie heartbreak equaled nothing but a fucken mess. Every bit of me was scattered from Blackwater to far beyond the heights of the Hudson Palisades, all the way up to Alpha Centauri. From the "Dawn of Man" chimp to the beautiful

Pepsi people cruising Venice Beach. From busted bongs to nuclear bombs. From sexual bombshells to wedding bells.

Finally Callie said: "What if you never get out?"

"I will."

"But what if you don't? Then all that ring'll do is remind me of how you never left." She handed it back, then leaned into me.

I wrapped an arm around her, smoothed a hand along her back.

In a whispery voice, a voice as thin as the few strands of blonde hair caught in her lips, she said, "It's only that if you left I hope you'd come looking for me, not some ring. That's all."

"But I want *you*," I said. "How'll I find you?"

She told me she'd write.

I told her that'd be nice, but secretly I didn't buy it.

Then we just sat there listening to the low, driving thump of The Replacements get all knotted up in the muffled chatter of customers walking into the diner.

Eventually, Callie lifted her head from my shoulder. "I should go."

Part of me wanted to start the car, do what I should've done from the very start. Forget my fears and obstacles. Forget everything. Just leave Blackwater in the dust. But I could still feel Mom's pills and Grandmother's death play that weird tug of-war inside me. No way did I want to chance going off the rails with Callie at my side. "I guess you're right," I said.

She took the ring from my hand. At first I thought she'd changed her mind. Then she slipped it back into my coat pocket. "Take good care of it, Mark. It's special. I can feel it." She kissed me on the cheek, then left.

As she hobbled toward home, I watched her intently. Callie of the pretty blonde hair; Callie of the liquid green eyes; Callie of the better Ophelia ways; Callie of the one good, strong leg, and sweet, lopsided smile.

And while it hurt like hell to see her go, I didn't look away. I had to prepare myself for when I'd watch her leave for real. Me minus Callie: zero. Callie minus Blackwater: life.

Drifting down Route 9, I did my best to block out all the leavings. I cranked the stereo. Rolled down the windows. Gunned the engine. Nothing worked. Callie, my grandmother, and Mom kept coming back to me. I sensed Callie in the unusually strong momentum of the engine, and in the achingly beautiful songs blasting through the stereo. Grandmother's spirit I sensed in the blur of passing scenery, and in the hum of wheels against road. As for Mom, I felt her in the cold air. I felt her in the last bit of downers floating through my blood.

Chapter 18

FOR THE REST OF the day after leaving Callie, I cruised Blackwater. Normally, I would've steered clear of places like the power plant and Satan's Tree, but not that day. When it got darker and colder, and the downers had completely abandoned me, I felt far lonelier and alone. Normally, I would've headed to Jimmy's. I chose a different destination.

Once I'd pulled into the vacant lot across from the Third Lake, I called out: "Julie's Been Working for the Drug Squad!"

Mad Man appeared. Beneath the overhead streetlight, his partially lit, weathered, and pockmarked face resembled a waning crescent moon. In addition to his trademark jeans, boots, and swoop of hair, he was also sporting a huge, black, puffy down coat—Michelin Man gone punk rock. He scoped out my ripped jeans and equally ripped face. He knew I wasn't there to sell socks. "Looks like you've been through the meat grinder, Spicoli."

In a rush and jumble of words, I explained my day. Some of what I was saying I couldn't even understand, but I think Mad Man caught my drift.

He slung an arm around my shoulder. "Damn. That's a rough one." He glanced down at the dirt lot riddled with tire skid marks, and the occasional spent condom and busted beer bottle. During the summer, those objects would've served as grim artifacts left by Blackwater's Third Lake denizens. But being winter, they looked like diamonds, the way everything shimmered in glittery, icy white. Right then, I figured Mad Man was considering some wise words to offer, but out of the blue, he said: "Wanna see what I do with my socks?"

Later, his offer would make a bit more sense, but right then, that proposition seemed like the biggest mindfuck of the day. For years, Jimmy and I had done practically everything except torch Mad Man's super Aqua Net'ed hair, trying to make him reveal his sock secret. Up until that moment, all kinds of rumors had been going around town—everything from Mad Man using the dirty cotton for extra pillow stuffing to achieve wilder, kinkier dreams, to placing the socks on his TV antenna to receive alien transmissions.

"You serious?" I said.

He gave my shoulder a meaty squeeze. "Sure, Spicoli. You've waited long enough."

◆ ◆ ◆

THERE WERE ALL KINDS of odd homes throughout Jersey—the House With the Chair on Top, the Cookie Jar House, and the Palace Depression. Add Mad Man's to the list. Once through the front door of his place, we were already in the living room/kitchen/bedroom area. In addition to the record albums, tubes of paint, spray paint cans, and dirty socks scattered about, there were four rocking horses hanging from the ceiling—four for the number of Horseman of the Apocalypse. All over the walls: a collection of velvet Elvises, in various stages of his career—from lean hip-swinger to Fat Vegas days—painted with Cheetos dust and lacquer-sprayed. In the center of the room: a pulled-out sofa bed, topped with an assortment of Winnie-the-Pooh plush dolls, hair dyed blue. A grimy hotplate and mini fridge sat against the far wall. The air reeked of spray paint, foot-funk, and stale bong water. Atop some day-glo painted milk crates was a portable TV with bent rabbit ears, minus socks. The TV was turned on its side so that if you wanted to view it normally you'd either have to cock your head to some weird angle, or be sprawled out on the sofa couch. Either that or sit up straight and let *Cheers*, *Growing Pains*, and *Wheel of Fortune* spill all over you horizontally.

Mad Man tossed our coats over a hot-pink fiberglass replica of the Statue of David—a freaky distant cousin to Jimmy's ceramic gnome. Then Mad Man swept the blue Poohs from his sofa bed, and folded it up. "Here. Sit."

"That's cool," I said. "I'll stand."

He grabbed a couple Millers from the mini-fridge, offered me one.

Since my nerves were still jangly from the downer comedown, I gladly accepted. I cracked it open, swigged brew.

Mad Man dittoed. Then he picked up a pill from the floor— a black beauty. After tucking it into his front pocket, he said: "Know how old Van Gogh was when he died?"

"No idea," I said. "Fifty?"

"Thirty-seven," said Mad Man.

"He looked a lot older in his paintings," I said.

"Tell me about it," said Mad Man.

I eyed him as he continued drinking. Through the years, he hadn't changed much. Not much had changed with me either. "What's Van Gogh got to do with socks?" I asked.

Mad Man shrugged. "Maybe nothing. Maybe everything. But here's something to consider. He actually didn't start creating art until he was about twenty-seven. But in those last ten years of his life, Van Gogh created two thousand pieces, including around nine hundred paintings and over a thousand drawings and sketches." He paused, took a long last pull off his Miller.

I'd already experienced enough confusion that day. I was growing tired of playing Twenty Questions. I wanted to tell him to get to the point, but I waited and downed more brew.

He grabbed some art canvases propped up against the wall behind the TV. He spread them across the warped hardwood floor.

Our old socks hadn't been used for religious, sexually perverse, or ritualistic voodoo shit. They hadn't even been used as a radiation screen. They'd been colorfully painted and glued across each canvas. I pounded the rest of my beer, then said: "Are you serious?"

There wasn't a hint of irony or apology in Mad Man's voice when he responded: "It's kinda like therapy."

Maybe it was because I'd sucked at finger painting in kindergarten. Or that I'd never watched *Oprah* or *Sally Jessy Raphael* to understand all the touchy-feely stuff he was getting at. But I was willing to try. "Why old socks?"

"That's the point exactly," said Mad Man. "It's the sweat, the stink, the way they've been lived in that makes each sock a living work of art." He pointed at one of the canvases. "Check it out. You're in that one."

Atop the canvas—reeking of spray paint, glue, and toe jam—I spied a pair of tube socks that I'd recently sold him. They had holes in the heels and big toes. Bits of their grime and gray color showed through the yellow they'd now been painted. There were other socks glued across the canvas, too. Sleek socks, battered socks. Baby socks, jock socks. Even a pair of women's fuzzy socks.

A pair that looked like Jimmy's had been sprayed blue. A pair of my old man's: green. Others I didn't recognize—red, orange, and gold. Collectively, the footwear resembled bodies: misshapen and elegant bodies intertwining, forming a circle. Those bodies were alternately loving and struggling, trying to liberate themselves from the canvas.

"It's my latest," said Mad Man. "I call it *Love From Space*."

"Why's that?" I asked.

"You tell me," said Mad Man. "Look at it."

I got down on one knee, studied my socks on the canvas. As I did so, I was reminded of a Bruce Lee quote, something about how art is the expression of the self. And how the more complicated and restricted the method, the less opportunity for the expression of freedom. In Mad Man's case, it was all about that expression of freedom, or at least potential freedom. There I was on the canvas, all tangled up in Jimmy's, my old man's, and everyone else's lives. We were struggling to bond, struggling to break free. The longer I stared at the artwork, the more intensely it brought up all the love and dissatisfaction I'd been dealing with my whole life. I grabbed the canvas. Wanted to worship it, shred it to pieces.

"Easy, Spicoli. You'll wreck it."

"Sorry," I said, coming to my senses. I handed it over.

Mad Man placed it, along with the others, back behind the TV. "It's okay," he said. "It affects me that way, too."

For a moment, Mad Man didn't speak. Then his brow crease deepened, as if his thoughts were digging a ditch right between his eyes. "Look," he said. "I know what people say about me. That I'm just some freaky-dressing, sock-buying, SSI check–collecting nut job. That's fine. Everyone's entitled to an opinion. Me, I'm a walking advertisement for what makes me feel good and that ain't gonna change. As for taking my work to New York and other places, I tried all that stuff. Didn't work out. But I ain't getting weepy about

it. As long as I've got my art I could be on the moon for all I care."
He paused, pressed a paint-splattered finger into my chest. Bull's-
eyed my Social Distortion T-shirt-covered heart.

"Check it out," I said. "I once heard this story you were sewing
all our socks into radiation blankets."

Mad Man howled over that one. "I've heard a lot of stories
around town. But that one beats 'em all." He cracked open a couple
more beers, then said: "Of course you didn't believe it, right?"

I didn't respond.

"What?" he said. "You didn't think that was crazy?"

Still no response.

Mad Man placed a hand on my shoulder, gave me a friendly
shake. "Damn, Spicoli. You're nuttier than me."

I shrugged. "I was kinda hoping it was true." After taking
a long pull off my beer, I launched into still another one of my
nuclear rants. Went off about the massive power excursion at
Chernobyl earlier that year, sending radioactive fallout into the
air, four hundred times more powerful than the Hiroshima bomb.
After that, I railed on Three Mile Island, then much closer to
home, Crab Creek. Said how easy it would be for a disgruntled
worker to flip a few switches in the nuclear facility's control room,
shutting off pumps and key valves, causing a meltdown, sending
poisonous gasses into the atmosphere. Within days, high levels of
radiation would annihilate the body's actively dividing cells. Signal
acute hair loss, severe vomiting, diarrhea, bleeding from every
orifice. Early deaths within a ten-mile area would number two to
twelve thousand. Add to that the tens and hundreds of thousands
of cancer deaths that would occur over the next two to sixty years.
And forget about the food grown in the area. It would remain
radioactive for hundreds and hundreds of years.

Mad Man rolled his eyes. Told me about a book he'd once read,
In The Belly of the Beast, by Jack Henry Abbott. Said the guy wrote

about his time in prison and how it totally sucked, but how he'd made his peace with it. Mad Man followed that up with a laugh.

"What's so funny?" I asked.

"The screwed thing is," he said, "once Abbott got out of jail he ended up murdering some other guy."

"So much for freedom," I said.

We toasted beers over that one, then Mad Man said: "I'm real sorry to hear about your granny and Callie, I really am. But while you're stuck in Blackwater, you gotta try to make peace with it all. There's beauty in all the shit if you look deep enough."

Part of me wanted to believe him, but another part highly doubted his plan would work for me. I didn't have prison confessionals or sock art to grant me inner contentment after such a fucked day. All I had were beers, bong hits, Jimmy's mom's codeine cough medicine, and Mom's downers to help me get along. "I dunno," I said.

"For real," said Mad Man.

Chapter 19

JUST A FEW DAYS after Callie had left Blackwater, I was sitting in math. It was another one of those days, like most every day in that class, where the fluorescent lights made everyone appear washed out, dead. The teacher droned like an EKG machine flatlining. Rather than copying the problem-of-the-day into my journal, I created my own word problem. It went something like this:

Callie flies against the wind from Blackwater to Tucson in eight hours. She then returns from Tucson to Blackwater, in the same direction as the wind, in seven hours. Find the ratio of the speed of Callie (in still air) to the speed of the wind.

That word *speed* got me to Speed Racer. *Jake Speed. Vanishing Point.* Steve McQueen. *Bullitt.* Bullet in the brain. Brainwaves. Ocean waves. Other words for waves are surf, breakers, rollers, whitecaps. Waving goodbye. *Au revoir. Goodbye Yellow Brick Road.* "Hit the Road." "Thunder Road." *The Road Warrior.* Kung-fu warrior. Bruce Lee. Leech. Leery. Gleeful. Lee Marvin. Lee jeans. Lee Press-On Nails. Nails in the coffin. Coughing up blood. Coughing up a loogie. The Bogeyman. Batman. Airman. News anchorman. Man overboard. Bored stiff. Bored to death. Bored as hell. "Highway to Hell." "Run Like Hell." "Hell is Living Without You." Hellbound. Hellbender. Return to Sender. Going to Hell in a handbasket. A-tisket, a-tasket, a green and yellow basket. Breadbasket. Wastebasket. Dorothy traveling to Oz with her pretty handbasket. Dorothy blown away by a hurricane. "Hurricane" the fighter, a botched conviction. Hurricane Gilbert. Hurricane Gloria. Or that troubling wind blowing Callie away. "Against the Wind," "Blowin' in the Wind," "The Wind Cries Mary." *Mary Poppins.* Popeye. Pop-Tarts. Pop gun. Poppies. Popsicles. Pop Goes the Weasel. Diesel. Diesel trucks. Long-haul travel. Blackwater to Tucson, and back. "Back in Black." Backflip. Backdate. "Backstreets." Back dive. Dive bar. Set the bar higher. "I Want to Take You Higher." "Rocky Mountain High." "High on Rebellion." "Highway Patrolman." "Highway Star." Starlight, starbright. Asterisms. Andromeda, Cassiopeia, Pegasus. Some constellations are only visible in the northern hemisphere, while others are only visible in the southern hemisphere. Some constellations have families: Hercules, Ursa Major, Perseus, Orion. Lion. *Androcles and the Lion.* The Lion and the Mouse. Mousetrap. Shrewmouse. Mickey Mouse. Walt Disney. Cryonics. *The Dark Side of the Moon.* A "Moonage Daydream" frozen in time and space. "Time in a Bottle." "Message in a Bottle." Sending out an SOS.

Chapter 20

THAT ONE SUNDAY MORNING—JUST a week before high school graduation—began with a ringing telephone. Those bells sounded almost exactly the same way they did that day I'd learned my grandmother had died. I stumbled out of bed, grabbed the phone.

It was Mr. Gigliotti. "Is Jimmy there?"

Still rubbing sleep from my eyes, I croaked: "No. Why?"

In his exhausted and cigarette-thrashed voice, Mr. Gigliotti told me Jimmy was gone. He continued explaining how just the day before he and Jimmy had been home watching Mr. T. At one point Mr. Gigliotti fell into one of his coughing fits, and coughed up some blood into his handkerchief. That alone was bad. But what he told Jimmy next was far worse. In a choked-up voice, he repeated the same thing to me: "Son, I have cancer."

The Big C plus Jimmy's dad: death. My life minus Jimmy's dad: far worse than a head-on crash with Satan's Tree. I couldn't speak. Couldn't move. Could already feel myself becoming just another shadow in my already way too ghostly home.

"You there?" asked Mr. Gigliotti.

I felt my lips say yeah, but I could barely hear the words. Then, fearing the worst, I asked: "What kind of cancer?"

"Lung. Stage one."

With all my power plant research, I'd learned a little about cancer. Stage One was confined to the lungs. As the numbers grew, so did the risks. Stage Two: the cancer has spread to the chest. Stage Three: add bigger, more invasive tumors. Stage Four: the real killer. That's when the cancer has spread throughout the body. If Mr. Gigliotti had to have the Big C, Stage One was the place to be. And while removing the cancer from the lungs didn't guarantee its total elimination, it offered him at least another five years if the Gods of Life were on his side.

Feeling a bit more hopeful, I asked: "What next?"

"Before anything," said Mr. Gigliotti, "we gotta find my boy." Then, in an even more choked-up voice, he added: "All the years Jimmy tried making me quit those coffin nails. And now look at me."

"Don't be so hard on yourself," I said. "Maybe it's not just the—"

Before I could even complete my thought, Mr. Gigliotti was all over me. "There you go again with your conspiracy theories. It's like I've tried to tell you—" He tried to say more, but launched into one of his coughing fits.

Whether or not he wanted to listen, I knew Blackwater had the highest cancer incident rate in all of Jersey. And despite the power plant's multiple safeguards and backup systems to prevent meltdown, it sometimes leaked radioactive poisons into the air, including cesium-137, iodine-131, and strontium-90. Once entering the body, the cesium went for the muscles. Iodine attacked the thyroid gland. Strontium marauded the bones. Had Mr. Gigliotti been healthier, I would've argued the facts. Instead, I said: "I'm sure Jimmy'll come home soon."

"I don't know," said Mr. Gigliotti. "He was pretty scared when he left."

"But graduation's coming up," I said.

Starting junior year, then into twelfth, as his dad's health had fluctuated so had Jimmy's grades. One report card: B average. The next: D. On Mr. Gigliotti's insistence, Jimmy had attended summer school, and had received endless hours of after-school tutoring. I'd even pitched in with extra help in English and History. It had all been enough to get him back up to a solid, steady C average.

"I'd like to think Jimmy'll be back," said Mr. Gigliotti. "But I got a bad feeling about this one, son."

"Don't worry," I said. "I'll find him."

I did my best to keep my promise. I dumped a few quarts of oil into the Vega, zoomed past Mad Man's, the Dump, the cemetery, all three lakes, you name it. Everywhere I went—no Jimmy. That's when I began worrying bigtime. I sped home. Sought out advice from higher sources—prayed to the St. Jude statue Mom had left behind. Even dug out my Ouija board, laid it out on my bed. Instead of giving me that same cryptic message it had in the past—E-A-T—all the board did was sputter to L, then U, then stalled out. I flashed on some possibilities: *lunch, lunatic, Lucifer*. No help at all. My two Bruce posters offered no assistance either. They just stood there, barely looking at me—striking poses of toughness and cool so beyond my ability to mimic or embody. I paced the halls, muttering other possible Ouija clue words: *luggage, lucid, lullaby*. Those words only dragged me further from Jimmy. *Luggage* got me recalling Mom. *Lucid*: Grandmother. *Lullabye*: Callie. The thought of Callie got me bolting back to my room, rummaging through my dresser. Good to her word, she'd written a number of times since settling in Tucson. I grabbed her very first letter—the one where she'd said she'd always love me and hoped that I'd one day leave

Blackwater—and shoved it into my jeans pocket, then rocketed back down the hall into the living room.

The first thing I spied—an acrylic painting Mom had left behind, something she'd once created at a church-sponsored weekend art class. It depicted a crude two-sailed pink sailboat on a placid teal sea. Above, the birdless, sunless sky was all colors of the rainbow, with hints of blacks and grays swirling in from the right. Whenever Jimmy had visited for sleepovers or to do homework, we'd always joked about that crappy painting; we'd say a blindfolded, Benadryl-dosed kindergartener could've done a better job. Mom, however, had her own take on that artwork. She'd said it represented how life's joys were fleeting and that sooner or later everything led to trouble. Whatever the interpretation, screw that painting. I swiped it off the wall. Just as I was about to send the huge monstrosity sailing like a Frisbee, the phone rang.

It was Jimmy.

"Where the hell are you?" I said. "Your dad's worried sick." As soon as I'd spoken those last four words, I regretted having said them the way I did. But I don't think Jimmy noticed.

His voice was scraped raw. It machine gunned me with hysterical sobs. "I-I-I…d-d-don't…w-w-want…" Between all his tears and gasps for air, I could just make out that he didn't want his pops to die. Said he'd kill himself if it happened. It was all so chaotic right then, the way he'd choke out random words— *seagulls, windows*—and me trying to hastily assemble them into a clear picture. And when Jimmy wasn't sobbing or speaking, I was listening for environmental clues that might reveal his location. There was a long sustained *BOOM*, like wind rushing into the phone receiver. There was the roar of passing cars. An occasional honking horn. High-pitched squeals like brakes going bad, or maybe kids laughing. Then there was Jimmy sobbing: "I don't want my pops to die…"

I told him it wasn't going to happen; his dad would be around for a good long time. Then I asked: "Where are you?"

More fits and starts of choking and sobbing. It was all such an emotional Morse code I couldn't completely translate. Then, *click.* He was gone.

Standing with the dead phone in my hand, I racked my brain, trying to determine his location. Right away, I knew he wasn't with a girl. And since I hadn't spotted him in any of our hangouts, it was clear he'd left town. But that one confused me. Unlike me, Jimmy had never been a big fan of getting out. Then I flashed on some of those clues—ones he'd stated, or ones I'd picked up on my own: *windows, seagulls, wind, children, L-U.* That's when I realized that my Ouija board had been spot on. Unlike that jinx we'd suffered as kids—when all our pets were croaking left and right—Jimmy was now with the one-and-only friend that would never die on him. Lucy the Elephant.

◆ ◆ ◆

ABOUT MY TRIP.

On that hazy, humid mid-June day, where gray mixed with blue to create an anemic-looking sky, I cruised along Route 9— past the Little Red Dollhouse, the Dump, and the power plant. With each mile, the heady aroma of pines, swamps, and cranberry bogs whipping in through the open window lessened. All the things I'd ever loved and hated about my little town grew smaller and smaller in the rearview mirror.

I continued driving.

Through Waretown and Barnegat, I studied the world around me. It was a lot like Blackwater, with gun shops; bait and tackle shops; muscle-bound dudes in John Deere caps and flannel shirts; teenage girls, sporting tattoos and hickeys, halter tops and short shorts. In a week, with high school diploma in hand, and eighteenth birthday just around the corner, I'd be kicked out into that world.

Once there, I'd have no idea what to do next. College, JC, scoring some shit job, it was all a toss up. And whether that coin landed heads or tails, every option seemed a big, fat loser. Granted, leaving Blackwater didn't guarantee a sure win either. I could easily end up out in LA not so much a bong loader to the stars, but a gas jockey to the washed-up and lonely.

Fine, I thought. I'd take that risk. It was like the wise words Mad Man had once offered, regarding my life in Blackwater. Quoting the Clash, he'd said: "If I go there will be trouble. And if I stay it will be double."

As I sailed down through Parkertown and Tuckerton, I did my best to keep that mantra going strong. But once I reached Smithville my brain began entertaining all kinds of strange scenarios. What if Mr. Gigliotti died sooner than later? What if I couldn't find Jimmy? Worse yet, what if he'd Code 10-51'ed himself? Then what? Would I return home to help take care of Mr. Gigliotti, or just keep driving?

◆ ◆ ◆

I EVENTUALLY FOUND JIMMY'S Ranchero parked in the gravel lot beneath Lucy the Elephant. That made sense. Ever since he'd first heard how that nearly hundred-year-old, sixty-five-foot-high wood and sheet metal pachyderm had survived fires, storms, and renovation after renovation, he was hooked. Through the years, Jimmy had occasionally taken a bus, or had his old man drive him down to visit the elephant whenever life got him down.

I rapped on Jimmy's driverside window.

He didn't respond. Real or legendary, Jersey has had all kinds of odd creatures roaming about—Big Red Eye, the Hoboken Monkey Man, and its most popular beast: the Jersey Devil. After the night he'd had, you could add another to the list: Jimmy. Since he'd spent the last twenty-four hours smoking and driving non-stop, his posture was slouched and stiff; his big brown eyes wilder and sadder than usual. Decked out in that photocopy outfit of his pops, he resembled a younger, more ragged, and spaced-out version of Mr. Gigliotti. He just kept taking drag after drag off a joint, the smoke cloud around his head growing bigger and bigger. Through that cloud, he just kept staring up at the gray wood and sheet metal elephant with drippy, gooey eyes—marshmallows that had been roasted too long at a Dump bonfire party.

I knocked again.

Jimmy rolled down the window. Smoke spilled out and was immediately escorted away by the fresh, clean ocean breeze. He didn't utter a *hi*, or *howdja find me?* As he'd later agree with me, our friend magnets were so highly tuned to each other's frequencies, it was really only a matter of time before I found him. He went back to smoking and staring at Lucy.

It made sense he'd put himself through so much grief for his dad. Mr. Gigliotti was the best. He'd never smacked me or berated me. Had never smacked or berated Jimmy. He'd always made his home my home. As for my own home, all I had back in those days was my old man. My attitude used to be that if he were sick or dying, I wouldn't run away or contemplate suicide. I'd just party. Equally jealous as sad, I asked Jimmy: "Want some company?"

He shrugged.

I hopped in the passenger seat, noticed the ashtray—filled with smoked and unsmoked joints. As for the car, the stench of rank BO and mindbomb weed had the interior reeking like a Grateful Dead concert. I kept my window down.

Once Jimmy polished off his joint he reached for a fresh one. He took a nice, long drag, then exhaled. The smoke sailed over the dash, slinked up the windshield, then separated into two thin ghosts, one drifting out of Jimmy's window, the other out of mine.

"You should take it easy," I said.

He just kept smoking. The more he did, the duller his eyes grew.

I reached into my jeans pocket, the one not containing Callie's letter. Inside was Grandmother's ring that I'd begun carrying with me everywhere. Whenever I'd get worried or anxious, I'd touch that ring. It would calm me. Set my head on straight better than any drug, or smack from my old man. Once I'd touched that ring, I snatched the joint from Jimmy and snubbed it out in the ashtray.

Jimmy collapsed back into his seat, motioned toward the salt air–weathered elephant: "She's different."

"How do you mean?" I asked.

"Since the last time I was here. She's not as big as I remembered."

"She is," I said. "Look how happy she's making everyone." Laughing children scurried beneath Lucy's feet. Up in the riding carriage perched high atop her massive frame, a few tourists stood, excitedly pointing toward the ocean.

"So what," Jimmy huffed. "She's making me feel like shit." He reached for the keys in the ignition.

"What're you doing?" I said.

"Whudya *think*?"

I placed a hand firmly over his, tight enough so it couldn't move. "Where? Home?"

Jimmy struggled to turn the key. Grunted: "No way."

I tightened my grip, grunted back: "What about your dad?"

Jimmy called truce. I released my grip on him. His spaced-out eyes grew clear. His slouched posture: now erect, shoulders back. So weird and sudden, that calmness and clarity. I figured he'd stumbled upon some revelation concerning his dad he was about to share with me. Instead, he reached over, popped open my door, and insisted: "*Out.*"

I slammed the door shut.

He tried opening it again.

I seized his arm, executed the reverse wristlock—that useless move I'd used on my old man back when we'd gone out shooting. It had barely worked then; the same could be said for Jimmy.

He jerked free. "Is that one of your bullshit Bruce Lee moves?" He slumped back into his seat, only moving occasionally to shake off the lingering pain from his wrist, elbow, and shoulder.

I slumped back into my seat, glanced up at Lucy. I recalled that age-old pet jinx Jimmy and I had shared. When I was seven, I won a goldfish from the Wilbur Brothers Family Circus. Before I'd even gotten it home, the doomed fish had already gone belly up in the plastic bag. The following year, I used three weeks worth of allowance to buy a rabbit. It soon died of monkeypox. When Jimmy was eight, he had a pet garter snake die of mouth rot. When he was nine, wet tail got his hamster. Then, when Jimmy and I were ten, his dad brought us down to Margate to visit Lucy for the very first time. Now, some eight years later, I motioned toward that elephant. "Let's go inside."

"Fuck that," said Jimmy, rolling his shoulder, still trying to shake the leftover pain from that reverse wristlock.

"C'mon," I said. "It'll be like the old days."

"No way. She ain't like that no more."

"Give her a chance," I said. "If you do I'll buy you your weed for a whole year."

Jimmy's right hand, feeling much better, flipped me off. Then he said: "I grow my *own*, you douche."

"Whatever. I'll buy you a new bong. Or a real grow light."

After what seemed like hours of deliberation, and the final moments of shoulder rolling, wrist flicking, and elbow massaging to send off the last bits of pain, Jimmy finally said: "Deal."

We headed over to Lucy. After I paid the four-buck admission fee, we were assigned a tour guide. She looked to be pushing thirty or so, tanned and weather-beaten to an almost leathery red. Sported a blue windbreaker, screaming-yellow Bermuda shorts, squeaky-clean white sneakers, and a baseball cap squashed over an afro perm.

"I'm Jean," she said. "How're you boys?"

I didn't respond right away. Instead, I marveled at her entire presence. Her face: big and round. Her torso: thin. From the waist down, everything got big and stayed that way. The more I studied her, the more she resembled the inside of my old lava lamp. How those falling blobs of liquid wax used to get really thick up top, then slender in the middle, then all blobby again down at the bottom. And because she so reminded me of that lava lamp, I liked Jean all the more.

"I'm great," I beamed. "I'm Mark. This here's Jimmy."

"Well hi, Mark and Jimmy," chirped Lava Lamp Jean. "Ready to see Lucy?"

I nodded like my stupid head was about to fall off.

All Jimmy did was stand there, sullen faced, staring at his checkered Vans sneakers.

Jean glanced back at me. "Seems your friend forgot to take his happy pill."

I shrugged. "He's had a rough couple days."

"Well all that's gonna change," said Jean. "Let's go, boys."

She led us through a doorway into the elephant's hind leg. After traveling up a spiral stairway, we found ourselves in a large open area.

Forget the plywood floors, the angle irons holding the walls in place, and the exposed ceiling air ducts. I was completely mesmerized. There I was, once again, deep inside the massive beauty of Lucy the Elephant. "Wow," I said. That's all I could say: wow.

"Darn right 'wow,'" said Jean. She went on to tell us all kinds of facts about Lucy, facts Jimmy no doubt already knew, but I'd never been aware of. Like how back in 1881, inventor and real estate mogul James V. Lafferty had originally built Lucy as a way to lure potential buyers to his properties. And how the elephant was later converted into a summer cottage, after that a bar. She told us how Lucy's ears were seventeen feet long, ten feet wide, and each weighed two thousand pounds. How a million pieces of lumber, two hundred kegs of nails, and four tons of bolts had been used to build her. The elephant had even once been raised with special house jacks and moved from one part of town to another.

Jean pointed at one of the many windows built into Lucy's massive frame. "Know how many she has in her?" she asked Jimmy.

Even though he knew the answer and then some, all he muttered was: "Who cares."

"*Okaaaay…*" Jean looked my way, hoping for a more positive response. "How 'bout you?"

I had no idea. I took a wild guess: "Thirty-six?"

Jimmy flashed me a look. It wasn't so much code for *dumbass*. It was a pretty obvious *dumbass*. He grumbled: "Twenty-two."

Jean beamed. "Howdja know?"

"He knows a lot of things," I chimed in. "Ain't that right, Jimmy?"

"Whatever," he muttered. He went back to staring at his shoes.

Jean shook her head. "You two really are a pair." She took us up some stairs that led us into Lucy's head. "Look out her eyes, boys."

I manned the right one. Jimmy didn't bother manning the left. Being a Lucy aficionado, he already knew the only thing he'd see were some lousy old buildings. So he just stood there, arms tight across his chest, telling me to hurry.

What I saw through Lucy's right eye was ocean. So endless and so many different shades of blue. That ocean sparkled brighter than Grandmother's ring. Suddenly, I was filled with a sense of calm I'd never before experienced. It was like my life had started all over again clean. But it hadn't. Deep inside me, I could still feel Callie, Mom, Grandmother, and all the other ghosts and flesh-and-bone beings that made up my life. And no matter what I did—drive three thousand miles away or take a rocket to the moon—I realized I'd never shake them. Fine. Especially right then. Because instead of dragging me down like they often did, I was happy to have each and every one of them with me. Happy to have them look through the elephant's eye and witness that ocean—blue ocean, sparkling ocean, an ocean big and wide enough to not only hold all my happiness, but to drown all my bullshit.

Jimmy shook me from the good and bad of it all. "C'mon already."

While Jimmy had seen that ocean view countless times, it seemed to affect him differently that day. Once he'd pressed his right eye against Lucy's right eye, his grumbling stopped; his tight shoulders eased down away from his ears a bit. "You see?" I said, taking full advantage of his body language. "Lucy's still great, huh?"

At first, Jimmy didn't respond. He just kept staring out at the ocean. Again, I said those words. That's when his shoulders completely dropped into their relaxed, natural state, and all other signs of tension left him as well. He wiped at his face, nodded.

Jean even picked up on Jimmy's change. She gave his back a pat, and said: "I told you the best was yet to come. Let's get you two up top."

She guided us to the open-air riding carriage atop Lucy's back. For as far as you could see there was ocean, and the cheerful summer cottages, and dilapidated structures dotting the Margate landscape. The ocean breeze whipped all around us. Carried up on its chilly currents were the smells of salt air, cotton candy, and fresh-squeezed lemonade. Those smells always made me feel so electric and alive. Like summer would never end, and everything was possible.

Jean asked me: "Got any questions?"

I did. "What do the locals think of Lucy?"

"Some folks love her," she said. "But others take her for granted. Even when she was whipped into shape, they still couldn't care whether or not she was torn down."

"Sounds like where I'm from," I said.

"Oh yeah? Where's that?"

"Blackwater."

Jean made an *euw* face. "Man, I feel for you."

"You're telling me," I said.

I approached Jimmy, slung an arm around his shoulder. Whether due to exhaustion or the cold, he was shivering. I drew him closer. "Remember when your dad brought us here? How you wanted to take Lucy home?"

"Of course," he uttered.

"You were right," I said. "She's the perfect pet."

"The best," he said. "I love Lucy." Then, for the first time that day, an inchworm of a grin slinked across his face.

"Don't worry," I said. "Your dad'll be okay."

He jerked away. "He's got *can*cer."

"But there's surgery," I said. "And chemo. There're all kinds of things to help."

"You don't know for sure." With that, he shot down the stairs.

I bolted after him. We ended up on the beach, sprinting past tourists, scrub pines, palms, and dune grass. Seagulls cawed and circled overhead. An old man combed the sand with a metal detector. Families collected seashells. We kept running.

All that rushing through sand felt like we were moving in slow motion while our muscles worked double time. I finally caught up to Jimmy, wheeled him around. "Your dad needs you," I said out of breath. "And all you did was run off like some chicken shit."

Jimmy shoved me.

I shoved back.

Next thing we knew we were a sweaty knot of flying fists and curses, the two of us tangling like we were fighting for the same heart. We crashed to the sand. More punches to the gut, head, and ribs.

At one point, I got him in a headlock. "Give up?"

"Fuck you," Jimmy sputtered, through a puffy lip.

"What about going home?"

Another "fuck you."

I doubled my grip on him. "What about your dad? Or graduation?"

Jimmy tried saying more, but all that came out were grunts and gasps for air.

I let him go.

Struggling to catch his breath, he wiped some blood from his lip, and hissed: "You're lucky I didn't *Westinghouse* you."

He was referring to George Westinghouse. Back at the turn of the twentieth century, after securing the patent for AC electricity, he challenged Thomas Edison's DC system. In retaliation, Edison tried influencing public opinion by displaying the dangers of alternating current electricity. Utilizing AC, he electrocuted animals up at his West Orange lab. His displays of AC's killing potential did nothing to scare off the public. They did, however, help to create the electric chair, and the frying of Coney Island's Topsy the Elephant.

"Yeah right," I said. "You better watch it or I'll go Bruce Lee on you again."

"Dude," Jimmy shot back. "You couldn't go Pee-Wee Herman."

After that, we just sat there in the sand, nursing our war wounds, and occasionally joking about our lousy fighting skills.

Finally, Jimmy said: "If I go home what if my pops dies? He'll never see me graduate."

"Trust me," I said. "He will. And there's an added bonus."

"What's that?"

"There'll be tons of graduation parties with hot girls."

"You're *al*ways talking about that," said Jimmy. "Don't you ever think about anything besides getting *laid*?"

"Yeah. Getting *you* laid."

"Don't rush me," he huffed. "I just ain't found the right girl yet."

Perhaps that was true. For years, I'd tried hooking him up with different girls: fellow students, waitresses, even a clerk—a young ringer for Stevie Nicks—I'd encountered at Spencer's at the Ocean County Mall. But with each and every girl I'd introduced to Jimmy, he'd either said they weren't cute enough, or didn't like Tolkien, smoke weed, or share his particular taste in music. Or maybe, like Mom had speculated, he was gay. Being the early days of AIDS, I didn't fully get all that entailed. It would take me a little while to sift through the tons of fears and few reliable news sources swirling around to better understand how something like Jimmy's sexuality could seriously affect the safety of his future health and well-being in Blackwater. In that moment, however, I erred to the side of straight. I snatched up a stick, sketched a crude picture of a girl in the sand. "When it comes to the opposite sex," I said, "the thing you gotta remember is that you can be a lot of things, but the one thing you can't be is scared."

Jimmy swiped the stick, swished it back and forth through the picture. "I ain't scared."

"I ain't saying you are," I said. "I'm just saying sex is a big deal. Like a rite of passage."

"How do you mean?" he asked.

"It's like once you do it," I said, "you're a man. No one can take that from you. It's better than a DWI. It stays on your record forever."

Despite his messed-up lip, that one made Jimmy smile a smile I hadn't seen in a while. But then that smile vanished. He shook his head. A mess of curls spilled down into his eyes. "Don't bother with girls," he said.

"Why?"

"I don't think I'm that much into them."

"Like the girls I choose," I said, "or no girls at all?"

Jimmy didn't say anything. He just kept swishing that stick through my drawing.

I repeated my question.

Finally, he mumbled: "No girls at all."

"You mean you're—"

Jimmy whipped the stick into the wind. "I *knew* I shouldn't have told you," he said. "You hate me now?"

I flashed on all the times we'd hung out in his basement, wrestling and rolling around on the floor. I couldn't help but wonder if he'd had a thing for me then, or even now. What if he did? How would that affect our friendship?

Jimmy knew what I was thinking. "Don't worry," he said. "I'm not into you. Only guys that like Stevie Nicks."

That one made me smile. That one made us both smile.

"I don't hate you," I said. "I'll never hate you." I scooped up a handful of sand and let it slowly sift through my fingers. "How long have you known?"

"A while," said Jimmy. "That's one of the reasons I spend so much time in my room." He let fly a sound somewhere between a laugh and a sob. "Some people have problems coming out of the closet. I can't even come out of the basement."

"Why didn't you tell me sooner?" I asked.

He shrugged. "I thought maybe I'd change."

After that, we fell silent. End of The Day Silent. Setting Sun Silent. Had I been in LA right then, I would've been watching that sun slowly sink into the Pacific. But since I was still stuck in Jersey, facing the Atlantic, it was setting behind me.

"What'll I do now?" Jimmy asked.

"I dunno. You're kicking butt in school. I'm proud of you for that."

Jimmy beamed. He dabbed some blood from his lip with the collar of his flannel shirt, then sat up a little taller.

I sat up a little taller, too. That's when I noticed the pre-dusk sky streaked with shades of blue-gray, orange, and rust red. Distant storm clouds moved in from the east. Vibrant waves crashed in front of us. The cool, crisp salt air whipped around the laughing children running along the beach. At that moment the world seemed such a peaceful, picture-perfect place.

"You didn't answer my question," Jimmy said.

I pulled Callie's letter from my pocket. I didn't read Jimmy all the stuff about Callie telling me how much she missed me, and how she hoped we could see each other again some day. Instead, I fast-forwarded to a part toward the end. "Listen to what she says here," I told Jimmy. "'All in all, life doesn't get any easier, it just gets different.'"

He shrugged. "So?"

"I mean look at us," I said. "We're sitting on the beach. We've got Lucy with us. We're not sick or nothing. No one's giving us any shit. It's great, right?"

"Not really," said Jimmy.

"Think about it," I said. "Right here. Right now. We're okay. I guess it's just strange to think this might be one of the best moments of our lives. And after this…who knows."

"Exactly," said Jimmy. "After this I gotta go home and watch my pops die."

The sun fell further to the west. That once colorful sky veered toward black. And from the east, storm clouds drew closer. The salt air became laced with the smell of deep dampness and sweet electricity.

I glanced back toward Lucy. From out of the gathering darkness she loomed high above all else, staring out at the water with sad, knowing eyes.

As for Jimmy and me, we weren't secured in one place. If we'd wanted, we could've bolted. Forget Blackwater. Forget everyone. We could've just hopped in our cars, and headed off in separate directions, never looking back.

"Hey," said Jimmy. "You feel that?"

At first I didn't know what he was talking about. Then I felt a single raindrop land on my arm, then another crash-land on my head. After that, a whole ton of them fell from the sky.

"Hey," said Jimmy. "It's raining."

I glanced up. "Yep."

"It feels nice," he said.

I agreed.

"Think we should leave?" he asked.

"Not just yet," I said.

Chapter 21

WITH DIPLOMAS IN HAND, and high school in our rearview mirrors, Jimmy and I were immediately sucker-punched by the real world. As planned, we gave JC a shot. But after just a couple semesters of mind-numbing classes like Survey of Mathematics and Computer Science, we were spun. Could hardly tell a tombstone from the Rolling Stones. So we dropped out. From there, our options grew bleaker.

It was either ship out for the military or find work in town. Since we weren't keen on jarhead buzz cuts or getting shot at, we voted for day jobs. There was the power plant. Next, the Exxon station. Yet, since we figured we'd do more gas huffing than pumping, Jimmy and I vetoed that one, too. Ditto with Bob's Bait and Tackle, Nora's Knit Shack, and 7-Eleven. That pretty much left Sole Survivor Shoe Store and the Rainbow Casket Company. Jimmy took the shoe route. I followed the dark Rainbow.

"It's about time," my old man said when I first got the job from his buddy, Mr. Delaney. "It's taken you eighteen years, but you're finally serving the public."

I'd end up working at Rainbow for two years. Didn't think I'd last that long, but I did. I never got wasted at work. Never left early. Was always on time. Had my morning routine wired.

To be at work by ten, I'd wake at eight. Didn't perform my two-Bruce ritual anymore, not since twelfth grade. But I'd give the posters a well-deserved nod, then get down to my own version of kicking ass. Since my old man would already be at work, I'd haul the Kenwood speakers from my bedroom, into the hallway. One morning I might crank Springsteen's *Nebraska*. The next day: Pixies' *Surfer Rosa*. It all depended upon my mood. Then I'd shower, brush my teeth, drag a comb through my hair. Slap on slacks and a fresh white button-up, which would be sweated out well before the end of the day. Then a tie, black jacket, and black Florsheims: clothes my old man bought me when I first got the job. Next, I'd chow down on coffee, cereal, an English muffin, or whatever edible leftover was available. Just before I'd head off in my Vega—which I'd topped off with oil the night before—I'd down some Listerine. Not only did it make for better customer relations, but that mediciney shot would also recall the vodka I'd snuck from Mom's Bloody Mary back when I was six.

As for the Rainbow Casket Company and its neighboring businesses, they had their own memorable qualities.

Located in a strip mall in the center of town, Rainbow was flanked by Dandy Dry Cleaners on one side, Three Brothers Pizzeria on the other. That walk through the parking lot, I'd be marauded by all kinds of smells: pepperoni, sausage, ground beef. The nasty cherry on top was a kerosene stench. And the sounds: customers bitching about the rising prices of dry cleaning and how their clothes smelled all chemically. High-school dropouts and burnouts—guys not that much unlike Jimmy and me—hanging in front of the pizzeria, bumming smokes and spare change.

Once through the door of Rainbow, it was a whole other world. Sobs, carefully measured words, and Muzak. Scented candles, Softique Kleenex, and Stargazer lilies. Holden Caulfield once said: "Who wants flowers when you're dead? Nobody." Apparently, my boss, Mr. Delaney, never read *Catcher in the Rye*. Those Stargazers were everywhere. Stuffed into vases on the counter. On various shelves, stuck in between urns, Hummel figurines, and crosses. That densely sweet smell was what Mom used to say that's what she'd imagine Heaven to smell like. As a child, I believed her. Only a day into working at Rainbow, I thought she was full of shit.

Stargazers and Muzak aside, Mr. Delaney wasn't bad. Was in his late fifties. Tall, thin-lipped, lean-faced. Bowl-cut gray hair, gravelly voice, raised left eyebrow when making a point. Think Lurch from *The Addams Family* repackaged: less severe, no eyeshadow, far better vocabulary.

That first morning when I walked through Rainbow's front door—which sounded an electronic *ding* when opened—Mr. Delaney was waiting for me in the showroom, right between two of Rainbow's best-selling caskets—the Legacy and the Starlight Slumber, the coffin in which my grandmother had been buried. In his own crisp white shirt, black suit, and shoes, Mr. Delaney stood tall, stern, his hands gathered behind his back. He seemed ready to quiz me on death-related matters—perhaps the grieving process, or why it was better to say *casket* instead of *coffin*. Instead, in that rough voice of his, he asked: "What's a shark's favorite illegal substance?"

I knew the answer, but didn't respond. I just let his question hang heavy in the air like the stench of Stargazers.

Mr. Delaney repeated it with a bit more gravel and gravity.

What the hell, I thought. It was a decent enough joke. "I dunno. What *is* a shark's favorite illegal substance?"

Left eyebrow raised, Mr. Delaney said: "Reefer."

I let fly a sly grin. "Not bad, sir."

That's the way it was with my boss. As severe as he could appear at times, he said if you didn't start the morning with a joke, selling caskets could wear you down, fast. Then he'd throw in a bit of trivia. Like how with all the steel caskets buried in the US each year, we could use that metal to build a new Golden Gate Bridge. Or how the Bo people of Southern China don't bury their caskets. Instead, they hang them vertically off the side of cliffs.

But once the jokes and trivia were out of the way, Mr. Delaney was all business.

"Death is the final chapter of our lives," he told me that first day, as he guided me through the showroom past all the pink, black, antique white, platinum, and natural-wood display caskets. "The loss of a loved one is devastating. Our guests need to be treated with dignity and respect." With that Lurch-like voice of his, he went on to explain how at the time of a loved one's death, that's when family members are faced with overwhelming financial decisions that must be made quickly. Said it's our job to help those families, in whatever way possible, honor the lives of those they loved so dearly. Once he'd relayed his Rainbow ethic, Mr. Delaney's thin lips eased into a smile, but only a slight one. He offered me a pat on the back. "Think you can do it?"

I gathered my hands behind my back, just like I'd seen him do when I first walked through the door. "I'll do my best, sir."

And I did. I stayed well read and up-to-date on current casket information. To improve my customer-relation skills, I read *Solid Gold Customer Relations*. To better understand death and dying, I read *On Death and Dying*. Employing a calm and measured voice, like I'd witnessed Mom do while selling Mary Kay, I could readily explain to my customers how copper caskets were resistant to corrosion and stronger than stainless steel. How excellent strength and stability made poplar a better choice than elm. How mahogany was one of our finest buys due to its hardwood durability and resistance to termites and rot. How fiberglass caskets were extremely light and most commonly used for infant burials. In my free time I'd polish the display caskets to perfection, fluff the pillows, make sure the inner crepes were frilly and stain free. I did whatever I could to provide my customers with the perfect eternal resting place for their dearly beloved.

Other times, whenever death got me down, I'd visit Mad Man. One time after handing me a beer, he offered wise words by Gandhi: "'Each night, when I go to sleep, I die,'" he said between Miller swigs. "'And the next morning, when I wake up, I am reborn.'" Another time, just after I'd given Mad Man some of my old socks, no charge, he served up some Victor Hugo: "'It is nothing to die. It is frightful not to live.'" Still another time, while taking a break from using those socks I'd given him to create another masterpiece, he reminded me of something Jimi Hendrix once said: "'I'm the one that's got to die when it's time for me to die, so let me live my life the way I want to.'" Or that Ambrose Bierce line: "'Death is not the end. There remains the litigation over the estate.'"

Mad Man's pep talks; Mr. Delaney's jokes, trivia, and experience; along with all the information I'd accumulated on my own; everything helped me through my entire stint at Rainbow. There was, however, that one day where it seemed nothing could save me.

Was a Monday, mid-October, a good few months into the job. Mr. Delaney had gone home early with a headache. That meant me alone for an hour until closing. I drifted through the showroom, polishing and re-polishing the caskets: the Amber Mist, the Queen's Lair, the Starlight Slumber. Back in those days, the way I'd constantly fret over those caskets, it was as if I was hoping to wipe away the big deaths and only consider the little ones—where each day we lose hairs, slough skin, or get the beginnings of a wrinkle around the eye. With only ten minutes left until closing, believing I was customer free, I heard the *ding* of the front-door bell.

It was a middle-aged black couple. Black families had always been scarce in Blackwater. Broke my heart to see one of them in Rainbow—especially this one. The man, Mr. Dixon, I immediately recognized as one of Blackwater High's janitors. Unlike the other custodians, he never grumbled. Always managed to whistle a cool tune—like Bessie Smith's "Me and My Gin"—while vacuuming entryway carpets, wet mopping hallways, replacing light fixtures, and disinfecting toilets and urinals. Constantly had good jokes to share. After Grandmother's death, he'd even helped me figure out how to solve a particularly troublesome math word problem, which scored me a B- on a quiz, by far one of my highest grades ever in that subject.

His eyes, like his wife's eyes, were overflowing creeks. Their furrowed brows: the eroded shores of those creeks. My chin trembled. I discretely positioned myself by a vase of Stargazers. Breathed in that despicable scent to ward off tears.

Mr. Dixon loosened the top button of his sweated tan shirt to speak, but couldn't bring himself to do so. I grabbed one of the many boxes of Softique Kleenex placed throughout the showroom, swiped out a number of tissues, handed them over to the couple. I trembled the words *take your time*. None of us needed to speak anyway. We all knew what was up. Not only was that fall of '88 already going on record as racking up the most number of new photos on Satan's Tree, it was also the fall that had acquired the first photo of a black person—nineteen-year-old Dawn Dixon.

About Dawn Dixon.

She and I were the same age, had known each other since ninth grade, when her father first started working at Blackwater High. Since Dawn and I shared many of the same classes through the years, we'd often discussed one of our mutual loves: music.

We agreed Stevie Wonder's *Innervisions* kicked ass. Thought the DKs sounded much better with D.H. Peligro. The first record we ever listened to was Barry White's *Can't Get Enough*, owned by our mothers. There was only one area where we differed. On occasion we'd joked about what song we'd want played at our funeral. I'd said, "Spirit in the Sky." Dawn: "Amazing Grace."

Other things about Dawn.

She wasn't into partying. Would always say *ma'am* and *sir*. Had a piccolo voice and eyes smokier than bonfires. Possessed a wit sharper than a Chinese throwing star, and a smile that could make the Jersey Devil weak-kneed. Like her father, Dawn had sometimes assisted me with math. My parents had also invited her over for a few of my birthday parties, even after they'd witnessed certain neighbors shaking their heads, and turning their backs while watering their late June lawns. My parents never gave a shit about their ignorant behavior. Neither did I. Whenever a Piney thug cracked wise about Dawn in my presence I was always quick to speak up. Told them to keep their bullshit remarks to themselves, or to save them for when they were hanging with their buddies, knitting rebel flags. Sure those remarks got me into a few scrapes over the years. But dealing with Terry had prepared me for those.

Standing in the Rainbow showroom with Dawn's broken-hearted parents, all those facts came flooding back to me: How Dawn had been so smart and funny, so well-versed in music and math. And how certain assholes had ridiculed her simply because of her skin color. All that reminded me, still again, how insane life was, how kind and cruel it could be, how short and unpredictable. Which then brought up Callie, Mom, my grandmother, and Jimmy's dad. Which led me to wonder why I'd ever decided to work at Rainbow in the first place. At least at Exxon I could've spent my days floating along in a gas-huffing haze. With Rainbow, I had to deal with loss and death, sober. Once all those swirling thoughts reached critical mass, I could feel that I was a goner. Forget Mr. Delaney's jokes, Mad Man's wise words, or all the hours of reading I'd done. While I'd been able to draw upon those resources when dealing with strangers, they eluded me when dealing with Dawn and her family. That moment felt so surreal, like what it might've felt like to witness, firsthand, those Bo people in Southern China, and all their caskets hanging off sheer cliff walls. That's when I totally shut down. Drifted through the Rainbow showroom like a numb, stupid cloud. Kept handing tissue after tissue to Dawn's parents. I even used a few myself. Mumbled words I can barely recall saying. Somewhere in there, though, I think I said "Amazing Grace." All I know for certain is that I must've possessed enough wits to steer the Dixons to the Starlight Slumber. I only know that to be true because that's what the sales receipt said when I handed it over to Mr. Delaney the very next morning.

Chapter 22

A S THE RED SWAMP maple leaves changed from vibrant blood red to shriveled, crunchy brown, then gradually back to bloom, so changed the ways I dealt with customers at Rainbow. With Grandmother's ring in one suit pocket, and Callie's latest letter in the other, I continued absorbing and applying everything I learned from Mr. Delaney, Mad Man, and my own readings. Whenever I'd deal with customers of Jewish faith, I was sure to first suggest caskets and burial containers that were as simple and natural as possible, no metal. Whenever I'd deal with adult children purchasing a casket for a parent, I'd often share an Einstein quote: "'Death is not an end if we can live on in our children and the younger generation. For they are us, our bodies are only wilted leaves on the tree of life.'"

Time and again, all those broken-hearted customers made me realize how I truly missed certain people that had left me in some way or another. Those customers also made me appreciate the people still hanging strong, namely Jimmy's dad.

It had been nearly two years since his lung cancer surgery. Things had been touch-and-go for a while. Good days consisted of no infection, easy breathing, minimal hair loss. Bad days: chest pain, puking, blood clots. With time, however, the chemo regimen and other drugs had begun working their magic. The cancer hadn't returned. He was up and about a bit more every day. Was even doing some light taxidermy, small game like bass, pheasants, and foxes. The doctors said he was lucky. Said he might actually be around for a while.

In fact, there was that one weird phone call from him, just after I'd gotten home from Rainbow one day back in May of '89. Hadn't even yet changed out of my work clothes and was still reeking of Softiques and Stargazers. When I first heard Jimmy's dad's voice, I expected bad news. But then he surprised me by saying: "I got something for you."

When I asked what it was, all he said was: "Meet me at Duffy's at eight tonight." Then, *click.*

I spent the next couple hours—whether showering, changing into my street clothes, cranking tunes, feeding my old man, or doing dishes—wondering about that mystery gift. Maybe it was some funky stuffed animal—a hedgehog or a skunk. Or maybe reading materials related to my job. Or some pain meds he didn't need anymore. Once my Vega's dashboard clock struck 7:45—8:00 p.m. in bar time—I crunched through the stone and dirt parking lot, into Duffy's.

About Duffy's.

It was nut jobs, dye jobs, and hand jobs in the alley behind the bar. The ding of a pinball machine, the clicking shut of lipstick, the crack of pool balls, and the clicking open of a lighter. Duffy's was where 21A on the jukebox gave you Metallica wailing "Seek & Destroy," while 17B was Louie Armstrong crooning "It's a Wonderful World." It was ragged flannel shirts and crisp button-ups. Tattoos and tears, come-fuck-me pumps, and a skanky girl becoming belle of the ball at last call. It was drinking elbow-to-elbow with the Chief of Police, his son, an ex-con, or a man who'd just lost his wife, child, or parent to cancer. Duffy's was that 7:00 a.m. Budweiser on tap before heading off to work at the power plant. It was the lights down low, mistaking cigarette smoke for ghosts, and a cemetery worker with the dirt of freshly dug graves still on his shoes.

Mr. Gigliotti was seated beneath a neon Budweiser sign hanging from a dingy wood-paneled wall. Like other times I'd seen him out and about, he wasn't carrying his portable oxygen tank. Kept it in the cab of his pick-up, where he'd take periodic blasts from it. He motioned toward the empty seat across from him, and the Rolling Rock already waiting for me. We clinked bottles, took great gulps, squinted from all that cold going down.

At first we discussed mundane stuff like the weather; how all the pines and oaks, along with the cranberry and bayberry shrubs were blooming. All the tree frogs, white-tailed deer, and swamp darters, well, darting. The whole time, Mr. Gigliotti and I remained huddled close so we could hear one another over the rowdy crowd, the jukebox, and the hard crack of pool balls. At one point, I asked: "How're you feeling?"

He shrugged. "A little older every day."

There was some truth to that. His sober face: lined, ravaged. Plowed by life's heaviest machinery. What little was left of his once coal-black hair was now white and stuffed beneath a camouflage-colored Joe Camel baseball cap. The meds he was taking to ward off the cancer would sometimes make him puke and had even made him suffer some hearing loss. Despite his better sleep and eating habits, his trademark overalls and flannel shirt hung a little loose on him. Through it all, though, he still possessed his intense Dillinger-like gray eyes. Those eyes studied me intently. "How's the death game, son?"

I took a blast of beer, then said: "Sold an oversize today."

While regular caskets measured between twenty-four to twenty-seven inches, oversize caskets measured between twenty-eight to thirty-one inches and higher. The one I'd sold that day clocked in at the lower end—twenty-eight.

Once I mentioned that measurement, Mr. Gigliotti knew exactly whom it was for—a buddy of his, a mountain of a guy that worked as a power plant operator. The local paper had said he died of a heart attack. I, of course, had my own theories. For a change, I kept them to myself. Just took hit after hit off my Rolling Rock, waiting for Mr. Gigliotti to reveal his mystery gift.

He must've noted how I was doing my best to exercise self-control, because after sparking up a cigarette—the second of three he allowed himself in a day—he motioned toward the ten-point buck head hanging above Duffy's entrance—a shoulder mount he'd created a good ten years ago. "Now there's an exercise in patience," he said.

While I hadn't witnessed him create it, as I was only nine at the time—only months before meeting Jimmy—I'd later heard all about the process. First he'd skinned the deer, cut off its antlers. Sent out the hide for tanning. Then he created a Styrofoam mannequin of the deer's bust. Mounted the antlers on it with Bondo and drywall screws. Cut tear duct slits and a lip slot into the mannequin. Created nostrils. Cleaned it all up with a file. When the tanned deer cape was ready, he trimmed the nostrils and eyes of excess skin and cartilage. Used a whipstitch to sew up any bullet holes or other holes. The process went on and on. Once the deer cape was stretched over the mold, he made sure the brisket was aligned. Made sure the upper and lower lip of the form lined up with the hide. "The skin will tell you everything you need to know," Mr. Gigliotti would always say. "The secret is learning how to read it." Once he'd stitched up the animal and allowed the hide glue to dry—which could take weeks—it was still another series of labor-intensive steps: apply the air-brushed colors, carefully blend the browns, whites, and blacks. Complete any final grooming and cleaning. The entire process was so time consuming. "If you can't accept delayed gratification," Mr. Gigliotti would say, "you can't be a taxidermist."

As he eyed that shoulder mount, I could practically see him reliving each and every step it had taken to create it. Could hear his mind working, wondering if he still had it in him to do it all again. "One of these days," I said, "you'll create an even bigger one."

What was left of Mr. Gigliotti's Camel bobbed up and down between his lips, as he said: "Not so sure about that, son. But it's nice of you to say." He squashed out the last bit of that cigarette, then said: "Let's go."

The magnolia-scented, cricket-singing night air was alive. It was the perfect accompaniment as we trudged to the far end of the lot, where Mr. Gigliotti's pickup was parked well out of the reach of streetlights.

He popped open Bessie's passenger-side door, pulled something out. In the shadowy dark, all it looked like was a big lump of nothing in his hands.

"What is it?" I asked.

"A lead vest."

I shoved my hands into my jeans pockets. "Jimmy put you up to this?"

Mr. Gigliotti shook his head. "I got it from one of my buddies at the medical center."

Hands still stuffed in pockets, I gave him the once over. His lips weren't lifted at the edges. The laugh lines around his eyes and mouth, slack. He seemed sincere, but I still didn't get it.

"Well?" he said, with a wheeze. "This ain't getting any lighter."

I took the vest off his hands.

He eased himself inside the pickup, turned the key in the ignition. Not to fire up the engine, but the tape player. He popped in a Bessie Smith mix-tape he'd put together. First up, "Nobody Knows You When You're Down and Out." Over the low strains of piano and muted trumpet, Bessie sang such achingly beautiful blues—the aural equivalent of the heart's most pained and precious honey. As she continued singing, Mr. Gigliotti held his oxygen mask to his face and took a few slushy pulls from the tank. Once done, he stepped out of the truck, but left Bessie singing. Gone, for the most part, was that wheeze in Jimmy's dad's voice. Only a throaty quality remained—like he was imitating that muted trumpet in Bessie's band—when he said: "Let's see you with it on."

I figured any minute Jimmy would jump out from behind a parked car, and yell: "You're on *Candid Camera*, dumbass!" I sat the lead vest down on the ground.

"Go ahead," said Mr. Gigliotti. "There's a method to the madness."

The way he said those words—far more enticing than the vest itself. When I slipped the bulky mass over my head, it only covered my torso area down to my groin. Most of the back of my Springsteen T-shirt, with that pink Caddy on it, was exposed.

Mr. Gigliotti secured the Velcro straps over my shoulders, but had problems cinching up the ones around my back. "It's kinda old," he said. "The fasteners are a little messed up." His patient taxidermy hands worked a bit longer. Finally, he wheezed: "Done." He got back in the pickup, took a couple more hits off the tank.

I hopped in, alongside him. Bessie Smith was now singing "Graveyard Dream Blues."

Mr. Gigliotti turned the stereo down. Over the low sounds of Bessie saying something about going to the graveyard and falling down on her knees, Jimmy's dad said to me: "You're spooked by the power plant. I don't get it, but that's fine." He glanced down at his oxygen tank and mask sitting between us on the black leather bench seat. Keeping time with Bessie's blues, he drummed lightly on that tank with his thumb. Every time he hit it, the tank made a dull, sick-sounding *ding*.

That unnerving sound reminded me that Blackwater had been coined the cancer capitol of Jersey for a reason. And while I believed cigarettes had been the main cause of Jimmy's dad's cancer, I was certain the power plant had contributed to his illness as well. But that vest he'd given to me, both of us knew it would barely protect me from an X-Ray. "So whydja do it?" I asked. "The vest."

Mr. Gigliotti pointed out his Joe Camel baseball cap. "This is my way of saying 'fuck you' to death, son. I figured the vest could be your way." He paused, chuckled, then added: "Yours is just a heavier way of saying it."

That was for sure. The vest was making my shoulders sag, my chest sweat. I flashed back to my church-going days with Mom. There was Jesus and his burden of the cross—all to take away the sins of the world. No way was I on that level. But the vest definitely felt like a burden; my cross to bear, so to say. I gave it a test run. I flashed double middle fingers, directed them toward the power plant. "*Fuck you*, death!" I intoned.

And even though Bessie was moaning something about a gravedigger and last goodbyes, that didn't stop the laugh lines from returning to life around Mr. Gigliotti's eyes and mouth. He flashed his own double middle fingers. Repeated those words: "*Fuck you*, Death!"

Chapter 23

WITH THE EXCEPTION OF work, sleep, and shower, I wore that lead vest—which vaguely resembled a bulletproof vest—most every day. Didn't bother concealing it beneath my clothes. Just strapped it on over whatever I was wearing. Every time my old man would see me in it, he'd shake his head. Whenever Jimmy spotted me, he'd laugh his ass off, call me *Leadbelly*. The times Mad Man saw me he'd offer that Woody Allen quote, which never got old: "'I'm not afraid of death; I just don't want to be there when it happens.'" I definitely freaked out some people around town. The first time I wore it into 7-Eleven, the cashier—figuring me for some Piney wackjob gun enthusiast—dove behind the counter, and called out: "Don't shoot!"

I raised my hands in the air, flashed peace signs. "I just want a sixer of Rolling Rock!" I called out. "Gonna pay for it even!"

Luckily, I got through those situations, and others like them, no problem. But then came that one July day, only a couple months after Mr. Gigliotti had given me the vest. It was a Friday, after work. I was out by Barnegat Bay reading Callie's latest letter. I'd just finished the part where, referring to my dumpy little town and me, she'd written: "What doesn't kill you makes you stronger." That's when I spotted Terry.

He was prowling the streets in his '78 black Trans-Am two-door coupe. Sounded like a full-on riot under the hood as he sped by. I prayed he'd just keep going, into the next town, the next state, the next life. He skidded over to the side of that lonely stretch of road. His brake lights glowed bloodshot red until they grinded into the burning white eyes of reverse. Burning white eyes bearing down on me. He screeched to a stop, leaned out the window. His voice was all thuggish, like it was packing tattoos and brass knuckles. "Yo faggot," Terry called out. "What's with the vest? You becoming a pig cop like your old man?"

I flashed him the middle finger.

Terry revved the engine. Made that riot under the hood go wild. "Let's go for a ride," he called out over that noise.

I crammed Callie's letter into my jeans pocket. "Forget about it," I said.

He gunned the Trans-Am's turbo horses. "Last chance, dickweed."

Nothing much had changed that summer. Warblers and mosquitoes still swarmed the humid air. Cars still crashed into Satan's Tree. Jimmy continued getting wasted, working at Sole Survivor, and helping his mom take care of his dad. Dump parties were big, loud. The once full and colorful cemetery flowers wilted to a shriveled-up brown. And though I was twenty and Terry twenty-two, nothing much had changed with us either. "Fuck off," I called back.

Terry leapt from his car, got in my face. Dilated pupils, sweating, clenched jaw muscles, nerves scraped raw: Meth-o-mania. "Got a problem following directions, faggot?"

I glanced around. Not a car in sight, only massive storm clouds bruising the far edges of the eastern sky. Equally as pummeled was the air. It reeked of salt, rotten fish, and dead sea lettuce that had washed ashore. "I don't got any problems," I said. "But it seems you do." Sure the vest bulked me up in some ways, but over the last few years I'd also done some additional bulking up in the Courage and Attitude Department. As for Terry—the same old trashed James Dean looks, along with solid muscle and cool packed into stonewashed jeans, scuffed-up work boots, and a *Shit Happens* T-shirt. The only new addition: a naked Baby tattoo on his forearm.

"Well?" he raged. "What's it gonna be, faggot?" He shoved me. I shoved back.

"Let's see how well your vest works," said Terry. From the waistband of his jeans, he produced a .44-caliber Bulldog pistol; the same model David Berkowitz, aka The Son of Sam, had used to snuff out his victims back in the seventies. He pressed the gun into my chest.

That was definitely a moment I could've spun into a mind-numbing math word problem. Something like:

Terry can unload all the bullets in his Bulldog in four seconds. Mark can unload them in six seconds. How fast can they unload the bullets together?

But I wasn't thinking math, or Mad Man's wise words, or even Mr. Delaney's death trivia. All I was recalling was a solid piece of advice my old man had once shared—If ever threatened by someone with a weapon, never agree to go to a second location. So I stood my ground. "What're you gonna *do*?" I said. "*Shoot* me? It's just a lead vest, you *id*iot!"

I wasn't in the mood to explain why I was wearing it. Terry wasn't in the mood to hear it anyway. He seized me by the collar of that vest, bullied me to his car. The more I resisted, the more that indigo-blue naked Baby tattoo on his muscled forearm danced. Her hips shook, hair tossed, massive torpedo tits blasted. Terry popped open the car door, flipped up the seat, then punched and shoved me into the backseat.

He hopped behind the wheel, locked both doors, and turned to face me. "I bet your old man's got some pretty good weed, huh?"

"Whudya mean?" I said.

"He's Chief of Police, faggot," Terry insisted through grinding teeth. "I bet he gets his hands on some kick-ass shit."

That's when I realized what he was up to: he wanted to trade me for weed. "Go score off one of your friends. Or Jimmy."

"What're you talking about?" Terry shot back. "There's no better weed than cop weed." He slapped Black Sabbath's *Sabotage* into the cassette player, and peeled out.

The whole time he was driving, I was scheming my escape. But seeing as his coupe was only a two-door—both seats blocking the doors—a clean getaway would've been impossible. And even if I'd managed to escape, vest or no vest, a flying leap at sixty-five miles an hour would've reduced me to mangled roadkill. Mr. Gigliotti wouldn't even have been able to stuff and stitch me back together. So I just sat there, awaiting Terry's next move.

As he continued driving, he flew off in a paranoid rage, going off about how everyone and everything—from the cops, to Satan's Tree, to the Jersey Devil—were out to get him. He spouted conspiracy theories concerning Jesus, Jimmy Hoffa, AIDS, alien abductions, the Jonestown Massacre, and JFK's assassination. He ranted about hating school, then taking that lame-ass janitor job at the power plant where, everyday, his nuts got nuked by uranium fuel assemblies, reactor vessels, and spent fuel pools. All he wanted to do now was get super wasted. Erase his brain. By the end of his tirade he was almost bawling.

"Take it easy," I said. "Things aren't that bad." I didn't know what else to say or do. In all my years of knowing him, I'd never seen him so nuts. Sure the vest was making me sweat, but there was also fear sweat. That rank scent mixed with the lingering odor of Stargazers I hadn't yet showered off that day.

Terry spun the wheel sharply, skidded to a stop by a payphone at the side of the road. He locked eyes with mine in the rearview mirror. "I'm gonna call your pig old man. Don't try anything funny. I'll be watching you."

"I'll be watching you, too," I said.

Terry lunged through the space between the bucket seats, seized me by the throat. Worked the Bulldog's barrel between my lips and teeth until it pressed against my tongue.

I could barely breathe. All I tasted was bitter gunmetal. And forget speaking; my utterances had been reduced to mangled, mumbled vowels. Warm trickles of piss ran down my right leg.

"Listen, smartboy," Terry seethed. "Just 'cause I ain't flashin' my piece don't mean I ain't ready to use it. Got it?"

More trickles of piss. More grunted vowels and gasps for air. My teeth clicked hard against the barrel as I nodded yeah.

Terry withdrew the gun, noticed my piss-stained pants. I figured he was about to blast me bigtime. Brand me with every name in the book, tons worse than Jimmy had ever done. Instead, all he said was: "Better not get any on my seats, faggot." Then he leapt from the car. Kept his gun hand trained on me, and his other hand on the phone while speaking with my old man.

Once done, he hopped back behind the wheel. Over the riot of that engine, he blasted: "Your pig father went for it."

I didn't buy it. My old man was a by-the-book cop that played by the rules, even when Blackwater's lowlife didn't.

"You're a fucken liar."

"Sorry to disappoint you, faggot. We're meeting him out in the Dump." Then Terry slapped Motorhead's *Iron Fist* into the cassette player. "Go To Hell" blared through the car as he blasted through town. We blew past Duffy's and Callie's old house. Satan's Tree, the three lakes, and the cemetery. With the acrid taste of gunmetal still in my mouth, I regarded all those places—the ones I loved, the ones I hated. I said a quiet prayer to St. Jude, the patron saint of lost causes, hoping that wouldn't be the last time I'd ever see those places.

Eventually, Terry veered the Trans-Am onto the Dump's bumpy entrance road. The car bounced, bucked, and weaved. Then it came to a stop. Over the throaty idling of engine, I heard the echoed whoops and hollers of faraway partiers.

Then I heard my old man. Normally, his voice was Sergeant Carter times ten. Now it was that times a million. "Outta the car, Terry!" he boomed.

"Screw that," Terry shouted. "You c'mere."

My old man approached the car. Though he was sporting normal-looking street clothes—tan slacks and a starched white button-up, sweat staining both underarms—the blood-red setting sun, combined with all the shadows cast by the Dump's trees, made him look way more renegade. Packed with far more tactics, marksmanship, and decisional shooting training than Terry, he was all business. He had what appeared to be a quart-size plastic bag packed with weed in one hand, and his Smith & Wesson .38 in the other. The gun was drawn on Terry, but his eyes were on me. He observed my piss-stained pants, the lead vest, the wilder than usual look in my eyes. He shook his head, grimaced. Despite that, and even when he said, "If this is a plan you've cooked up to break my balls, I swear to God if Terry doesn't kill you, I will," I still felt relieved.

My old man glanced back at Terry. Gone his look of fatherly disappointment. Now: badass glare. He had his thumb resting on the .38's hammer, but chose to not yet cock it into action. With a voice equally as steady as his aiming hand, he said: "I don't know what you're up to, hotshot. Scoring weed's one thing. But kidnapping, attempted murder, and possession of an unlicensed firearm are a whole other ball game. A good fifteen to twenty hard time. You may as well give up before things get any worse."

Terry wasn't about to do that. Neither was the meth. It had suddenly made him more alert. Eyes trained on my old man, gun steady on me, he said: "Where's the big pig parade, Chief? Got everyone in hiding? The marksmen in the trees? Or maybe they're all at Dunkin' Donuts."

My old man could've easily produced a cut-down, telling Terry that was the oldest, most lunkheaded joke in the book. But he could see Terry was wired, ready to explode. Code 10-50: *use caution.* All he said was: "I figured I could handle this alone."

"Fine," said Terry. "Just gimme the goods and I'll be on my way."

After tossing the plastic bag through the open window, my old man said: "Gimme my son."

Terry glanced down at the weed, then back at my old man. "How do I know it's good?"

"Why don't you put the gun down and try it?"

Flashing a greasy grin, Terry said: "Nice one, Chief McDaniel." With his free hand, he grabbed the bag, sniffed it. "Not bad. Wheredja get it?"

"Some thugs working outta the diner," said my old man. "Philly Greek mob."

That answer seemed to satisfy Terry. "I'll leave your pants-pissing faggot son out by the entrance."

"Be sure you do," said my old man. "And whudya have in mind after that?"

"Smoke this fine weed of yours, Chief. Then who knows? The sky's the limit."

"Well don't dream too high," said my old man. "We'll be seeing each other real soon. Remember, I know where you live."

"And I know where you live, too," said Terry. He jammed the Trans-Am into D and peeled out.

Yet as we neared the main road, Terry slammed the car to a crawl when we spotted a police cruiser parked by the Dump's entrance. As the kicked-up cloud of dust surrounding the Trans-Am dissipated, I noticed the cop was one I'd occasionally seen at the police station those times I'd gone there to take my old man dinner when he was working late. On any other occasion, I would've signaled to the officer for assistance. But that big bag of cop weed in Terry's lap made me think twice.

Terry wasn't as clear-headed as I. His eyes were darting around like he'd just bought them off the lot, and was taking them out for a test drive. He reached for his .44 in the passenger seat. Made that Bulldog snap its teeth. Keeping that gun low, Terry told me: "Be cool, faggot."

"Speak for yourself," I said. I sat up in my seat, flashed a thumbs up to the police officer.

That stony-faced officer, suited up in steely blue, had two hands on the wheel—one at ten and one at two. His head: barely moving. His eyes: carefully tracking the slow movements of Terry's Trans-Am.

I turned away from the officer, stared straight ahead, did my best to remain calm.

As for Terry, the meth wouldn't let him relax. Sweating. Jaw-grinding, wobbly eyes. He kept one twitchy hand on the Bulldog, while the other gripped the wheel. The fingers on that hand: white in certain places, red in others. "I swear to Christ," Terry uttered, "if I go down for this, we all go down."

That's when the officer flipped on his takedown lights. They turned the dusk-dirty air into a dangerous carnival.

Suddenly, time slowed bigtime. Like it had just downed some of Jimmy's mom's codeine cough medicine. I could sense every creeping moment so clearly.

A crow flew by. I could practically count every one of its pearly black feathers. There was a smudge of red on its beak, maybe the blood of some dead possum or skunk. The bleeding sun, like a great big wound in the sky, sank a little lower. I smelled honeysuckle and bonfire smoke, dust and gasoline. The bleeding wound sank still lower. I heard crickets and bullfrogs tuning for evening's symphony. The hiss and crackle of a distant bonfire. The harsh, clear crack of a far-off partier's gun. And just when it seemed like Terry was about to fire off his own gun, my old man pulled up behind us, waved to the officer to let us through.

The officer's head remained unmoving, while his eyes nodded yes. He killed his takedown lights.

Terry eased us out onto the highway, back toward town. Once we'd cleared the Dump, Terry wasted no time in establishing his own authority. He shoved the .44 in my face. "We got some partying to do, faggot."

Chapter 24

TERRY PUNCHED THE GAS. The Firestones bit hard and fast into highway. Pine trees blurred by. So did highway mile markers, grazing deer, and all the cars that Terry passed.

I glanced out the rear window, witnessed a world of dusk's bruised light.

Dusk—I felt akin to that time of day. Maybe it was because my own life had always felt like one great big in-between. I spotted a car a ways behind us. Looked to be my old man's, but I wasn't sure. Right then, I was reminded of one of his old Irish sayings. "It's better to be a coward for a minute than dead for the rest of your life." But when it came to Terry, screw that. I'd played that fearful role for years. It was finally time to change that equation. Atom bomb times neutron bomb: Me. Me to the power of ten: Superfly TNT Dynamite.

I lunged for Terry's gun. Wasn't clear-headed enough to utilize any of the jiu-jitsu moves, special grips, and other close quarters combat skills my old man had tried teaching me in the past. But I did manage to get a good grip on Terry's shooting hand. He tried jerking free. I held on tight. Was pulled through that space between the seats. Even with that bulky vest on, I still managed to punch and kick wildly. So did Terry. The car swerved from one side of the road to the other.

At one point, a wild gunshot exploded through the roof.

Terry muscled the Bulldog away, stiff-armed me into the backseat. "You stupid motherfucker," he hollered. "Look what you done to my car. You're *so* dead." With eyes on the road, he reached back, squeezed off a shot. It blew through the seat next to me.

"Holy shit," I yelped, flailing my arms in a frantic semaphore. "Just cool it. O*kay*?"

"Don't tell me to *cool* it, faggot." Terry cold-cocked me upside the head with the .44.

At first I saw stars. Then I saw Baby. Dancing. Not dancing. Then I didn't see her at all. All I saw was black. Black like the farthest-reaching night sky: heaven's dark, dirty doormat.

When I came to it was completely dark out. I was slumped over in the back seat. Wind rushed in through open windows. Ozzy Osbourne's "Crazy Train" pounded through the stereo speakers. My head pounded, too. Like every thought was laced with glass. I touched the place where Terry had hit me, pulled my hand away. Spotted blood mixed with shadows and moonlight on my fingers. As for my piss-stained pants, they'd mostly dried, so the denim didn't stick to my thigh when I sat up. They did, however, faintly reek. Think old shoes crossed with ammonia, volume turned down. "Fucken hell," I said, my voice sounding worlds away. "I thought you were gonna let me go."

Terry continued driving. He was absolutely mesmerized by all the broken white highway lines speeding toward us. "I will," he said in a voice there and not there. "I just don't like partying alone."

"What're you, serious?" I said.

Terry snapped out of his highway hypnosis, caught my eye in the rearview mirror. "I dunno," he said. "Maybe. Yeah." He flipped open the glove compartment. Produced a palm-sized pot pipe. It was made of white glass. The stem resembled neck vertebrae leading to a human skull bowl.

I leaned between the seats. "At least you're gonna pull over, right? You ain't gonna smoke while you're driving. We could both of us get killed that way."

"What're you nuts?" Terry spit back. "I ain't gonna pull over and be a sitting duck for your old man. I'll drive with my knees." As he did so, he packed a bowl of cop weed, sparked up. The stash smelled like blueberries crossed with burnt rope and pine trees. Luckily, it was strong enough to drown out the smell of my pants. Terry took one hit after another. Very soon the car was consumed by a dark undertow of pot smoke and stereo.

I collapsed back into my seat, rubbed my aching head. "This is nuts. I can't believe you went through all this shit for weed."

"Weed, booze, pills, whatever," said Terry.

I knew what he was getting at. A sensitive subject, for sure. One I would've numbed myself to had I been in his shoes. On numerous occasions I'd witnessed Terry pummel guys for barely mentioning his dad. Still, I couldn't help myself. "If you feel like talking about …you know…your past—"

Terry flashed me a look in his rearview mirror, like he was ready to reach back, either with his fist or gun, and dust me. Instead, he just swiped a hit off the pipe. And another. Each hit took a little edge off his meth high, but did nothing to erase his hardened appearance, or haunted eyes. As all the broken white highway lines continued rushing toward us, he said: "I don't know what it's like with you and your old man, but with mine he used to get wasted all the time, and beat the shit outta me. Beat the shit outta my mom, too. Then the next minute he'd be all nice, saying things were gonna be okay, that he'd get a job, or lay off the booze, or be a better father and husband. Then *BOOM*. His shit would start all over again." Terry took another drag off the pipe. He opened his mouth just enough so the smoke could ease out, drift momentarily through the car before streaming out the open window. He continued. "And if that's not bad enough, then you wake up one morning to find your old man sitting in the kitchen with a gun to his head, and when you ask him what he's doing, he can't even look at you. All he does is pull the trigger. Next thing you know you've got his blood and brains all over your pajamas. Man, lemme tell you. No matter how much you can hate a motherfucker, shit like that still messes with you." He took another hit, then held up the pipe for my inspection. "I keep thinking the more I smoke, the more I'll forget. But it doesn't happen. So I just keep smoking."

I had no idea how to respond, though I could feel that Terry was waiting for me to speak. I glanced out the back window. Saw fuzzy spinning headlights in the distance. If those lights belonged to my old man instead of my rattled mind, then our bond was stronger than I'd thought. Not only had he seriously bucked police procedure to hand over confiscated weed, but he'd also risked his life to save mine. And while we definitely had our share of problems, I was thankful my old man was alive, and that I was his son. I turned back around. "Hey, Terry. Don't Bogart the weed. My head's killing me."

He handed over the pipe, along with the plastic bag and Zippo. "Knock yourself out, faggot."

I pinched off some weed from the stash, packed the bowl. Then I cupped a hand over the pipe to block out the rushing wind, and sparked up. Hit after hit, I studied Terry's reflection in the rearview. I wondered whether his hard-bitten appearance was due to partying, seeing his old man off himself, or from the power plant—where plutonium, the key element in nuclear waste, was so deadly that, if properly distributed, just half a kilo could cause cancer in everyone on Earth. I blew out a nice long stream of smoke, then said: "Why do you even work at Crab Creek? Surely you could get a job doing something else."

Terry popped his Doors *Strange Days* tape into the player. As the eerie strains of organ, thundering drums, and Morrison's voice floated through the car, he said: "Like Jim here, and my old man, I guess I got a death wish." He glanced out the window, watched our dumpy little town drift by in a blur. The more our town blurred, the more Terry seemed at peace.

Ditto with me.

That blur: that's when Blackwater was at its best. When you were moving so fast that Satan's Tree, the cemetery, and everything else was there and not there; like the whole town had swallowed a handful of Mom's downers, and had sailed off into a peaceful, dreamy blur. But once we got stopped at a red light, that's when all the dreaminess morphed back into the same old reality of the power plant, and billboards advertising retirement homes and funeral homes.

Terry locked eyes with mine in the rearview. "Why's a smart fucker like you still here?"

"What the hell do you care?" I said.

"Easy, faggot. I was just asking."

Right then, a Bruce Lee quote popped into my head: "If you spend too much time thinking about a thing, you'll never get it done." I gave Terry the same old answer I'd always given myself: "I'm still trying to figure that one out."

"Well don't think too hard," said Terry. "All you gotta do is this." He bashed the gas, barreled through the red light, barely missing an oncoming car. The speedometer climbed to sixty-five in a thirty-five mile zone.

"What the hell're you doing?" I hollered

"Getting you out."

I didn't buy it. It was the weed talking. Not Terry. "But I thought you hated my guts," I said.

"Maybe I owe you, faggot. For beating the shit outta you as a kid."

At the next light, he spun the wheel. The tires skidded, squealed. The car slid sideways. I braced myself against the passenger door. For a moment, my 33 ⅓ RPM life slowed to 16. Everything around me tuned in loud and clear. I heard the buzzing of the liquor store's neon sign, every single chirp and grunt in that comforting cricket and bullfrog symphony. Could see all the stars in the summer night sky. Those stars were so luminous, so close that I could practically hold all that roaming silver in my hands. But then the Trans-Am tires bit hard and fast into road, and Blackwater sped up to 78 RPM. We zoomed down Route 9. The warm, fresh air rushing through the open windows temporarily cleared my stoned and aching head.

"Where to?" Terry asked. "Seaside? Asbury? The Big Apple?"

"How 'bout LA?" I said, flashing on the California roadmap in my back pocket. In addition to Grandmother's ring and Callie's latest letter, I carried that map everywhere.

"Why not," said Terry. "I hear LA pussy's solid gold."

Whether it was the gun butt upside the head, the shock of being shot at, or my own stupidity, I actually believed him. Thought he'd changed from my lifelong tormentor into my liberator. I was ready to erase our dreaded past, start all over again clean. I imagined the two of us cruising Venice Beach and the Sunset Strip bars. I let fly a whoop.

The speedometer climbed to seventy. Eighty. The glow of oncoming headlights and streetlights, like liquid pearls, streaked across the windshield, then were gone.

At the edge of town, Terry skidded into the Dollhouse parking lot.

"What the hell?" I said. "Keep driving."

"Relax, faggot. We gotta make a pit stop first."

"What about my old man?"

"Screw him," said Terry. "We gave him the slip. Besides, he ain't gonna do nothing with this around." He flashed the Bulldog. "Might have to use you as a body shield, bro."

I punched the back of his seat. "I thought we had a deal."

Terry howled over that one. "If you believed that, you're not as smart as I thought, Bright Boy." He jerked me from the car. Jammed the gun into my belly.

Had he been packing a .22, I wouldn't have been as freaked out. If he'd pulled the trigger, the bullet would've just rattled around in my belly. But he was packing a .44. Forget my vest warding off Death. Considering the closeness of range and velocity, the bullet would've expanded when entering me. In a flash, blast fragments everywhere. Massive tissue damage. Internal, external hemorrhaging. Acute respiratory compromise. Next stop: the pearly gates. I went weak kneed.

Terry jerked me back to standing. "Make one stupid move in the club, faggot," he thundered, "I swear to Christ you're *dead*." Gun trained on me, he popped open the trunk with his free hand, pulled out a gallon of distilled water. The plastic jug and cop weed he handed over to me. Then he snagged a three-foot-high, blue acrylic bong. It was a near doppelgänger for the red one I'd whipped across my room that day Grandmother died. Bong and gun in tow, Terry muscled me through the parking lot.

Across the street I noticed a billboard for the Rainbow Casket Company. Right then, I said a silent prayer, hoping I wasn't Mr. Delaney's next customer.

◆ ◆ ◆

NORMALLY, THE DOLLHOUSE WAS a dancer's cheap-wine breath in your face asking if you wanted some company, or if you had any pills, weed, or needles to share. It was Prince's "Little Red Corvette" and dizzy swings around the stripper pole. Fingerprint-smeared mirrors lined the back of the stage, wadded-up toilet paper and gnawed-on cocktail straws littered the dingy red carpet. It was beer-bellied guys with faces more used-up than high school math erasers, and pale bands around their fingers from where they'd removed wedding rings, just before tossing crumpled dollars at a dancer's feet. A cigarette machine you could fool with slugs, and junky girls slinking through the club like butterflies with wings pulled off. The Dollhouse was all those things and more. But due to my current condition—all weeded and whacked-out—I barely detected a thing. Just a swirl of disco ball light, along with the comforting thud of Springsteen's "Brilliant Disguise" filling the room.

Making no attempt to hide the bong, Terry shouted a hey to Jack behind the bar. As for the gun, he discretely jammed it into my back, and whispered: "Keep walking, faggot. No funny stuff."

We made a beeline for the bathroom. Terry had me load the bong with distilled water. In just a while, that water would cloud up, reek like weed. Right then, though, the water—smelling mildly of plastic—glugged from the white container, and sloshed down the bong's long blue acrylic cylinder, crystal clear.

From there, we ended up in the back of the club, just out of reach of the stage lights and swirling disco ball light. Bulldog still trained on me, Terry had me cop a squat in a horseshoe-shaped booth. The sound of Terry's relieved sighs mixed with the creaking and scooching of vinyl as we eased into our seat. Once settled in, Terry sparked up another bong bowl of cop weed. Then another. And another.

Once he'd polished off his fourth bowl, Baby took the stage. She was a flash of hot pink bikini bottom, and pale flesh wrapped in a swirl of colored lights. The way she moved, like she had ghosts in her blood. Ghosts in her hips and heart. No way did she resemble the tattoo on Terry's arm: a clearly inked sex kitten, dancing wildly to the tune of Terry's rage. This Baby, the one in front of me, was disappearing.

Terry waved his gun in the air, and yelled over the music: "Yo, bitch! You gotta quit that junk! It's messing up your moves!"

After catcalling Baby, Terry made a big mistake—he flipped his gun on the table, just out of reach.

That's when I did something pretty stupid myself. I sprang to standing, gripped his three-foot bong like a baseball bat. Instantly, dirty water rushed from its massive base, down the long tube, and spilled all over my vest and pants.

At which point, my old man emerged from behind a massive stereo speaker. Later he'd say he'd been there the whole time, just waiting for Terry to screw up, and take his gun off of me. "You see," my old man said, his .38 pointed squarely at Terry's head. "I told you I knew where you lived, dirtbag."

Terry was so stunned by my old man's reappearance and my stupid bong move he didn't know what to do. Glassy-eyed, he sat slumped in his seat, mesmerized by the swirling disco ball throwing bubbly shards of light across the walls.

As for the few customers in the club, they were a stumbling rush toward the exit.

The chaos brought Terry back to his senses. He lunged for his Bulldog.

I brought that bong down hard on his gun hand. The bong didn't break. But it sure did a number on his hand. Later I'd learn that I'd broken it in a couple places.

Immediately following that bong hit my old man seized Terry by the throat.

Terry tried fighting him, but was too wasted, and his right hand was hurting too much to properly battle my old man. That 16-cylinder rage machine kicked into overdrive, repeatedly bashing Terry's head against the wall.

Which tore Baby from her junky dream dance. She leapt from the stage, tried coming to Terry's defense.

My old man shoved her away. "Get that damn girl outta here," he called out to Jack.

The bartender struggled to hold Baby still. "Want me to call for help, Chief?"

"Forget about it," said my old man, now holding Terry in something far more crude and deadly than a police-approved chokehold. "I'll handle this myself." Then he looked to me. "Let's go."

I followed him as he dragged Terry to the bathroom.

Once inside the john, he slammed Terry up against the drab tiled wall. He punched him in the face. The sound was dull, thick. Nowhere near as bright and firecrackery as movie punches. Terry tried calling for help, but my old man crammed the .38 into his mouth. "You make one more sound, punk, you're dead."

"Yeah right," Terry sputtered.

My old man cocked the trigger. "Make no mistake about it. I'll blow you away if I have to. But I'd rather send you off to Rahway and let you rot." Then he glanced over at me. "C'mon," he said. "Take a few shots. We both know you've wanted this for years."

There I was, suited up in a bongwater-soaked lead vest and piss-stained jeans. Definitely not Bruce Lee-approved fighting attire. But I was ready.

Just as I was about to respond, Terry spit blood and coughed out: "Your faggot son doesn't have the guts, Chief."

My old man jerked the gun from his mouth, and said: "I wasn't talking to you, *Fonzie*."

Terry shot back: "Well I was talking to you, *Dirty Harry*."

Reasserting his grip on Terry, my old man said: "Make it fast, Mark. We don't got all day. What's it gonna be?"

No way would it be a fair fight with him holding Terry at gunpoint. "Only if you wait outside," I said.

"Forget about it," he said. "I'm staying right here. But I won't help." He holstered his weapon, took a few steps back.

"Well?" Terry said, trying to shake off the pain from his right hand. "What're you waiting for, faggot? It's like your pig old man said. We don't got all day."

I removed the vest, revealing my Hoboken Pest Control T-shirt with a big cockroach on front. I got into Terry's mangled face. I seized him by his bloody shirt.

He got me in a bear hug.

For the second time that day, forget all the close quarters combat skills my old man had tried teaching me. I was so wasted, and everything was happening so fast with Terry, that I couldn't recall a one. I just punched and kicked wildly.

Our shoes skidded and squeaked across the piss and water-stained floor littered with crushed-out cigarettes and wadded-up toilet paper. We bounced off a couple tiled walls like full-tilt pinballs, then slammed into a john door. My back took the brunt of it. A blast of pain shot up and down my spine as we crashed through that steel door. Huddled over the toilet, we continued fighting. Sure there was the rank smell of shit and piss, but mostly what I smelled and tasted was my own rusty blood. Terry's fists plus my face: black eye, busted lip. My fist missiles times Terry's face: cauliflower ear, broken jaw.

We blasted out of the stall, and across the bathroom. I shoved Terry against a graffitied wall. Barely flinching, he doubled his grip on me, hefted me off the ground, and brought me down hard onto one of the sinks. The porcelain basin and I crashed to the ground. From the busted pipe sticking out of the wall, water shot everywhere. I slipped and slid my way to standing.

Strangely enough, the more I fought, the more I came to my senses. It was like those fists of mine were great big paintbrushes, and I wanted to keep working Terry over until no signs of life bled through.

Good to his word, my old man just stood there, arms folded tightly across his chest, and back against the exit door so we couldn't leave, while Baby—kicking and screaming on the other side, as Jack struggled to hold her still—couldn't get in.

Terry and I continued brawling. Even with that screwed-up hand of his, he fired off a fist missile to my gut that doubled me over. I fired off a shot to his head that made his eyes wobble in his skull.

Sure he had the edge on me in the Muscle and Crazy Department. But I had the edge when it came to stored-up anger. Gun me. Squib me. My bottled-up rage blasted all over the place.

We continued fighting.

At one point, I glanced over at my old man. He shot me a look. I shot one back. While his look wasn't one that said *you're my son*, and mine wasn't one that said *you're my father*, it was close. Real close.

Chapter 25

THERE'S NOTHING LIKE SUCKING on a gun lollipop and surviving to make one feel they've been granted a new lease on life. That's what those first few months felt like following my escape from the Terry penitentiary. I was kicking ass at home and at work. Was flipping Death off left and right. But once summer had ended, and autumn's crisp, clear colors had morphed into the gray skies of December, I began ruminating about family. More like lack thereof.

Maybe that's why that one near-Christmas night, there was a particular chill in the air. Not so much like winter cold, but death cold. Over a thick green flannel shirt—a shirt much like Mr. Gigliotti's trademark shirt—I slapped on my lead vest. Popped a couple Vicodins I'd swiped from Mom's place earlier that day. I strapped myself aboard the slow upward drift of those pills. As I cruised Blackwater, those pills turned my head into dreamy feedback fuzz—"Purple Haze" on a morphine drip. That soundtrack accompanied me as I drifted past the cemetery and Satan's Tree. A retirement home, a funeral home, and the Rainbow Casket Company.

On the brighter side of things, there was the Rotary Club holiday tree lot, and all the aluminum-sided ranch and colonial-style homes wreathed in blinking lights and tinsel. I didn't bother swinging by Jimmy's place. He was working late that night, taking inventory before Sole Survivor's pre-Christmas sale. So I just kept driving. A giant Douglas fir, decorated to the hilt, stood outside the police station where, like Jimmy, my old man was working late.

Everything continued shimmering. On the gravel lawn of Callie's old house was a beat-up, doorless fridge. Inside it was an illuminated plastic Jesus. As for the traffic lights, all the brilliant reds, yellows, and greens—the colors of the stop-and-go rainbow. My whole town was glowing. I was glowing, too. Comfortably Numb Me. Dizzy Star Atop the Downer Tree Me. I kept driving until I spotted the most radiant place in town: the Little Red Dollhouse.

Once through the door, I shielded my eyes from all the shattered disco ball brightness, and headed straight to the john. The stench of unflushed toilets and sickly sweet deodorizer filled the air. So did the dull hum and flicker of the overhead fluorescent lights. My low-fi high tuned out, tuned in. I splashed water on my face, studied myself in the mirror. Gone my wild eyes, disheveled hair. In the place of it all I saw fire. Fire more brilliant and blazing than the flames shooting from Newark factory smokestacks. I reached into my right front jeans pocket, the pocket that didn't contain a Callie letter, roadmap, or pills. I touched Grandmother's ring. It set my head as straight as it could get at the time. I splashed more water on my face, ran wet fingers through greasy hair. Was ready to see the brightest bright that cold and hazy night could offer: Baby.

Seeing as it was a Tuesday, with money still needing to be spent on family presents instead of strippers' rent, the place was dead. Just Jack behind the bar, a cocktail waitress filling orders, and a handful of guys seated up front. Most people like Jack, that had already seen me in my vest at some point or another, just ignored me, considered me another eccentric Piney. The ones that hadn't yet encountered me, though, flashed nervous looks—like they figured me for an undercover cop, or a crazed sniper on the loose. I flashed them double peace signs as I floated to the bar.

Short and stocky Jack, with his grimy ashtray of a face, said: "Look what the cat drug in. Captain X-Ray. You look a little better than the last time I saw you."

That was the night Terry and I had tangled, just five months prior. I'd ended up with a bloody nose, a fat-lip, a few bruised ribs, but my dignity intact. Terry wasn't as lucky. He'd wound up with a black eye, a busted jaw and hand, and being hauled off to jail.

I managed a smile. "Can I get a beer, Jack?"

He handed one over.

I popped another Vicodin, washed it down.

Jack raised an eyebrow. "You ain't going Karen Ann Quinlan on me, are you?"

"Don't worry," I said. "It's just a vitamin."

"Yeah, right," he said. "Vitamins." He wiped his hands on a dirty bar towel, then popped David Bowie's *Low* into the cassette player.

As "Always Crashing in the Same Car" pulsed through the speakers, I made my way to that shadowy booth in the back of the club—the place where Terry had held me hostage. The acrid taste of gunmetal came back to me. I downed a couple swigs of beer to chase away that bitterness.

On stage, bathed in a hazy chaotic swirl of colored lights, was a dancer. Called herself Brandy. Was pale, skinny-waisted. Had wavy jet-black hair, dark eyes. She slithered across the stage, pressed her tits together to grab the rolled-up dollar bills customers had placed in their mouths.

Once done, AC/DC's "You Shook Me All Night Long" blasted through the club. In time with the thunderous beat and slash-and-burn of guitar, Baby took the stage. Up top, she was blue eyes and straight brown hair. Below: an electric-green bikini bottom. She swung on the stripper pole. Became a beautiful blur, a pale-white dream begging to be real. Taking front center stage, she briefly came back into focus. In the shattered light, she shone brighter than all of Blackwater's holiday lights. She soothed hands over breasts. Ran those hands down along ribs, to hips. On one of those hips: a butterfly tattoo. Had big colorful wings: swirls of purple, jade, and gold. Like Baby, those wings were flowing freely, yearning to fly away. I wanted to fly away, too. That's when all the downers I'd taken kicked up a notch. Made each wild shake of Baby's hair, each hip sway and pelvic thrust fade to black. I banged a fist against my thigh to bring her back to me. But the pills took over and, again, I was off on my Vicodin flying carpet.

Those sleep-dealing pills and I played that game for a while: the surfacing and drowning in black. Baby finally interrupted that game. Looming over me, she was decked out in a long-sleeve, lacy-white top and cut-off shorts. Her pale, smooth legs spilled out from beneath those shorts like melt-in-your-mouth piñata candy.

She brushed sweaty strands of hair from her face, and asked: "What're you doing here, Sugar Smack?"

It was a fair question. Ever since that run-in with Terry I'd gone through all kinds of mood swings. There'd been times when I'd felt invincible. Still other times when I'd relive the Terry kidnapping— either in nightmares, or fully awake, tasting that harsh gunmetal in the back of my throat. No amount of pills, booze, or Jimmy's mom's cough medicine could chase away those feelings. I kept thinking they would, but they didn't. That night with Baby was one of those nights, where I'd thought those pills would help me shed my pains.

"I wanted to see you," I said to her, my voice sounding there and not there. "Wanted to wish you a Merry Christmas."

She gave me a good, long look. Never mind the vest, she'd already seen me in it. She was more concerned about the drugs. "What're you on? Downers?"

I nodded.

Baby slid into the booth next to me, brought her face close to mine. While certain things about her had changed through the years, her breath had remained the same: Boone's Farm Apple Wine and Marlboros. "Got a taste for me, Sugar Smack?"

I handed over a couple pills.

After downing them with the last of my beer, she said: "I spoke with Terry a few days ago."

"Oh yeah?" I said. "What did he have to say?"

"When he sees you again you're a dead man."

We both knew that would be a while. Penal system math adds up fast.

"I know I shouldn't," said Baby. "But I miss him."

"Screw that," I said. "You deserve better."

"Like who? You?"

I nodded.

"It's like I keep telling you," she said. "You're not my type." She tapped a chipped black-polished nail against the tabletop, then added: "Tell you what. I'll meet you halfway. Wanna dance?"

That one caught me off guard. It had nothing to do with the pills. We'd just never touched in real life. Only in my dreams. The polynomial equation of sleep and me: Baby. The exponentiation of wide-awake fantasy: Baby. "I guess," I said. "Sure."

"It'll cost you, Sugar Smack."

"How much?"

"I usually charge forty. But for you, thirty."

I didn't argue. I handed over a crumpled Jackson and a ten.

"What about the vest?" she asked.

I shrugged. "I'll keep it on for now."

"Have it your way, Sugar Smack."

Baby guided me to the edge of the booth, straddled my lap, and slipped off her top. She didn't have massive Vargas Girl–like breasts as had been displayed in Terry's tattoo, or in all those pictures I'd drawn of her back in high school. Still, they were full, with light-brown nipples.

"You think I'm pretty?" she whispered.

Maybe it was the pills, or maybe just me wanting to always remember her that way, but Baby was, once again, in full possession of her radiant high school moonglow: full cheeks, luscious cherry lip-glossed lips, and teeth as white as the sparkling whites of her eyes. "Absolutely," I murmured. "You're beautiful."

Baby took my hands, guided them around her waist. In time with Springsteen's "Candy's Song" lingering through the room, she extended her arms, glided them through the air. Hip grind, hair toss. She swayed back and forth.

As amazing as she felt, it was difficult to concentrate on her movements. All I could think about were Bruce's words, about how there's a sadness hidden in Candy's face, a sadness all her own where no man can keep her safe. I wanted to be better than Bruce. Better than any of his songs. I wanted to save Baby from everything. I tried to kiss her, but she leaned back. Her hair fell off her shoulders, as she shook her head no to the rhythm of the song.

"What's the matter?" I asked.

"Nothing, Sugar Smack. I just don't wanna kiss you. You're not my boyfriend."

"But I wanna be," I said. It was a foolish thing to say. It was also stupid of me to believe that our dance was the only thing that costs. Everything costs. Words cost. Love costs. The cost of living. The cost of war and peace. The cost of smoking. Manhattan Island had cost the settlers twenty-four bucks worth of trinkets, while the Manhattan Project, and all those nuclear bombs, had cost two billion. All those bombs going off. Like I was going off, too. I continued running my fingers up and down Baby's back, reading the bones of her spine like a lover's Braille.

When the song ended every bit of her glowed holy.

"Let me take you somewhere," I whispered. "Anywhere."

"How much you got, Sugar Smack?"

I pulled out the rest of my cash. I was too fucked up to count it. All I knew was that it was the wadded-up remains from my most recent Rainbow check. I tossed the stash on the table.

Baby eyed it. "Sure you wanna do this?"

"Absolutely."

"Fine," she said. "Let's go."

◆ ◆ ◆

BABY LED ME DOWN a dark hallway that led to her bedroom. It wasn't very big, about a third of the size of the Rainbow Casket Company showroom. The room had blood-red walls, and a curtainless window facing a bare-brick wall. It reeked of stale cigarette smoke and old sex. Besides a simple oak dresser upon which were scattered votive candles, necklaces, lipsticks, fortune cookie fortunes, and a bent-up spoon, the only other furniture present was a mattress on the floor. Rumpled sheets covered it. By that bed was an open suitcase. Clothes spilled out of it, all over the place. Instead of flipping on the overhead bare-bulb light, Baby clicked on a floor lamp covered in a sheer white scarf. Its soft glow was almost swallowed whole by those red, red walls.

"Any more pills?" she asked.

I grabbed what I had left: three. Two for her, one for me. We downed them dry.

Then Baby floated through the room, collecting up the bent-up spoon, some heroin, a syringe, and other supplies. She poured the smack, and some citric acid into the spoon. Mixed it with water, then cooked it up. It reeked of vinegary skunk. She snapped a filter off a Marlboro, placed it into the mixture, stuck the needle into the filter, and drew up the poison. After rolling up her sleeve, she strapped a belt around her arm, and guided the needle into her vein. Her eyes rolled back into her head like plums in a slo-mo slot machine. She offered me the syringe.

I waved it away. "That shit'll kill ya."

"You're one to talk," she said, "with all your pills." Then she got quiet. Just stood there, like a flesh and blood statue. Her pale neck thrummed at the place where her slow pulse beat just beneath. She wasn't so much looking at me as admiring all those doped-up clouds inside her mind. Then she came to. Her foggy eyes: now crystal blue. She eyed the lead vest. "You gonna take it off or what, Sugar Smack?"

Nothing else mattered at that moment. I wanted to go all the way. I stripped out of the vest and everything else.

Baby stripped all the way, too. All shaved below, she was like Barbie. A living, breathing Little Red Dollhouse Barbie.

She flipped off the floor lamp. Only a whisper of moonlight spilled into the room.

We collapsed onto her bed, became a puzzle of arms and legs. I couldn't tell which hand clawing at the sheets was mine, which leg drowning in the river of clothes was hers. It took a few minutes to get hard. But once I did, it was pedal-to-the-metal all the way. I slid inside Baby. Grabbed at her breasts. In her blurry face, I glimpsed Callie. My heart burst wide open. All the tiny lights of me, far brighter than that trickle of moonlight leaking into the room, spilled out all over Baby. She became luminous.

"Is this just about the money?" I asked.

All Baby could say was: "It's too much work fighting you anymore, Sugar Smack." She turned, rocked hard on her side and kept going. Took me along for a ride that ended with her on top.

I drove deeper into her.

She blazed wilder, brighter. Her hair, like a dark waterfall, streamed down across her face. In time with the heroin slinking through her veins, she ground her hips into mine. Our bodies writhed, turned inside out, outside in: orgasmic origami.

I slurred I loved her. That I'd always loved her. Told her even though I'd given part of my heart to Callie, I was ready to hand over the rest to her. Then I woozily told her how I wanted to take her away. Said we could be like a Springsteen song, where we'd bust the night wide-open, head out on the highway, and leave all our problems behind. I continued babbling all my hazy, crazy love talk.

Baby stopped her grinding. Through sluggish lips, she said: "Easy, Sugar Smack. What're you saying?"

"I, uh…I was wondering if you…uh, you know…you'd marry me." I groped for my pants by the bed, produced Grandmother's ring. The faint sliver of moonlight streaming in through the window made that ring sparkle.

Beginning to drift off on her own drug-induced flying carpet, Baby didn't seem to recall seeing that ring from back when I was seventeen. Back when I did all I could to honor Grandmother's dying wish. Yet with Callie long gone, and all the pills now making my mind go satellite, even the wrong girl seemed right. I took Baby's hand, slipped that sparkling ring on her finger. Again, I asked her to marry me.

"Christ," she said, wiping at her nose. "I wish I had a dollar every time some guy asked me that."

"But I'm serious," I said. "I wanna take you to California."

Baby's wasted eyes drew into slits. "I'd never make money out there. Those girls are prettier than me."

"Fuck that," I said. "You're way prettier."

For what seemed like hours, days, aeons, she didn't respond. Then she did: "Flip on the overhead, will ya."

Once bathed in the harsh, unforgiving bare-bulb light, Baby just looked at me. It was the first time I'd ever seen her so clearly. She lay on her bed, drowning in that sea of clothes and crumpled sheets. Her eyes: sad, bleary, ringed in runny mascara. Her moon-face: eclipsed, out of orbit. Her arms: pale, bruised, needle-marked. She looked like a dream, as if she were seeing herself in a really bad dream.

With all the blue draining from her eyes, she said: "This is me, Sugar Smack. This is it." She dragged the crumpled sheets across her even more crumpled body, and added: "This was a fucked idea. You gotta go."

No way was that happening, not without her at least. Since high school, I'd deemed her my savior. Perhaps she'd been an accidental one, but still a savior nonetheless. I knelt by her side. Got an even better look.

Gone the illuminated beauty I'd so adored back in high school. Gone the girl who'd given me the guts to score with Callie. Gone rebel attitude and rock-n-roll cranked to ten. Now Baby was just static. Pure static. But I didn't care. I'd take that static with me anywhere. Nurse her back to pure quadraphonic sound.

"Please," I pleaded, shaking her from a nod. "I need you."

She slipped off the ring, placed it in my hand, and closed my fingers around it. "You don't need me," she murmured. "You gotta leave."

I continued pleading. But she wouldn't have any of it. She hadn't gone Code 10-88, *OD*, but she did gradually drift off into a junk-fed oblivion. I stumbled into my pants, slapped on my shirt. Threw on my vest. Then I left.

The whole drive from Baby's place, everything was dead. The roads were empty. Duffy's was closed. The darkened, empty high school was lonelier and more eerie than the cemetery. As for the decorations wreathing homes and businesses—lights out. I popped Deep Purple into the cassette deck. "Highway Star" seared through the speakers. My car swerved back and forth. I rolled down the window. The slap of cold air revived me enough to keep me on my side of the road.

I recalled that final word Baby had said to me: *leave.* That's exactly what I needed to do. What I'd needed to do for years. I hit the gas. Red lights led to green lights led to exits: Out. Of. Town. I zoomed toward the Garden State Parkway. Once there, I'd head south, then pick up 76 West. It was just like I'd seen in countless dreams since I was a kid. Only this dream was real. In a few days I'd be out in LA, cruising Venice Beach. Just like all those beautiful, carefree people.

As I barreled down Route 9, toward the center of town, I leaned my head out my open window to get a blast of cold air and to glance up at the night sky. I spotted a brief, distant shimmer. It could've been Alpha Centauri, I figured. Or Venus. But it could've also been an alien spaceship. Even in my fucked-up state that night, I could still recall the Jersey lore I'd heard through the years, how UFOs had been sighted all across the state, even as far back as 1882. There were also those Bible passages from Revelations and Jeremiah that had confirmed alien existence. Also how alien technology had supposedly given rise to the Great Pyramids in Egypt. All that alien intelligence in the night sky—I wondered what those high-flying, super-minded beings thought of Blackwater. More specifically, what, if anything, did they think of me.

That's when I noticed my car heading straight toward Satan's Tree. Maybe part of me wanted it to happen. Or maybe the hulking tree—with its far-reaching bare branches, like wide-open arms—was heading straight for me. Suddenly, all the downers I'd taken slowed things to 16 RPM. I could read every timeworn and weathered "I love you" and "I miss you" contained in the notes marking the tree. Could see Dawn Dixon's face, along with the other faces of the deceased, their youth and innocence forever captured in the laminated yearbook and family album photos tacked into the scarred gray bark. I recalled those words from a Springsteen song: "...a state trooper knocking in the middle of the night, to say your baby died in a wreck on the highway..." I smelled the deep, smoky aroma of a distant maple-wood bonfire. Could distinguish between the night cold, and the deep chill of the nearby cemetery's moss-covered tombstones. I heard the silences between each vocal growl, drum fill, and guitar riff blaring over my stereo. I wanted to be that song. Wanted to be that Highway Star. I flashed Satan's Tree the finger. Yelled, "Fuck you." Then I slammed on the brakes, spun the wheel, and did all I could to avoid it. But it was no good.

Chapter 26

THE NEXT THING I remembered was the harsh smell of antiseptic. Disinfectant. A blur of drab, blue-gray medical scrubs. Gurney with wings. Squeaky wheels. Fly-by ceiling lights. Muffled commands crackling over the intercom. All that and a flimsy white bracelet, bearing my name, strapped around my wrist. The doctor got me out of my lead vest.

A sudden rush of sound and light hit my bare chest. Into my body rushed the noise and energy of the people around me: my old man, the Blackwater Medical Center attendants, the sick and healthy. It was all so much, so fast. My heart swelled. Not so much from pain, but joy. The sudden crush of the outside world now inside me felt good. I was relieved there wasn't a lead vest shielding me from it.

After a brief examination—some poking and prodding, checking my eyes and pulse—the doctor said: "The vest might've actually saved your life. It may have prevented your ribs from fracturing and puncturing your organs."

Before they got me into a hospital gown to run more tests, I managed to fish Grandmother's ring from my pants pocket. I handed it over to my old man.

"What the hell were you doing with that?" he said.

All I could say: "Just hold it for me, please?" Then I reached for his hand, gave it a squeeze. "Promise I'll be okay, dad?"

He nodded. "You'll feel better soon, son."

I told him thanks. He asked for what.

"For everything," I said.

After that: blood tests, X-rays, MRIs.

For once, the Gods of Blackwater were on my side. No head or back injuries. No rotator cuff tears. No fractured pelvis. Just a few scrapes and bruises here and there.

The doctor hooked me up to some machines. Those machines beeped and whirred. Buzzed and blipped. It was all a crazy racket at first. Soon, the noise leveled out to a steady rhythmic song. Those singing machines—one administered a morphine drip.

I drifted off. As I lay on the gurney, I couldn't tell whether I was in my body or out of it. Couldn't tell whether or not I'd truly survive. Then came a sign to let me know I'd remain among the living. From out of nowhere, in flew an angel. Not my guardian angel old man, but an angel nurse. That angel was equally as glittering and glorious as Grandmother's ring. With hypo in hand, that angel took me by the arm. Said, "Your veins are smiling at me."

Chapter 27

JUST LIKE HOW WHEN Mom left home, it felt like ghosts and shadows had taken her place. That could've been my life following my crash. I could've become a puff of smoke, a patch of dust, an unexplainable creak or groan in a once sorta home sweet home. What really saved my ass, though, were all my angels. Sure there'd been that angel nurse and my guardian angel old man. But there'd also been other angels along the way. One had made his home my home. One had exemplified love. Another had given me her body, but then flew away. All those angels: I did my best to offer them thanks each and every day after my accident. But then there were those two other angels, my dark angels, the ones on the Heaven-Sent casket.

On first glance, the Heaven-Sent's natural brushed copper finish, welded corners and bottom seams, crushed velvet pillow and finely woven satin interior, adjustable bedspring and mattress for perfect positioning of the body, along with those two angels painted on the interior panel and exterior lid, made it seem like a bed in a rich kid's home. But the more I stared at it, the less precious it became. Though barely bigger than a sneeze, that casket meant business. The sight of it alone broke my heart. I couldn't imagine it with a body inside.

In all my time at Rainbow I only had to sell one, to a woman whose eight-year-old daughter had been Code 10-16—*hit-and-run*—while riding her bike. Happened just a couple months after my crash. Standing before that heartbroken mother, I went numb, almost as numb as I'd gone with Dawn's parents. Except this time, I could hear myself give my Heaven-Sent pitch, which I'd often practiced, but had hoped to never use—how it was made of 20-gauge steel. Had a half-couch or full-couch lid option. Was leak-proof. Its white exterior was accented with brilliant gold traditional corners and full swing-bar handles. The pitch went on and on. When I was finally done, that poor mother wrote a check for the Eterna-Lux—the child-sized Eterna-Lux.

For the next few months, I couldn't shake that numb feeling. None of Mr. Delaney's jokes or Mad Man's wise words could snap me out of it either. Not even those times when business was slow and Delaney had clocked out for the day, when I'd crash out in one of the coffins in back and read casket manuals and books on the stages of grief. On Mad Man's recommendation, I'd even read *The Autobiography of Malcolm X*. In it, I'd learned that, while in prison, the civil rights activist had copied the dictionary by hand to help set him free. Since that knowledge-equals-power formula had worked so well for Malcolm in such dire circumstances, I figured it could also help me escape in my own way. So on slow days at work I began cruising *Webster's*. A word I discovered while on my travels: *hubble-bubble*. But unlike its namesake—that high-flying, space-minded telescope—this Hubble got you high and spacey in a different way. It was an East Indian hookah with a bowl made from a coconut shell. It was built in a way so that when smoke passed through the water, it made the noise for which it was named.

While all that reading had offered its fair share of entertainment and illumination, none of it helped me to shake my numbness. It still felt like all those angels that had once served me so well, before and after my crash, had abandoned me. Or maybe I was the one that had abandoned them. Then, whether I was dealing with my old man at home, Jimmy and his dad, or customers at work, it felt like I was there and not there. A shadow, a ghost, an unexplainable creak or groan.

Once that grim feeling set in deep, I began having nightmares. It was the same thing over and over. I kept seeing that little girl on her bike, so happy, so full of life. Next moment: nothing but a chalk outline on the road. Then there was my own crash: one moment I'm flipping off Satan's Tree, then I'm just a weathered photo alongside Dawn Dixon. Through it all, I drank more in my off hours, thinking that might help shake the nightmares. All it did was achieve massive hangovers, the spins. Abruptly excusing myself from sales pitches to puke in the alley behind work. I'm lucky Mr. Delaney didn't fire my sorry ass during that time. I guess my only saving grace was that, at the heart of it all, he must've recognized I was driven to serve the public. Still, it got to the point where every morning when I'd look in the mirror, all I'd see was a minimum-wage flunky doing the Grim Reaper's dirty work. A low-life coffin-pusher buried six feet under in failure.

Then came that night Jimmy and I went to the Wilbur Brothers Family Circus.

Chapter 28

BY THE TIME JIMMY and I had returned to his place with
Mr. Jeepers, we'd already sung, sweated, and run off most
of our high during our great circus escape. Gone were the
weed and codeine wings we'd worn earlier that evening.
We were back on solid ground. Senses rewiring. Disconnecting
from the fuzzy electricity of drugs. Reconnecting with the clarity
of the moment.

After we'd fed the chimp some food from the fridge, we headed
down to the basement. We sparked up Rhiannon, the crappy
Sears, and some Nag Champa. Then Jimmy promptly headed back
upstairs to continue searching for his dad.

As for Mr. Jeepers and me, we sat across from one another
on the clammy basement floor, right by Rhiannon and Jimmy's
bed. Up until that point in my life, I'd only hung out with primates
of the *Homo sapien* variety—ones I'd argued with, partied with,
loved, and lost. So I just sat observing the chimp.

Beneath the bare overhead light bulb, Mr. Jeepers seemed
slightly out of it at first. Like he was slowly emerging from a circus-
tranq haze, only to discover himself in a strange new world. He

did this slight side-to-side sway as if he were listening to a soft, sweet song. Eventually, he began working his tongue carefully over all parts of his hair, even the random bald and ashy patches, removing the remaining bits of circus mud and hay. Once he'd cleaned himself, he shifted so that he sat facing Rhiannon. The scene reminded me of that moment in *2001: A Space Odyssey* when those great apes crowded around that monolith rising from the earth. Except Mr. Jeepers wasn't going batshit crazy like those apes. He simply cocked his head side to side, completely mesmerized by the rumbling dryer. He sniffed it. Reached out a craggy black finger to touch the pulsating puke-green appliance, then quickly jerked away.

"It's okay," I said. I scooted closer to Rhiannon, pressed my hands against her warm, tumbling hum. In the past, I'd often given Jimmy shit about her. Said the dryer was a complete waste of space and electricity. That night, however, her soothing song was medicine.

Mr. Jeepers went through that ritual a few more times: touching Rhiannon, jerking away. Finally, he rested a palm against her, then the other. He bobbed his head, grunted softly. Regarded me with dozy, slow-blinking eyes perched beneath a hooded brow. His big ears stuck out from the side of his head like small radar saucers. His flat nose, fleshy bulging mouth, and black face were lined with intricate highways and bi-ways of wrinkles. That look of his—at once comical and sober—settled around me like the incense smoke drifting through the room.

The chimp scooted closer to Rhiannon, rested his left side against her.

I rested my right side against her so that I could face Mr. Jeepers.

For a few moments, he was able to give himself over to the dryer's warm vibrations, and tune out the sounds of the crappy stereo and Jimmy clomping around upstairs. The chimp's eyes closed. His shoulders eased down from around his ears. His fleshy belly, dappled with random patches of hair, pulsed softly.

Somewhere along the line, I drifted off, too. When I opened my eyes, Mr. Jeepers was looking right at me. Not in an aggressive, territorial way. Just observing me like I'd done with him.

I sat up, stretched.

Mr. Jeepers dittoed. Then he opened his mouth, yawned. I spotted places where he was missing some teeth. The ones that remained: dull, yellowed. He closed his mouth, settled his hairy arms into his lap. His jaw worked slowly, as if chewing food. He sniffed the air, let fly a series of soft hoots. Then he settled back into studying me with his intent, curious look.

"My name's Mark," I said, pointing at myself. Then I pointed at him. "You're Mr. Jeepers." I repeated his name, letting each syllable claim its own turf in time and space: "MIS—TER—JEE—PERS."

I could've left things at that—just the two of us chilling by the dryer, discovering more and more about one another—until Jimmy returned. Instead, I made the boneheaded decision to reach for the nearby coat-rack gnome. I slid it between Mr. Jeepers and me. "Welcome to Jimmy's world," I said.

The chimp picked at the silly cement fixture: its worn rose-cheeked face, red hat, white beard, blue jacket, green pants, and black boots. Once done, Mr. Jeepers flashed me a look. On a facial map, it would've been located somewhere between Boredom and Annoyance.

I did my best to mirror his look.

That one began pulling Mr. Jeepers out of his haze. He grunted, smiled a toothy smile. Then he slapped at the gnome. It wobbled, crashed against the concrete floor. The gnome's red cap busted off; spun away. Mr. Jeepers bobbed up and down, grinned even more.

I was so caught up in trying to make him laugh, that I didn't even think twice when reaching for Jimmy's prized *Bella Donna* record sitting within arm's reach. I slipped the Stevie Nicks LP from its jacket, handed it over to Mr. Jeepers. He sniffed at the white paper sleeve. Worked a wrinkled finger into it, ripped it away, leaving only the black disc in hand. The record was dotted with fingerprints and scratches from all the times Jimmy had stopped the disc to play various sections in reverse to search out hidden messages. Mr. Jeepers tapped the disc against the floor. Tapped it against his forehead. He pressed it to his ear, held it there as if Stevie were serenading him. The chimp bobbed his head, wriggled his toes. Then, whether due to my body language, or the chimp tapping into some primal wavelength communicating my truest, deepest feelings regarding Jimmy's musical tastes, Mr. Jeepers sat bolt upright, screeched, and whipped the record like a Frisbee. The disc sailed wobbly over the bed, nailed the concrete wall, right by Jimmy's oddball poster collection. The record splintered into a few pieces, each one sailing off in different directions.

That one cracked me up bigtime. That one cracked Mr. Jeepers up, too.

Suddenly he had tons more energy. He leapt to his feet, grunted excitedly, stuck out his tongue. Then he slapped a hand against his chest, slapped a hand against the floor. But when he heard Jimmy upstairs, thudding around, calling out his dad's name, the chimp got quiet. His hair stood on end. He whimpered, made a pouty face.

I felt myself make a worried face, too. Wasn't trying to mirror Mr. Jeepers. It was just odd that Jimmy's dad was gone. Especially with his poor health. Surrounded by the wreckage of Jimmy's busted record and trashed gnome, my mind spun off in different directions. I pictured Mr. Gigliotti crushed and bloodied in a totally wrecked Bessie. Or sprawled out dead at the base of Satan's Tree. Maybe Code Blue at Blackwater Medical Center.

I must've fallen too far into my worried look because the next thing I knew, Mr. Jeepers was plopped in front of me again, tapping me upside the head with a craggy black finger. He brought his face close to mine. I lurched back, afraid he might bite. Instead, he reached out a hand, curled and uncurled his fingers like he needed something from me.

I scooted closer.

Mr. Jeepers gently hooted as he fussed with some loose threads hanging from the knee area of my ripped jeans. When that lost its appeal, he latched onto my Who *The Kids Are Alright* T-shirt, pulled himself into my lap. He grabbed a fistful of my dirty-blond hair hanging down around my shoulder. It didn't hurt. But it didn't feel that great either. It took almost all my strength to pry his fingers loose.

He wobbled back on his butt, settling once again on the concrete floor, right in front of me. He puckered his lips, hooted. I followed suit. He sniffed the air between us, slapped a hand against the floor. So did I. He sat bolt upright and shot off an excited grunt far louder than Rhiannon. I dittoed. Then, as if testing me to see how far I'd go, he stuck a finger up his nose. Picked it, ate it. I didn't think twice. I did the same.

That's when Jimmy returned back downstairs. When he spotted his busted gnome and record, his worry flipped to its B-side: annoyance. And when he observed Mr. Jeepers and me huddled close, cracking one another up, that only cranked his anger. "What the hell?" he blurted out.

I got up on my feet, grabbed Mr. Jeepers by the hand. His grip was firm, yet not overpowering. It perfectly matched my own strength as we tottered over to Jimmy. Referring to the record and gnome, I said: "Things got outta hand. I'll replace them." Then I told Jimmy I was sorry. And I meant it. While my dumbass antics had seemed hilarious at the time, it was clear to see I'd gone bungle in the jungle. Again I apologized, then asked: "Wanna go look for your pops?"

Those words did little to ease Jimmy's worry or resentment. His jaw tightened. His sleepy eyes drew into slits. His hands curled into fists, then relaxed. Fists, relaxed. I'd rarely seen him so upset, the only other time being when I'd discovered him at Lucy the Elephant after he'd first learned of his dad's cancer.

Observing Jimmy's fists, Mr. Jeepers latched his arms around my thigh, burrowed into me.

I stood there as calm as possible. If Jimmy threw a punch, so be it. I deserved it.

It was during one of those moments when Jimmy's hands weren't all bunched into fists, or his face wasn't wadded up in frustration, that he brought an index finger to his mouth and chewed the nail. One of his Vans sneakers tapped rapid-fire against the concrete floor. Regarding my question, he uttered: "Let's wait a little longer." Then he glanced down at Mr. Jeepers still latched to my leg. Despite his concern and dissatisfaction, Jimmy couldn't help but let fly a tiny smile—a smile as miniscule as a roach joint. Looking more at the chimp than me, he said: "Fucken lovebirds."

I shrugged. "Just killing time waiting for you." Then I added: "Let's give Mr. Jeepers a proper tour of his new home."

We led Mr. Jeepers through the basement. He sniffed and picked at the milk crates chock-full of family photos and board games, including my Ouija board that I'd brought over a few days prior to screw around with whenever Jimmy and I were bored. The chimp knuckle-walked across the messed-up pool table, slapped at the poster collection. He even explored The Dark Side of the Moon. There, he climbed all over the water-stained cardboard boxes stuffed with rusted tools, banged-up kitchenware, old clothes, and other family junk. He tore open one box, yanked out one of Jimmy's dad's moth-bitten flannel shirts. He brought it to his face, sniffed it, flashed another toothy grin.

Seeing that shirt made Jimmy brighten. He bolted back upstairs. When he returned he didn't have to say a word. His face—unplugged from fun—said it all.

We continued introducing Mr. Jeepers to his new home. But it was hard for us, especially Jimmy, to completely enjoy the rush of being brand-new chimp parents. Every time the house would creak or groan, Jimmy would shoot upstairs, thinking his dad had returned. Every no-show only made his mood grow more and more dismal.

At one point, I said: "Let's do like the Great Adventure drive-thru safari. Let's let Mr. Jeepers roam free." I figured if nothing else, watching Mr. Jeepers explore the basement solo might provide a few laughs. Maybe take our minds off Jimmy's dad for a while.

Right off the bat, Mr. Jeepers returned to Jimmy's poster collection. He sniffed at Chuck Norris and *Lord of the Rings.* When he got to *Bella Donna*—Stevie Nicks standing in a sheer, dripping chiffon dress, a huge white cockatoo perched atop her upheld right hand—he licked Stevie.

Jimmy brightened. "You see, asswipe," he said, firing off an elbow nudge to my ribs. "At least he's got good taste in music."

Just as he'd said that, Mr. Jeepers ripped the poster from the wall.

I nudged Jimmy back. "You got that right, fuck face."

The chimp made a beeline for the milk crates. He yanked out my Ouija board. Ripped the lid from the box. Took a dump right on the board.

That one cracked Jimmy up to no end. "E-A-T *that* one!" he roared.

His laughter excited the chimp even more. Mr. Jeepers hopped atop Jimmy's lumpy mattress—sans box spring and bed frame— sitting on the basement floor. The chimp latched onto the down pillow; the one that, for so many years, had concealed Jimmy's stash of his mom's codeine cough medicine. Mr. Jeepers raised the pillow above his head, brought it crashing back down onto the bed. He repeated the gesture, then tore and bit at the pillow. Feathers went flying. Sure it bummed Jimmy out a bit, but he didn't make a move to stop Mr. Jeepers. Neither did I. We were thoroughly entertained by the chimp's unpredictable antics. He continued ripping at the pillow. More feathers went flying. He bounced up and down on the bed, grabbing at those feathers, tossing them about wildly. Then, armed with a blanket and sheet, he leapt to the floor. Sat cross-legged by the bed, encircling himself in those feathers and other soft, warm, Jimmy-smelling items.

As the night wore on, Jimmy and I gained more energy and alertness. Mr. Jeepers dittoed. Shedding layer after layer of inhibitions, grogginess, and worries, the three of us sang and danced along to Pink Floyd. Hopped up and down on Jimmy's wrecked bed. Leapt repeatedly over the broken gnome. We pulled out the Twister board—left hand, red; right hand, yellow; left foot, blue; right hand, green—as Mr. Jeepers clambered all over us. At one point Jimmy tied a blanket to an overhead pipe, let the chimp swing from it. He kept one hand gripping that blanket, while the other slapped at his chest. When he tired of that, he launched off, bounded through the basement. Grunted, hooted, smacked his lips. Bobbed his head, swatted his hands against the floor and cinderblock walls. Jimmy and I did our best to keep up, mirroring his actions; trying to experience that musty old basement with new primal eyes and ears. Had Jimmy's dad been home, he would've been yelling for us to *shaddup*, let him get some sleep. But with Jimmy's mom, she never heard a thing. She continued snoring away in her bedroom. Through it all, Jimmy and I were finally able to forget about the time. And those moments when we did think to glance out the BB-cracked window, all we saw was a dark world, gradually blending into shades of blue.

Finally, the three of us collapsed onto the dilapidated sofa. Jimmy passed out almost immediately. Mr. Jeepers crawled into my lap. The smell of mud, circus hay, and clear night air still clung to him. He was all huge ears and bulging mouth. His flat nose wriggled and sniffed. Wriggled and sniffed. His bright, brown eyes were perched beneath a Frankenstein-like massive brow. Beneath those attentive eyes: an intricate webbing of wrinkles. He reached for my arm, began picking away bits of dirt and debris. That led to him cleaning bits of trash from my hair. Once done, he wrapped his strong skinny arms around my neck. Hugged me like a baby might hug its mother. I drew Mr. Jeepers closer.

Everything about my life prior to that night had always felt like a huge waste of time: day in, day out, my head continually spun by drugs, loss, and math word problems. Then there was that hug from Mr. Jeepers. It sounds strange to say, but if it took all that bullshit from my former life to lead me to that hug, fine. It was all worth it. Because right then, that hug with Mr. Jeepers felt so real, so pure, so simple, just two breathing bodies burrowing into one another, digging down deep, seeking warmth and comfort.

Then came that Friday morning sunlight spilling in through the basement window. Not only did it signify a day when Jimmy and I would have to phone in sick to work, it also meant it was time to search for Mr. Gigliotti and chimp supplies.

Jimmy, Mr. Jeepers, and I crept up the basement stairs. Once outside, the early morning May air felt good—the right combination of warmth and chill to launch us into our day. I fired up my blue Toyota Corolla—a used car my old man had helped me purchase after the crash. Didn't have the sweet pinstriping, chrome-plated wheels, and blow-your-eardrums-out Kenwood speakers like the Vega had. And its wheel wells were slightly rusted from Blackwater's salt air. But it was tons more dependable in the engine department, and its tape player and dash clock weren't bad either. The clock read 7:30 a.m.

The three of us cruised around town. It was one of those rare and beautiful Blackwater mornings where the sky had painted everything—the Dump, the three lakes, Mr. Gigliotti's taxidermy shop—all shades of oranges, reds, and golds. Even the places I dreaded were stunning.

Jimmy held Mr. Jeepers in his lap. The whole drive, the chimp never struggled to break free. Instead, he kept his nose glued to a small crack in the window. He smacked his lips as we passed tall stands of pine trees; hooted as we passed the Little Red Dollhouse; let out a sharp cry as we passed Satan's Tree. And when he wasn't doing that, he was reaching for the steering wheel, trying to jerk it in the opposite direction from where I was driving.

As beautiful as Blackwater was that morning, as funny as Mr. Jeepers was, Jimmy and I couldn't help but fear that at every turn in the road, we'd spot Bessie crashed into a tree or phone pole. Or maybe Mr. Gigliotti sprawled out dead along the highway shoulder.

We continued our nerve-racking drive. Each and every place we checked: no Mr. Gigliotti. Finally, we spotted his empty pickup in Duffy's parking lot.

I shielded my eyes, glanced through the windshield, which wasn't as immaculately clean as it used to be back in those days when Jimmy's dad had the time and energy to baby the pickup. The oxygen tank, I noticed, wasn't on the bench seat. That was a good sign. I checked inside Duffy's. Only the bartender, along with a couple power plant employees and a cemetery maintenance worker.

Suddenly, I got an uneasy feeling—like my throat was stepping on my stomach, my heart reaching down to my toes: internal Twister. Call that feeling a hunch or a wild guess. Whatever you name it, it made me slap some coins into the bar payphone, punch numbers.

My old man picked up halfway through the second ring.

He'd only been able to get out the *hell*— of *hello* when I said: "Let him out."

◆ ◆ ◆

THE WAY MY OLD man told the story, it went something like this:

That night in question—the Thursday night when Jimmy and I had first discovered Mr. Jeepers at the circus—he'd been at Duffy's downing a few brews with a couple off-duty cop buddies. He spotted Mr. Gigliotti at the end of the bar. When Jimmy's dad left, my old man noticed he was a bit unsteady on his feet. He ran the usual field sobriety tests on Mr. Gigliotti in the parking lot: balancing, walking a straight line, and reciting the alphabet backward. The way my old man put it, Jimmy's dad didn't do so well. So he hauled Mr. Gigliotti down to the station, gave him a breath test. He was over the legal limit.

For a change, I felt like the cop in the family, analyzing my old man's fluency and response time, whether or not he corrected himself when speaking. I didn't detect any huge red flags. But I did notice a couple glaring omissions. Like how much was Mr. Gigliotti over the legal limit, a lot or only a little? What about Mr. Gigliotti's unsteady footing: how much had been due to alcohol versus the side effect of one of his many meds? And perhaps the most important question: were my old man's actions purely based on Mr. Gigliotti's drinking, or something else? Or maybe it was a combination of the two. I had no idea how to answer any of those inquiries, and I wasn't sure my old man knew how to either. Even if he did, I'm sure there would've been more glaring omissions.

When stating my case, I simply referred to Jimmy's dad as Mr. Gigliotti. And I never let my voice get too passionate; I kept it as even-toned as possible. Since formal charges hadn't yet been filed, I asked my old man to please give Mr. Gigliotti a break on account of his cancer. I also told him that if he breathalyzed every Blackwater resident, more than likely he'd find a number of them to be over the legal limit, to one degree or another, any hour of the day. No bullshit, no stumbling over words, no huge gaps between thoughts in anything I said.

My old man must've detected that, too, because after careful consideration, he said: "You can pick him up at the police station."

◆ ◆ ◆

Luckily for Jimmy and me, Mr. Gigliotti was waiting for us outside. Had Jimmy and I gone into the police station with a stolen chimp in tow, and still wearing our clothes from the night before—rumpled, reeking of weed and sweated-out alcohol—my old man would've been first in line to add black and white stripes to our wardrobe.

When Mr. Gigliotti spotted Jimmy, Mr. Jeepers, and me pull up to the curb, he did a double take. Then he shook his head. I flipped my seat forward, leaned against the steering wheel as Jimmy's dad grunted his way into the back seat, portable oxygen tank in tow.

As he did so, Mr. Jeepers' hair raised. He bobbed up and down in Jimmy's lap, imitating Mr. Gigliotti's grunting noises. Then he glued his face back to that crack in the window as I pulled us out onto Route 9.

The sun climbed a little higher in the morning sky. It streaked the passing cars, Callie's old house, and the rest of Blackwater with so many shades of yellow—yellow ochre, chrome yellow, and cadmium yellow, all the yellows Mad Man once told me Van Gogh had used in the second phase of his art career. I glanced in my rearview mirror. Mr. Gigliotti's Joe Camel cap still screamed *fuck you* loud and clear. Though his flannel shirt and overalls seemed slightly baggier and more weathered than usual. As for his face: pale, drawn. Drab as the hospital gown my grandmother had worn that last day I'd seen her in the hospital. "Sorry about all that," I said to Jimmy's dad.

His lips drew into a tight thin line, then relaxed, but only a little. "It's not your fault, son." He paused, then asked: "You have a hand in springing me?"

I nodded.

I could sense he wanted to say more—maybe thank me, tear into my old man, or interrogate Jimmy and me, find out what crazy shit we'd done to end up with a chimp. Instead, he sat there quietly, drumming on the oxygen tank sitting next to him. One dull *ding* after another, he watched his son fuss over Mr. Jeepers— tickling the chimp's chest, cooing, playing Piggy, patting him atop his slightly bald head. All things Mr. Gigliotti might've done with Jimmy when he was just a baby.

When our eyes locked in the rearview, I said: "We took him from the circus last night. His name's Mr. Jeepers."

Doing what he did for a living, one might think Mr. Gigliotti would rather see an animal dead sooner rather than later. Not so. He quietly sang that old standard: *Jeepers creepers, where'd you get them peepers? Jeepers creepers, where'd you get those eyes?* While doing so, he continued drumming and observing his son and the chimp. Whenever Mr. Jeepers bobbed his head and hooted, so did Jimmy. Whenever Jimmy glanced out the window, marveling at the passing scenery, so did Mr. Jeepers. In response to it all, Mr. Gigliotti's stony face gave way to a craggy smile.

At one point, the chimp opened his mouth wide, closed his eyes, and sneezed. He did it a couple more times. Each sneeze sounded so human.

Up until that point, things had been going fairly well, at least in regards to the chimp's health and well-being. But when Jimmy and I heard those sneezes, we freaked. We'd had other pets in the past whose final days had also started with a simple *ah-choo*.

Jimmy flashed me a look. I flashed one back. Code for: *What now?*

I glanced in the rearview. "Whudya think, Mr. Gigs?"

All too familiar with our lousy pet track record, Mr. Gigliotti did his best to ease our concern. "Probably just something in the air."

Mr. Gigliotti continued his singing and drumming. But when the chimp sneezed again, he zipped it. So did Jimmy.

What happened next was a byproduct of my ridiculous Tilt-a-Whirl brain, once again, spinning out of control. Only this time it had nothing to do with math. It was all about Mr. Jeepers and that sneeze. As I continued driving along Route 9 toward Jimmy's place, I imagined all kinds of nightmarish pet-jinx scenarios: the chimp had caught some strange disease from the Wilbur Brothers. Maybe a strain of that swine flu which had killed a Fort Dix army recruit back in '76. Or far worse: that freaky disease which had ravaged a Philadelphia Legionnaires convention, also back in '76. That disease had killed thirty-four. I silently enumerated all the symptoms that Mr. Jeepers, or any one of us, might soon exhibit: chronic cough, fever, chills. Next: muscle aches, tiredness, loss of appetite and coordination. Signal diarrhea and vomiting. Soon afterward: confusion and impaired cognition. Finally: death.

Mr. Gigliotti noticed my sweaty brow, the way I was gripping the wheel, and stepping deeper into the gas. Maybe he was trying to ease my spinning mind, or perhaps he'd caught a strain of my pet-jinx fever, too. Because just as I was about to turn left down his street, he tapped me on the shoulder, and said: "Keep straight, son. Let's go see my vet buddy, Doc Morton."

Chapter 29

BECAUSE OF THAT PET jinx Jimmy and I had shared since youth, we'd already encountered Doc Morton. I'd even heard about him through Jimmy's dad. In addition to being an animal vet, he was also an army vet. Had served alongside Mr. Gigliotti in the Korean War's Seventh Infantry Division, which had taken part in the Battle of Pork Chop Hill. Doc Morton had been injured in that battle. Walked with a limp, but refused to use a cane. As for his meaty hands, they hadn't wielded scalpels or treated injuries in the war, they'd operated all kinds of weapons: a 120mm mortar, a Browning Automatic Rifle, also an M20 super bazooka. One might think such strong hands, as Doc Morton's hands, would've been better suited for plumbing, construction, or even law enforcement like my old man. But actually, he handled animals with the utmost care.

Doc Morton's office smelled like wet dog crossed with flea collars. The sunshine-yellow walls sported a veterinary medicine degree from Rutgers, a cork bulletin board filled with happy animal photos, and two Korean War certificates: one declaring his service, another for his Purple Heart.

Right away, the good doctor informed us that Mr. Jeepers hadn't caught a killer strain of flu, or some still undiscovered, unnamed deadly disease. He merely echoed what Jimmy's dad had said in the car: probably just something in the air that made the chimp sneeze.

Mr. Gigliotti observed the relieved look on my face, his son's face. He brought an index finger and middle finger up to his Joe Camel cap, gave a little salute to his war buddy. "Appreciate that one, Doc."

Doc Morton: long weathered face, wild white hair, a lover of dogs. He was Emmett "Doc" Brown from *Back to the Future* repackaged: far less eccentric, far more animal science, no DeLorean time machine. He mirrored Mr. Gigliotti's salute with good humor, but once he saw Jimmy and me with Mr. Jeepers, his right eyebrow raised, a field of wrinkles sprouted across his forehead. He scooped Mr. Jeepers from Jimmy's arms, and sat him down on a bare-bones, wooden examination table.

Doc Morton's voice was as rough as a potholed road. But whenever he spoke with animals, it was placid as the Third Lake on a calm day. "Howya doin', little fellah?" he said to Mr. Jeepers. He carefully extended a meaty index finger.

With most pets I'd had in the past, they all would've been cowering, whimpering, or trying to bolt for the door. To them, vet equaled death. But that wasn't the case with Mr. Jeepers. He leaned forward, sniffed Doc Morton's finger. Then he reached for the stethoscope hanging from the vet's neck. He sniffed that, too. Then he bobbed up and down in his seat, hooting delightedly.

"There you go, little fellah," Doc Morton said. "You got good taste in humans." The vet grabbed a clipboard from his desk, swiped a black pen from his lab coat pocket. That coat was so well starched it rustled every time he moved. In that harsh voice of his, Doc Morton asked Jimmy and me to join him at the table. He noticed our bedraggled appearance—our rumpled clothes and weary eyes. "Looks like you two soldiers had a wild night," he said.

Jimmy and I looked at one another, then back at the vet, and nodded.

He then asked how we got the chimp.

Jimmy and I tag-teamed, going back and forth, recounting the story. When one of us forgot a detail, the other would jump in and complete it, then add a new detail, or part of one. The other one of us would then complete that detail and move the story forward. It went back and forth like that until we'd assembled all those pieces into a complete picture.

Instead of lecturing us like I thought he would, Doc Morton said: "I might've done something like that when I was your age."

He ran some basic tests on Mr. Jeepers: took his temperature, checked his heart rate, and pupil response. After each test, he'd click that black pen of his a few times, then jot down notes and check various boxes on an intake form attached to his clipboard.

The whole time, Mr. Jeepers sat patiently on the exam table—alternately looking at Doc Morton, then at Jimmy, then his dad, then me, then back at the vet—all the while, gently hooting, making kissing sounds, and occasionally playing with his toes. He barely flinched when Doc Morton drew blood.

"I won't be able to test it here," the vet said. "I'll have to send it out."

The last thing Mr. Gigliotti wanted right then was to have his name associated with a stolen chimp—especially if the Wilbur Brothers ended up filing a missing animal report with the police department.

Doc Morton placed a hand on his shoulder. "Don't worry, Frank. I'll have a zoo vet buddy take care of it. It'll all be hush hush."

As Doc Morton continued examining Mr. Jeepers, that lab coat of his rustling, he asked Jimmy and me more questions. Stuff like: "What did Mr. Jeepers look like when you found him?" "What was his health like?" "Did he seem happy?" "Did he exhibit any odd conduct?"

Again, Jimmy and I tag-teamed: "The chimp was dirty…" "He seemed kinda out of it, like maybe a little drugged…" "He was wobbling on his feet…" "He wasn't vicious…" "He seemed friendly…" "No weird behavior."

Based on our responses, Doc Morton said that the circus workers had probably given the chimp a mild sedative, which had probably worked to our advantage when kidnapping Mr. Jeepers. "From what I see so far," he continued, "your chimp seems to be in decent spirits and exhibits no real injuries."

It was when Doc Morton said that last word that I flashed on his Purple Heart certificate. I knew Mr. Gigliotti was involved with it on account of his Silver Star displayed in his hallway at home. But whenever I'd asked Mr. Gigliotti about that award, or any of his other ones, he'd only offer up so much information, then deflect. Why dredge up old war stories, he'd always say, when there are so many brave people all around us—doctors, nurses, power plant workers—fighting their own battles every day, so we can live a little better. Referring to that Purple Heart, I asked Doc Morton to tell the whole story.

He took a break from examining Mr. Jeepers, motioned toward Jimmy's dad. "If it weren't for this brave man, I wouldn't even be here to tell it."

Mr. Gigliotti waved away Doc Morton's commendation. "Aww, Doc, you always do this. It was nothing, really. You would've done the same for me." He leaned against the sunshine-yellow wall. His hands remained shoved deep in his overall pockets, his eyes on the drab gray floor, as Doc Morton recounted the incident.

"In the spring and summer of 1953," the vet began, "the Americans, along with the Chinese and Koreans, were negotiating a peace treaty. That's when Pork Chop Hill happened." He explained how on July ninth and tenth, the Chinese divisions were engaged in battle. So was the Seventh Division. But on the morning of July eleventh, a US commander decided to abandon Pork Chop Hill. He withdrew his troops under heavy gunfire. That's when Doc Morton took a .30-caliber bullet to the leg. Luckily Jimmy's dad came along, dragged the vet to safety. That's when Doc Morton pressed pause on his story. He shook his head; his voice grew soft and somber. "So many good men killed for a lousy nine-hundred-and-eighty feet of land," he said. His already weathered face wilted even more when he added: "So strange people call the Korean War a forgotten war. I can't forget it at all."

Jimmy and I had no idea what to say after something like that.

The same could be said for Mr. Jeepers. He sat motionless on the exam table, regarding Doc Morton with those huge, soulful eyes of his.

Mr. Gigliotti was actually the one that brought some life back to the room. For a change, he served up his own war memory. "Pork Chop Hill wasn't the literal translation of the Korean name for that hill, ain't that right, Doc?"

As Doc Morton considered that one, an easy smile slinked across his face. He stuck out a thick index finger, lightly tapped Mr. Jeepers on the nose.

The chimp swayed side to side, then rolled onto his back and waggled his wrinkled feet in the air.

"Go ahead," said Jimmy's dad. "Tell the boys about it."

Doc Morton explained how Pork Chop Hill had sounded a lot like the Korean phrase—*bok jop hae*—which meant *it's complicated.* "That's what the Korean officers would say when referring to the situation on Hill 255," the vet said. "'It's complicated.'"

The two war buddies—not bitter about the past, just grateful to be alive and going about their business—had a good laugh over that one. Then they got quiet.

Doc Morton went back to observing Mr. Jeepers. As he checked the chimp's reflexes and limb range of motion, he asked: "How's the cancer these days, Frank?"

Jimmy's dad thought about that one, then said: *"Bok jop hae."* He launched off a sly grin, then his tone grew more serious. "I think I got it on the run."

"Good to hear," said Doc Morton. "What about your animals?"

Mr. Gigliotti shrugged. "A little here and there. What about yours?"

"Saving Blackwater's finest one dog, cat, and chimp at a time." Doc Morton tickled Mr. Jeepers' belly. The chimp brought his knees into his chest, extended his arms, tried tickling back.

Once Doc Morton had completed his tests, he concluded that, while circus life had left Mr. Jeepers a little rougher for the wear, he at least seemed to be in fairly decent health and spirits. "But we won't know everything until we get the blood work back," he said. Again, he noted my rumpled appearance, Jimmy's too. Raised right eyebrow, wrinkle farm. "I get it, you boys wanting to help an animal in distress. But chimps aren't like the ones you see on TV." The vet related how primates are incredibly strong and fast and can easily overpower humans. "If you're going to keep him," the vet continued, "you better get some books and do your homework. Think you're ready?"

Jimmy and I weren't so much concerned about Mr. Jeepers flipping out on us. We were more worried about him falling prey to our pet jinx. Jimmy flashed me a look. Code for: *Maybe this wasn't such a good idea.* As for me, I figured since we'd dodged that sneeze scare, we were golden. I flashed my own look: *Don't sweat it. We've outgrown it.* Then I glanced over at Doc Morton. "Absolutely," I said.

The vet advised us that we should start with simple things like bedding: hay perhaps, shredded-up newspapers and magazines could work, too. Also plenty of mental, physical, and visual stimulation: TV, games, running around, placing the chimp's cage near a window. And make sure he gets plenty of fluids: water or fruit drinks. Don't forget food: stuff like fruits, vegetables, seeds, and nuts. Beyond that, Doc Morton said he'd make a few calls, see what additional advice he could offer.

Once we'd scooped up Mr. Jeepers, had given our thanks, and were heading for the door, the vet said to Jimmy and me: "Let's hope this fellah lives a long and happy life."

Chapter 30

THAT PHRASE, "IT'S COMPLICATED," could sum up so many areas of my life. It could also sum up my next seventy-two hours, in a big way.

Immediately following that vet visit, Jimmy, his dad, and I drove around, gathering up chimp books from the library, along with hay, a cage, and other supplies from various businesses. Then, Jimmy and I left his dad and Mr. Jeepers in the car, while we bolted inside Shop-Rite supermarket.

That Friday afternoon—like most Friday afternoons—the usual Blackwater party crowd was stocking up for the weekend: teenaged and twenty-something guys decked out in *Smokey and the Bandit*-era trucker caps, biker jackets, ripped jeans, and Springsteen facial hair circa *Born to Run*. With them were pale, doughy girls sporting equally ripped jeans, Doc Martens, feathered hair, flannel shirts, and wasted, unfocused eyes. The store's fluorescent lights offered an additional creepozoid effect, made everyone look like they'd taken an injection of plutonium straight to the heart.

Jimmy and I made a beeline for the fruit section. We tossed apples, bananas, and melons into our shopping cart.

Once we encountered the coconuts, I was reminded of that *Webster's* word I'd learned while cruising the dictionary at work—*hubble-bubble*. One would expect that since Jimmy and I were new parents, we'd put aside all our partying, at least for the time being, and get serious about life. Maybe it was our lack of sleep, or our inability to completely shake our old numbskulled ways, but once I told Jimmy that story about coconut bongs, he was sold. We tossed four into our cart.

Armed with all our supplies, we waited in line behind a couple of customers buying dog food, Preparation H, Liquid Plumber, TP, and Miller Tall Boys. Inching our way closer to the cashier, Jimmy whispered in my ear: "Check her out. She's *hot*."

"But I didn't think you liked—"

Jimmy shrugged. "A guy can change his mind."

What was even more surprising than his sexual reorientation was the cashier. Whether due to my exhaustion or the harsh fluorescent lights, she seemed a mess to me. Her furrowed brow, extra junk in the trunk, and eyes as crazed and off-kilter as a turbot fish I'd seen in the Ts of *Webster's* gave her that all-too familiar look of still another recent Blackwater High School graduate, already ruined by the radioactive real world. Add to that: her hair was an auburn wrecking yard. Her mouth: crammed with braces. Her face: a billboard for acne. Just below that face—which resembled so many of the faces that hung out at the First Lake every summer—on a polyester-shirted chest that looked to be about a 28A, she wore the nametag Marlene. That was a name that sounded like a type of fake butter or feminine hygiene product. I leaned into Jimmy. "I dunno," I said loud enough so he could hear me over the store's Muzak version of "Lost in Love." "If you're gonna go girl hunting, I think you can do better."

"You don't know what you're talking about," he said. "You're dumber than a Jackson White."

The Jackson Whites were a group of outcasts living up in the Ramapo Mountains. Jersey lore had it that, as far back as the Revolutionary War, they'd been the descendants of crazed Indians, escaped slaves, Hessian deserters, and prostitutes, which, over time, had been inbred to the point of mutation.

"You're the Idiot Wind," I shot back. "Either that or you're blind, stoned, or both."

Up close, though, I realized Marlene was pretty hot. Definitely Second Lake material. Possibly even Third, depending on her partying skills. She was clean-cut *Sears* catalogue model-type, crossed with extra sassy *Tiger Beat*. Fair skin. Clear brown eyes. And her breasts: they'd grown to 32Cs. Her auburn hair: straighter, more lustrous. The acne: mostly freckles. The junk in the trunk: chalk it up to a brush and a wad of keys in her back pockets. And when she smiled, she didn't bother concealing her braces. All that perk and self-confidence was light-years beyond most local girls. Had I been alone, I would've hit on her. But since Jimmy saw her first, he had squatter's rights. I grabbed him by his shirt, yanked him in front of me. "Marlene, I'd like you to meet Jimmy. Jimmy, Marlene."

Marlene didn't seem to mind our rumpled appearance. She giggled. Had you frozen the moment it could've been her cheery high school graduation photo. "Glad to meet you," she squeaked. She began ringing us up, her shimmering red lips quietly counting as she pushed the repeat button on the cash register.

"By the way," I said, wanting to speed things up in the Let's Get It On Department, "Jimmy thinks you're cute, Marlene."

"Shut up," Jimmy said, punching me in the arm. "No I don't." He glanced at Marlene, then down at his checkered Vans, fidgeting about.

"Then what?" Marlene said, glancing up from the cash register keys. "You don't?"

"Don't what?" Jimmy said to his sneakers.

"Think I'm cute," said Marlene.

Jimmy's brow scrunched so that his two dark eyebrows drew close like two little furry beasts kissing. "No...I mean yeah," he mumbled.

Marlene blushed. Her face was a freckle-faced time bomb. She began bagging all the fruits. Referring to the coconuts, she asked: "You guys going to a luau?"

"That's *way* too upscale for Blackwater," I replied.

"Easy," said Marlene. "The town ain't *that* bad." The way she spoke—it wasn't so much out of ignorance or blind admiration. It was more like she could find something good in even the worst situation.

I put that to the test. "Name one thing not so bad about it."

Marlene mulled it over, then offered: "Well, *you* guys are here. And you seem okay."

Now I was the one to blush. I grabbed a coconut, tossed it from hand to hand. "We've got a new pet chimp. Ain't that right, Jimmy?"

Jimmy—all stoner-dozy eyes, tousled mop of dark hair, and baby-faced looks slowly crawling toward manhood—nodded dreamily then shook his head.

"You're so wasted," Marlene chirped. She flashed a bracey-bright smile, then said: "Are you serious? An actual chimp? Like a real one?"

Jimmy brushed a sweep of curls from his eyes. "His name's Mr. Jeepers."

Just then, some skinny dude in ripped jeans and a Harley T-shirt got behind us in line. He was armed with a quart of JD, a six-pack of Schlitz, and breath that smelled like old cat litter. Suffering that breath, I leaned in close, and said: "Go to the other line, will ya. I'm trying to help my friend score."

Mr. Cat Litter Breath flashed a *right on, bro* look and took off.

As Marlene continued bagging everything, she asked: "Can your chimp open the coconuts, or do you?"

Still looking more at his shoes than her, Jimmy responded: "Oh…those are for hubble-bubbles. Something we got from the dictionary."

Before Jimmy could continue, Marlene interjected: "You read the *dic*tionary?"

Not sure whether to feel proud or ashamed, Jimmy didn't respond.

Marlene offered another silvery smile. "That's so *cool*. I do that, *too*."

Jimmy looked at me.

I smiled a: *See, I told you words could help set you free.*

He turned back to Marlene, looked her straight in the eye. In that one moment, he possessed more confidence than he ever had in his entire life. "Do you know what it means?" he asked. "Hubble-bubble?"

When Marlene said she didn't, Jimmy said through a snicker: "It's a coconut bong."

"*Rad*," Marlene cheeped. "How'd it get its name?"

Had he not been sleep deprived and hangover hazy, Jimmy could've easily responded. Instead, he flashed that sad smile of his.

I jumped in to salvage the moment. "It's 'cause of the sound they make when you smoke them."

"Wow," said Marlene. "Like onomatopoeia."

Jimmy grew more nervous. He flashed me a look: *What the hell's she talking about?*

Ever since I'd learned that word—*onomatopoeia*—in high school English, I'd fallen in love with the sound of those six bouncy syllables. Kept them on replay in my jukebox brain. "That's when something gets a name that sounds like what the thing does," I said.

"Exactly," said Marlene. "Like 'tinkle' or 'buzz.'"

"Or 'chickadee' or 'murmur,'" I said.

Marlene beamed at me. Her face was more incandescent than a Duffy's Budweiser neon sign.

I brightened, too. Not only was she cute and optimistic, but smart. And while she didn't possess Baby's pedal-to-the-metal sex appeal, or Callie's quiet charm, she had a certain *snap crackle pop* that rendered me even more weak-kneed and stupid-headed than sleep deprivation and Jimmy's weed.

"What?" said Marlene. "Why are you looking at me that way?"

"No reason," I said. I left it at that. If our flirting continued, she might be trading her brainy DNA with me instead of Jimmy. Now I was the one staring at my shoes.

Marlene turned back to Jimmy. "Well I think it's cool you read the dictionary. And that you've got a chimp and that you're making coconut bongs."

"You mean it?" said Jimmy.

"Of course," said Marlene.

What I said next was a total violation of bro code. But I couldn't help myself. "You should stop by tomorrow night, Marlene. You can meet Mr. Jeepers."

Jimmy flashed me a look that screamed: *What the hell are you doing? I don't know the first thing about making it with a girl!*

I continued. "And maybe Jimmy'll make you one. You know. A hubble-bubble."

"Great," said Marlene. "I'd *love* it." As she spoke those last words she was looking mainly at Jimmy, but a little at me, too.

Chapter 31

O NCE WE GOT BACK to Jimmy's place, we immediately flipped on Rhiannon and the Sears. Then it was double duty in every department. When we weren't assisting Jimmy's dad with his needs; or I wasn't rushing home to tend to my old man's needs; or when Jimmy and I weren't napping; or plowing through chimp behavior books; or setting up Mr. Jeepers' cage by the basement window; or creating a play area out of hay, branches, and leaves that we'd set up by Jimmy's bed; or looking for all the chimp-related shows we could find on TV, I was helping Jimmy make a hubble-bubble.

We cut PVC pipe, copper tubing, and wire mesh. Wielded hammer, chisel, vice, and pliers. Drained milk from coconuts, matched drill bit sizes with tube and pipe dimensions. We calibrated the weight, balance, and airflow of each fruit to align with the strict demands of our party needs.

After numerous hammer-whacked fingers and broken coconuts, Jimmy held up his first completed hubble-bubble. "Whudya think?" he asked.

Leftover milk was dripping from the copper tubing he'd whacked into the coconut. The PVC-pipe mouthpiece was cracked from when he'd jammed it in the vice to saw it.

The look on my face must've said it all, because Jimmy's face grew dark as New York City during the '77 blackout.

"Don't worry," I said. "I know you can do better."

He gave it another go. And another. Eventually, with the last remaining coconut, he produced a hubble-bubble: no leaks, no cracks. It was perfect. Again, he asked for my opinion.

"It's totally prodigious," I told him. *Prodigious*—another word I'd learned from *Webster's*.

"You think Marlene'll like it?" Jimmy asked.

I didn't think she'd like it. She'd love it. Marlene had become Jimmy's muse. Like Suze Rotolo had been for Bob Dylan back in the sixties when he'd created *The Freewheelin' Bob Dylan*. Jimmy hadn't made just any old bong. He'd created his own version of "Don't Think Twice, It's Alright." And while I was happy for him, my only regret was that I wouldn't have anything nearly as cool to present to Marlene. "Don't worry," I said. "You're in like Flynn."

To celebrate, Jimmy and I gave the bong a test run on The Dark Side of the Moon. Sure it was all cold, shadowy, and cobwebby, but there was at least comfort in knowing that it was the farthest spot from Mr. Jeepers' cage and play area.

Since the hubble-bubble was Jimmy's creation, I insisted he take the first hit.

Fuzzy bong in one hand, he sparked up with the other. The Zippo lit up the cold shadows as Jimmy sucked in deep. The water inside the coconut burbled madly. Jimmy's eyes grew wide. He took his lips away from the PVC-pipe mouthpiece, capped the opening with his hand. After a whoosh of a smoky exhale, he said with a greasy grin: "There's that sound. Hubble-bubble."

"Absolutely," I said. Then I swiped my own hit. While that spacey coconut was coarse and bristly to the touch, each hit off it was smooth and sugar sweet.

With each following hit, Jimmy and I held the coconut bong as if it were a trophy. The trophy we'd never received in grade school, high school, or JC. It was better than any outstanding sporting or academic achievement award. It marked us as winners. Made us victors in the Stoner Olympics.

◆ ◆ ◆

THAT FRIDAY EVENING, I discovered something that got Mr. Jeepers stoned off his ass: a song. I stumbled upon it completely by accident.

Once Jimmy and I had finished all our rushing around—creating hubble-bubbles; setting up the chimp's cage and play area; sweeping up stray hay, broken branches, and shattered bits of coconut—we chilled out. While Jimmy hubble-bubbled on The Dark Side of the Moon, I spun tunes. Earlier in the day, I'd played just enough Stevie Nicks to keep him off my back. Later, though, I mainly played stuff that I'd planned on spinning at our Marlene party the following night—everything from Springsteen to Lou Reed. Jane's Addiction to Patti Smith. "It's the End of the World As We Know It (And I Feel Fine)" to "Sowing the Seeds of Love."

Throughout all those tracks, Mr. Jeepers was out of his cage, roaming free. Either grooming himself in his play area, or wandering through the basement. In one hand: a baby bottle filled with apple juice. In the other: a skinny branch used to dig out stray ants and spiders from tiny cracks in the walls.

But once I cued up Norman Greenbaum's "Spirit in the Sky," everything changed.

As soon as Mr. Jeepers heard that fuzzed-out guitar intro, the bass, simple drumbeat, and handclaps, he froze. When that trippy beeping guitar riff began, his hair stood on end.

And then Greenbaum's voice kicked in:

When I die and they lay me to rest / Gonna go to the place that's the best / When I lay me down to die / Goin' up to the spirit in the sky...

Mr. Jeepers dropped his baby bottle and branch and knuckle-walked over to the stereo speakers. He squatted in front of one, cocked his head side to side. He reached out a thick black finger. Instead of jerking away, like he'd done the previous night when first encountering Rhiannon, he touched the speaker, placed a hand against it.

I crept over to Jimmy, who'd just finished his last hubble-bubble hit on The Dark Side of the Moon. Referring to Mr. Jeepers, I said: "Check it out."

Once Jimmy observed the chimp's absolute fascination with the song, his sleepy, doped-out eyes grew wide as two beer-bottle bottoms. "Wait," he said. "Ain't this song about death?"

"Sort of," I said. "It's about other things, too."

Greenbaum continued singing:

Prepare yourself / You know it's a must / Gotta have a friend in Jesus / So you know that when you die / He's gonna recommend you to the spirit in the sky...

To the rhythm of the music, Mr. Jeepers bobbed his head, smacked his lips. Let fly a series of soft pants, grunts, and hoots.

As for Jimmy, the combination of weed, lack of sleep, and all his pet jinx worries wouldn't release their grip on him. "What if," he began, "this is Mr. Jeepers way of...you know... making peace with death."

"Relax," I said. "Maybe he just likes the beat."

That was the short answer. Because if Mr. Jeepers was anything like me, there were so many appealing things about that song—the trippy guitars, the Stovall Sisters' high-flying background vocals, its elements of blues, folk, gospel, and psychedelic rock. Not only did it reference the afterlife, but also the idea of finding redemption, getting clean in this life. From the moment I'd first heard it, back when I was twelve, I could already hear it playing at my funeral. In his own way, maybe Mr. Jeepers was feeling all those things, too. Far better than that, though, perhaps he was hearing that song like I was hearing it that night in the basement. Why wait till I'm dead to go to the place that's the best. I wanted to discover it while I was still alive.

When the second chorus kicked in, Mr. Jeepers blasted off to the heavens. He leapt to his feet, bounced up and down, twirled in circles, rolled around on the floor.

Jimmy and I didn't budge. We just stood there on The Dark Side of the Moon, alternately nervous as hell and completely in awe, wondering what the chimp would do next.

At the halfway point of the song, when the searing guitar solo and rolling drums kicked in, the chimp went ballistic. He screeched, slapped his hands against his thighs, and against the floor. Even rocketed over to his play area; repeatedly grabbed handfuls of hay and pillow feathers, chucked them into the air.

And when the final verse kicked in and things got quiet, Mr. Jeepers got quiet, too. He plopped back down in front of the speaker, leaned his head against it.

Never been a sinner / I never sinned / I got a friend in Jesus / So you know that when I die / He's gonna set me up with the Spirit in the Sky...

More soft pants, grunts, and hoots from Mr. Jeepers. Then, in the final forty seconds of the track, when that thunderous electric guitar kicked in, the chimp, once again, sprang to his feet. He bounded up and down the creaky wooden stairs. Bounced up and down on Jimmy's bed. Swung wildly on the blanket secured to an overhead pipe.

But once the song faded out, Mr. Jeepers came to rest in the middle of the basement. He sat staring at that stereo speaker sporting a sad, crushed look. Like his face was a balloon, and someone had let all the air out of it.

That's when Jimmy and I figured it was time to intervene. We bolted upstairs and snagged some of the fruit we'd bought at Shop-Rite—apples, bananas, and melons. We hid the snacks throughout the basement.

Still again, Mr. Jeepers became enlivened. He knuckle-walked over to Jimmy's crappy Sears, discovered a banana behind his favorite speaker. He bit into the top part of the fruit, where the stem met the yellow peel, then opened it pretty much like a human would. Once he'd finished it and had tossed the peel aside, he swiped one of the bigger branches from his play area. He cracked open a melon he'd discovered beneath the pool table. After he'd consumed it, he made a beeline for the portable TV with coat hanger rabbit ears. Playing on that TV was *Bedtime for Bonzo*, sound down low. But Mr. Jeepers wasn't interested in Reagan and his chimp. He wanted the apple slices atop the set. Fruit in hand, he crawled onto the bed, right next to Jimmy. The chimp took slow bites off the apple. That fleshy, wrinkly mouth of his carefully worked the fruit until it was almost mush. He swallowed. Then he handed Jimmy a slice.

What happened next I can only attribute to all the weed Jimmy and I had smoked, along with our lack of sleep. Over Lou Reed's "Vicious" warbling on the Sears, Jimmy said all bitchily: "Looks like Mr. Jeepers loves *me* more than *you*. Just like with Marl*ene*." Then he took a teasing bite of that apple slice.

I told him he was nuts. Said I'd been the one making Mr. Jeepers go ape shit on the dance floor. As for Marlene, I told Jimmy I had a turntable in my pants that could make her boogie all night long.

Next thing we knew we were in each other's faces.

I threw a punch. Jimmy blocked it, threw his own. It caught my upper arm. Didn't really hurt, just pissed me off even more. I got him in a headlock. He sputtered out *motherfucker.*

Mr. Jeepers got so freaked that he zoomed across the room, swinging from one basement pipe after another, until he landed behind Jimmy's sofa. He curled up into a tight ball, and began barking.

For the chimp's sake, Jimmy and I called truce.

Jimmy scooped Mr. Jeepers into his arms, brought him over to me as I sat on the bed. "It's okay," Jimmy cooed into the chimp's ear. "Mark's our friend."

But Mr. Jeepers wouldn't look at me. Only Jimmy.

I coaxed, pleaded, even made the Play face. No dice. Finally, after more begging, and feeding the chimp a couple Jell-O Jigglers and some of Jimmy's mom's garlic and onions, we were friends again.

After that, the three of us plopped down onto the couch. Mr. Jeepers crawled into my lap. His age-old brown eyes looked right into my eyes. He cleaned bits of trash from my arms and hair. Then he wrapped his arms around my neck, gave me a full-on hug.

Suddenly, that clear sense of calm and joy I'd experienced the night before—when we'd first brought the chimp home from the circus—returned to me. I foolishly figured that easy feeling could spin on forever and ever, be the perfect soundtrack for my life. Very soon, however, I'd see how reality could be one cruel-ass DJ.

Chapter 32

Once Marlene and her friend, Susan, showed up Saturday night, the first thing Jimmy did was to extract that hubble-bubble from beneath his Sex Pistols *Sex Pack* T-shirt. "There," he said, handing it to Marlene. The way he sounded: all the years of yearning for a companion were bottled up in that one syllable.

Marlene's lips puckered into a perfect circle. The circumference of those lips: bliss. "You're so sweet," she said. "No one's ever done anything like this for me before." She held the bong like she'd just received her own trophy.

At that moment, no amount of onomatopoeias or literary references could've helped me. Erased Me. Invisible Man Me.

"So now what?" Marlene asked, looking only at Jimmy. "You gonna show me how it works?"

"Sure," said Jimmy.

The two of us led Marlene and Susan down to Jimmy's toxic basement room, reeking of weed, mildew, Nag Champa, chimp shit, and pine-scented Glade.

Jimmy sparked up Rhiannon and another stick of incense. I sparked up the Sears. Cheap Trick's *Live at Budokan* warbled throughout the room.

Once Marlene spotted Mr. Jeepers she abandoned Susan and rushed over to the chimp's cage. "He's so *cool*," she cooed. "Is he friendly?"

That's when I committed my next two violations of bro code. The first: before Jimmy even had a chance to get to Mr. Jeepers, I was already at his cage, flipping the latch, and lifting him into my arms. I ignored Jimmy's stink eye as I sidled up next to Marlene. "This here's Mr. Jeepers," I said. "Mr. Jeepers, Marlene." I then committed my second violation by charming Marlene with the French I hadn't spoken since Callie left town. With a slight bow, I said: "*Tu es belle ce soir, mademoiselle.*"

Having also studied some French, Marlene blushed a thank you. Then she brushed strands of dark hair back behind ears way too big for her small, soft face. To Mr. Jeepers, she squeaked: "Pleased to meet you."

Mr. Jeepers turned away, burrowed his head into my shoulder.

"Don't be shy," I spoke softly into his big fleshy ear. "Marlene's a friend. Ain't that right, Jimmy?"

As Cheap Trick's "Big Eyes" played over the stereo, Jimmy flashed his own eyes. That dirty look he'd given me earlier had escalated into throwing daggers.

Unaware of the exchange, Marlene still had her own eyes on Mr. Jeepers. She was softly cooing his name, telling him she only wanted to play. Then she cautiously extended the top of her hand, wrist first, in a supplicating gesture.

The chimp lifted his head from my shoulder. At first he only stared at her hand. His flat nose worked overtime: wriggling, nostrils flaring. Like he was taking in all of Marlene's various smells—her light peppering of sweet perfume, her assemblage of sex pheromones, auxiliary steroids, and the rest—to see if they all added up to a trustworthy person. Those calculations must've come back positive because the next thing I knew Mr. Jeepers was hooting, cooing, smacking his lips. He leaned forward, touched Marlene's hand, then licked it.

She blushed, shivered. "*Oooh*, that tickles."

That's when Jimmy whisked the chimp away from me, and said: "I think Mr. Jeepers wants to be with Marlene and me for a while."

I shrugged a *whatever*, grabbed a Rolling Rock. Popped it open, took a couple swigs. "Need Your Love" was up next on the Sears. On any other sound system, it would've been a massive wash of chunking guitars and deep swampy beat. On Jimmy's system, however, it was the aural equivalent of biting into tinfoil. I gulped down more brew. Then I noticed Susan still standing by the basement stairs, right where Marlene had left her. She seemed vaguely familiar. Like someone I might've seen at the Third Lake and thought was kinda hot. As she scoped out the room, she had a dull look on her face. Like she was watching really boring TV. I went over to her, introduced myself.

That bored look on her face barely changed as she told me her name.

Her breath reeked of cigarettes and sickly-sweet peppermint schnapps—two strikes against her. But I couldn't deliver the third. Susan wasn't half bad. Had a sweetly dimpled, slightly chubby-cheeked face. Big, wide-open blue eyes behind super-slinky, cat-eye glasses, a beautiful mop of golden locks tied up in pink ribbons, and luscious 36Cs dwelling fitfully beneath a yellow blouse. She was a Cabbage Patch Doll repackaged: made sexier, sassier, drunker.

The two of us made random small talk. Then we plopped down on the couch.

Susan produced a small stainless-steel flask from her purse, and uncapped it. The schnapps smelled like Jimmy's mom's codeine cough medicine gone napalm. She took a swig, offered me some.

I waved it away, told her thanks but no thanks. Then I swiped my California roadmap from my back pocket. I unfolded it in my lap, dropped some weed and a Zig-Zag paper onto it. The rolling paper covered LA. A big green bud of Jimmy's homegrown lay atop Bakersfield. Seeds were sprinkled amidst San Jose, Sacramento, and San Francisco. Once I'd rolled the joint and sparked up, I offered Susan a hit.

She declined, took another swipe from her flask.

"You should take it easy," I said. "That stuff's a killer."

As Susan downed more schnapps, I spotted Jimmy, Marlene, and Mr. Jeepers across the room. Jimmy had the chimp cradled in one arm while his free hand held Marlene's small freckle-splattered hand. Over Cheap Trick's "Ain't That a Shame," I could hear Jimmy proudly display his poster collection to her. And I could hear Marlene respond: "Pretty cool. I mean my room's different. I have Go-Go's and *21 Jump Street* posters. And I'm more into Harrison Ford than Chuck Norris. But that's okay."

Recalling that night, Jimmy and Marlene were such polar opposites. Especially when it came to fashion. Decked out in well-worn jeans and that Sex Pistols T-shirt, stoner-eyed, basement-dwelling Jimmy resembled a hard-living, punk-rock roadie in training. Conversely, fair-skinned, freckle-splattered, clear-eyed Marlene sported a black-and-white striped T-shirt, a simple black skirt falling just above bare knees, and Doc Martens Mary Jane flats. She was a photocopy of the early '80s pop bubblegum likes of Bananarama and *Sixteen Candles*. What Jimmy and Marlene shared, however, was that both seemed innocent almost to a fault—a rare and wonderful quality in Blackwater.

As for Marlene's friend, Susan, she continued drinking. With each swig, she drunkenly eyed Jimmy's room. With the exception of Mr. Jeepers, a brand-new copy of *Bella Donna*, and a new Stevie Nicks poster to replace the one Mr. Jeepers had torn from the wall, that room hadn't changed much over the years. There was still Rhiannon; the ceramic gnome, chipped red hat plastered back to his head; the tower of milk crates containing albums, bongs, board games, and family photos; the messed-up pool table; the grow lights shining down on two of Jimmy's latest pot plants—Samwise Gamgee and Legolas Greenleaf, both characters from *Lord of the Rings*. There were also the poster-covered cinderblock walls, The Dark Side of the Moon, and the maze of overhead copper and PVC pipes.

"Jeez," Susan said, not quite loud enough for Jimmy to hear. "This party *sucks*."

Sure our impromptu soiree didn't live up to Dump parties I'd attended where there'd been raging tunes blaring from parked muscle cars, dreamy-eyed stoner girls sporting jean jackets reeking of pot and wood smoke, seemingly endless bottles of booze, and joint after joint being passed around a massive bonfire. "It's not bad," I said. "I've been to worse."

I glanced over at Jimmy. He'd just locked Mr. Jeepers in his cage, and was staring at Marlene with big, dopey eyes.

Marlene had that coconut bong trophy in her hands. Over the warbly Sears and the chimp's occasional hooting and screeching, I heard her say to Jimmy: "Would you like to show me how it works?"

He looked over at me, flashed a troubled look: *What now?*

Part of me wanted to say: "Step aside and let Grand Master Party Flasher show her how it's done." Instead, I flashed him a look: *What're you waiting for, dumbass? Go for it!*

He escorted Marlene to his bed. The two sat cross-legged on the lumpy mattress.

Between hits off the hubble-bubble, Jimmy relayed to her the most recent shoe fact he'd learned at Sole Survivor. How in the Middle East heels were added to shoes to lift the foot from the burning sand. Then, in all earnestness, he said: "You're that heel. And I'm the foot. You save me from the burning sand."

Clouded over in pot smoke, Marlene screwed up her face, smiled. "In a weird way," she said, "I think that's one of the nicest things anyone's ever said to me." She kissed Jimmy on the cheek.

Me, I gave the tip of my joint another kiss, then considered the situation. With all my heart I wanted Jimmy to be happy. I also wanted Marlene to be the one to make him happy. But then there was Marlene and me. I got so lost in those thoughts that I'd completely forgotten about Susan. She leaned into me, hiccupped in my face. In that napalm cough medicine voice of hers, she said: "You're kinda cute."

That night I was on top of my fashion game. For a change, my face was well washed, zit free, my mess of hair combed. I sported strategically ripped acid-washed jeans, along with my Bruce Springsteen & The E-Street Band T-shirt—the one where Bruce is leaning into Clarence Clemmons while he's wailing away on sax. That whole ensemble was topped off with a few squirts of Calvin Klein's Obsession.

Maybe it was that Obsession, my clothes, or something else. Whatever the case, Susan grabbed my right hand, guided it beneath the back of her blouse, up toward her bra strap. "Go for it," she slurred. Then she slammed her lips against mine, got me deep-docked in liplock. Her tongue went Code 10-30, assaulting the inside of my mouth.

I jerked away, gasped for air, wiped at my lips. "Let's take it slow," I coughed.

"Whatever," Susan huffed. She got up from the couch, polished off her schnapps. Then she started in on the Jameson whiskey I'd bagged from my old man's liquor cabinet.

Still woozy from that brutish kiss, I sat slumped on the couch, unmoving. I glanced across the room, spotted Mr. Jeepers. He sat squat in his cage, looking right at me through his prison bars. He appeared as sad as he was when I'd first spotted him at the circus. That got me considering his new home. Sure Jimmy and I had given him fresh food, loads of love and attention, exercise, and hadn't given him sedatives like the circus had probably done. That meant something, I figured. But really, all Jimmy and I had basically done was switch the chimp from one cage to another. I got up, released Mr. Jeepers. Then I slapped "Spirit in the Sky" onto the Sears.

Like the night before, the chimp went ballistic. He made a beeline for his play area, right by Jimmy's bed. He bounced around; grabbed handfuls of hay, twigs, and leaves; tossed them in the air, then gathered them back up again as Jimmy and Marlene looked on in amazed delight. Once bored with that, the chimp seized an old *Playboy* Jimmy's dad had offered up as visual stimulation. Mr. Jeepers flipped through the magazine, all the while hooting and grunting. Once he'd gone through it forward and backward, he began ripping up all those beautiful bunnies, gleefully hollering and smacking his lips as he gathered up the shredded bits to add to his play area.

That's when Susan changed into a total ice queen, far colder than The Dark Side of the Moon. She flashed Jimmy and me a look as unwelcoming as crime-scene tape. She slurred loud enough for everyone to hear: "Chuck Norris and Stevie Nicks posters. A monkey. You guys are fucken *idiots*."

Mr. Jeepers stopped what he was doing. He glanced over at Susan, let fly a loud screechy cry, then shot a stream of diarrhea, barely missing Jimmy's bed.

I could totally relate to how the chimp was feeling right then. It would've been one thing for a true-blooded Ivy League girl to say something like Susan had said. But she was just some rude, Cabbage Patch Doll–looking, plastered-off-her-ass Blackwater girl. I got in her face, launched a *Webster's* slam I'd put together from the J, K, L, and M words. "Listen, Susan. You're nothing but a kerosene libidoed Judas hole meandering through a mackerel sky of morphiomania."

"Good one, dude," Jimmy cackled.

Mr. Jeepers jumped up and down in his play area, imitating that cackle.

Susan snorted a laugh. "That don't even make sense. None of this makes sense."

"You're dead wrong," I shot back. "Consult the dictionary and you'll see."

With that, Susan said: "I'm outta here, Marlene."

No one argued with her. That's what we did in Blackwater. We drove drunk. We let our friends drive drunk.

Marlene glanced over at me. With lipstick smeared well past the city limits of her lips, she said: "Sorry. She gets like that sometimes."

"No problemo," I said. Then I said we needed some new tunes to liven things up.

When I asked what they'd like to hear, Jimmy said: "Whatever."

Of course he'd say that. All he needed was Marlene and his hubble-bubble and he was set. As for me, another thing I'd learned from all those K-Tel Records ads I'd seen when I was younger was the importance of playing the right tune at the right time. Take that Kinks song: "Give the People What They Want." It got girls' libidos moving faster than a Corvette engine flywheel. And another: Pink Floyd's "Wish You Were Here." It was great for wooing slinky stoner chicks. Aerosmith's "Toys In the Attic" could tame the most rebellious, feather-haired rocker babes. 'Til Tuesday's "Voices Carry" was an instant leg-spreader.

Once I'd cued up that 'Til Tuesday record, I cleaned up the chimp shit. Then I placed Mr. Jeepers back in his cage. Afterward, I just stood there, right by the BB-cracked window—the wild and bright full-moon light spilling in all over the place—wondering what to do next.

Marlene glanced over at me, flashed her adorable bracey-bright smile. "Wanna join us?" She gave the lumpy mattress a pat.

"Yeah," Jimmy said. "Join us." When Jimmy spoke those words, he didn't have his hands on his hips signaling aggression, insularity, or frustration. Didn't even have his elbows propped atop his knees and head in hands signaling frustration, sadness, or the desire to be left alone. Instead, he was sitting in a relaxed way, his back against the cinderblock wall, his legs stretched out across the bed.

All in all I took that as a sign to join them.

Marlene sat between Jimmy and me. Her light peppering of perfume had grown muskier, less flowery as the night had progressed. "Here," she said, handing me the fuzzy bong. "Go for it."

It was an exceptionally killer batch of Jimmy's mindbomb weed, a new strain he'd appropriately titled Across the Universe. With each hit, my head grew lighter. The room tilted and hummed. Sparkled and shimmied. I handed the bong back to Marlene.

She sparked up, then said: "So, guys. Now what?"

Jimmy shot me a quick look. Code for: *Holy shit, dude! Does she mean what I think she means?*

Regardless of what she'd meant, or what Jimmy was hoping for in that moment, I was picturing my own possible scenario. It was pretty kinky. We'd continue smoking, drinking—anything and everything to further blur our awkwardness. Next, shy kisses between Marlene and Jimmy. Then between Marlene and me.

Kisses would lead to the three of us groping one another. Clothes would fall away. Naked bodies would intertwine, becoming a complex puzzle of desire. Eventually, a puzzle piece would fall away: Jimmy. That made sense for a number of reasons. And while that remaining picture of Marlene and me would look pretty cool, it would only confuse Jimmy even more. "I should go back to the couch," I said.

"But you just got here," said Jimmy.

"Yeah," said Marlene. "You just got here." She gave me a good long look.

I gave her one back. Though I was weed-whacked, that's when I realized what she meant to me. Her goofy, yet adorable eighties outfit, braces, and those ears a little too big for her face killed me. But not in the way you'd think. With time, she'd shed the mouth metal for straight white teeth. Her fashion sense would develop. She'd grow into her body a little more. Become a woman. And in the process, hopefully remain innocent and undamaged. *Sure it was all a long shot*, I thought that night. But it was possible. Anything was possible. That was the thing I wanted to touch, taste. The thing so sorely lacking in my life: possibility.

I whispered that word in French—*possibilité*—then kissed Marlene on the cheek.

Mr. Jeepers must've sensed something was up because he rattled his cage bars, sounded a series of low grunts.

Which caused Marlene to giggle.

Jimmy giggled, too. Then he kissed Marlene's other cheek.

As for that kiss I'd given Marlene, it hadn't equated into tasting possibility. It hadn't even meant I was firing off the starting gun for a threesome. The reality of the situation was that all I'd done was kiss a very stoned girl, and had misled my best friend in the process. "Shit," I said. "I'm sorry. Lemme help." I wobbled over to the Sears, slapped on Nazareth's *Hair of the Dog*, cued up "Love Hurts." Then

I clicked off the lights. The only illumination: that full-moon light spilling in through the BB-cracked window. I grabbed Mr. Jeepers, the bottle of whiskey, and plopped back down onto the couch, directly across from Jimmy's bed on the other side of the room.

While I could only faintly see them, I could feel Jimmy and Marlene looking at me, both wondering what to say or do next. I just sat there in the near dark, comforting the chimp, and taking swig after swig off the bottle.

Jimmy and Marlene continued taking hits off the hubble-bubble. All those hits led to making out. Signal sounds of kisses and faint delighted moans.

I flashed on Jimmy's dad right then. Figured him to be where he usually was as of late—crashed out in his easy chair in the middle of his quiet jungle. Bathed in the TV's dull blue flicker, he'd be wearing his oxygen mask, and pulling one raspy breath after another off the tank. And while Jimmy and I had our own drugs and diversions to help us escape the real world, Mr. Gigliotti had his own to help revitalize him—Cyclophosphamide, Adriamycin, and Cisplatin to ward off cancer tumors; Compazine and Benadryl to beat the nausea; Coumadin to dispel heart attacks.

Jimmy and Marlene's make-out session grew more intense. Shoes were kicked off. Shirts were shed. Their dark shadowy figures cast even odder shadows against the wall behind them. Part of me wanted to continue watching and listening, but another part of me wanted to shut my eyes and ears to all of it.

Mr. Jeepers knuckle-walked over to their pile of clothes. He swiped Jimmy's Sex Pistols shirt, dragged it across the room, and back onto the couch. He balled it up and placed it beneath his head like a pillow.

With a quizzical look, he lay there studying me as I took a few more hits off the Jameson. When the room began to spin a bit, I sat the bottle on the concrete floor, right by the couch. Then I lay down next to Mr. Jeepers, making sure to keep one foot planted on the floor so those basement spins wouldn't get any worse. I gently scratched behind the chimp's ears. He picked random basement debris from all over me. It was no small job, but he kept at it until it was complete. Then he slung an arm across my chest, and lay there, making small, wet lip-smacking sounds. Despite a case of the spins, all my worries slipped away. The only thing left: the music, Mr. Jeepers, and me. Each and every one of Nazareth's bluesy and dreamy guitar riffs, each and every little hoot and hug from the chimp lifted me higher and higher out of Blackwater. Somewhere along the line, however, I drifted off a little too far.

Chapter 33

HAD MY FEW HOURS of drifting been a math word problem, it might've gone something like this:

A tightrope of three feet is tied to Mr. Jeepers' cage at one end, and Mark's ankle at the other. Mr. Jeepers walks along the tightrope toward Mark, who at the same time is floating away at three feet per second. Assuming that the tightrope can be stretched infinitely long, will Mr. Jeepers ever reach Mark?

That word *reach* would've led me to stars. *Stars* to Callie. Then, gone. Grandmother. Mom. My old man. Gun. Terry. Biting taste of gunmetal. Heavy Metal. Blue Cheer. "Summertime Blues." The Blues Brothers. The Wilbur Brothers. Mr. Jeepers.

Before I could drift off any further, I was yanked back to earth by Marlene's screams. I sat upright. My head was pounding, stuffed full of cotton balls and wrecking balls. The basement: still spinning. I rubbed my eyes, focused in on Marlene. She was bathed in a swirl of shadows and moonlight. Had a blanket wrapped around her tilt-a-whirling bare body. Her eyes: pinned open wide. Her hand that wasn't clutching the blanket: pointed in my direction. That's when I spotted Mr. Jeepers on the floor by the couch. He was vomiting and shaking. Next to him: my empty whiskey bottle.

I stumbled to standing, gathered the chimp into my arms. Did my best to keep him calm and still. Kept telling him everything would be okay.

Marlene rousted Jimmy from bed. He threw on his clothes, bolted upstairs, shook his dad awake. Jimmy's dad promptly phoned Doc Morton.

Then Jimmy, his dad, Mr. Jeepers, and I crammed into the pickup. During the whole drive to the vet no one spoke. No Bessie Smith on the stereo either. Just a series of fleeting fever-dreamed snapshots: black-and-blue bruised night with glimmers of cadaver-white along the horizon. The wide-open arms and scraggly fingers of Satan's Tree. Wolf-howling winds rushing in through open windows. Passing cars' headlights bleeding blazing streaks across our windshield, as Mr. Jeepers lay trembling in my lap.

Once we reached Doc Morton's office, I scooped the chimp into my arms, rushed toward the door. Suddenly, time slowed to a Vicodin crawl. Milliseconds stretched into minutes. Minutes expanded into lifetimes. Mr. Jeepers' shuddering paused, or at least that's what it felt like in those creeping moments. His wandering and unfocused eyes: crystal clear, but cracked with panic. Those pleading eyes seemed to ask: *What happened? Why am I here again?*

Had I been straighter, I would've told him that I would've gladly traded places. Let him have his old life back while I was the one getting poked with needles, hooked up to drips and machines, all the while knocking on heaven's door. Instead, all I could do was to keep running for the vet's door as time rushed back to real-life speed.

Doc Morton ushered us into the exam room. Since Jimmy's dad had only been able to offer minimal details over the phone, the vet needed more specifics. And fast.

"What exactly did he get into?" Doc Morton asked.

Before I had a chance to offer that it was my booze, and probably all my drinking that had prompted the chimp to do the same, Jimmy piped in: "We had a party. Somehow Mr. Jeepers got into some whiskey."

I glanced over at Jimmy. He briefly looked at me, then looked away.

Doc Morton continued speaking. But I was only able to catch bits and pieces of his plan of attack. He said something about an IV to ward off organ collapse. Said he'd also have to induce vomiting, which is what I felt like doing right then, too. The vet's lips kept moving, but I couldn't catch all his words. But I did hear him mention something about blood tests to see how badly the chimp's kidneys were hurt. Next thing I knew he was whisking Mr. Jeepers down the hall to the procedure area.

That left Jimmy, his dad, and me in that examination room with sunshine-yellow walls, photos of happy animals, and Korean War memorabilia. While we'd been there just a couple days prior, it felt like it had been aeons.

Later Jimmy would confess that he hadn't gotten laid at the party. He wouldn't say much more than to offer that it didn't feel right. Said he couldn't get it right. That's how I felt that night at the vet. Slumped in a chair, I kept shaking my head and apologizing, saying I'd fucked up massively; the whole thing had been my fault. Then I made the mistake of glancing up at that cork bulletin board sporting all those happy photos—a beaming woman, one arm curled around a grinning Golden Retriever, the other arm wrapped around a fat, serene Calico cat; a weathered, trucker cap-toting, snaggle-toothed, smiling Piney with his wrinkle-faced bulldog by his side. The sight of those happy pets and owners, and more, made the wrecking ball in my head swing wilder. I closed my eyes, felt the room drift. I gripped the sides of my plastic chair, planted my feet firmly on the dull floor. But that wasn't much help. I opened my eyes. Again, that damned bulletin board. More mental wrecking ball busting my brain to bits. At the time, I couldn't come close to figuring out why that bulletin board had disturbed me so much. Later, though, when I was straighter and saner, I'd get it. For most of my life when people had left me it had been for reasons out of my control. All I could do was down more booze, pills, weed, and go another shade of numb as I witnessed person after person leave in their different ways. With Mr. Jeepers, though, his record had been spotless in that regard. Not only had I been the one to instigate his leaving from the circus, I'd also been the one to instigate his leaving from Jimmy and me. Never would the three of us be as happy as all those pets and owners in those photos. Never. And though I couldn't understand the situation so clearly in the vet's office that early Sunday morning, I could still feel there was something about all that happiness that was completely alien to my way of life. In fact, it was all so strange and unnerving that I reached for a nearby garbage can and puked into it.

Jimmy, who'd been pacing the small room to pieces, swiped some paper towels from a gleaming metal dispenser on the wall. He handed them over.

Again, I caught his eye. Instead of guilt-tripping me, he offered in a low voice: "Try to relax, dude. It could've been me instead of you." He paused, then added: "Or maybe it was the…you know…"

Even in my massively messed-up state, I understood one thing for sure. No matter what Jimmy said, no matter what his dad or anyone else said, this all had to do with the way I'd been wired. Just like how guns will continue to fire bullets. Or how people will continually leave one another. Or how nuclear bombs will always obliterate. All it seemed I'd been programmed to do my entire life was get wasted and watch my world slip away. That's what really fucked up Mr. Jeepers, I concluded, as I threw up once again into the trashcan. It wasn't so much the alcohol. Wasn't even the pet jinx. It was more the way I'd been living.

Chapter 34

OME THE NEXT DAY, Monday, I was back at Rainbow. It was a slow morning, thank God. Still, it was wall-to-wall caskets and burial urns. Stargazers and Softique Kleenex. For the last ninety-six hours, practically all I'd had in my system was drugs and booze; little sleep, little food. I drifted through the showroom as if I were bareback riding an earthbound cloud, a three-legged one at that. My brain kept replaying the last four days on an endless loop. My head ached. My sweat reeked. The combination of my lingering hangover plus those hellacious Stargazers equaled me rushing for the toilet every few minutes. When I wasn't in the john I'd continue drifting. Would continue mentally kicking my ass for how everything had gone down. At least my nightmare had a silver lining: the vet had said Mr. Jeepers would pull through. I did my best to hold on to that thought as I continued pacing and beating myself up. Through it all, however, I'd somehow managed to keep my black suit clean and wrinkle-free. Yet, my haggard and worried face was far lousier than a driver's license photo.

Instead of passing along a joke or wise words, Mr. Delaney asked: "What's up?"

I wasted no time in relaying the entire Mr. Jeepers saga.

Once done, Mr. Delaney's thin lips got a little thinner, more pinched at the edges. He glanced down at his well-polished black Florsheims. They reflected shards of the early-June morning light spilling in through the huge storefront window. Still looking at those shoes, my boss didn't mince words, when he said: "I know you and your friend meant well. But it seems you both have some growing up to do."

I couldn't argue with him, at least when it came to me. So much of what had happened with Mr. Jeepers, my car accident, and all the other crash-and-burn moments in my life had come down to choices I'd made. And others I hadn't made. Though I was my father's son—the son of a cop—in no way had I retained any of his upstanding DNA. My moral compass was on the fritz. My up was my down. I'd been left stranded in a no-man's land where it seemed no guardian angel or North Star could get me back on the right path.

And though I hadn't said any of that to Mr. Delaney, he must've sensed some of those dark thoughts when he offered: "At least it's good that Mr. Jeepers is on the mend."

I flashed a relieved smile, told Mr. Delaney that Doc Morton had even made a few calls while I was at his office. He'd phoned a friend of a friend that runs a chimp sanctuary deep in the Pine Barrens. Once Mr. Jeepers was up and about a bit more, the vet had said, the chimp would be transferred to that sanctuary to spend his remaining days in leisure. I considered what I'd just told my boss, then said: "Mr. Jeepers is tough. Also lucky. He's escaping Blackwater."

Mr. Delaney offered his own satisfied smile. "Reminds me of a trip I took," he said. A few years back, Delaney had visited his sister in Clearwater, Florida, not long after she'd left Jersey to retire in the Sunshine State with her second husband. That trip, Delaney related, had been the first time in a very long time he'd allowed himself to leave his business behind for a few days and simply relax. In Florida, he said, he'd experienced loads of sunshine; blue skies; people greeting him with smiles, saying hello; and orange trees everywhere. "Even pretty girls on the beach in bikinis, if you're into that sorta thing," he offered with a wink.

As he continued speaking, he walked through the showroom. While I felt like fried death with a side of shit, I did my best to keep up with him. My hope was that his story, which had been pretty boring so far, would somehow offer a wise gem like so many of the other anecdotes he'd passed along during my time at Rainbow.

I shadowed Mr. Delaney as he moved past the Legacy casket and Starlight Slumber. He paused at the Silver Gemini, shook his head. His voice grew somber and gravelly: "Then I had to go and ruin my great vacation by returning to Blackwater." He continued walking past the Blue Moon, the White Lily, and Ambassador. Finally, he came to rest at the Heaven-Sent. "I never realized how terrible it was here," he remarked. Then, realizing how he could've been misinterpreted, Mr. Delaney rested a hand on that child-sized casket. "I don't mean here in the shop," he said. "Sure it can be heartbreaking at times, but I love what I do." He explained how it was Blackwater that had felt so bleak with its power plant, and drunk Pineys armed to the teeth, speeding around in pickups and hotrods. "Even a killer tree," he added, "if you believe the local lore." Again he paused, shrugged. "Who knows," he offered softly, as if speaking to himself. "Maybe I'll leave one of these days."

To anyone else hearing Delaney's story their reaction might've been something like *yeah, so what?* But when he said those last few words—the words I'd been telling myself, and so many others, for so many years—they hit me hard. Those seven words—*maybe*

I'll leave one of these days—dug right through all my bullshit, all my good and bad intentions, and suddenly unlocked something deep inside me. Recalling that moment, it was like everything in that Rainbow showroom—all the caskets, burial urns, sickly sweet flowers—along with all the bright sunlight outside had flooded into me, formed very distinct boundaries. On one side of my life: shadows and ghosts. On the other side: golden light and wide-open road. Once and for all, and without any hesitation or second-guessing, it seemed I had to pick one of those sides. Truly believe in it. Fight for it with all my life. That fight didn't necessarily guarantee me true freedom either. But it did guarantee action. Motion. Delaney's words—which had been my words for way too long—had lit a giant rocket under my ass. Made me realize that the last thing I wanted was to be a Blackwater casket pusher for the rest of my days. It was finally time to escape my dumpy little town's grim, flat, boxed-in radioactivity, and experience California's fresh-aired, wide-open spaces. See if they could open my mind to a new way of life. Sure it was all a long shot. But up to that point in my life, all it felt like I'd ever done was roll snake eyes. Right then, a long shot seemed like a sure win. I was ready to take a chance, shed the skin of my losses. Not so much to shake my name or memories, but instead to take the subterranean route far from my homesick blues, and arise in a new land where the sun would shine down on me most every day. And while Mr. Delaney had in no way offered his story, or those ominous words—*maybe I'll leave one of these days*—as a means to start the chain reaction of thoughts and events that would greatly affect the rest of my life, that is indeed what happened when my hangover fog suddenly lifted, I finally woke the fuck up, and told my boss in the kindest, most respectful way possible: "I quit."

Chapter 35

THAT DAY I QUIT Rainbow officially marked the fourth day of June. Just twenty days shy of my twenty-first birthday. Like all the other Junes I'd witnessed in my dumpy little town, lawns smelled sweeter, greener. Bluebirds and warblers sang louder. Tulips and roses exploded in Technicolor bliss. And the way everyone dressed: it had been one long, slow striptease since December. Sweaters, wool pants, heavy socks, and boots had been shed for shorts, T-shirts, halter-tops, and flip-flops.

While those changes of seasons had been quite captivating at times, they amounted to little more than a fleeting pop song on the *Billboard* chart of life; a sickly-sweet melody reminding me I'd been stuck in Blackwater still another year.

Finally, all that was about to change. First things first: once I left Rainbow, I bolted over to Jimmy's.

As usual, his house was filled with all those amazing Missing Mom smells—simmering garlic, sausage, onions, and tomatoes. While Mrs. Gigliotti tended to her cooking, Jimmy's dad sat in his living room easy chair, taking slow, easy breaths off his oxygen tank. On the tube: John Wayne's *Rio Bravo*.

Mr. Gigliotti—decked out in his trademark outfit, which had been fitting him a bit better as of late—observed me in my black suit. His still intense Dillinger-like eyes creased into a slight smile as he slipped off his oxygen mask, and asked: "Going to a funeral?"

"Actually just leaving one," I said. I got down on one knee by his chair. Caught a slight whiff of Joe Camel. Nowhere near as noxious as the old days when Jimmy's dad would chain-smoke three packs a day or more. "How're you feeling?" I asked.

While he'd been up and about a bit more—eating better, getting rest, and breathing easier—he knew better than to sugarcoat the truth. "Getting older every day, son."

For a moment, we remained quiet. Quiet as all those animals surrounding us in Mr. Gigliotti's taxidermy jungle.

Jimmy's dad broke our silence by saying: "I'm glad your chimp'll be okay."

"Me too," I said. Then I offered: "How's Jimmy?"

Mr. Gigliotti shrugged a *who knows with that boy?*

On the TV, Dean Martin—the town drunk and former deputy sheriff—along with John Wayne—the sheriff—were shaking down some sinister cowboys in a bar. John Wayne, with that classic voice of his, was urging those cowboys to get out of town.

That's when I told Mr. Gigliotti I was leaving soon.

Like his son, Jimmy's dad had heard me utter those words countless times before. But there must've been something in the way I'd said them on that particular day because a seedling of a smile bloomed across Mr. Gigliotti's face. "Good for you, son." But then that seedling smile withered. "Jimmy won't be too happy though."

Again, silence. We surveyed that quiet jungle surrounding us.

Standing in the corner: a mounted gray fox. Hanging on the wall: a huge striped bass. On another wall: a ten-point buck head. Through the years Mr. Gigliotti had given all those unclaimed animals a home. Through the years he'd done the same for me.

As for Jimmy, I found him downstairs decked out in that photocopy outfit of his pops. He was sweeping up hay, branches, and pillow feathers while Sly & The Family Stone partied out on the Sears with "I Want To Take You Higher."

I grabbed a second broom from upstairs. Then I stripped off my tie, suit jacket, and joined Jimmy.

It was an odd thing with the two of us. Practically all of our past conversations had focused on getting wasted. But since neither of us felt like partying right then, it was difficult for us to address everything that had occurred over the last number of days. So we just kept sweeping.

Every so often we'd glance up at one another, thinking that might be the moment when we'd find the words to speak. Still a no go. So we just kept sweeping.

But when Jimmy's broom kicked up a tuft of Mr. Jeepers' hair, that's when he finally uttered: "This sucks harder than the Blue Hole."

The Blue Hole was a body of water located deep in the Pine Barrens. Legend had it that the mysterious swimming hole was not only a hangout for the Jersey Devil, but would also suck unlucky swimmers down into its chilly depths.

"You got that right," I said.

We continued sweeping.

As we did so, I recalled a Bruce Lee quote: "To know oneself is to study oneself in action with another person." It was so true. All those moments Jimmy and I had spent with Mr. Jeepers—playing Twister, bounding through the basement, chilling out, never going to bed angry—had been rare and welcome instances when we'd felt truly human and alive. Not the lost losers we'd felt like so many other times in life. Over the sounds of the crappy Sears and our brooms' scritchy-scratchy soundtrack, I told Jimmy I was leaving.

That's when he got that sad smile on his face, the one I'd first noticed back in fourth grade—the one that broke my heart if I stared at it too long.

"You should leave, too," I said. Right as I'd offered that suggestion, I knew it would be a tough sell.

Just as I'd predicted, Jimmy said: "I can't leave until my pops gets well."

I stopped sweeping. "Do you think that day'll ever come?"

Jimmy plopped down on the floor. Said he needed a hit right then. As I continued working, he fired up a bowl. At first he didn't say a word. But after a few hits he became more talkative than I'd ever seen before. Hit after hit, his words got all tangled up in the pot smoke and dust clouds drifting through the room. "I'm sorry you weren't ever close with your pops like I am with mine," he began. "And I'm sorry your mom left. But my family needs me. I don't care if I don't fit in here in Blackwater. I can deal. I'll miss you, but I'd miss my pops tons more if I left and he died on me."

When he was done, it dawned on me that all those times I'd tried to hook him up with girls, or score him a chimp companion, had been for naught. Jimmy never needed my saving. All he'd ever wanted was to be right by his dad. I couldn't argue with that. So the two of us hung out in silence while the pot cloud, music, and stray dust particles drifted around our heads. And while part of me couldn't completely shake the idea that he'd probably never break free of our backward little town, another part of me admired the hell out of him for staying with his family. With Jimmy, blood was far thicker than water. With me, leaving had always been in my blood.

Just as I was heading out, Jimmy asked: "Want your Ouija board back?"

While that board had done well by Jimmy, practically all it had ever offered me was that one useless word E-A-T whenever I'd asked it when I'd know things were going to be okay. "Keep it," I said. "It's all bullshit."

◆ ◆ ◆

THAT EVENING I DIDN'T bother knocking on my old man's study door. I just walked right in. Hefted a stack of *Police Chief* magazines from a wooden chair, and pulled up next to him. Before I could get too comfortable, I said: "I'm leaving."

My old man rubbed his tired face, chuckled through his hands. "I'm serious this time," I said.

My old man leaned forward in his chair. The lines across his forehead dug in deeper. His button-up grew more wrinkled. The gray around his temples: grayer. My old man minus Mom: rough. The sine of him strapped with solo parenthood added to the cosine of me: a thousand times rougher. "Your whole life you've gone from here to there," he said, "drugs, drinking, screwing up. And I've always been the one left to clean up your messes."

"But I never asked you to do any of that," I countered.

"It's because I love you, Mark."

With those words, I spied that dreaded photo on his study wall. The one that most summed up our relationship: him handing me back over to Mom in those first few hours after my birth. Referring to that photo, I said: "Look at you. You couldn't even hold me."

My old man removed the print from the wall. "I was handing you back to your mother," he said. "You'd just pissed yourself, and I didn't know how to change you." He handed over the photo so I could see for myself.

Up close and personal, that picture told a different story. There was Tiny Seed Me. My face was more bunched-up than a busted balloon. I was crying hysterically. My old man—only twenty-five at the time, not much older than me—seemed equally as lost and clueless. Like he didn't know the answers to life's big questions. Or didn't even know the questions. Couldn't figure out his left from his right. Couldn't find the exit door, the escape hatch. Yet through it all, his meaty hands remained gently secured around my waist. He was passing me over to a very tired, but relieved, Mom. Her hands were reaching out to me, but not quite holding me. Captured in that moment, suspended in mid-air between the two of them, it seemed I'd already found a home in my old man's secure grip, and it was Mom I'd never truly reach.

"What's the deal?" I asked. "If it's me just pissing myself why's it even on the wall?"

My old man regarded the photo. He was almost smiling. "Look how young we were. So innocent. We had our whole lives ahead of us. Anything was possible." He shook his head. "We had no idea what we were in for."

I considered that one, then told my old man I'd be leaving tomorrow, or the next day at the absolute latest.

◆ ◆ ◆

THE VERY NEXT MORNING my old man shook me awake. "Get up. You got company."

I threw on some clothes, headed to the door.

Mom was standing on the porch. In the hazy sunlight, she was decked out in Stepford Mary Kay. Her pink, knock-off Chanel suit was so glaring it made my teeth hurt.

"What're you doing here?" I asked. "You should be working."

"Your father called," she said. "He says you're leaving."

Just then, my old man appeared behind me.

"Buzz off," Mom snapped at him. "Mind your own business."

"Look, Sylvia," he said. "I tried to be civil and invite you over. But don't get nasty with me. Especially when you're standing on my porch."

"Well it used to be mine, too," said Mom.

"Not anymore," my old man shot back.

More arguing. It was just like old times. Like old times, my usual response was to puke. I stumbled onto the porch, alongside Mom. Ralphed my brains out into the rosebushes.

"You see," said my old man. "This is the kind of son we raised, Sylvia. All he's good for is getting wasted."

"I ain't wasted," I said. I looked to Mom for backup.

While she'd blown it in many ways in the Mothering Department, she at least knew the difference between stress sick and booze sick. Her hardened eyes softened. Then all at once, those gentle eyes flashed back to molten metal. "You don't even know your son, Mike."

"You're one to talk," said my old man.

Their arguing could've continued for days. But having dealt with numerous domestic violence cases in the past, my cop old man had observed how family disturbances could easily escalate from zero to ninety in a heartbeat. He corralled us inside, shut the door. "What do you want me to say, Sylvia? Do you want me to apologize?"

Mom stamped a high heel against the living room carpet. "I don't want *any*thing from you, Mike."

As for me, I wanted something big. A miracle product Mom could pull from her Mary Kay bag—a perfume, a deodorant, something my parents could smear on their skin, spray in their hair—to eliminate all their pain and abuse. "Can't you two say anything nice to each other for once?"

My old man was the first to speak. "Look, Sylvia. We both know I can be a real bastard sometimes. But you gotta admit we both had a hand in this."

Mom didn't respond. She was as stunned as me. My old man, normally a man of so few words, was actually trying to make sense of our lives.

In a voice as deep, clear, and resonant as the chiming of our grandfather clock, he continued: "I know I haven't been the best father to Mark. But I'm trying. And with you, Sylvia, I know I haven't been the best husband. I'm sorry I wasn't there for you."

"You're damn right you weren't there for me," she blasted.

My old man could've easily counterblasted. Instead, he calmly replied: "Even when you were there you were hardly there. But that was you. We loved you anyway. But when you left you may as well have put a bullet in our heads."

My parents looked to me for some kind of response.

I had no idea what to say right then. Which came first, my old man's anger and absences, or Mom's pills and distances, I wasn't sure. As for my whole family, it was hard to say what had happened to any of us. "You know what?" I said. "Screw this shit. I'm outta here."

"Oh no you're not, young man," said Mom. She seized me by the arm. Yanked me out the door, and out to the street to her car.

I could've easily resisted. But I figured it might be the last time I'd see her for a while.

She stuffed me inside her Caddy.

Once behind the wheel, she slammed the Hostess Snowball into D and peeled out. She ran the stop sign at the end of our block, then barreled through a yellow light turning red, as she sped toward the Garden State Parkway.

I didn't ask where we were going. And as much as I hated her smoking, I didn't stop her when she reached for one Virginia Slims after another.

Through a smoky haze, Mom offered up one of her usual self-centered thoughts: "How dare you do this to me."

"I'm not doing anything to you," I said. "I'm doing this for me."

When we hit the Parkway North, she revved the Caddy up to seventy-five. All the way to Exit 82 she remained sullen and silent. Even after we'd left the highway's mad rush and floated effortlessly along Highway 37 toward the ocean, her mood remained as miserable as the incoming storm clouds.

We ended up in Seaside Park, not far from where Callie and I had lost our virginity.

Mom parked on a lonely stretch of road by the ocean. Instead of speaking, she swiped another cigarette from her purse, and sparked up. The red tip bloomed into a fiery red star, then faded. Fiery star, faded.

As she huffed the Virginia Slims down to the filter, I studied her car's interior. The knobs, dials, upholstery: immaculate. Right then, it would've been so easy to flip her off and bolt. But if I'd done that, I would've lugged all my old rage and guilt to California. No way was that happening. When I reached the Golden State I wanted to start out clean.

After snubbing out the last of her cigarette into the nearly overflowing ashtray, Mom reached for another.

I snatched the pack away. Tossed it out my open window.

"Get it," she said.

I crossed my arms in front of my chest, shook my head.

Mom repeated her command with bigger teeth, more bite.

I still didn't budge.

That's when she said: "Do you have any idea how many of my clothes you ruined?"

I had no idea what she was talking about.

"When you were a baby," she said, "you'd throw your shit at me. You ruined so many of my blouses and pants suits."

"You're one to talk," I said. "All those times I tried brushing my teeth only to find my toothbrush gone because you'd used it to clean the tile grout."

That's when Mom's Jackie O-like looks, the ones she'd spent so much time moisturizing and powdering, crumbled all to hell. "Can you ever forgive me?" she said. "For leaving."

I recalled that day she left home. She was standing at the door in her flower-print dress—all those beautiful flowers forever fading away. That memory alone could've put a chokehold on the rest of my life if I'd allowed it. But that wasn't happening. "Maybe," I said. I looked away. Spotted great gray and black storm clouds drifting in from the east. They darkened the sky, the water, everything. "Tell me something," I said, turning from that sky. "For real. Whydja leave?"

Mom glanced down at her hands bunched up in her lap. Those hands worked a worried prayer. In a frail but measured voice, she told me how, even as a little girl, she'd never been good with expressing her feelings. And how that led to her constantly questioning her abilities as a mom and wife. Add to that all my old man's bullshit. All she ever felt like was a failure.

"So what?" I said. "My life's screwed up, too. You should've taken me with you."

Mom regarded me. Her bleak eyes grew even gloomier. "Why would I do that? At least your father knows how to be a parent."

Until then, I'd managed to stay pretty cool. But after years of having heard her repeat that ridiculous phrase ad infinitum, I lost it. "Your pills are making you *nuts*."

"Hardly," she said. "You and your father love each other. Think about it."

I did my best to follow her insane line of reasoning. I scanned the family photo album lodged deep in my mind, flipped through its dusty, old pages. There was me at five: my old man beaming when he found me brandishing a plastic gun and tin badge, pretending to be him. Me at nine: alternately admiring and fearing him while he did his best to teach me how to fight. There were other memories, too—him showing me how to ride a bike, drive a car, telling me old Irish tales at bedtime, and occasionally helping me with schoolwork.

About schoolwork.

There was a time in eighth grade. My old man had given me a lead pencil he'd brought home from a police chiefs' convention in Atlantic City. "Use it on your algebra test tomorrow," he'd said. "Maybe it'll bring you luck." It did. That was the one and only time I'd ever gotten an A on a math exam. My old man was so proud. But then there were those other memories of him hitting me and berating me.

Mom swiped a pill from her purse. After downing it, she held out the bottle for my inspection. "You've been taking them from me, haven't you?"

I didn't respond.

"Well?" she said.

I nodded. "Howdja know?"

"A while back," she said, "I found one of your letters from Callie in my bathroom. That, and I've noticed pills missing here and there."

"Why didn't you ever stop me?" I asked.

She thought about that one, then said: "They helped me feel a little better. I guess I'd hoped they'd do the same for you." She slipped the bottle back into her purse. "Look, honey, I know your father and I have made some big mistakes. But we love you very much."

Perhaps that love was true. Maybe it had started out so well meaning. But having slipped from that twinkle in Mom's eye to the lump in her gut, to the bundle in her arms, to the burden in her life she had to shake, that love had crashed and burned. And though Mom, my old man, and I had shattered in the process, we were still connected in some ways. I had my Irish father's prominent chin and oval face. I also shared my Mediterranean mom's olive complexion, full lips, and sad but hopeful eyes. The reflexive property of Mom: Me. The symmetric property of Me: Mom. Wherever we went, no matter how far we ran from one another, there we'd be—together again. That's when I said what I hadn't yet been able to tell her, only her empty house on those days when I'd broken in to steal her pills. "Even with everything that's happened," I said, "I still love you. And I miss you." I reached across the seat to hug her.

She tried pulling away, but I wouldn't let her. "It's okay. This is us. This is all we got."

In my embrace, Mom trembled. As I did my best to console her, I recalled all those times she'd never been able to hold me. The way she could be so cold, as if from very early on her skin had been wrapped around ice. Maybe that's why she feared such intense warmth and affection. Maybe too much love would've melted that ice and there would've been nothing left of her.

Just then, I recalled her cigarettes. Figured she could use one right about then. I reached for the doorknob.

"Don't leave," she pleaded.

I grabbed the cigarettes, hopped back in the car. "Smoke 'em if you got 'em."

With shaky hands, Mom lit up, swiped a few deep drags. Once the nicotine and that pill had cast their calming spell, she pointed toward the beach. "It's beautiful, isn't it?"

Again with the crazy talk. All I saw were stray beer bottles and crumpled fast food bags littering the sand, along with densely overcast skies and a tourist, sporting a tinted sun visor, and an *I Heart the Jersey Shore* T-shirt strolling by.

"The water," Mom said. "Look at it. What do you see?"

"Gray," I said. "Everything's gray. It's depressing as Blackwater."

She crushed out the last bit of her cigarette in the ashtray. Then she told me how when she was a little girl she used to love gray days at the beach; the water would blend into the sky and make it hard to tell where one thing ended and the other began. It was like all she had to do was walk out to the edge of the surf, and the sky was already within reach.

I made an *euw* face. "Sounds like a Hallmark card."

"Easy," Mom said. "That's my life you're talking about." She torched up another Virginia Slims, sighed out a cloud of smoke. The smoke slinked up the front windshield then tumbled back down, and out her open window.

We spent the next while, sitting quietly, staring out at the dark water and gray sky. Eventually, the sky dropped a few raindrops. They clattered softly against the Caddy.

"I love that sound," said Mom. "And the smell."

She was right. Those were two things I'd miss out in LA: that sweet, electric smell of the air, and the sounds leading up to a good old-fashioned Jersey Shore summer storm.

"Be honest," Mom said, doing her best to be cheery. "Isn't it nice out?"

"It looks like crap," I said.

"C'mon, honey. Be serious."

I was. Because if I allowed myself to tell her she was right, that all the gray made the sky appear so huge, that all we had to do was walk down to the surf and could touch it, I may never leave. "You're wrong," I said with a lumped up throat. "This ain't beautiful. This is all messed up."

Chapter 36

ONCE I SAID MY final goodbyes to my old man and Mad Man, and left some roses at Grandmother's grave, I took off. All the things I'd ever loved and hated about my little town grew smaller and smaller in my rear view mirror. Then they vanished.

From Jersey, I roared through Pennsylvania, Ohio, and Indiana. By day, it was farmlands, cities, and truck stops. Dust, diesel, and verbena. Late at night, when highway hypnosis transformed solid highway lines into mirages, the landscape became a stranger— something grim, shadowy, angular. Passing headlights and taillights: blood trails and hungry ghosts streaking the dark. That's when I'd roll down the windows. Get a blast of clear, fresh air. Crank the radio, spin the dial. Cruise beyond the late-night wash of infomercials swearing they'd help me grow hair, lose weight, find God, until I was plugged into a sonic rush of Skynyrd, Petty, Van Halen, and, occasionally, "Spirit in the Sky."

I kept driving. Beyond St. Louis, Salina, and Oklahoma City. Every so often I'd pull into a rest area, or a motel parking lot to catch some sleep. But whenever I'd close my eyes, all I saw were those broken white highway lines rushing at me. Heard the steady hum of wheels against road. Felt every skin pore, every nerve ending and hair on my body, buzzing. So I kept driving.

All the while, heading west. Closer and closer to the place that was the best.

During those late-night hours of driving, my fuzzy, buzzing mind would sometimes wander off, go California dreaming. I never put the brakes on any of those glorious hallucinations. How once I crossed over into the Golden State the skies would open up with a thunderous roar. There'd be sunshine pouring down, angels singing psalms of salvation. This would segue into Guns N' Roses, plugged in, electric and alive; Axl Rose wailing, "Welcome to the Jungle." Also bikini'ed beauties, spotlighted in all that liquid sunshine, holding up their own welcome signs, and dancing to the rhythm of that Guns N' Roses song.

I kept driving. The Texas panhandle: dusty fields for as far as the eye could see. Brilliant blue skies far wider than my eyes could ever hold.

Certain days I witnessed flashes of Mom, my old man, Jimmy, and his dad in the faces of people I saw at diners, gas stations, or in passing cars. Certain nights, when the dark sky was riddled with holes of plentiful light, I created constellations for those I'd left behind—Mr. Jeepers Perseus, Baby Andromeda. And the brightest of all, Grandmother Major.

I kept driving. Pre-dawn Albuquerque glittered like a field of diamonds. The Colorado River: a jeweled scar cutting across the rugged belly of Mother Earth.

What surprised me was that the further I got from my old life, the closer it felt. All the good and bad of it: friends, enemies, and families. Those evening symphonies of crickets and bullfrogs, the hard-rock acoustics of sudden thunderstorms, the laughter, the weeping at Satan's Tree, the roar of guns, and the booming of souped-up hotrods. All those things and more had been my second skin since birth. Some of it I knew I'd always carry with me. The rest I'd shed like excess baggage.

I kept driving. Steady mantra of wheels against road. Faster and faster until all those broken white highway lines became one clean, unbroken line.

There was no great parade when I finally crossed over into the Golden State. The skies didn't tear open with a deafening roar. No Guns N' Roses. No bikini'ed beauties. Angels didn't sing psalms of salvation. But at least it was a sunny day. Suddenly, a great weight lifted from my shoulders. My head cleared. My hands eased up on the wheel. Felt like that old language deep inside me was making room for my new vocabulary of deserts, beaches, earthquakes, and beautiful weather. With each mile, my old New Jersey Me was intermingling with my new California Me, becoming one shared breathing in and out.

Springsteen once said, "It ain't no sin to be glad that you're alive." And while I'd heard those words countless times before, I never truly understood what they meant until I witnessed a huge sign posted above the Wheel Inn around Cabazon. It sported those three letters I'd seen for years: E-A-T. That sign was the greatest sign of all. So I pulled into the parking lot, slapped some coins into a pay phone. While I had no idea what my future held—maybe I'd roll lucky 7s for a change, or maybe more snake eyes—everything was perfect in that moment. One shared breathing in and out. So much so, in fact, that when Callie answered, the first words out of my mouth were: "Everything's gonna be okay."

A World of Thanks

THIS NOVEL COULDN'T HAVE been possible without the assistance of so many wonderful people. To those who offered invaluable feedback during this book's various incarnations: Wayne Reynolds, Brendan Schallert, Milo Martin, the Chautauqua Writers Group (Sid, Karen, Ted, Dyanne, Dianne, Linda, Mary Pat, Andrew, Lia Schallert—RIP), Jenny Burman, Kathi Flood Martin, Ginny Fleming, Lara Hopwood, Erika Rae, George Langworthy, and Alex Smith. Thanks to my fantabulous blurbers: Aimee Bender, Jamie Blaine, Jessica Anya Blau, Antonia Crane, Shana Nys Dambrot, Tony DuShane, Jonathan Evison, Jack Grisham, David Kukoff, Brad Listi, Ben Loory, James Morrison, Greg Olear, Patrick O'Neil, Rob Roberge, David Rocklin, Jim Ruland, Jodyne L. Speyer, Heather Woodbury, Lenore Zion, and Adrian Todd Zuniga. Thanks to Brett Hall Jones; Mark Childress; Michael Pietsch; Andrew Tonkovich and Lisa Alvarez; my peeps Tony Saavedra, Gwen Goodkin, Sandra Ramirez, Renee Thompson, and all the other amazing folks associated with the Community of Writers at Squaw Valley. Thanks to Jessica Trupin (aka: Col. Trupin) for believing in this book when no one else did. Karen Ford: huge thanks for your super-keen editorial eye!

For their research assistance, thanks to: Bob Amberg (regarding the trees, plants, and vegetation of the Jersey Pine Barrens); Dr. Erna Toback (Mr. Jeepers); Patricia Lane—aka mom-in-law (Mary Kay fact-checking); Dr. Bob (drugs); Dr. Massimo Rossetti (veterinary medicine); Chuck Testa (Ojai Taxidermy); Mukti Garceau & Ishmael Gonzalez (fact-checking my rusty French); Chief Thomas R. Darmody & the Lacey Township PD; Mark Sceurman & Mark Moran, editors of *Weird NJ*.

My thanks continue: Stephen Elliott, Ashley Perez, Megan Nico DiLullo, Joe Daly, Reno Romero, Stephanie Barbé Hammer, Nick Belardes, Chevalier's Books, Jace Daniel, Eddie Gomez, and Aris Janigian—thanks for supporting this book and my writing over the years. Cat Gwynn, thanks for your amazing photos and Buddhist cool! Rev. Dave Stambaugh (inspirational Jersey conversations); Jersey pals—Steve Cronin, Mark McGovern, and Mike Madonia (bits of you are in this book). Scott Rodas of the Ocean County Library and Richard D. Helfant, Executive Director and CEO of Lucy the Elephant (thanks for your long-distance support). *Merçi beaucoup* to the amazing musicians that have assisted in the recording of various portions of this novel, or have accompanied me while performing it live: Tyson Cornell (guitar), Butch Norton (drums), Jeremy Toback (bass), Josh Haden (bass), Michael Barsimanto (percussion), and Andrew Bush—producer/engineer extraordinaire (Grandma's Warehouse, Echo Park).

Much love and gratitude for my parents: Mom, thank you for teaching me how to read, and always nurturing my creativity. Dad, thank you for your support, especially during the hard years, and for always reminding me to keep a sense of humor. Brother Bob, bits of you are in this book, too. Ruth and Steve, thanks for being you, Jersey true, love you both.

To my wife, CLS Ferguson: thank you for your love and support, and for giving me the courage and inspiration to pull this book out of the drawer, to finish the job I started. A shout out to my dog, Sadie, for remaining faithfully by my side as I typed and typed all my rewrites. To the dynamic ladies at Rare Bird: Julia Callahan, Hailie Johnson, Winona Leon, Alice Marsh-Elmer; thank you for your wonderful work and support. To my publisher, Tyson Cornell: a world of thanks, my friend, for believing in me, and my book when it was a glorious mess.

Lastly, I am forever indebted to my editor, Seth Fischer, and my writing mentor, Sid Stebel. You are truly two fine gentlemen that kicked my ass until I bled a story.